Praise for **PLAGUE** by Julie Anderson

The first Cassandra Fortune Mystery

If it's excitement and mystery you're after, try the bang up to date and very topical 'Plague'.

Time and Leisure magazine.

Gritty and gripping. Carefully blending mystery and intrigue, power, scandal, money, sex and corruption.

The Yorkshire Times

'Plague' is good fun, with some lovely insights into how the historic buildings and some of the people in the Palace of Westminster work.

Mike Naworynsky, former Deputy Sarjeant at Arms, Palace of Westminster.

Few fictional scandals involving Parliament would surprise anyone these days, but 'Plague' offers a humdinger.

Literary Review

A fascinating and authoritative insider view of modern power politics that is all too frighteningly prescient

V.B. Grey, author of Tell Me How It Ends

A tense parliamentary thriller with the sour tang of authenticity.

Annemarie Neary, author of The Orphans

The story gripped me right to the end. Very accurate description of Westminster and how easy i~~t is to get lost!~~

Lord Collins of Highbury

Pacey, suspenseful and ric̶ ̶ ̶ ̶ ̶ ̶ ̶ ̶ ̶ ̶ ̶ ̶ ̶)elling. If you're unlucky enough tc̶ ̶ ̶ ̶ ̶ ̶ ̶ ̶ ̶ ̶ ̶'n.

Clapham Society

CLARET PRESS

Copyright ©Julie Anderson
The moral right of the author has been asserted.

Cover and Interior Design by Petya Tsankova

ISBN paperback: 978-1-910461-48-8
ISBN ebook: 978-1-910461-49-5

A CIP catalogue record for this book is available from the British Library.

This paperback can be ordered from all bookstores as well as from Amazon, and the ebook is available on online platforms such as Amazon and iBooks.

www.claretpress.com

ORACLE

[signature] 24/11/21

Julie Anderson

He who learns must suffer. And even in our sleep pain that cannot forget falls drop by drop upon the heart, and in our own despair, against our will, comes wisdom to us by the awful grace of God.

"Agamemnon", Aeschylus

C O N T E N T S

Delphi

Athens

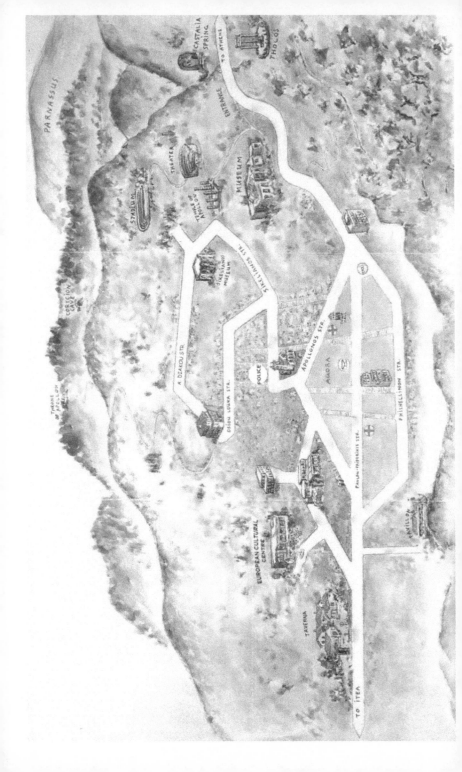

Delphi

P R O L O G U E

There was a certain look, a tilt of the head, a glint in the eye... he could always tell. He hadn't quite caught her name, but she was something at Delphi Museum, to do with the temple complex. Slim and stylish, she seemed to be in her mid-twenties, with large, brown eyes and creamy skin. The russet red highlights in her long brown hair caught the late autumn sunlight.

Maybe this trip wouldn't turn out to be so bad after all. Delphi might be in the back of beyond, but it could have its compensations, there was nothing to stop a little enjoyment. If he could get rid of his colleagues once things were sorted out, he would see what she had in mind.

'Did you come up from Athens?' she asked, her lips parted slightly.

'Yes, just arrived.' He was looking down at her. 'The scenery is beautiful, so dramatic, very different from the dust and grime of the big city.'

'Oh, Athens has other attractions. So much more interesting, so much more *fun* than a quiet little place like Delphi.'

'Do you know it?'

'Not as well as I'd like to,' she said, one eyebrow raised. 'I get away when I can, on the occasional long weekend, for the shopping and the nightlife. I do a little translating on the side, it pays well.'

'I'm staying–'

'I know.'

'Why don't you come over for a drink later? You can tell me all about your trips to Athens, the nightlife.'

'I'd like that.'

Her eyes fixed on his own as he looked her up and down. Her crooked smile revealed small, even teeth. Yes, he hadn't misread the signs, she was definitely interested.

It was no surprise to him. He had authority, glamour even, to a small-town girl with a bit of education like her. Aware of his own good looks he knew that women found him attractive, especially young women. She was younger than he was, but so what?

'I'll see you later then,' she said.

'I'm looking forward to it.'

And he was.

MONDAY

◊ ONE

Cassandra Fortune jolted awake.

The soft leather seat and the powerful purr of the engine had lulled her into a doze, but now the engine had stopped. Through the tinted windows she saw a forecourt beneath a floodlit concrete canopy, but dark, moving shapes obscured the light. People. They were surrounding the car and pressing up against the glass. There was a pounding on the roof above her head.

What? What's the hell's going on?

With an oath the driver shoved his door open, allowing in a rush of icy air, accompanied by the sound of shouts and yells. Seconds later her rear door was opened.

Cassie slung her satchel and handbag over her shoulder and began to climb out of the car, clutching her laptop case close to her chest. She placed her palm against the heavy door, anxious that it wouldn't be forced closed and trap a leg or an arm, but the driver held it open long enough to pull her out into the mass of bodies. It slammed shut behind her. Together, they struggled through the chanting mob in the direction of the brightly lit glass entrance doors.

The glow from the building was the only light to be seen. Beyond the forecourt was absolute blackness. High on the slopes of Mount Parnassus the European Cultural Centre nestled snugly in the middle of its own illumination, glistening in the surrounding darkness. Now it was under siege.

Cassie felt someone grab at her upper arm and yank her sideways. She yelped and pulled back, gripping the precious laptop even tighter. In the confusion she couldn't see who had hold of her, there were too many people crushed together, faces straining. A shouted order sounded harsh above the din and the grip on her arm slackened. Now the movement of the crowd changed direction, carrying them forwards. The driver battled his way, swearing and shoving, to one side, dragging Cassie in his wake, but the attention of the crowd had shifted and no one bothered them further. They stood beside a concrete pillar and watched.

The besiegers reached the glass doors, which shook at their pounding, but didn't open. A knot of people formed, creating a battering ram to try and gain entry. Within, Cassie could see other people, youngsters dressed in jeans and camouflage jackets, struggling with uniformed Centre staff. Protesters. More instructions rang out as a large man in combat fatigues strode forward. Older than many in the crowd, a leonine mane of unruly brown hair framed a strong, bearded face. He wore a determined, if sardonic expression as Cassie watched him. She knew a man in charge when she saw one.

With a hiss the glass doors suddenly slid open and jeering protesters spilled into the high-ceilinged hall. Those already inside were clinging, limpet-like, to whatever they could grasp, wooden banisters or brightly upholstered furniture. Men, some in Centre uniforms, some in kitchen whites, were trying to drag them towards the doors to eject them into the night. High-pitched screams of protest sounded as fingers were prised loose, chairs screeched, sliding across the floor tiles, all the sounds amplified by the rough stone walls. Slipping into the reception, Cassie ducked behind her half-raised arm, fearing that missiles would soon start to fly.

The protesters seemed to take heart as their reinforcements arrived, but the blare of a police siren caused anxious looks, dismaying them all. A battered police car drew up beneath the canopy on the forecourt, its flashing lights fracturing the darkness. Those demonstrators still hovering outside decamped at speed into the surrounding shrubbery.

From the car a heavy-set man in his late forties, his dark hair streaked with grey, stalked into reception. He wore a protective police gilet and carried a wooden baton. Two black-suited men with walkie-talkies strapped to their belts ran around the side of the building to join him.

Security detail. Is the Minister here early?

More men wearing kitchen whites arrived to help the Centre security staff haul protesters away. They took much greater care than the two ministerial security men, who were far less gentle. Cassie winced as one of them brought an elbow down sharply on fingers which clutched a wooden sofa arm, causing their owner to shriek in pain as she was pulled away.

Increased numbers and the mounting violence persuaded some of the protesters to leave, while others were ejected. Cassie and her driver scurried to one side as the last of them, a young man with dreadlocks, was pulled to the doors and thrust out into the night. A black-suited security man slapped his hands together as the policeman questioned the man behind the reception desk.

Exasperated, Cassie looked at her driver for help. She spoke several European languages, but Greek wasn't one of them and she was unaccustomed to not understanding.

'He asks if that is all of them?' the driver explained.

The clerk, suit neat and hair unruffled, replied in the affirmative, but added something Cassie couldn't understand. She frowned.

'The leader seems to have gone missing,' the driver translated. 'They're going to do a sweep search.'

The policeman man pointed at two of the kitchen staff, giving orders.

'They are to help him search the ground floor. He,' the driver pointed to the desk clerk, 'is to lock the doors and see that no protesters get back in.'

As the first security man set off up the stairs, Cassie and her driver picked their way between overturned chairs toward the desk.

'May I help you?' The desk clerk's voice was absurdly bland.

'My name is Cassandra Fortune. I'm here for the public administration conference. I'm afraid I'm late, my suitcase didn't arrive in Athens and I missed the conference coach.'

Her voice didn't convey the rising panic she'd felt at the airport when she realised what had happened and that she had no way of getting to Delphi on time. Encountering the protest was nothing in comparison to her fear of failure on her first mission for David Hurst, Prime Minister of the United Kingdom. Many anxious calls to her secretary back in London had resulted, to her immense relief, in the arrival of the dark grey ambassadorial Rolls Royce at the arrivals bay, a stately thoroughbred among the tooting local yellow taxis.

'Ah, yes.' The man consulted his console. 'Welcome, Ms Fortune, we have been expecting you.' He reached below the desk and handed her an old-fashioned key on a large metal fob marked 17. 'First floor, upstairs and turn right.' He gestured towards the foot of the staircase then turned to the pigeonholes behind the desk. 'You have a message.'

He handed her an envelope.

'Also we have managed to find a room for your driver. It wasn't easy, the guesthouse is fully booked for the conference.'

A torrent of Greek between the two men followed. Cassie waited, foot tapping.

'I'll go park the car,' the driver said to Cassie, pocketing his room key. 'You need me?'

'I don't think so, thank you, unless...' she turned to the man behind the desk. 'I've lost my luggage and need to buy things, something casual and warm to wear.' She indicated her formal suit and mackintosh. 'Will the shops be open in Delphi?'

'No, madam. It's much too late. The town will be closed now.'

'I thought it might be.' She spoke to the driver. 'No, I don't need you any more tonight, though it would be good to go into Delphi tomorrow morning. Thank you for all your help out there.'

'It's my pleasure.' The man gave a crooked smile. 'Good night, Ms Cassandra.'

Cassie climbed the staircase, which was made of the same glossy red wood as the smart modern reception furniture. A solitary security man scowled as he passed her on his way down, his search for the missing protest leader evidently fruitless. Room seventeen was along the corridor on the right.

Tossing her laptop and handbag on to the bed, Cassie ripped open the envelope. The message was from her secretary, Siobhan, saying that Cassie's bag had never made the flight. She had arranged for it to be flown to Athens and forwarded to Delphi as soon as possible. Cassie thought about phoning her, it was about eight o'clock in London, but the lack of bars on her mobile showed that she didn't have a signal. She sighed. It was being in the mountains. She didn't want to speak over a public line, so she'd try and make contact tomorrow from different places around the Centre.

She removed her laptop from its case, added a European adaptor to her charger and plugged it into a wall socket. Her hotel-type room held a bed, bedside tables, a wooden unit of drawers and cupboards and a wall-hung TV. A fan of glossy brochures lay on the desk next to her laptop.

She picked one of them up. It was about the Centre, she recognised the lobby from the photograph on the cover, though the image looked a great deal neater than the real thing currently did. Built in the late 1970s, at a time of forward-looking optimism, the Centre was a showcase of a new and civilised Greece, she read. This was after the military dictatorship had been toppled and its generals put on trial for crimes against their own people, before Cassie had been born, but she'd seem grainy TV images of the trials. The age of the authoritarian strongman was over; Greece was ruled by law, it had joined the European Union. The Centre was a symbol of the new democracy, a promise to the younger generation, many of whom had suffered for their opposition to the government.

What would those young people downstairs say to that?

She sighed and dismissed the thought, massaging her upper arm where it had been grabbed. A bruise was already forming. She riffled through the other booklets; there was one on the nearby Temple of Apollo, a guide to the Delphi Museum and a map of Delphi town. She'd take a look at them tomorrow.

Within minutes she was standing under the jet of hot water. It was only afterwards, wrapped in a bath towel, that she remembered that she didn't have a hairbrush or comb.

Damn.

Working her fingers through her tangled hair she wondered if the night manager could find something for her. The guesthouse wasn't a hotel, it was accommodation attaching to the Centre, but it might have something, a vanity set, maybe. Perhaps he could also rustle up a sandwich – the kitchen staff was still here, she'd seen some of them – and she hadn't eaten since lunchtime. It wasn't quite ten o'clock. She picked up the bedroom telephone.

No reply. Perhaps he was dealing with another guest. She gave it ten minutes and tried again. The phone rang but no one picked it up.

I'll have to wait until breakfast.

She switched on the hair dryer, then switched it off as she heard a noise. Her neighbours had arrived in the next room, a man and woman, talking in low voices. She heard gentle laughter. The walls of this place were certainly thin. She returned to drying her hair.

Tomorrow morning she would go into Delphi to buy clothing and other necessities. The conference would be opened in the afternoon by Theo Sidaris, Greece's Finance Minister. He was the reason why she was here. She had to make a good impression.

Cassie still couldn't quite believe that this was for real, the international jet-setting on behalf of the Prime Minister. It was a long way from her previous post overseeing minor procurement projects.

Her smile of satisfaction faded as she picked up and sniffed the blouse she'd travelled in.

Ugh.

But she had to wear it tomorrow morning; she had no choice.

Her hair dry, Cassie placed her little bottle of sleeping tablets on the bedside table, along with the diazepam.

She was very tired, even though for her body clock it was still early. Her nap in the car aside, sleep had been hard to come by after the end of her last assignment and she was still weary with a deep exhaustion. She'd helped solve a criminal investigation, which had wide ramifications in government. In doing so she had aided the rise of David Hurst to become Prime Minister and attracted his notice and his confidence. Now she was a member of a small group of people who Hurst trusted to do his personal bidding. It was an odd collection, ex-intelligence agents, fast-tracked PAs and Cassie supposed, herself, until recently a disgraced civil servant.

Halfway up a mountain and far from London, she'd surely be able to get a good eight hours sleep. She climbed into bed and switched off the light.

◊ TWO

Cassie breathed deeply and let her muscles relax.

Her room was in complete darkness, there was no ambient moon or starlight peeping through the gap between the floor length curtains. She closed her eyes and consciously began to set aside the cares of the day: the loss of her luggage, her anger and anxiety at missing the coach and then arriving at the Centre into the middle of a demonstration.

Now she was here, where she had planned to be, and tomorrow she could begin her mission. All would be well. She was to make a presentation at the conference on taxation reform, although this was not her true purpose.

When she had last seen David Hurst, the Prime Minister, he'd been sitting at his desk in the private study in Number 10, a room which a lot of people knew existed, but very few got to visit. Even now Cassie felt a frisson, a thrill at being one of them. A big man, still physically powerful in his middle years, Hurst's hair was grey, almost tonsure-like. He'd been chewing the end of a pen.

'You're up to speed,' he'd said as he came to join her on a sofa. It hadn't been a question. 'I'd like to add my own perspective.' And he'd removed his spectacles, sliding them into his shirt pocket.

'We need to regain influence with our European neighbours, especially given forthcoming trade negotiations. Greece has the Presidency of the European Council next year and will set the agenda for those negotiations and other things. Theo Sidaris, the Greek Finance Minister, is anglophile. He went to the London School of Economics, plays cricket in his spare time, he's the man to approach. Get him on side, persuade him to visit the UK for some off-the-record conversations.'

Sidaris was regarded as the heir apparent to the current Greek Prime Minister. Cassie would be meeting him and his main economic advisor and long-time friend, Professor Diomides Matsouka, the following day.

'Tax reform is a good reason for the Minister to visit London and you will offer help in introducing the new system in Greece, though he will know that we want to talk about other things as well,' Hurst had continued. 'It's your job to get him here. Impress upon him my own special interest in his visit. You are my personal envoy, something he will be made aware of through the usual channels however much the Ambassador mightn't like it.'

Cassie hadn't expected that managing relations between Number 10 and the rest of government would be easy, but an apoplectic British Ambassador to Greece wasn't what she'd had in mind. Somehow the PM had got wind of the outburst.

'The Foreign Office is under strict orders to facilitate your trip and give you whatever support you need. I'll want to know if they don't.' The Prime Minister had stood, signalling the end of the conversation. 'Come back with good news.'

This was her mission. Get the Greek Finance Minister to London to talk to the PM.

The cost of failure? Don't think about that.

She chastised herself. She had let her thoughts run away with her when she should have been lulling herself into sleep, putting the anxieties of the day behind her and being positive. Instead she had returned to her fear that she would fail.

Irrational.

She turned on to her other side and plumped the pillow before settling down again.

Half dozing, she could hear the people in the next room again. They seemed to be having some sort of disagreement and their voices rose. The words were Greek – indecipherable. She wouldn't be able to understand them even if she could hear them clearly, but their tone was accusatory and the anger in them unmistakable. The noise level increased.

Cassie reached out and flicked the light switch.

A domestic. All she needed at – she consulted her watch on the bedside table – eleven thirty. She was tired and she had to rise early the following day.

Bloody annoying.

She reached for her sleeping pills then stopped. She had to be awake and firing on all cylinders in eight hours; pills were not the answer. Perhaps the night manager could do something, telephone next door and ask them to desist. She lifted the telephone and dialled reception. This time he picked up.

'Yes madam,' he said calmly, as if calls to reception at eleven thirty were commonplace. 'How can I help?'

'The people in the room next to mine are shouting at each other. They seem to be having an argument,' Cassie said.

'Do you want me to come up?'

'It might be a good idea, or perhaps you could telephone the room... no, wait, they've stopped.' Cassie waited, the noise had died down. 'They've probably heard me speaking and realised how loud they are. Thank you anyway.'

'Good night, madam.'

'Good night.' Cassie replaced the phone on its cradle and settled down again. She had just switched off the light when the noise began again.

So much for getting eight hours sleep.

Cassie climbed out of bed and pounded on the wall.

'Can you keep the noise down? I'm trying to sleep in here!'

All went silent, until she heard the slamming of a door. Someone had left the room, were they coming to apologise or to confront her? Cassie waited, but there was no knock upon her room door.

Thump!

She jumped back as the wall shook. Someone had hit it very hard on the other side. Someone was still in that room and she had succeeded in enraging them.

Cassie took two long strides back to the phone, eyes still trained on the wall, every muscle tense. It had gone quiet, but she wasn't entirely convinced that it would stay that way. As the seconds extended into minutes and there was no further sound she began to relax and climbed back into bed.

Keep calm and carry on.

She jerked upright at another noise. It was the same door again, she realised, either the occupant of the room had left or someone else had entered. She lay back on the pillows and waited to hear more, straining for any sound.

Nothing.

After a few minutes she switched off the lights and snuggled down beneath the duvet.

TUESDAY

◊ THREE

A phone was ringing, growing louder.

Too early!

Cassie groaned. She groped for the phone on the bedside table to swipe the 'Off' button. The ringing stopped and she flopped down onto the bed.

Eyes open! You'll only go back to sleep.

She pushed herself up on her forearms, eyelids barely apart. Morning light filtered, mouse-grey, through the long curtains.

Clambering out of bed, she grabbed the large bath towel and shuffled to the bathroom. In the mirror she saw the smudges of tiredness underneath eyes still crusted with sleep. Her skin looked putty-like and lifeless. Not good, especially today. She had a Minister to impress. She needed to be confident and assured, not worrying about how she looked. She was the UK delegate to the 27th European Convention on Public Administration.

She slapped cold water on to her cheeks and shivered. The water was icy. She ran the tap until it warmed then filled the basin to wash. Returning to the bedroom she pulled on yesterday's clothes and dragged her fingers through her sleep-flattened hair, binding it back with a band found at the bottom of her handbag. There were cosmetics in there too, she thanked her lucky stars that she had decided to take them through airport security, not pack them in her case. At least she could make her face more presentable.

Slipping on her shoes, she pulled back the curtains.

Wow!

A huge expanse of pale blue sky filled the upper third of the window, arching over a snow-covered forest on the mountainside opposite, its shadowed slopes dropping to a valley floor so far below she couldn't see it. The valley wound away to her right, around mountain spurs and hills towards a coastal plain. In the far distance there was a smudge of a large town or city in a curve of a coastline. Beyond the promontory a glint on the low horizon was the sea, merging with the western sky still purple with night.

She was in a different world.

Cassie stepped out on to her balcony. Below lay a narrow terrace, its trees, shrubs and steps ice-encrusted and glittering in the first rays of the sun. Above the soaring birdsong she heard the clanking of goat bells. She breathed in the sharp, clear morning air and her irritation fell away.

So magical.

But cold.

Dropping her room key into her handbag Cassie headed down to reception to see if there was any news from the Embassy in Athens about the interpreter she had been promised. The well-groomed young woman behind the desk produced a message to say that the interpreter would be arriving that morning.

'Thank you,' Cassie said. 'I'll go and get some breakfast, if you could let me know when they arrive. Oh, one more thing, my neighbours, the people in room eighteen, the room next to mine, were very noisy late last night. Could you let me know who's in that room, please?'

'I'm sorry, we can't give out personal information,' the desk clerk adopted a pained and patient expression.

'Of course.' Cassie turned away.

'Though... actually... room eighteen isn't occupied.'

'I thought the guesthouse was full?'

'It is, though the people who should have had that room didn't arrive last night. They're arriving late this morning'

'So who did I hear arguing?'

'Are you sure you did? It couldn't have been a television?'

Someone banged on my wall.

'Completely sure.'

'I – I can't explain it.' The desk clerk began to look flustered. 'Do you want to speak with the manager?'

'No, no, that won't be necessary,' Cassie said. 'The man who was on the desk last night, is he the manager?'

'Christos? I think that's who you mean,' the desk clerk answered. 'He's the night manager.'

'Thank you. I spoke with him about the noise, he'll remember. Will he be around later?'

'Yes, madame.'

'Thank you.'

Her tummy rumbling, Cassie headed for the dining room.

◊ FOUR

The dining room was laid out refectory style with an array of hot food available from a long counter. Tall glass doors and windows opened on to the terrace that Cassie had seen from her balcony. She collected a tray and helped herself to cereal, toast and coffee and looked around the room.

The type of diner varied, ranging from a group of middle-aged men in sweaters and jeans, obviously a single delegation, to young men and women who seemed to be students or staff at the Cultural Centre. Hearing American English spoken nearby, Cassie chose a table occupied by two men and a woman.

'Good morning,' she said as she unloaded the contents of her tray. 'I'm Cassie Fortune. May I join you?'

'Jim Norton,' a blond, long-faced man wearing a check shirt and jeans half stood and offered his hand, which she shook. 'My partner, Elise Forché.' He indicated the small, dark-haired woman sitting next to him.

Had she imagined it or had he stressed the word "partner"?

'Enchanté,' she murmured, her brown eyes narrowing almost imperceptibly as she looked Cassie up and down. Cassie acknowledged the introduction with a smile, which the woman didn't return.

'Mike Robbins,' the second man said, in a distinctive American drawl. He nodded briefly but continued to shovel up his scrambled eggs. He was a big man. 'Is there a Brit delegation?'

'No,' Cassie replied. 'Only me. Are you the US version?'

'We're not a delegation,' Norton said. 'Elise and I are from the OECD, the Organisation for Economic Co-operation and Development. We're based in Paris.'

'I'm in renewables,' Robbins added. 'Here to listen. You?'

'I'm presenting tomorrow,' Cassie said. 'Taxation reform.'

'Tax!' Robbins crossed his large index fingers in the universal sign against the evil eye.

Probably a small-state marketeer. Well funded. They got everywhere, even half way up Mount Parnassus.

'Did you arrive last night?' he continued. 'D'you see the half-assed protests?'

He's in renewables yet dislikes environmental protesters?

'I–'

'Why do you call them "half-assed"?' the Frenchwoman interjected. 'The young people are doing something that they believe in, exercising their right to protest, to take a principled stand.'

'Their leader is a hero of Elise's,' Jim explained. His voice dripped with sarcasm.

'*Bien sûr*, I admire someone who holds true to their beliefs, who stands up to the powerful and can't be bought,' Elise countered. 'Why shouldn't I?'

'You admire him so much that you let him into your room?' Mike Robbins snorted.

So that's why the security man couldn't find him.

Jim clamped his lips together.

'I helped him out,' the French woman said, glancing in Cassie's direction. 'What of it?'

'Just when Jim and I happened to be out for a smoke,' Mike countered, one eyebrow raised, to his compatriot's increasing discomfort.

'*Va te faire foutre*! What do you know about any of it?'

'And where were you when I came back?' Jim gave up his attempt to say nothing.

'I told you – we've gone over this already.'

She pushed back her chair and reached to pick up her mobile and leave, but Jim got to it before she did. He turned his shoulder so as to prevent her from taking it from him and tapped in a password as Cassie watched, open mouthed.

'Give that back!'

Heads were turning, people's attention attracted by the sharp voices. Cassie looked at Mike Robbins in embarrassed sympathy but he was too busy watching his fellow American with something, she thought, like glee.

'What's this?' Jim demanded. 'You've been tweeting him.'

'So?' Elise tried to grab her phone. 'Look how many followers he has. Lots of people tweet him.'

In the doorway to the dining room the young desk clerk appeared, scanning the room. She spotted Cassie and headed towards her table.

With relief, Cassie excused herself, placed her breakfast tray in the rack and moved to intercept her.

'Ms Fortune,' the desk clerk said. 'Your interpreter is in reception.'

A woman was perched on the edge of a sofa in the lobby, fidgeting with the rings on her fingers. She looked to be of average height, not as tall as Cassie and slim to the point of being angular, with jet black hair falling in corkscrew curls to her shoulders. Her skin was alabaster pale and she had a small mole at the right-hand corner of her mouth. Attractive and well turned out, rested and ready for work. Cassie felt a surge of resentment. Right now this woman was everything that she, Cassie, was not.

Don't be silly, it's not her fault you're shattered.

'Hello, I'm Helena Gatakis, from the embassy.' The woman stood and held out a neatly manicured hand.

'Cassie Fortune, pleased to meet you.'

'You've had some bad luck in transit, I understand.'

Cassie sensed pent-up energy and tension. It had probably been impressed upon Helena Gatakis how important it was to please Cassie. Almost certainly a freelancer, as British embassies didn't take on many local permanent staff these days, Helena's future work would depend on her success now.

'Yes. Have you been to Delphi before?' She made small talk to put Helena at her ease.

'I was going to ask you that,' the interpreter smiled. 'No, I haven't. It's spectacular landscape, isn't it? I understand that we may have a trip to the Museum later today.'

'Oh, good, that'll be interesting. I didn't know about that.' Cassie noticed the flash of pleasure on the woman's face at being informative and useful. Yes, she was nervous. 'But before then I need to go into Delphi town to buy some things. As you know, my luggage went missing and I'm not sure when it will arrive.'

'It isn't far. The chauffeur can drive us there on his way back to Athens.'

Cassie raised an eyebrow.

'The ambassador wants his car back,' Helena explained, with a tentative half-smile.

Bit of a blow.

'Of course.'

It was quite something having her own driver and car, especially when the car was a Rolls Royce, but it couldn't be helped.

'We'll need to go soon, the Minister will be here by midday. I want to go through my briefing notes with you, but we can do that on the way. I'm looking for any details about Minister Sidaris and his advisor, Professor Matsouka, that my secretary hasn't already given me. I'll go and get my coat.'

'Right,' Helena said. 'I'll wait here, Ms Fortune.'

'It's Cassandra. Actually, please call me Cassie.' Cassie got to her feet. 'Cassandra, like....'

'The princess of Troy, daughter of King Priam.' Cassie wondered how many times that would arise during the trip. 'And no, I can't tell the future, as she did. I wish I could.'

Helena smiled. She was quick and intelligent, picking up on Cassie's mood. She'll do very well, Cassie thought.

'Five minutes,' she said and hurried up the stairs.

When she returned she found Helena listening to an animated discussion between the receptionist and another guesthouse employee. Cassie raised a questioning eyebrow.

'It's nothing,' the interpreter replied, flustered. 'Someone's late for work this morning.'

'Not our business.'

'No,' Helena hesitated. 'It's just... they asked if I might be able to do some translating for them if she doesn't show up. Apparently she's very reliable so they're really quite taken aback and at a loss that she hasn't arrived.'

'Helena, if I may call you Helena?' Cassie didn't wait for a reply. 'You're here to assist me, that's what the Embassy sent you for, I–'

'I told them I couldn't.' Helena's cheeks were flushed pink. 'Of course.'

'Good. Now, Delphi.'

◊ FIVE

Clothing shops in Delphi were in limited supply so the car dropped Cassie and Helena outside one selling outdoors gear. Cassie bought T-shirts, socks and a waterproof jacket to wear against the cold, as well as jeans, a track suit and trainers. A pharmacy supplied toiletries, a hair-brush and tights. As she handed over her credit card she wondered if she could charge it all to expenses, her civil service *per diem* wouldn't cover it.

Delphi town was built on one side of a jutting ridge, its streets clinging vine-like to the steep mountain side. The fortunes of the town were closely linked with the Temple and its visitors as, she supposed, they had been for millennia. Around the other side of the ridge, along a lane branching off from the new road which circled the mountain, lay the Cultural Centre.

'It's very beautiful up here,' Cassie said. In the sharp, bright light and thin air she could see the brown leaves of the trees on the opposite side of the deep valley as if they were close enough to touch. 'Though isolated. I can't get a mobile signal.'

'The reception is very poor, especially when the weather is bad, I'm told,' Helena replied, looking at the clear blue sky. She sniffed the air. 'There are storms forecast, though it's hard to believe.'

'Who's that?' Cassie shaded her eyes the better to see a figure running on the side of Mount Parnassus above them.

'It's a woman,' Helena said, doing similarly. 'Jogging.'

Helena was right, it was a woman, though she was as tall as a tall man, fit and rangy. Her strawberry blonde hair was drawn back from a strong face, with a jaw cut clean as a knife and a high bridged nose.

Shuffling down the gradient then striding along the trail as it flattened, she leaped from rock to rock with the grace of a gazelle. She turned off before she got as far as the road, though it wasn't clear whether she was deliberately avoiding them, or following some predetermined path. They watched as she crested the brow of the mountain ridge, a long plait bouncing between her shoulder blades.

Like an Amazon. Where do I know her from?

'The Olympics,' Helena answered her thought and Cassie remembered.

Meg Taylor, winner of the ten thousand metres gold medal at the Beijing Olympics. She was Greek born but had married the successful British long jumper, Guy Taylor. Cassie remembered an iconic photograph of them celebrating in the Athlete's Village, dressed up to the nines, each wearing their gold medal. Later there'd been some scandal and divorce. Now little was heard of her.

'Is she from Delphi?'

'I don't believe so,' Helena said. Then she stepped back from the road, stretching out her hand to draw Cassie back alongside her. 'Look.'

A motorcade of black limousines was snaking its way around another arm of Parnassus along the highway. Two helmeted motorcycle outriders preceded the cortège, others followed at its rear. The head of the convoy disappeared behind a fold of the mountain, reappearing just beyond the edge of Delphi town. The large machines swept passed them, tinted windows hiding their occupants.

Cassie and Helena watched until the motorcycles and the first cars rounded the mountain spur and were lost to sight. There's my mission, Cassie thought as her eyes followed the cavalcade. Her heart began to beat faster.

Then the procession ground to a halt.

'Come on.' Shopping bags rustling, Cassie hurried up the slope at the road-side to the path which the runner had followed over the ridge.

At the top they saw why the motorcade had stopped. A large herd of goats was being driven down the mountain, bells clanging. The animals at the front had already crossed the road and were heading down to the valley, but the rest of the herd was following behind, walking and trotting across in front of the outriders and the convoy. A young boy and an older shepherd, carrying a staff, were chivvying them along.

'As ancient as the mountain,' Cassie exclaimed, smiling. 'The Homeric meets the twenty-first century.'

The goats finished crossing and with a wave of thanks, the goatherd disappeared down the mountain side. The motorcade moved on.

'I wish I'd taken a photograph,' she said as they walked back down to the road.

But who would I share it with?

The thought came to her, unbidden.

'You'll find plenty of examples of the timeless meeting the modern here,' Helena said. 'Many of my fellow citizens would say that we are only now emerging from a real-life Greek tragedy in which a lot of people suffered.'

Cassie grimaced in sympathy. The Greek debt crisis had been very hard on the ordinary Greek people, especially those like pensioners and public sector workers who, through no fault of their own, were dependent on a state, which no longer had the means to support them. The wealthy had placed their money abroad to avoid paying taxes, but everyone else had to bear the pain. The country was only now recovering and there was a lot of discontent at the injustice, some of which found a focus in populist and nationalist rhetoric.

'I understood that things are improving.'

'They are, but there are plenty of people living on the breadline, though the Minister won't say that. There are also plenty willing to exploit people's anxieties. You've read about Golden Dawn?'

The violent, ultra-nationalist and racist body, with ties deep into organised crime, Golden Dawn had been banned as a criminal organisation wrapping itself in a mantle of politics. Cassie nodded, but her thoughts were elsewhere. The tax reforms she was to talk about were a cost-cutting measure, but maybe clarity and transparency were also strong cards to play? So everyone would know the system and how it applied. An aid to social justice might be relevant and appealing to the Minister.

The idea of fairness. Also as old as time.

Her thoughts were interrupted by shouts and voices up ahead. Cassie automatically quickened her pace to see what was going on.

They rounded a curve in the lane to see the motorcade stationary once more. Protesters surrounded the cars while others stood in front of the gates to the grounds of the Centre, chanting, waving placards and fists. This was a well-organised ambush, Cassie realised, almost certainly the demonstrators from last night. What had Elise Forché called their leader, a man of conviction? It seemed he was also a man of considerable organisation. She had a sneaking respect for him.

The outriders from the back of the convoy were forcing their motorcycles between the protesters and the limousines, while black-suited security personnel climbed from their cars to help clear the way. So far the violence had been minimal.

'Is there another way in?' Cassie asked. 'That runner must have got inside somehow. If she'd gone through these gates we'd be able to see her now.'

Helena shook her head. 'If there is, I don't know of it.'

'Let's wait then,' Cassie stepped off the road towards a grove of trees. 'Here, out of sight. We don't want our faces to be associated with anything that might embarrass later.'

The two women watched from their hiding place as the noise increased, the chants turning to yells and screams as the security people began to haul protesters away. A tall, broad-shouldered man wearing mirrored sunglasses was directing security operations; he spoke into a walkie-talkie and his shirt blazed white against deep olive skin.

'Security Chief Iraklidis,' Helena said. 'He's quite high profile.'

Cassie couldn't imagine any of the security personnel she knew being "high profile", but then, none of them was as obviously handsome as Iraklidis.

Some of his men were keeping the protesters away from the ministerial car, others were trying to clear a way to the gates. It was there that the leader of the protesters stood, booted feet firmly planted, surrounded by seated protestors.

After avoiding capture last night with a little help from Elise.

'Why are they protesting?' she asked, not understanding the chanted slogans.

Helena gave a dismissive shrug. 'The environment.'

'Climate change, or something more specific?'

'This is probably about the big US fossil fuel companies. They're on the prowl, wanting to sink testing wells for fracking.'

'But Greece is an earthquake zone, the whole region is.'

'Madness, isn't it?' Helena said. 'But after the financial crisis Greece couldn't afford to be choosy about its international partners. Repayment of the national debt is the priority. It makes for some unusual alliances. That's why Sidaris, as Finance Minister, is a focus for these protests.'

Cassie's thoughts shot back to Mike Robbins, the American she'd met a breakfast that morning. Now she understood why he was there: he also wanted to catch the eye, or ear, of the finance minister, to urge the case for renewable energy.

People were hurrying towards the gate from inside the Centre. A siren sounded and Cassie turned to see the approach of the police car she had seen the night before. She wondered if the same burly policeman was inside, a small place like Delphi wouldn't have many police. His life wouldn't be easy while this conference was on.

'We won't be waiting long now,' Helena said. 'The leader will be arrested and the others dispersed.'

The gates were opened and staff began to help the security men move the protesters away. The same policeman forced his way through to the protest leader, handcuffed him and, with the help of a couple of the security men, led him to the police car. The motorcade resumed its course. The remaining protesters retreated to either side of the road still waving their placards but shouting with less enthusiasm now that their leader was arrested and their blockade ended.

The two women made their way back to the dirt lane where despondent groups of protesters were now making their way back to the main road, dragging their placards behind them. They all looked young, in their twenties at most. Two security men stood at the gates, watching them leave and taking photographs.

'What will happen to the leader of the protest?' Cassie asked, thinking of Elise's comments at breakfast.

Helena shrugged. 'He'll probably be charged with a public order offence and will spend the next few days in Delphi jail, at least as long as the conference lasts. After that, who knows? If he's well-known he might be made an example of. I wouldn't be surprised if he's been arrested plenty of times before.'

Environmental protests at a public administration conference. A disgraced Olympic gold medallist. And, no matter how much she tried to focus her thoughts on her mission, bubbling away at the back of her mind was last night's row in the unoccupied room next to her own.

This was shaping up to be quite a conference and she hadn't even met the Minister yet.

◊ SIX

'Follow me, please.' The neat young man raised his hand to usher Cassie and Helena through the clutch of press people, out of the lobby and up a set of stone steps along the side of the main building. Cassie noticed several security men on patrol carrying walkie-talkies and firearms.

He trotted up the steps to a smaller building and opened a heavy wooden door. The Minister had opened the conference and Cassie had been invited to meet him.

The young man led them into a spacious lounge area with yet more huge windows and a balcony looking out on another spectacular view. The other side of the valley, which had looked so near in the clear morning light, now seemed distant, its wooded slopes far away.

Don't look at the scenery. Focus.

'Ms Cassandra Fortune of the United Kingdom and Ms Helena Gatakis of the British Embassy.' He introduced them and withdrew.

The Security Chief was silhouetted, jacketless now, against the window, facing into the room. He appeared relaxed, but Cassie wasn't fooled, he was still watchful. A doe-eyed, brown-haired man in his late forties sat on a sofa speaking with the runner Meg Taylor, who was perched on the arm of the sofa opposite, elegant in pale trousers and top. Another man of similar age to the seated man, was standing at a side table with his back to them, also without a jacket, pouring drinks. At the announcement he swung round to look at them.

Theo Sidaris was compact of build and of middle height, with wavy black hair swept back from his forehead, above a face scarred and pitted down the left side, the result, Cassie knew, of a youthful climbing accident. His stance was as relaxed as everyone else but it didn't hide his innate energy and physical power. His black eyes were sharp and twinkled with intelligence as he smiled.

'Welcome, Ms Fortune,' he said in heavily accented English, then continued his welcome in Greek. As Helena translated, he and Cassie studied each other, more or less openly. He was alert and engaged, an accessible and attractive figure, but with a certain detachment.

'Thank you, Minister,' Cassie said. 'And thank you for inviting me to meet you. May I also congratulate you on a most illuminating and interesting speech. I found the sections on historical parallels particularly relevant.'

Sidaris smiled and gave a little sardonic bow, familiar with diplomatic flattery.

'Please come and sit down,' said the man rising from the sofa, in uninflected English. 'I'm Diomides Matsouka, economic advisor to the Minister.'

'Pleased to meet you, Professor Matsouka.' Cassie shook his hand. This was Sidaris's lifelong friend and fixer, a man with no official government position, but who was recognised by all as the Minister's right hand.

'Yannis Iraklidis, Head of Ministerial Security,' the Professor gestured towards the Security Chief, who nodded a greeting. 'And Meg Taylor, formerly Meg Aertos, of whom you may have heard.'

The former athlete stood.

'Hello.' Her handshake was firm. 'I'm an old friend of the Sidaris family, in case you're wondering why I'm here,' she said. 'Theo and I are related in a very extended way.'

'Ms Taylor,' Cassie said as she and Helena sat. 'I believe we saw you out running on the mountain this morning.'

'Really, I wasn't aware of you. I was in a little world of my own.'

'Meg is well known for ignoring the world around her,' Professor Matsouka said and everyone laughed. It was obviously an old joke between them all.

'Would you like a drink? Coffee? Water?' Meg moved to take the space which Sidaris had vacated by the side table.

'No, thank you.'

Helena also declined.

Sidaris took the sofa opposite Cassie, by the side of Professor Matsouka.

'Well, Ms Fortune,' the Professor prompted.

'I am here as personal envoy of David Hurst,' Cassie began. 'As well as doing a presentation.'

Helena translated but Cassie got the distinct impression that Sidaris understood what she was saying, though her briefing notes had told her that he had long since forgotten the English of his younger days.

'Mr Hurst is, as you know, new in post,' she smiled. 'But he is most anxious to meet you.'

'I am merely Finance Minister of a country recently much impoverished.' Sidaris spoke and Helena translated. 'Why does the Prime Minister of the United Kingdom send envoys to me?'

'You are being modest, Minister. You are widely believed to be the heir apparent to the premiership and your proud and ancient country is now resurgent.'

'It has the Presidency of the European Council next year.'

No point in pussyfooting around it.

'Yes.'

'Then we understand each other.' Sidaris sat back on the sofa and, having looked at Professor Matsouka, turned his astute gaze on Cassie. 'What does David Hurst want?' he said in English.

'He wants you to come to London to speak with him. Before you ask me, I must tell you that I am not party to his private thoughts on any discussion the two of you may have, but I believe it is about strengthening the position of the centre-left across Europe and how it may address certain global issues.' Cassie paused.

'And your presentation? Is that relevant to any discussions?'

'In part,' Cassie said. 'Its subject is tax reform.' She glanced at Professor Matsouka, who had leaned forward. 'We are introducing a new, transparent tax regime in the UK, making it easier for people to understand how everyone contributes towards the common good. Perhaps this system may be of use to you in Greece.' She paused, recalling the brochure about the Centre. 'It's fitting that we discuss this here, at a Conference Centre built to celebrate democratic principles, even if the ancient Temple to Apollo nearby exemplifies the arbitrary rule of the gods. But then Athena, goddess of wisdom and the symbol of democracy, was Apollo's sister,' she smiled. 'We would be happy to share our new system with you, should you wish to explore what it has to offer.'

'Charming,' said Sidaris, chuckling. 'So appropriate for the setting. You are a practiced diplomat, Ms Fortune.'

Cassie smiled and shook her head.

'It might be of use,' Matsouka said to his friend. 'I'd like to know more.'

'Good.' Sidaris slapped his hands on his knees and rose, indicating that the interview was over. 'We will speak again, Ms Fortune. Thank you, Ms Gatakis.'

'Thank you, Minister.'

Helena murmured her thanks in Greek.

'I look forward to your presentation,' Professor Matsouka said as he accompanied them to the door. 'But... perhaps you are coming on the visit to the temple complex later this afternoon?'

'I was unaware of such a visit,' Cassie said. No point in pretending otherwise, Helena had mentioned a visit to the Museum, but not this.

'But I'd be very interested to see the ancient site.'

'It's happening soon,' Matsouka said. 'Before we lose the light.'

'Then I'll certainly come along. Will the Minister be going?'

'No, much as he would like to, that would attract too much attention.'

And more demonstrations.

'One of the downsides of high office, Ms Fortune, as I'm sure you're aware. Meg and I will be going with Yannis and a couple of his men, of course.'

'Cassie, please call me Cassie.'

'A diminutive of Cassandra. I'll say nothing more in case you tell my future.' The Professor paused for a moment. 'And near the Temple of Apollo too. But the obvious comments will already have been made. That's the problem with a classical name, though it's better than Clytemnestra or Medea, I suppose.'

All victims, some more guilty than others.

The door closed behind them.

'Ok?' Helena asked, as they walked back to the guesthouse. 'Was that ok?'

'Yes,' Cassie responded. 'You can report back to the embassy that so far all is on track.'

Helena's face fell and Cassie immediately regretted her sharpness. The woman was only doing her job, even if that meant reporting back on her performance. Being reported upon was part of the package and the Ambassador would certainly be watching for any misstep. Helena would be his eyes and ears; as a contract worker she had no choice, she couldn't afford to offend him or his people. It wouldn't be personal.

'It was ok,' she said. 'You're right.'

It hadn't gone badly, she reflected, but she hadn't learned much she didn't know already, other than that the Minister spoke English but liked to pretend that he didn't. Not so bad a beginning but if she was to achieve her goal and get the Minister to London she'd have to do better next time, once they'd seen her presentation. And if that wasn't enough... she'd have to think of something else.

◊ SEVEN

Half an hour later a group of a dozen people, including Cassie and Helena, set off on foot. As they passed through the Centre's gates the shadows of the cypress trees were already long and Cassie shivered and zipped up her newly purchased jacket. The temperature was dropping.

Cassie and Helena walked with Jim Norton and Elise Forché. Mike Robbins hadn't come but there were other delegates, including a small group of older men who, Helena told her, were the Austrian delegation. They were timetabled to present immediately before Cassie's session on the following morning so she scrutinised them with interest. Nondescript and stolid, probably competent, but not exciting, she decided.

None of the ministerial party had appeared.

'Maybe they'll come by car,' Helena suggested. 'After this morning's demo, I wouldn't be surprised. Some of the demonstrators are probably still around.'

The temple complex was a twenty-minute walk along the main road through Delphi town and around another spur of the mountain, just beyond the modern Delphi Museum. Tucked into a fold of Mount Parnassus, it was nature's secret. Despite the increasing secularism of society, the place had kept its mystery.

'How old is the Temple?' Jim asked.

'The temple ruins you'll see today date back to 320 BCE,' Nico, their guide, answered. He looked tired, with bags beneath his eyes. 'It's the sixth Temple of Apollo to stand here, though the site has been sacred for millennia, initially to the great Mother Goddess, Gaia.'

Having turned off from the main road they arrived at a set of high metal gates topped with spikes. Nico unlocked them, standing up straighter as a black limousine pulled up at the side of the road below. Meg Taylor, Professor Matsouka and Yannis Iraklidis, the Security Chief, got out and strode towards the tour group, flanked by two security men.

'Enter, please,' Nico said and ushered them all through the gates, closing them thereafter.

They stood in a relatively flat open space, with a wide pathway of large flat stones leading from it across and up the mountain's slope. On either side of this were the remains, sometimes only foundations, of stone and brick buildings, now partly overgrown with greenery. Cassie could see the huge base of the Temple much higher above, with its polygonal masonry and she glimpsed the marble columns upon it.

'All the peoples of the Mediterranean world made precious offerings here, even the Great Pharaoh of Egypt. The ruins on both sides of the Sacred Way are treasuries.' The young man led them along the rising path, which zigzagged back upon itself up the mountainside. 'The most complete is the Treasury of the Athenians.' He pointed to a temple-style building higher up. 'It was restored in the nineteenth century.'

'How did they ensure no one stole the offerings?' Iraklidis asked. He bestowed his flashing white smile on Elise and Helena and, briefly, herself.

'The sanctuary was looted several times,' Nico answered. 'But the whole of the Mediterranean world honoured Apollo and to steal from him was blasphemous. Traditionally, those who blasphemed were flung from the top of the Phaedriades cliffs, called the Shining Ones.'

'Those cliffs there?' one of the Austrians asked, pointing to the massive rock faces looming over one side of the temple site. A tall, lean man with piercing blue eyes and a shock of white hair, he looked older than his colleagues, but spoke easily, without the shortness of breath which walking up the incline had caused for the others.

'That's right,' Nico said.

'Why are they called the Shining Ones?' the Austrian asked again.

'You can't see it now, the sun is in the wrong position,' Nico said. 'But when it's higher in the sky it reflects off the white rock and the cliffs appear to shine. They're over fifteen hundred meters high.'

'Are there any remains of temples to Gaia?' Meg Taylor asked, as the group resumed walking.

'Sadly no,' Nico answered. 'Offerings to her were found at the Castilian Spring dating to about the fifth century BCE, but her association with Delphi goes back long before that. Apollo came along later. Legend has it that he wrestled successfully with the Pytho, the great snake belonging to Mother Gaia, so he took possession of the sanctuary.'

The group rounded another switchback in the trail, walking past the bottom of the steps leading up to the Athenian Treasury.

'Where's the spring?' the tall Austrian asked.

'Between the Shining Ones.' Nico pointed to a cleft in the mountain at the foot of the cliffs. 'The Pythia, the priestess of the Oracle, would bathe there to achieve ritual purity before she made her prophesies.'

The group was now at the top of the sloping path, on a terrace next to the massive base of the Temple itself, with its six very large marble columns or half columns. Here the wind whipped around them as clouds obscured the low sun. Cassie pushed her hands further into her pockets.

'Did the Pythia operate inside the temple?' Helena asked, shivering inside her coat.

Cassie hoped so. It was one thing to be the mouthpiece for a god, quite another to do so at fifteen hundred metres when snow lay on the ground in November, especially if you had to bathe in the open air first.

'Vase paintings show the Pythia divining the god's messages in a special area, probably subterranean, called the *adyton*.'

'Where's that?'

'We're not sure.' The guide made a rueful face. 'There's a fourth century BCE plan of the Temple showing a small chamber which could be the *adyton* and there are a number of small nooks, but none really fits the plan nor the descriptions. Ultrasound imaging suggests there are a number of chambers beneath the main structure, but it'd cost millions to excavate while preserving the existing ruins.'

'Was the Pythia in some sort of trance or mania when she prophesied?' asked the same lean Austrian.

'It seems so, yes. Dionysus was the god who brought mania,' Nico answered. 'He ruled here during the winter months, not Apollo. So perhaps it was Dionysus who created the trance. However, geologists have found that two geological fault lines cross beneath Delphi, with fissures under the Temple itself which allow small amounts of naturally occurring gas to rise to the surface. Rock testing showed ethane, methane and ethylene – formerly used as an anaesthetic – to be present. These would create a calm, trancelike state and, if a lot was consumed, a form of wild mania.'

Basically, the Pythia was stoned. No wonder people thought she prophesied in riddles.

'Not a lot to see really,' Jim said, handing Elise down the ramp and jumping down after her.

'The Temple was the centre of Delphi life,' Nico reclaimed their attention. 'It had a philosophical as well as a religious element, its stones carry the three famous edicts: Know Thyself, Nothing in Excess, which is sometimes translated as Moderation in All Things and finally, An Oath Leads to Mischief.'

'Isn't there an athletics stadium?' Meg Taylor asked. 'I'd like to see that.'

'It's much further up,' Nico said. 'I don't think there's time today, the light is going.'

Meg looked as if she was about to argue.

'Quite right,' Professor Matsouka said, as the wind ruffled his hair. 'We should be getting back soon. But perhaps you'll let my colleague see it tomorrow? She has a professional interest.'

'I want to run on it,' Meg said.

Nico's eyes widened.

He's just realised who she is.

'It's outside the boundary fence,' Nico offered. 'You can get to it from above, using the path from behind Delphi town, the one which goes up to the Corycian Cave. Just take the right-hand turn before the path really starts to kick upwards.'

'Thanks, I will,' she replied. 'Anyone want to join me?'

She looked directly at Cassie, who blinked in surprise.

'Yes, I wouldn't mind a run before breakfast,' she replied, deciding to take the hint. 'Though I'm sure I won't be able to keep up with you.'

'Oh, I'm very slow these days. Seven thirty? It should be light by then.'

'The guesthouse lobby at seven thirty it is.'

'Now, if you'll follow me,' Nico began again.

◊ EIGHT

That night the conference attendees were the only diners in a local restaurant, located along the mountain road within its own grove of olive trees. Cassie was seated between Helena and, according to his place card, one Dieter Freyer of Salzburg.

'You're next to the handsome Security Chief,' she said to Helena, pointing to the next card along.

'Am I?' The interpreter looked at the place card too.

'You seemed quite taken with him this afternoon. And he with you. Have you met before?'

'Only in a general sort of way.' The interpreter's cheeks reddened.

'He doesn't wear a wedding ring.'

'You've looked!' Helena raised her eyebrows in mock horror.

'Neither do you.'

'Me, no, I'm footloose and fancy free.' Helena's laughter ended abruptly with the arrival of Yannis Iraklidis.

'Ladies,' he greeted them with that smile. 'Did you enjoy this afternoon's visit?'

'Very much,' Cassie said pleasantly before turning her attention to the man on her left.

'Herr Freyer,' she said. 'Cassandra Fortune of the UK.'

'Ms Fortune,' the Austrian shook her hand. 'You are presenting tomorrow.'

'Yes, taxation reform.'

'Not my area of expertise,' the man said. 'Very technical, I don't understand it.'

That makes two of us.

'You're with the Austrian delegation?'

'Indeed. We are the largest, I think.' Freyer puffed out his chest to afford this the status of an impressive achievement. 'We arrived yesterday and present tomorrow morning on the restructuring of our transport and cultural projects. It has been a major undertaking.'

Cassie was tempted to ask how big his budget had been, as she strongly suspected that HMRC's was much larger, even though the British delegation consisted only of herself and Helena. She forbore and instead asked, 'Do you live in Salzburg city? It's very lovely, I'm told.'

'Yes, I'm very lucky.' He smirked.

'Wine?' A young woman, one of a clutch of black clad waiters and waitresses, asked.

'Do you have beer?'

'Yes, of course, if *kyriakos* would prefer.'

It's going to be a long evening.

The arrival of the ministerial party provided a distraction, with

Professor Diomides Matsouka and Meg Taylor seated at the centre of the long table, as the guests of honour.

'Hm, Sidaris doesn't show his face, I see,' Freyer sniffed. 'Not very hospitable.'

'Given the demonstration earlier, maybe the Minister thought it would attract less attention and be more enjoyable for all concerned if he didn't attend,' Cassie answered, trying not to sound sharp.

Freyer grunted and turned to speak with the person on his right.

After the ministerial party was seated the meal began. Beside her Helena's attention was focussed on Iraklidis and, as far as Cassie could tell, the Security Chief was paying court in return. He seemed the sort of man who was entirely aware of the effect he had on women in general and some in particular. He was the one member of the ministerial party who had been at the restaurant ahead of time, probably checking security.

And rejigging the seating place cards?

The waiting staff served hot flatbreads with hummus and tzatziki. The food was good, the wine flowed and the volume of talk and laughter grew louder. Even Herr Freyer mellowed sufficiently to praise the meal, possibly under the influence of several steins of foaming lager. After finishing with a gossamer light syllabub Cassie sat back, replete.

Soon diners were asked to move to smaller tables at the edge of the room. The long table was to be cleared and the space used for dancing. A four-piece band set up on a dais at one end of the room. To loud applause they struck up a waltz.

As she rose Cassie was approached by the tall Austrian who had been on the Temple tour.

'Ms Fortune, Stefan Schlange,' he said, offering his hand with a smile. 'We met this afternoon. I'm the main presenter of the session before yours.'

He was polite, but Cassie had glimpsed him looking her up and down in a way she hadn't enjoyed.

'On project restructuring, I understand,' she said. 'Are you a project management specialist?'

'No. I'm a historian.'

'Stefan is an expert in the history of the EU.' The sharp-faced Austrian appeared at her elbow, a watchful terrier to his colleague's rangy afghan hound. He introduced himself. 'Dr Josef Wild.'

'Dr Wild.' She acknowledged him, then addressed Schlange. 'So you're not a classical historian?'

'No. Modern history, twentieth century Europe mainly: the Cold War, the EEC, the fall of the Eastern bloc and the triumph of democracy, a turbulent time but a positive one.'

Schlange moved a little closer towards her, glancing down, his eyes slightly hooded. At well over six feet tall, the Austrian would have been used to looking down at people, she thought. She mightn't be as tall, but she certainly wasn't going to lower her gaze.

'Stefan,' Dr Wild interjected. He gestured towards a large, round table at the other side of the room, where Herr Freyer was beckoning them over.

'Ah, would you excuse us,' Schlange said, as he and Wild left her and went to join their delegation.

Briefly Cassie joined Jim and Elise. Each had the bright-eyed perkiness of the slightly drunk. She sensed a tension between them too, but this was all part and parcel of a febrile energy within the tavern. The very air of the place crackled with it. Mike Robbins hovered at their table but did not sit. Instead, he button-holed Cassie as she rose to move on.

'I heard that you spoke with the Minister earlier,' he said. 'What did you talk about?'

What sort of question's that? Is he drunk already?

Robbins must have seen the astonishment on her face because he qualified his question. 'You didn't happen to discuss energy policy, did you?'

'No.' Cassie made to move on, but Robbins stepped into her path.

'Did he say anything about the environmental lobby? Anything about the demonstration?'

'No. Excuse me,' Cassie pushed past. She felt Robbins grab her wrist and she tried to tug it away, turning to protest.

'Cassandra,' Professor Matsouka was approaching. Robbins let her go. 'May I have the pleasure?'

'Of course,' she said.

The Professor whisked her around the dance floor, away from the American.

'A little too eager, our American friend,' he said. 'Drink, I suspect. I do apologise.'

'There's no need. It's not your fault.'

'No, but you are, in a manner of speaking, my, or our guest. Have you ever danced Greek style?'

'No,' she smiled at the change of subject. 'But I think I might be about to.'

Professor Matsouka produced a large white handkerchief from his pocket and, holding Cassie's right hand in his left, struck a pose, with the handkerchief above his head. He resembled a slightly Bacchic master of ceremonies.

'*Kalamatianos!*'

There was a cheer and people hurried on to the dance floor. The band began to play a folk tune, in seven-eight time.

'Here,' he held Cassie's right hand. Her left hand had already been claimed by a young staff member from the Centre. 'Just follow my steps.'

Professor Matsouka led the dance, taking three steps forward and two back, then leaping into the air with a flourish. Caterpillar like, the motion proceeded along the line of dancers until everyone was moving almost in unison, people stamping and leaping in a steady rhythm. They interlaced.

In the shadows at the edge of the room, onlookers clapped and shouted as the Professor lead the chain around and around. Cassie saw Helena and Iraklidis on the other side of the circle, laughing together as they danced, Elise and Jim, Meg, the tall Austrian and lots of others were joining in, catching the tail of the chain. Feet rose and fell. Air and light vibrated, and faces grew rosy. Old timbers quivered to remembered cadences. Slowly the tempo of the music increased.

She concentrated on getting the dance right, but the music got faster and faster and she missed steps. Laughing, she saw that she wasn't the only one in difficulty. Everyone was stumbling to keep up, smiling and joking as the chain wound round the room and back upon itself, its movement becoming ever more frenetic. Cassie lost herself in the measure and the motion, the repeating steps, the jerking rhythm. Then the music reached a crescendo and... stopped.

Breathless and sweaty she clapped and cheered. The room filled with rambunctious applause, whistles and shouts.

The band began a modern ballad and, a few couples aside, the hot and happy dancers went to claim cold drinks and to collapse into chairs.

'That was amazing,' Cassie said to Matsouka and Meg.

'I'm getting too old for it,' the Professor mopped his brow with the, now wrung out, handkerchief.

It was very hot and airless, despite all the windows and doors being flung open. Her T-shirt clung to her body and her hair had escaped its chignon. She rebound it.

'I need some cold water.' Cassie strolled over to the bar, where glasses of chilled water had been set out. She drank one, took another and turned to survey the room.

Elise and Jim were now entwined around each other and Helena and Iraklidis were standing so close to each other that they may as well have been. There were young couples embracing in the shadowy corners of the room.

Those who had not paired off were indulging in some serious drinking. Mike was sitting alone, steadily knocking back beers with whisky chasers, as was a group of Austrians, red faced and sweating. This was unlike any conference party Cassie had ever been to. The atmosphere was anarchic and wild. Anything might happen.

For the first time in weeks Cassie felt unencumbered, liberated from some oppressive weight. The misery of losing Andrew, the man she had begun to love, the fear of Lawrence Delahaye, the criminal she had made an enemy of, the anxiety about failing at her new job, all dissolved. The cadences of the dance still coursed through her veins. The horrendous tension was replaced by a sort of euphoria. Exhilarated, she wanted to dance again, to lead the chain in a mad romp. She heard herself laugh aloud at nothing.

The band was playing another traditional tune and dancers were beginning to form a chain. A woman, surrounded by dancers, was whirling like a dervish in the centre of the room, her long black hair sweeping outward. There was no sign of Professor Matsouka.

Don't get caught up in it. Leave. Leave now.

She blinked. Maybe that was wise. Despite having had so little sleep she'd agreed to go running in the morning – which was only a few hours away. She looked around, indecisive. Helena and the Security Chief were holding hands, staring into each other's eyes, oblivious to her presence.

Hmm, someone's mind isn't on the job.

The sour thought sobered her. Cassie collected her things from the table where she had been sitting. Pulling on her new jacket, she headed towards the door.

◊ NINE

The cold air hit her like a slap.

Above her was a starry panorama, inky black but gleaming. A full moon hung above Parnassus, lighting the grove and the path to the roadway, casting her own faint shadow before her.

A few steps on Cassie turned back to look at the restaurant. Through the open door she could hear the strains of the Greek dance. Inside all was flickering movement and shadows.

It's like escaping from a spell.

There're undercurrents of madness in that room.

Was this what happened when you drank and danced near a shrine when Dionysus was in residence? She took a deep breath of cold air and shook her head to clear it. A brisk walk up the mountain road would dispel all thought of bacchanalia.

Her feet crunched fallen leaves as she walked to the road. She spotted two security men patrolling the garden of the restaurant; one raised a hand in salute, then spoke into a walkie-talkie. If he was contacting his boss, Iraklidis wouldn't thank him for it.

At the road she turned in the direction of the Centre. It was very quiet and cold.

So, Yannis Iraklidis... handsome, well connected and, yes, quite sexy.

Probably got a girl in every port, or was it the madness of the bacchanal? But so what. Maybe a fling was all Helena wanted, or a passing sexual liaison. Not everyone wanted to fall in love, not everyone fell in love whether or not they wanted to. She had. She felt a familiar ache and shoved it aside.

What's that?

Someone was walking through the dead leaves in the garden of the restaurant, back down the road, probably an over-heated dancer out to take the air.

She turned her mind to tomorrow morning.

What could Meg Taylor want to speak with her about? She was clearly part of the Minister's longstanding entourage, but Cassie didn't think the runner had any political function. Perhaps she wanted a favour from Cassie or more likely, from her boss.

Cassie tried to remember the circumstances of Meg's past. It was a damn nuisance that she couldn't get a phone signal or wi-fi; she would have liked to look up the runner's history. She could access the internet at the guesthouse via their landline, but the service was slow and she didn't want her interest to be logged and potentially public. It was a quarter to midnight, so nine forty-five in London. She would telephone Siobhan's mobile when she got back to her room and ask her to do some quick research, if that was possible.

Again, a noise – from back down the road – had someone else decided to return to the Centre?

'Hello,' she called.

No reply. But she heard the noise again, footfalls, light but distinct.

Her skin prickled, the hairs rising. There was someone there, but they weren't answering her hail.

Moonlight illuminated much of the road and the mountain side, but created deep shadows beneath the trees and bushes at the foot of the upper slope, where anyone could easily hide. The noise had stopped. Whoever it was, they were waiting for her to move on.

Cassie began to walk, more swiftly this time. Again she heard footsteps. She was definitely being followed.

How far to the gates of the Centre now? Two hundred metres, maybe three? Her heart started thumping. The footsteps sounded closer.

Can I make it if I run?

'Hello!' A distant call came from much further down the road. It was Helena's voice. 'Cassie?'

'Helena, is that you?'

'And me. Wait for us,' Iraklidis called.

She exhaled in relief and realised how scared she had been. In the moonlight she saw the couple round a bend, lower down the road in the moonlight and waved.

'Am I glad to see you,' she said as they drew level. 'I thought I was being followed.'

'When? Just now?'

'It was us,' Helena said.

'No, I don't think that's what Cassandra means,' the Security Chief said. He was watching her closely. 'It isn't, is it?'

Can he sense my fear? Andrew always could.

'The sound I heard was closer.'

Iraklidis reached for the walkie-talkie which he was wearing at his belt and spoke rapidly.

'We'll check and make sure there's no one around and do a full search in the morning,' he said to Cassie. 'It could be quite innocent, but you shouldn't be out here on your own anyway.'

'Whoever it was didn't answer my call.'

'I see, well, if someone was following you they will have left traces and tomorrow we'll find them. Let's go back to the Centre.'

As they continued up the road the Security Chief appeared relaxed and good humoured, but his gaze was never static, always searching. Cassie saw him scanning the undergrowth. It made her nervous and she was pleased when two security men came towards them from around the next bend.

Iraklidis issued orders and they walked on either side of the road, weapons drawn. Helena was subdued.

The small group took the lane to the Centre and, when they reached the gates, Iraklidis stopped.

'I must return to the restaurant,' he said. 'To the others. You will be safe now, my men will see you inside.' He added some words in Greek, an endearment to Helena, Cassie supposed.

'Take care,' Helena answered.

The two women watched him disappear into the night.

'Who would be following you?' Helena asked.

'I don't know,' Cassie said.

'And why?'

'I don't know that either.'

Don't snap. These are obvious questions.

'I'm sorry, I didn't mean to be sharp.'

Helena murmured acceptance, but she wouldn't be the only one asking the questions. Iraklidis would too and she would have to answer. There was one possibility she didn't want to consider.

It couldn't be him.

During her last assignment she'd incurred the wrath of the power-hungry psychopath at the heart of the criminal organisation which she'd helped expose. Her relationship with him, Lawrence Delahaye, was complicated, he'd been her lover and her captor. He had also ordered the death of DI Andrew Rowlands, for whom she still grieved. Yet Delahaye was still free. She had sworn that there would be a reckoning, that she would see him found and destroyed and she knew the feeling was mutual. It was really just a question of which of them got to the other first.

She ought to warn the Security Chief about Delahaye, but then he would tell Professor Matsouka and the Minister might find out. An unwanted complication which might not go down well. Would it imperil her mission? It certainly wouldn't help. She fervently hoped it was just someone blundering drunkenly around after having come out to empty their bladder, being stupid.

Concentrate on Meg Taylor and tomorrow morning's run.

In her room Cassie rang reception and asked for an outside line. She phoned her secretary's private number.

'Hello. I've been waiting for you to call!' It was good to hear Siobhan's lilting tones, even if she was scolding. 'I assumed that gorgeous Greece was claiming all your attention.'

'It is gorgeous, very spectacular,' Cassie said. 'I'm sorry I didn't ring last night, but there's no mobile signal here and it was late. I tried reception but no one picked up.' True, but she should have tried again or phoned via landline earlier, as she'd promised. 'I don't have private internet access and I need to do some research.'

'Okay, I'll just get a pen.' There was a pause. 'Fire away.'

'Meg Taylor, nee Aertos,' she spelled out. 'Won Olympic gold as half of Britain's "Golden Couple", the other half being Guy Taylor. Came out as gay and got divorced. I'm uncertain which order that came in. It was said that the marriage a way of maximising sponsorship. Can you find out exactly what happened to her – and to him, please.'

'Yep, by when?'

'Mmm, like now? It's after midnight here but I'm supposed to be going running with her tomorrow morning at seven thirty. It was at her invitation and I need to see if I can work out what she might want from me.'

'I'll do some digging and phone you back in ten minutes?'

'Speak in a bit.'

Cassie prepared for bed, thinking about the evening. An orgiastic collective madness seemed to have taken hold of everyone at the dinner. Then to be followed by someone who didn't want to be seen, whose purpose was unknown. Were the two things linked?

The room telephone rang.

'Hi, it's me. Megaera, not Megan, Aertos, born Athens, 1980, came to the UK on an Erasmus Scholarship in the late 90s, started running professionally and married fellow Oxford student Guy Taylor three years later, gold medallist in Beijing. A very high-profile couple until their divorce.'

'Children?'

'No. She came out as lesbian after the divorce was announced. She and Taylor were accused of making a fake marriage to get better sponsorship deals. Sponsors deserted her, not because of her sexuality, they claimed, but because of the deception. She resigned her executive post with Sport England, has gone to ground since. Guy Taylor suffered too, but once the scandal died down was treated more as a victim. He remarried a long-time lover and currently sits on the boards of several City firms.'

'Okay, thanks Siobhan. Sorry to impose on your evening.'

'No bother. Get some sleep,' the secretary said. 'You'll need it if you're running with an Olympic champion tomorrow, even if she's no longer young.'

She's not that much older than me!

'Goodnight.'

Cassie looked at her watch, it was half past midnight. Siobhan was right, she should get some sleep, but the events of the evening would not let her rest. She relaxed her mind and let her subconscious sift its way through all the information

Someone had been following her and there was only one person she knew who would do that, or would order someone else to do it for him. Could that be it – a hired assassin? She didn't think so, it didn't feel right. Lawrence Delahaye wanted her dead, but he would want to administer the *coup de grace* himself, not hand the task to someone else. The animosity between them was very personal.

She shivered and climbed into bed.

It had all taken place so recently, only a few weeks ago. She hadn't had time to process the experience properly and, she suspected, she suffered from some form of acute stress disorder, or "shock", since September. Her eyes strayed to the bottle of diazepam on the bedside table. She switched off the light.

So much had happened in the short time since. She had left her previous department, took up her new post with the PM, began working with different Whitehall departments and agencies preparing for this mission. Everything seemed to have happened so quickly. She had promised to talk with a counsellor and she would, it was just that she hadn't had time.

There was nothing she could do about that now.

Get some sleep!

WEDNESDAY

◊ TEN

Cassie yawned and stretched as she went into the bathroom.

A run was the last thing she felt like doing, but she didn't have a choice. She had about ten minutes before meeting Meg in reception. As she pulled on her clothes she realised she hadn't reminded Helena about her run. The interpreter might wonder where she was when she didn't appear at breakfast.

She telephoned room twenty-nine.

'Hello.'

A male voice. Did she have the right room? Of course she did. *Yannis Iraklidis.*

'Ah, hello, good morning. May I speak with Helena, please?'

'Cassie, good morning. She's in the shower, shall I...?'

'Cassie, yes.' Helena sounded breathless. 'Sorry, I was...'

'No problem. I'm just ringing to tell you...'

She couldn't mention the run. Helena would tell Iraklidis and there would be security men at every turn. That wouldn't suit her at all.

'I'm not going into breakfast so I'll see you later. That's all.'

'Okay,' Helena sounded puzzled. 'Is everything alright?'

'Yes, fine. Bye'

Within ten minutes she was downstairs, waiting outside reception, running on the spot to keep warm – it was distinctly cold. There were still stars visible, low in the western sky, but the night had passed. She checked her watch – seven thirty-five – Meg Taylor was late.

Cassie caught sight of her running towards the guesthouse. Her hair was pulled up into a ponytail and she wore a track suit, the top of which was partly unzipped, revealing the sweaty T-shirt beneath. There was the sheen of perspiration on her face and neck. It looked as if she'd already done a run that morning.

'Morning,' Meg said as she jogged lightly on the spot, full of energy and bearing no signs of the previous night's excesses. 'Ready?'

As ready as I'll ever be.

'Yes. Be gentle with me – I'm not as fit as I once was. And it was a late-night last night.'

'You'll be fine. I left the tavern shortly after you did,' the runner replied. 'This is a jog, not a race.'

Cassie was surprised when she didn't take the lane to the road. They jogged along a narrow path through the olive trees towards the wire perimeter fence at the back of the Centre grounds. Within minutes they arrived at a wire gate.

'Ah, this is the other entrance,' Cassie said. 'I knew there must be one.'

Meg withdrew a key on a ribbon around her neck, unlocked the padlock and pulled back the lever to open the gate. She slammed it closed once they had passed through.

'This goat path will take us over the ridge to the top of Delphi town, where we will join the track leading up to the Corycian Cave.'

'Have you been up there?'

'Not yet, though I plan to, I want to see all the complex. Come on, let's stretch our legs and get away from here. I'm constantly expecting one of Yannis's men to see me and insist on coming along.'

'Me too.'

For the next ten minutes she concentrated on not falling too far behind, though Meg kept glancing back over her shoulder and adjusting her pace. They reached the top of the ridge and Delphi town lay before them. Meg slowed to a walk and Cassie caught up. Sensing that Meg would welcome frankness, she decided to tackle things head on.

'So, what did you want to talk with me about?'

'No beating about the bush with you, is there?' The runner laughed.

'It seems simpler and more honest to get to the point,' Cassie replied. 'And, as you say, we could be spotted and tagged at any moment. So, how can I help you?'

Meg stared into the middle distance. This wasn't a person who found it easy asking for help. She was probably more comfortable being petitioned herself, something she would be used to, as the Minister's friend.

'You know about my history?'

'Why don't you tell me.'

'I'm lesbian. I guess I always knew, though I didn't really understand. I married Guy believing that I could change, become heterosexual. Things were different then and my upbringing was a conservative one. It wasn't acceptable to be gay in the way it is now and I wanted children. And to confuse the matter – I genuinely loved him. He was a lovely man and we shared so much. There was nothing fraudulent. That's why the legal threats came to nothing. The only person I deceived was him – and myself.'

She spoke very rapidly, her cheeks flushing pink.

'Children didn't happen and like so many former athletes I moved into sports administration. I'd realised that I couldn't change my sexuality and I wasn't prepared to become a nonsexual being, but before I could make any sort of announcement I was outed. I'm still not sure by whom, someone who wanted my job, I suspect. I never fitted the standard model, you see, I was a foreigner and a woman and now a lesbian. The old boys's network didn't like me. They were happy to cut me down.'

A familiar story.

'I had to resign. For a long time I blamed myself, not just for the deception, which *was* my fault, but for the failure. I realise now that it wasn't so much a failure, more a coup, by people waiting to exploit my vulnerability for their own advancement.'

That sounds familiar too.

'I loved my job. I've paid for my actions. Now I want to go back to doing something like it.'

'Forgive me, Meg, for asking, but couldn't you do that sort of work here, in Greece?'

'I could, even though I don't really know the system here. I left Greece when I was in my teens. But I have another reason for returning to the UK.' She hesitated. 'I've met someone and we want to marry. Her family commitments mean she has to live in Britain.'

'Does Theo know that you are speaking with me about this?'

'No. He would disapprove.'

'But the Professor does?'

'No, him neither. He suspects I want to return to my life in the UK, but that's all.'

'Let me think how I might help,' Cassie said. 'Such appointments are independently scrutinised.'

'I know,' Meg interrupted. 'Please understand that I'm not asking for favourable treatment, merely to be sure that, if I apply for roles, it will be a level playing field.'

'There are image consultants who help with matters like this.'

'And if I have to go to one of them, I will.' Meg swallowed hard. 'I just want to know I won't be blackballed. I want to be allowed to try to return to my career. That's all.'

This was something Cassie could identify with – her own career having taken a nose-dive before her recent return to favour. She'd been a rapidly rising star but had got sideswiped, kicked into the basement where everyone expected her to stay, quiet and grateful for a job. That was where she had stayed until she'd joined forces with Detective Inspector Andrew Rowlands and got her career back.

'Will you help me?'

Cassie was cautious. 'I need to consider how I might best do that. It's not clear to me how I can help you in any meaningful way. I can't say with certainty what the best way forward might be but I'll certainly do my best.'

'I'll take that. Thank you,' Meg said and, as if embarrassed by the conversation, stretched her legs and drew ahead. For a while they ran, skirting the higher part of Delphi town. The track merged with a wider trail, which switch-backed up the mountain.

'This is the route to the Corycian Cave,' Meg said, slowing. 'It quickly peters out into a dirt path, with a pretty fearsome gradient, but we'll hit the turn-off to the stadium before then.'

Conversation wasn't possible, at least for Cassie, as the trail rose. When they reached the fork she stopped and put her hands on her knees, panting and out of condition. She looked up.

Meg stood atop a hummock, watching her, her face showing no emotion. It looked haughty and very, very beautiful, but almost other than human in its coldness.

People won't warm to you. They will envy you, admire you, but not like you. Then there's your past to manage. You definitely need an image consultant and, even so, it'll be an uphill battle.

'This way,' Meg said.

◊ ELEVEN

'Did the guide say how old this was?' Meg asked. 'I can't remember.'

They were standing in the centre of the elongated oval of the narrow stadium. The stepped spectator seating to their right reached around the curve of the bend, against a mountainside covered with firs and cypresses. To their left only the base of the supporting wall remained, before the slope dropped away to the theatre and temple ruins below.

'Fourth century BCE I think.'

'This must be the starting point over here,' Meg said as she walked over to the eastern end, Cassie following.

'Look.'

There was a row of stone slabs, ancient starting blocks with two grooves incised in each, where runners would have placed their feet for grip. Meg took up a starting position, arms wide, fingertips on the ground, resting on one knee.

'On your marks, get set, GO!' Cassie shouted.

Meg shot forward from the stone blocks, arms pumping, her pick-up lasting for a few paces before she got into her stride. As she headed off to the other end of the stadium, Cassie walked to its edge and looked out.

She was above the rest of the temple complex and could see the temple platform below and, through the trees, the semi-circle of stone seats of the theatre. To her left were the Phaedriades, their white stone catching the light of the rising sun. Far, far below was the valley floor.

It was easy to understand why the place had been sacred for so long. It was so still, a sense of the divine so near to the surface. It had astonishing drama and beauty. The ancient Greeks had believed it was the centre of the world.

Meg was coming back towards Cassie and the finish line. Head held high, her powerful motion was fluid and controlled, knees lifting, arms bent and swinging, fingers pointing upwards. A fine sight, Cassie thought and very appropriate to the setting, a demi-goddess, not a modern-day former sports administrator.

Meg raised her arms in a faux victory salute and Cassie applauded. The runner slowed to a walk.

'Can we get into the temple site from here?' Cassie asked.

'Dunno.' Meg shrugged as they ambled down the path out of the eastern end of the stadium. 'I don't think so, it's fenced off. But we can still reach the main road if we take the path to the foot of the cliffs and follow it down, past the Castalian Spring. I've done that run.'

The path headed in the direction of the cliffs, although it was soon absorbed into a wide field of scree, a gradient of loose stones and small boulders which stretched to the foot of the Phaedriades, where the path resumed. The scree slope ran down the mountain until it plunged directly downward for about twenty feet to the temple complex below.

'We'll be ok once we're across this,' Meg said.

'Right, but it's too steep for me to run,' Cassie said. 'You trail run if you want to, but I'll walk.'

'I'll walk, thank you. I don't want to break an ankle.'

As they picked their way across the scree slope Cassie caught glimpses of the ruins in the temple complex below, the morning sunlight creeping down to reflect from the white marble.

'It's such a remarkable place,' she said. 'Just coming here must have taken people away from their troubles. Perhaps that's the secret, to get folk away from the hurly-burly, the irreconcilable issues, the impossible decisions, bring them here and let them see things in perspective.'

'Maybe.' Meg looked across at Cassie. 'And look at themselves...'

'Yes,' Cassie said. '"Know Thyself" - one of the Temple inscriptions – though I didn't see much evidence of "Nothing in Excess" last night and there wasn't a lot of "moderation". Some folk will have very bad heads this morning and others might find they have new bedfellows.' She grinned. 'Did you notice...?'

'Yannis and Helena, yes,' Meg smiled. 'She's single, I take it?'

'As far as I'm aware. Him?'

'Divorced. And lonely, I think.'

'Really? I wouldn't have thought he would have any problems attracting women.'

'He doesn't, but he's quite wary of commitment,' Meg said. 'His marriage didn't end happily. The job, the hours, the weeks away. His wife found someone else. I think there were betrayals on both sides.'

'Ah. What's the third Temple inscription: "An Oath Brings Mischief"? Does that include something personal like wedding vows? I'd assumed it applied to formal oaths, given that so many of the consultations at Delphi were about peace or war, treaties or contracts.'

'I thought "oath" meant a promise – and that would include the marriage vow.' Meg's voice was bitter. 'You see before you a living example of the third maxim. I broke my promises – to Guy, to the sponsors and to the public. All those promises to the people who supported me and followed my career. Maybe I deserved the "mischief" which followed?'

Cassie looked down at the rocky ground.

'What's done is done,' she said. '"Nothing in Excess", remember. And that includes self-criticism.'

Ironic. I know how that works.

'Cassie...?'

'What? Sorry, miles away.'

'Time's moving on,' Meg said. 'I think we ought to head back to the Centre.'

Cassie consulted her watch. It was almost nine and she was doing her presentation before lunch. 'Heavens, yes,' she said and quickened her stride. 'No time for the Spring today.'

'We're nearly at the road,' Meg said. 'Then we can run again. It won't take long.'

Skip breakfast, go straight to the Centre to check the set up. There's plenty of time.

Nonetheless, when they reached the road a few minutes later, Cassie was happy for Meg to set a strong pace

◊ TWELVE

'Ms Fortune, if you would just wait here a moment, please,' the young man at the Conference Centre Desk said. 'Mr Marios is looking for you.'

The conference organiser, what did he want with her? Cassie had been introduced to him during dinner the night before. He was younger than she had expected, a boyish fellow with a round face.

'Ms Fortune, Cassandra.' He looked anxious as he came towards her across the lobby. 'I'm very sorry to have to ask you this, but can you do your presentation earlier than scheduled?'

'Um, I suppose so,' Cassie said. 'Why?'

Marios took her elbow and steered her over to the side of the room. He lowered his voice.

'It's one of the Austrians, Dr Schlange. We can't find him.'

'What?' This was the tall man, the historian of Europe.

'No one has seen him since last night. He was scheduled to do the presentation ahead of yours and, apparently, no one else in that party knows enough about the detail to present in his place.' He pursed his lips. 'So we will have to juggle the schedule. He was supposed to present at eleven. Do you think you could take that slot?'

'Yes, though...' Cassie looked down at her sweaty track suit. 'Could we make that eleven thirty? I need to shower, change and check the set-up is ready.'

'We will ensure that it is, I promise you.' Marios clasped his hands in front of his chest. 'Thank you so much. Thank you.'

'I'll be back here at eleven,' she said.

'Yes, thank you.'

Cassie hastened back to the guesthouse, frowning.

Many of the Austrians had been absolutely ratted the night before – there was some seriously excessive drinking going on. He'd probably slunk away somewhere to recuperate and was still sleeping it off.

Very unprofessional.

There were several pasty-faced, ill-looking guests milling around in reception when she arrived, amidst rather a lot of security men. Iraklidis stood by the doors in his overcoat, speaking with the policeman who they had seen at the protest the day before and a man in climbing equipment. Was this a search for the Austrian? Yet Mr Marios's demeanour had suggested that his nonappearance hadn't been widely shared.

Helena hurried up to her. The interpreter seemed on edge, worried perhaps that Cassie might look unkindly on her for sleeping with the Security Chief.

'Cassie, are you ok?'

'Fine, I've just been out for a run. What's happening?'

'A local woman's missing. Her boyfriend hasn't seen her since the day before yesterday. He was our guide from yesterday, the young man, Nico, from the Museum. She worked there too.' Helena paused. 'The Delphi mountain rescue team is out and the local policeman, you know, the one we saw at the protest. He's also the missing woman's uncle. He's asked Yannis and his men to help. They'll start at the foot of the Phaedriades and move gradually westwards across country, above the road and below.'

'What about Delphi town?'

'The policeman is handling that with some local people, calling on all the households.'

'When and where was she last seen? Do we know?'

'On Monday morning, the day before yesterday, here in the guesthouse. She came to organise a trip to the Delphi Museum for the visitors. Nico took us to the Temple instead once the ministerial party showed an interest in going there.'

'So that's forty-eight hours, almost.'

Cassie knew that the missing, if they weren't missing of their own volition, needed to be found within the first twenty-four to forty-eight hours or they stood a much higher chance of being forever lost. And that was in an urban environment, not halfway up a mountain. The woman might have had an accident and be injured. Forty-eight hours was a long time to be outside, especially in sub-zero night-time temperatures.

'Yannis hasn't forgotten your follower last night, either,' Helena said. 'He's sent someone over to search the road and roadside already.'

'Yes, I need to speak with him about that,' Cassie said. 'But it can wait. Finding the woman is more important.'

'Where did you go running?'

'To the stadium, around Delphi town.'

Helena frowned.

'Even after last night? You didn't mention it when you telephoned.'

'Meg Taylor suggested it when we were at the Temple.'

'Ah, yes, I remember.' Helena looked sidelong at Cassie. 'Just as well Yannis didn't know.'

Cassie changed the subject. 'I've been asked to do my presentation earlier than I thought. There is some problem with the Austrian delegation which was supposed to go on before me. One of them is missing too.'

'Two people missing. That's a coincidence. Maybe they knew each other? Could they have gone missing together?'

'It's one possibility,' Cassie replied, frowning.

An ageing visiting academic and a young local woman? Unlikely.

'How much earlier?' Helena asked, looking at her watch.

'I've said I'll start at eleven thirty but I'm going over to the conference rooms at eleven,' Cassie replied. 'The theatre has translation, but it might be helpful if you were there, just in case.'

'I'll be there.'

'Right, see you here just before eleven then. We can walk over together.'

'One more piece of news,' Helena said. 'Good news. Your suitcase has turned up. It arrived when I was in breakfast this morning. I told them to take it to your room.'

'Excellent. Thank you.'

It would be good to have her things again and a fresh blouse to wear.

Cassie took the stairs two at a time.

◊ THIRTEEN

Her suitcase stood in the middle of the floor. She slid its long handle back down into its place and lifted the case on to the bed to open it. You've got plenty of time, just keep calm, she told herself. At least an hour to get ready and re-read her presentation. She needed to find her blouse. Less than an hour if she included the time it took to get over to the conference hall. She unzipped the suitcase. As she undressed she began to run through the presentation in her head. She flipped the top open.

An item lay on top in a plastic dry-cleaning wrapper. She couldn't remember packing any dry cleaning. She turned it over to reveal the transparent side.

The room tilted. All the air sucked out of it.

It can't be the same.

She gulped and breathed again.

It was a grey silk pyjama top, with navy blue piping around its edges. Not hers, though one she had worn, or one very like it.

He can't have retrieved this. It can't be the same.

She ripped off its plastic covering and grabbed at the fabric.

It had been cleaned, but there were still little marks, flecks of a substance in the silk around the collar and shoulders.

My blood.

She could hear it pounding in her ears.

The bedroom in Barton Street. The television on the wall with the midday news report of Andrew's death. Lawrence Delahaye looking down at her. Making love to her. It all forced its way to the front of her consciousness as if a dam had been breached.

Cassie flopped on to a chair, the garment still in her hands. She began to tremble.

Control yourself! Think!

Someone had taken her suitcase, opened it and added the garment, then closed it, so it looked as if it had never been opened. At Heathrow, she presumed. Then what? Just left it there until someone found the case and sent it on?

He must know where I am.

Her flight had been to Athens and the case contained a brochure and papers relating to the conference at Delphi. Whoever opened her case would have seen them, they were on the top. Of course, that mightn't have been Lawrence himself, so whoever did it may not have realised that the information was important.

She couldn't be certain that Delahaye knew her whereabouts. But she couldn't be sure that he didn't. The follower on the mountain road could have been another of his creatures.

Or Delahaye himself.

Her insides turned to liquid.

Her mission, her career, her life, all threatened. Again.

Her eye was caught by the laptop, shifting to screen save mode.

He'll take this too just like he took Andrew. Don't let him.

She reached for the bottle of diazepam on her bedside table and tossed back two pills. Closing her eyes she concentrated on breathing, in, out, lowering her thudding heart rate. She opened her eyes again.

Now prepare. Get cleaned up. Read the presentation. This is too important to make a mess of it.

Cassie stood. She put her hand to the wall for balance, not trusting herself. Then she straightened, until her shoulders were back and her chin came up. She removed her hand from the wall and walked steadily through to the shower.

◊ FOURTEEN

'Cassie, well done!' Professor Diomedes Matsouka walked over to her, hand outstretched, as she stepped down from the stage into a rapidly emptying auditorium. 'Excellent presentation. And I have lots of questions...'

Damn.

'I hope I can answer them,' she replied. 'If not, perhaps you could talk to the people responsible in London.'

'I will definitely be contacting them.'

'Perhaps in person, if you visit?'

'Theo wants to speak with you. Come.'

He led her out of the lecture hall, Helena hurrying along behind, to the private suite of rooms where the ministerial party was in residence.

'Ah, here she is,' Theo Sidaris said as she entered the large, light living room. 'Well done. A very good presentation. You have intrigued Dio here and I'm sure he'll be speaking with the people responsible.'

'Thank you, Minister. I thought, perhaps...'

'Now, I must take a series of calls. I just wanted to congratulate you personally. Please excuse me.'

'And did you enjoy your run this morning?' Professor Matsouka asked, gesturing that she should sit on the sofa beside him, as the Minister left the room.

'Yes, I did, but...'

'We won't be coming to London, Cassie. If David Hurst wishes to speak with Theo, we can always arrange a call. Indeed, Theo would be happy to speak with him at his convenience.'

Her face must have shown her disappointment because the Professor went on to explain.

'We're only a small nation, recently much impoverished and yet we're still part of the club, the European Union. It might be tarnished these days, not the bright, promising, new idea of the 1970s, but it's the best option for us and we still have a seat at the table. Having the presidency of the Council of Europe is a privilege as well as a responsibility and we wouldn't want to be seen by our EU partners to be jeopardising that by conducting unilateral negotiations with non-EU countries, even our allies like the UK.'

Fuck.

Failure stared her in the face – on her very first mission. Would she ever be given a second? Everything she had achieved, the access to the PM, the briefings, the chance to make a difference, all potentially lost.

What do I do now? What else can I offer them?

Before she had opportunity to counter, Iraklidis entered, still wearing his coat. His expression was grave.

'What is it? Yannis?' Professor Matsouka stood.

Iraklidis answered in Greek, his tone sombre.

Helena brought her hand to her mouth as she gasped.

'They've found a body,' she said to Cassie, her voice a whisper. 'Of the missing woman.'

'Where?' Cassie asked.

The Security Chief stared at her.

'Yes, where?' the Professor repeated.

'At the temple complex, in the Treasury of the Athenians.' Iraklidis switched to English.

'My God, we were there only yesterday afternoon,' the Professor said. 'Was it an accident?'

'She was strangled.'

'So she was there, her body was there, when we went to visit the Temple yesterday?' Helena said, her face chalk white against her black hair.

'Yes.'

Helena gazed wide-eyed at the Security Chief. Iraklidis moved towards her, then stopped. Cassie saw him struggle with the urge to take Helena in his arms. The professional won. Then his eyes narrowed in suspicion.

'Cassandra, who is the criminal who is hunting you?' he asked.

'How did you know about that?'

Helena winced. 'The people at the embassy told me. After the stalker last night, I – I thought Yannis ought to know,' she said.

So. Payback from the Ambassador.

'Who is Lawrence Delahaye and why is he after you?' the security man continued.

'He's a criminal I helped to expose. He would like to see me dead.'

'Could the killing of the local woman be his work?' the Professor asked.

'If you're asking me whether or not he is capable of committing murder, then the answer would be "yes" as he is responsible for many deaths. But if you are asking me if I think he did this, then my answer would be "no". It's my death he wants and he isn't a random killer.'

'And you didn't think to tell me about this?' Iraklidis's ground out the question between gritted teeth. 'I am responsible for security here, including yours.'

'You're right. I should have told you, but I didn't imagine that he would know where I was.'

'Let's focus on what's immediately important. Theo leaves now, if there's a killer on the loose,' Professor Matsouka ordered. 'Arrange a car and a security detail to take him back to Athens straight away, Yannis. Make sure he has your best men. We will follow later.'

'The police have asked that nobody leave,' Iraklidis replied.

'They will make an exception for the Minister.' The Professor was brusque. 'The rest of us, well, we will have to stay.'

'There is a Police Major coming from the regional HQ at Amfissa to take over the case.'

'Then best we don't present him with a difficult decision. Get Theo out of here now.'

The chief nodded, relinquished Helena's hand and strode out of the room.

'That would be usual, would it?' Cassie asked. 'To bring a high-ranking police officer to deal with a case like this?'

'I would imagine so, these small towns have only one or two policemen,' Professor Matsouka said.

'And the local policeman... isn't he the uncle of the young woman found dead?' Cassie said. 'So he wouldn't really be able to investigate.'

'Yes,' Helena said.

'What's going on?' Meg entered, looking to the Professor then to Cassie. 'Yannis is shouting orders at the security men. What's all the fuss about?'

'They've found the missing girl, at the temple site, strangled.'

'Bloody hell! We were so near this morning. And yesterday afternoon during the tour!'

'We don't know how long the body was there,' Cassie said. 'I assume that the Inspector will bring a forensics team and a pathologist. They'll be able to tell us.'

The three faces were all turned towards her. Her eyes flicked from one to another, eventually resting on that of the Professor who wore a thoughtful expression.

'You're an investigator too,' he said. 'A detective.'

'Of highly specific cases,' Cassie replied, making her point carefully. 'I'm not a police officer. Neither am I in Intelligence.'

They would know this already. Just as Siobhan had researched them, so someone working for the Minister would have looked into her background.

'Cassie, it seems to me that you should help us with this,' the Professor said. 'If this is the work of the criminal hunting you, you should certainly be advising, after all, you know about him and we don't. If not, well, your skills could be useful. The local man is, as you say, compromised and Yannis, excellent Security Chief though he is, hasn't done any police investigation work for years. Besides, I want this matter resolved quickly so it would be helpful if you and Yannis work together. That way the arriving policeman finds there is little to do.'

She knew exactly what was going on. The Professor didn't trust the police because he didn't know if they might be working against him or not. The Greek police had become politicised, with many belonging to the far-right, neo-fascist party, Golden Dawn. Now there was a murder in the same location as a high-ranking, recently controversial, left-of-centre politician. This would be catnip to the political opposition. Golden Dawn might no longer be in the Greek Parliament, but they still had their political supporters.

'I don't think I should intrude on anyone's investigation...' Cassie stalled for time, thinking.

The Professor needed the case investigating by someone he could be sure wasn't working for his opponents. Cassie had no axe to grind politically plus she had skills that Yannis Iraklidis didn't have. Her experience was recent. And successful.

'It's no intrusion,' he continued. 'I'm sure Yannis and the police will be grateful for any help you can provide. This matter has to be investigated, but it should be put to bed as soon as possible. The conference ends on

Friday morning and everything must be concluded before we leave for Athens later that day. I don't want this following us there.'

Not again. I can't cope, I can't cope with this again.

'Of course, if you don't wish to help us...'

She realised that she had been slowly shaking her head. 'I truly don't think I can.' She'd made her decision. The price she'd pay for this investigation was too high.

'I really think you should.' Professor Matsouka's eyes hardened. 'If you want me to reconsider the decision about visiting London. Your help would be greatly appreciated, especially given the urgency.'

The Professor was a heavy-weight political operator and it wasn't simply because of his friendship with Sidaris. He had a steely character to go along with his undoubted intellect. She had no choice and he knew it.

'I'm happy to help,' she said, her lips barely moving, her jaw tight.

'Good. I'll inform Yannis.'

◊ FIFTEEN

'No.'

Yannis Iraklidis's eyes were cold and hard, his mouth a thin line. They were in an office off the reception of the guesthouse, which he had been using as a base of operations. The desk was strewn with papers, the biggest of which was a large-scale map of the immediate area, held down at its corners by coffee mugs.

'I'm sorry,' Cassie said. 'It wasn't my idea.'

She didn't blame the Security Chief, it was difficult enough for him to have to maintain security for the ministerial party, even if the Minister – with a third of the security men – had left. But he was to work in tandem with the local policeman who was a relative of the deceased and possibly a member of a banned anti-government organisation. Many rural police were. Adding to the mix a high-ranking detective would soon be on the scene whose political allegiances were also suspect. And now he had to accommodate a foreigner, someone who didn't even speak the language.

'It's not her fault, she didn't want to do this.'

Irritation and tenderness flitted across Iraklidis's face in quick succession. Somehow, Cassie suspected, Helena's attempts to placate her lover might not be helping matters.

'I will speak with the Professor,' he snapped and stalked out of the room. His overcoat slid to the floor from the hook on the door as it slammed. Helena picked it up.

Cassie subsided into a chair. This had too many echoes, exhumed too many memories so recently buried.

'We don't have a choice,' Helena said. When Cassie didn't respond, she stooped to look her in the face. 'You've gone very pale. Can I get you some water?'

'Er, no, thank you.'

'Was it bad? Your last assignment?'

'My – a man very dear to me was killed. He was trying to rescue me.'

Helena crouched down and held Cassie's shaking hands in her own.

'I'm sure it wasn't your fault,' she said.

Oh yes it was.

Cassie's vision swam.

Don't cry. Get a hold of yourself.

The door crashed open, swinging back on its hinges and Helena rose, letting go of Cassie's hands. Iraklidis entered, followed by Professor Matsouka. The Security Chief walked over to the window, tension visible in every limb.

'I have explained to Yannis that you will be assisting him,' the Professor said smoothly.

The Security Chief bowed his head slightly, his only movement.

'You will be part of the investigation team,' he said, his voice acid and begrudging. He turned to look at Cassie. 'And work to me. I insist that you tell me about anything you discover.'

'Of course.'

'Good,' the Professor said. He turned to leave. 'I'm glad that's settled.'

The door closed behind him and, in two long strides, Iraklidis was standing over Cassie, glaring down at her. 'There'll be no more withholding information, on murderers or anything else! You will discuss your plans with me. No going running on the mountain without my knowledge either.'

Oh dear. Best up-date him on the unexpected package then.

'Actually, there is something else I should mention…'

As quickly and succinctly as she could she told them both about finding the pyjama top in her suitcase, hoping that they would not ask the obvious questions.

'Pyjamas?' Helena said.

'Worn when I was kept prisoner,' she said, her voice close to a whisper.

'Now he wishes to remind you of it and tell you that he can reach you,' Iraklidis said. 'I think also he is trying to get inside your head.'

He's already there.

'Early this morning my men found tracks at the side of the road to the taverna,' Iraklidis said. 'Intermittently, in the moss beneath the trees, a man, or a woman with large feet, walked up there. They probably stood in one place for a time too, perhaps when you stopped to listen.'

'So someone was following me.'

'Yes.'

'Where did the stalker go?'

'The footprints stopped,' the Security Chief said. 'Once all of us continued along the road whoever it was could have stepped out on to the road and walked down or up.'

So whoever it was could still be around.

Cassie took a deep breath. Now was not the time to lose any more composure. And the best way to do that was to deflect attention away from herself.

'What about the murder? What do we know about the woman, the victim?' she asked.

'The dead woman is Barbara Doukas,' Iraklidis said briskly, but only after he had given her a look which said that he knew exactly what she was doing. 'Twenty-six years old, born and raised in Delphi. Lived with her widowed mother and worked at the Museum, though she spent a lot of time with her boyfriend, Nico Vasilakis, who we've met. He took us round the temple site yesterday. A small-town girl.'

'I assume that the forensics team isn't here yet,' Cassie said. 'So we don't have a time of death.'

'No,' Iraklidis said. 'We'll have to wait for the pathologist. But we have an idea. Her body was frozen and her clothing soaked and we haven't had any rain or snow since the night before last. Monday night.'

'Could dew have dampened her clothing?'

'Unlikely, her body was found lying on a raised plinth, not on the ground.'

'Was that where she died, do we know?' Cassie asked.

'Not for certain, but it looks that way. I'm going over to the site, do you want to come?'

Cassie nodded agreement.

'Do we know why Barbara Doukas was in the Athenian Treasury building?' she asked.

'No, but she had a key to the temple site, so she could have let herself in.'

'Was the plinth beneath her body dry?'

'Yes.' The Security Chief answered, his mouth twisting into a knowing smile. 'She lay, or was placed there, before the rain and snow fell.'

'So… some time during Monday night or early Tuesday.'

'Before I arrived. And you,' Iraklidis said to Helena. 'But you, Cassie, came along the Delphi road late that night. Did you see anything?'

'No, I was asleep in the car. I only awoke when we pulled up outside here. It was very cold, but it wasn't snowing then.'

'Can I do anything here while you are gone?' Helena asked.

'Yes. We need a full list of guesthouse and Centre staff and of guests checked in here on Monday or before and, if possible, the time when they checked in,' Iraklidis replied. 'I want to know who our potential suspects are. Once we know the time of death for certain, we can release anyone who arrived later.'

'There was a complimentary coach from Athens airport,' Cassie added. 'I should have been on it. You might find a list of those who were.'

'We'll go now, see you later,' Iraklidis said.

Cassie took the stairs in a rush as she hurried to collect her coat. Inside the room she pulled on a thick sweater from her suitcase. The pyjama top still lay neatly folded on the bed.

It drew her gaze. She couldn't tear her eyes away.

They're waiting for me. I must go.

Yet still she stood, every muscle tensed. Round one had gone to Delahaye. He had rushed her before she'd known the fight had started. But she'd be waiting for the next assault; he wouldn't catch her off guard again.

Her rasping breath sounded loud in the quiet of the room and she felt the pounding of her heart. With an explosion of rage she pounced, grabbing the garment, twisting and scrunching its silk into a ball and flung it into the corner of the room. Then she strode out, slamming the door behind her.

By the time she descended the stairs her face was calm and composed, her chin up, her backbone straight. She was the Prime Minister's representative at an international conference and there was still a way to fulfil her mission. Find a murderer before the police did and the Minister would come to London. Nobody and nothing was going to stop her.

◊ SIXTEEN

'So this was where she was found?'

Cassie and the Security Chief stood in the portico of the almost roofless building, its stone walls and floor hard and unyielding. Police tape stretched across the doorway.

'There.' Iraklidis pointed to a raised plinth of marble, attached to the left-hand wall. 'Lying on her back with her hands crossed upon her chest. Someone had arranged her body.'

He handed her his mobile phone with a photograph of the victim. She was bedraggled, wearing a coat, a sweater, trousers and boots. Her formal pose suggested peacefulness.

A ritual killing?

'Her key to the complex wasn't found on her body. Constable Ganas has informed the Museum Director, who lives down on the plain during the winter months. Only a skeleton staff of locals like Nico and Barbara work here until March. Each of them has keys to the complex and to the Museum, but no one else.'

'The site was locked when we arrived yesterday afternoon,' Cassie said. 'Nico opened it up, just before you arrived. So the killer locked the place up when they left. That shows a cool head.'

'And someone familiar with the site, perhaps?' The Security Chief raised an eyebrow.

'Does Nico have an alibi, I wonder?' Cassie said.

'He took us round the site. If he killed his girlfriend and left her body here it took some nerve to lead that tour. He let the searchers in this morning as well,' Iraklidis added, as he removed the tape and they entered the roofless rectangle of the Treasury.

'And somewhere there is a missing key. Are we sure she carried it around with her, didn't leave it at home?'

'No, we haven't had a chance to check out any of this.'

'And what about her phone?'

'No sign of one.'

'But surely she had one, can't we check?' Cassie said. 'Unless her killer took it. It might contain evidence, an email, a text? Had she been abused?'

'Unknown. We'll go and look at the body once we've finished here.'

'Where is she now?'

'Delphi Police Station, which doubles as the jail. There was nowhere else,' Iraklidis said.

They stood in the centre of the building. Cassie turned slowly around, considering each side of it.

'The walls would give some shelter from the wind, allow the snow to settle. Was that why she came here, for shelter? With her killer?'

'Too many unanswered questions.' The Security Chief squatted on his haunches. 'The floor doesn't tell us much, it's stone. There are no obvious signs of a struggle.'

'The forensics team will help us examine everything,' Cassie said. 'Is that plinth solid?'

'It looks like it,' the security man said, as he knocked on the side of the stone plinth. 'Doesn't sound hollow.'

'So what was its purpose?'

'A shelf, for votive offerings.'

'Gifts to the god,' Cassie said.

The Security Chief met her glance. 'What are you thinking?'

'It's an unusual pose,' she replied. 'Is that what Barbara Doukas was? An offering? A sacrifice?'

'Sir,' a security man called as he approached. He spoke to Iraklidis.

Two people were striding up the Sacred Way towards them, a woman and a tall, raw-boned young man. Both wore the dark blue uniform of the Hellenic Police underneath standard issue greatcoats. The woman wore a deep red scarf at her neck. Her black hair was scraped back from a square-jawed face into a folded ponytail. Were they Golden Dawn members?

Iraklidis descended the portico steps to meet them and Cassie followed. She hoped they'd speak English, otherwise she'd be entirely reliant on Iraklidis.

'Yannis Iraklidis, *Epikefalis tis asfáleias*,' he said. 'Ministerial security.'

The woman shook the hand he offered and introduced herself as Major Tisiphone Lykaios and the man as Sergeant Chloros from the regional headquarters of the Central Greece Force. They had been assigned to investigate by the Inspector General for Southern Greece. Her dark eyes peered with curiosity and not a little suspicion at Cassie.

'May I introduce Ms Cassandra Fortune.' Cassie shook the Major's hand. Her grip was firm.

A cascade of Greek followed. Cassie assumed Iraklidis was explaining her presence.

'I understand,' the Major said in a flat voice. 'Thank you for your assistance, though we will take over now.'

Cassie wasn't sure if these dubious thanks were aimed at Iraklidis, herself or both of them. One thing was clear, the Major considered herself to be in charge.

What will the Professor say to that?

'This is where the murdered woman's body was found,' Iraklidis said, leading the police into the Treasury. 'Are forensics on their way?'

'Not yet,' the Major answered. 'We were given very little information when we left Regional HQ. I will request that a team be sent as quickly as possible. Meanwhile, we should cover this area to preserve any evidence.' She indicated the roofless room. 'The weather forecast is for storms. Can we arrange for a tarpaulin or something similar?'

'The local policeman should be able to do that,' Iraklidis said. 'Constable Ganas. He is also the victim's uncle. The body is at the Police Station. I suggest that we go there now.'

They left a security man to guard the scene of the crime and began the walk to Delphi town.

'I'll bring my colleagues up to date,' Iraklidis said to Cassie.

Cassie listened with increasing frustration at her exclusion and regretted not bringing Helena along. As he concluded Iraklidis switched from Greek to English.

'The Minister has left, but everyone else attending the conference remains here and, of course, there are the townspeople,' he said. 'There are also a number of environmental protestors in the town, there have been demonstrations. Constable Ganas will have more information on them.'

'Thank you.'

The Major sounded more genuinely appreciative this time.

'There is one more thing,' Cassie said. 'One of the Austrian delegation to the conference is missing. I didn't mention it before,' she looked apologetically at the Security Chief, 'because I assumed he was nursing a hangover somewhere – there was quite a party last night – but now I'm not so sure. '

'Why?' The Security Chief asked.

'It's something of a coincidence that two people go missing at about the same time and in the same place, although at first glance they appear to have nothing in common. He was with us yesterday when we were taken around the temple complex,' she said. 'This would have been after the murder, I think, when the woman's body was lying in the Treasury. You might recall him, Yannis, a tall, older man.'

'Him, yes, I remember him. He was asking a lot of questions, about the Phaedriades and the Castalian Spring,' Iraklidis explained to the Major. 'To distract us, perhaps?'

'Or just out of curiosity,' Cassie said.

'He could be the killer,' Iraklidis suggested.

'Or the killer's next victim,' Cassie pointed out. 'But we need to find him. I hope his body won't be the next to be found.'

'We'll track him down.' The Major's voice brooked no denial. 'Killer or not. My Sergeant will check for any missing vehicles in the town. Without transport he can't have got far.'

'Again, Constable Ganas will be able to help,' Iraklidis said. 'Delphi is only a small town so any vehicle theft is unlikely to go unnoticed.'

'To Delphi Police Station then.'

◊ SEVENTEEN

Delphi Police Station was a two-storey building in the centre of the town. The local policeman's small apartment was on the first floor. On the ground floor was a small office and, separated from it by a heavy door, a couple of jail cells.

The two small cells had bars on to a corridor. Balasz Kouris, the protest leader, was in the nearest cell. Behind a makeshift curtain of blankets, pegged to the intervening bars, the body of Barbara Doukas lay on a trestle table, a large puddle beneath it. Light came through high, barred windows. Constable Ganas sat at the side of the table on an upright chair his whole body curled in on itself. He rose to his feet as they entered, his face sagging, his dark eyes full of anguish.

Iraklidis grasped the policeman's hand in his, offering, Cassie assumed, his condolences.

'*Efcharisto,*' the policeman replied. Then he caught sight of the two police from Amfissa and he straightened up.

The Major stepped forward and repeated Iraklidis's words.

They stood in a half circle around the table. Barbara Doukas had been a slight woman; her long russet hair was plastered close to her skull and her skin was greyish white. Every few seconds a drip fell from her clothes into the water, its sound echoing from the stone walls.

'Her clothes should be removed and we need to take photographs.' Cassie said, thinking about Horseferry Road Mortuary and the examination of the bodies in her last case. 'By the time the pathologist arrives immediate indicators of what happened to her, like bruises and abrasions, may have diminished or disappeared, so we have to photograph these now.'

Cassie glanced at the Major, who was contemplating the body with an angry expression. The policewoman seemed reluctant to disturb the corpse and the Sergeant took his lead from her, standing well back. Iraklidis was staring at the body, frowning, he clearly didn't want to conduct a detailed examination. And Ganas – no one could expect the grieving uncle to do it.

'It needs to be done now. The body is already old.' Still no one spoke. 'Or we may lose what evidence there is. A local doctor?'

There was a brief exchange between Iraklidis and Constable Ganas.

'Has gone to attend a birth outside of town,' the Security Chief explained.

'Then it has to be us,' Cassie said. She looked across at the Major again, seeking acquiescence.

Come on.

'You have done this before, Ms Fortune?' the Major finally responded.

'No, but I've seen professionals do it.'

'Then please proceed.'

Me?

Sod it, get on and do it.

'We will need scissors, evidence bags, a notebook, a sheet and,' Cassie said to the Constable, 'do you have any plastic gloves?'

Iraklidis looked relieved, and in response to his translation, Ganas left the miniscule jail, returning moments later with sealed evidence bags and a sheet. He gave Cassie a notebook, a pair of scissors and some transparent surgical gloves. The Major took a second pair.

This isn't going to be pleasant.

'Could you and the Sergeant take Constable Ganas into the office,' Cassie suggested quietly to Iraklidis. 'I'll call you when we've done the examination.'

After the men left she said to the Major, 'I'm going to remove the clothing, touching it and the body as little as I can. If you could help me put the items into the evidence bags the forensics people can look at it properly when they arrive.'

Cassie hesitated. She hadn't touched a dead body before, though she had come close to doing so on her previous case. But it had to be done. It was only flesh, she told herself, the spirit of Barbara Doukas having already departed. She summoned the analytical coldness which had served her well in the past.

She reached first for the scarf and saw that it was Hermès – expensive. Barbara Doukas certainly liked nice things. For the next twenty minutes, she and the Major worked in almost complete silence, concentrating on cutting off clothing and bagging it. The policewoman was efficient and neat, but seemed to wear a perpetually sour expression, her mouth turned down at the corners.

'Are you often called to investigate cases in places you don't know?' Cassie tried to establish a rapport.

'Only at the moment,' the Major answered after some hesitation. 'I am on detached duty. My usual station is undergoing reorganisation.'

'So you're not from Amfissa then?'

'No, that's where regional HQ is located.' She bagged up the last item of clothing. 'I'm a homicide detective. I hunt murderers.'

Someone else out of place. At least she's doing her usual job.

'Shall we take photographs now?'

'Yes, but we should do it systematically, making notes as we go along. That way there are written descriptions of any marks or abrasions as well as photographic evidence.'

'You are remarkably efficient, Ms Fortune.'

'Not really, just copying what but I've seen others do. And it's Cassie, please.' She waited, but there was no reciprocation from the Major. 'Let's start with her head.' Cassie picked up the dead woman's head from above, feeling her skull and under her hair for any gashes or lumps. She could feel how cold and wet it was, even through the latex gloves. 'There's no sign of any injury on the skull or face. But the throat and neck are badly bruised.'

The Major took photos of the dead woman's neck as Cassie lifted her head once again.

'I'm not skilled or experienced enough to know for sure, we need a pathologist to tell us, but I would say that if asphyxia through strangulation didn't kill her, it prompted some sort of reaction which did.' Cassie said and began writing in the small notebook while the Major looked closely at the victim's neck.

'I can see bruising but no clear finger marks,' she said and Cassie nodded her head in agreement.

'No, me neither, but an expert might be able to tell more. Her front upper torso looks untouched, though there are bruises on her upper arms. My guess is that someone held her by the arms roughly enough to bruise her.'

'*They* look like finger marks,' the Major said, pointing to the victim's arms and snapping more photos.

'Yes.' Cassie stretched her hand as if to place her fingers in the bruise marks. Her hands and fingers were long for a woman, but not long enough to have made the marks on the victim's arm. 'If these are from a single grasp, they were made by someone with larger hands than I have, or longer fingers,' she said.

'A man?'

'Most likely, but it could be a large-framed woman. Whoever it was held the victim by the upper arms, though there are no similar marks on her wrists. Though we need confirmation that's what happened when the pathologist gets here. What's this?'

The Major leaned forward to see as Cassie held up the victim's right hand. Her fingernails were broken.

'Give me one of those bags.' Cassie placed the hand inside the bag and secured it with an elastic band. 'That must be our best chance for DNA,' she said. 'The other hand's the same.' She repeated the procedure.

The examination continued, Cassie trying to recall and copy what she had seen Bill Pottinger do, the forensic pathologist involved in her last case.

'I can't tell if she's been sexually abused,' Cassie said, examining between the legs. 'Superficially, there's no tearing or bruising, but this needs an expert. Help me turn her over.'

For a slight woman, Barbara Doukas was heavy to turn. A dead weight.

'No marks on her back,' the Major said. 'She faced her assailant.'

'It certainly seems so.'

They turned the body again, its skin was clammy to the touch. Cassie breathed a sigh of relief that the examination was over.

'Here,' the policewoman unfolded the sheet and the two women draped it over the lifeless form, folding it back beneath the chin. They stood back.

'Murder,' Cassie said, 'by strangulation. After a struggle, probably a brief struggle, with someone who was larger and stronger than she was and probably on Monday night or in the early hours of Tuesday morning.'

The Major picked up the evidence bag containing the victim's scarf.

'Strangulation by hand,' she said. 'When this was already around her neck. What does that tell us?'

Good point.

'That it was unpremeditated, a crime of passion? That the killer didn't calculate how best to kill?'

'Perhaps,' the Major said. 'We didn't find a telephone on her. Was one found at the crime scene?'

'Not that I'm aware,' Cassie replied.

'So, assuming that she had one, where is it?'

Cassie shrugged.

'Thank you for your help. I'll have Sergeant Chloros type up your notes.'

Not something to ask Constable Ganas to do.

'Should Constable Ganas be involved in this case at all? As the victim's uncle?'

'No,' Major Lykaios answered. 'But we have little choice. He is the police here. He knows this town and the countryside around. He can get things done.' Her peremptory manner was returning. 'Come.'

The policewoman led the way out of the jail, passed the other cell. Balasz Kouris was sitting on the low bed, his baleful eyes following them from a face which was beginning to discolour with bruising. It seemed that Constable Ganas, or the security men, had treated the activist roughly.

Did he speak English? If he did, they had just furnished him with a lot of details about the victim. He'd been in the area on Monday night, he'd been seen during the protest at the Centre but had then disappeared.

Cassie hesitated in front of his cell. He was a big man, young and strong, attractive to women, as Elise Forché had demonstrated. Yet surely he had a different agenda, focusing on his activism? Idealist he may be, but that wouldn't prevent him from killing if he had to, Balasz Kouris was no saint. Did he have an alibi?

Cassie's eyes focussed and she realised that he was staring at her, staring at him. With a flush of embarrassment, she ducked her head and hurried on after the Major. As she left she could feel his eyes on the back of her neck.

◊ EIGHTEEN

The office attached to the reception of the guesthouse was really too small for them all. One wall was external window, over-looking the gardens, where dusk had already fallen. Another held a pin-board, on to which was pinned the large-scale map of the area and one of the temple complex. The photograph of the body in the Treasury was next to it. The office desk was pushed to one side and an assortment of people sat in the remaining space.

Constable Ganas had been dispatched on an errand elsewhere in the guesthouse while the discussion about his niece took place. Major Lykaios and Sergeant Chloros sat in chairs brought in from the reception, Cassie and Helena had the office chairs, while Iraklidis perched on the end of the desk.

Andrew used to do that.

'Right, what do we know?' The Security Chief began. 'Barbara Doukas was from Delphi, she had lived here all her life and was well liked. She had a steady boyfriend, Nico Vasilakis, and they both worked at the Museum. No known enemies, no particular difficulties with any of the locals. Nothing out of the ordinary.'

'And yet,' the Major countered. 'Small places like this can have simmering feuds just below the surface. Normally we'd rely on local police to help identify any animosities, but Ganas is hardly an unbiased source, so we shouldn't rule anyone out. But we must consider the visitors too. There are three groups for consideration: the townspeople – including the family and the boyfriend – the protesters and the visitors to the Centre.' She counted them off on her fingers.

'There are over sixty people staying here for the conference,' Helena read from her notes. 'Of these, most arrived on Tuesday morning, the day when the conference started and therefore after the murder. Twelve people work at the Centre and guesthouse, from administrators to cleaners and all are local.'

'We believe Barbara Doukas was killed on Monday night,' Iraklidis added. 'So the people who arrived later can be ruled out as suspects, which includes myself, the ministerial party and Ms Helena Gatakis.'

He's got that in quick. Don't look at us.

'And you?' the Major asked Cassie.

'I arrived late on Monday night,' she explained, her thoughts returning to the argument in the bedroom next to her own.

'What?' the Major prompted.

'When I was trying to get to sleep on Monday night I was woken by an argument in the room next to mine – number eighteen. I thought it was a domestic quarrel – it was between a man and a woman. It became heated. I could hear them but they spoke in Greek, I didn't understand what they were saying.'

'So?'

'When I banged on the wall to get them to quieten down someone banged back, very hard. The anger, no, fury, was palpable. When I asked who was in that room at reception the following morning I was told that it was empty, its prospective occupants had been delayed and weren't going to arrive until Tuesday. It was suggested that I had overheard a television.'

'But you weren't convinced?'

'Televisions don't bang on walls. There'd been people in that room.'

'It may have nothing to do with the murder,' Iraklidis said. 'But it needs resolution. The couple, whoever they are, were moving around late on Monday night, they may have seen something useful.'

'Exactly,' Cassie agreed. 'I spoke with the night manager on the telephone about the noise.'

'Christos Katapodis was on the desk that night,' Helena said, looking at her notes again. 'He's an old boyfriend of Barbara Doukas apparently.'

'We'll interview Mr Katapodis,' the Major said.

'Don't we need to interview all the staff?' Cassie added. 'Any of them could have seen Barbara Doukas, if she was there.'

'Yes. Continue,' the Major ordered.

Iraklidis said nothing. His gaze was fixed on the Major.

'Please,' she added.

'Another twenty or so delegates were due to arrive for the later days of the Conference,' Helena said, eyes flicking from Iraklidis to the Major and back. 'I spoke with Mr Marios, the conference organiser. He or his staff have now contacted them and told them not to come.'

'Well done, thank you,' Iraklidis said to her. 'We don't need another tranche of people turning up. Also, it would be helpful if we could encourage those who cannot be the murderer to leave.'

There was a small silence as everyone waited for the Major to respond.

'I am reluctant to allow anyone to leave,' she said eventually. 'We don't yet know enough about this murder to rule anything out. I would like to check the list of those who you propose are in the clear, before anyone is advised that they can go.'

'The Minister already left earlier today,' Iraklidis said, deadpan.

The Major pursed her lips but made no comment.

'All our reasoning is based on the murder taking place on Monday night or the early hours of Tuesday morning. When can we have medical confirmation of time of death?' Cassie asked. 'A forensic pathologist...?'

'Is coming from Itea,' the Sergeant said. 'Tomorrow if he can. He has to cover a very large area and there will be other suspicious deaths to deal with, but this will be high priority.'

Their superficial examination had provided some information, but they couldn't do without a pathologist. Aside from the increasing decomposition of the body, and losing evidence along with it, any court case would be more difficult without expert opinion.

'Couldn't we get him or her here sooner?' Cassie said. 'After all, the Minister–'

'Has already left,' the Major said. 'No. We are not in London, or even Athens. However, Constable Ganas has asked the local doctor to give an opinion.'

Better than nothing.

'How about Schlange? Could he have left town? Are any vehicles missing?' Iraklidis asked.

'None,' the Sergeant answered. 'Or at least, none that have been reported.'

'He can't have got far on foot,' Iraklidis said. 'Perhaps he's found somewhere to nurse a hangover and isn't aware we're looking for him.'

'What about the protestors?' Helena said.

'We know about those who were staying in Delphi town,' the Sergeant said. 'There is a YMCA as well as a number of small hotels and guesthouses.'

'Are we sure that this is all of them?' the Major said. 'What is your estimate of the numbers?' She directed her question to Iraklidis.

'Outside the Centre gates when we arrived, I would say about thirty,' he answered. 'There were a couple of local coordinators, but, according to Ganas,' he gestured towards the Constable, who had entered the room, 'the others were from nearby. We took photographs.'

'Good. Their leader is well known to the police,' the Major said. 'Balasz Kouris arrived in Delphi, by his own admission, on Monday night, so is a suspect. He's an activist, a so-called zemiologist, with a high profile on social media.' The Sergeant went over to the desktop PC and began tapping on the keyboard. 'If Ms Doukas was mixed up with Balasz Kouris she was asking for trouble.'

The Sergeant swivelled the monitor around so that they could all see it.

Balasz Kouris's Facebook page showed a photo montage from the protest outside the Centre, with a video of the ministerial motorcade and demonstration. Cassie spotted Iraklidis, looking sinister, commanding the security men, but it was Kouris who dominated the scene. He shouted slogans, waving his clenched fist aloft or pointed his finger in accusation at the ministerial car. He twisted to see a banner unfurling and laughed. An aura of manic energy and righteous rebellion emanated from the shaky YouTube video.

A dangerous man some would say.

Just beyond the cars two figures ducked into a grove of trees – herself and Helena. At least they weren't immediately recognisable. If anyone was looking for her and saw this footage they wouldn't be able to identify her and pinpoint her whereabouts.

'How were those posted?' Helena asked. 'There's no public wi-fi up here.'

'Probably put up later by some of the group,' the Sergeant replied. 'There's landline internet in town.'

'Is there any evidence that Barbara Doukas was interested in climate change or protesting against it?' Cassie asked. 'Or that she knew Kouris?'

'She was a member of Greenpeace,' Helena translated the Constable's reply. 'But she wasn't an activist in any way. What's a zemiologist?'

'The latest fashion,' the Major responded, dismissing the question.

It was clear that she would be looking for a link between the activists and the victim. Everyone in Delphi on Monday night was a potential suspect, including Kouris, Cassie reminded herself.

'I've asked the team at Amfissa to identify all the protestors from the YouTube video. If your men could send their photographs to the Sergeant, that would be helpful,' the Major said. 'The Constable has warned them not to leave until they've been interviewed. He and my Sergeant will concentrate on them and on the townsfolk. I suggest you concentrate on the Conference Centre visitors and staff.'

That makes sense.

'Ok,' Iraklidis said. 'I'm happy that we share information.'

'Agreed,' the Major said. 'We'll reconvene tomorrow mid-morning to do that and to decide who can be sent home. The Sergeant and I, meanwhile, will return to Delphi.' She stood.

'Major,' Cassie also stood. 'Shouldn't we begin interviewing tonight? Any delay might mean that people forget things – or allow them time to synchronise their stories.'

And the Professor wants this resolved quickly.

'Tomorrow, please,' the policewoman reiterated, turning to leave.

Cassie frowned. She couldn't fault the Major's logic. Dividing up the suspects was the right thing to do, otherwise they would never get through the interviews, but the delay wasn't necessary. Something wasn't right.

'Wait. Aren't there other things to consider? What about the body and the way it was laid out?' Cassie pointed to the printed copy of the photograph Iraklidis had shown her in the Treasury. 'There may be an element of ritual involved.'

'What do you mean?'

'The body was laid in the classic pose of rest and in a place where offerings to the god used to be kept. Is that just a coincidence? Or does it tell us something about the killer, or why he or she killed?'

'It is something to bear in mind,' the Major conceded reluctantly. 'But this isn't a Hollywood movie, Ms Fortune. The body could just have been laid there, there doesn't have to be a more elaborate reason.'

'Have there been any other deaths in Delphi with a ritual element?' Helena translated Cassie's question for the Constable.

It was obvious before the translation came that the answer was 'No'.

'The last homicide in Delphi was twenty-five years ago,' Helena said. 'A crime of passion involving a group of campers.'

If this was a ritual murder then it was the first, Cassie thought. Would there be others? Where was the Austrian?

'My Sergeant and I will go back to town now.' The Major rose and led the way to the door.

'Just stay here a moment,' Iraklidis said to Cassie and Helena and hurried after them. 'Major!'

'Why isn't she considering everything?' Helena said, her chin raised.

'And she shouldn't try to order Yannis around either, he's a policeman too and probably a higher rank than she is.'

'I rather think he might be pointing that out to her even as we speak,' Cassie said, arching an eyebrow. The Security Chief was entirely capable of looking after himself. 'She's unhappy at having to share the case. It's understandable, I suppose.'

We won't be able to control things as Professor Matsouka would like.

'Does the positioning of the body suggest anything to you?' Iraklidis asked as he returned. 'Just because it's on the plinth doesn't necessarily mean it's a ritualistic killing.'

'It's on a religious site,' Cassie shrugged. 'Not a modern religion maybe, but still a place once dedicated to a god and Barbara was closely associated with the Temple. It takes only a little imagination to see her as a priestess. Plus, there were environmentalists here at the time, some of whom might embrace ancient religions. Admittedly, I've never heard of modern Apollo worshippers, but maybe she fell prey to a visiting killer for whom the Temple, or Apollo, signified something. Yet, statistically,' she concluded 'it's more likely she was killed by someone she knew. Can we run background checks on the visitors who were here on Monday night?'

'Once we have our short list of suspects based on arrival times I'll arrange for checks to be done, whatever the Major thinks,' Iraklidis answered. 'Schlange's disappearance is worrying too. Is it linked to Barbara Doukas's? If he doesn't turn up tonight, we'll have to search for him. Tomorrow, not now, the light will soon go and my men are unfamiliar with the terrain.'

'And we'll interview the night manager tomorrow too,' Cassie said.

'Oh yes,' he replied. 'But among the other staff, I think. We don't want to single him out. If our perpetrator is still here...'

Helena paled.

She's only just realised.

There was a good chance the murderer was still amongst them and that he, or she, might try to eliminate anyone with any evidence against them.

◊ NINETEEN

As Cassie entered the dining room heads turned and she felt all eyes upon her. The room was full, but voices were low and subdued. The conference had been curtailed and, by now, everyone had heard about the death of the young woman and the Minister's departure. Diners were quiet but jittery.

'Cassie, over here.'

Helena waved, half standing. She had a small table to herself by the wall.

'Where's Yannis? Is he joining us?' Cassie asked as she joined her.

'Later. He's briefing the Professor.'

'Do we know if Major Lykaios and her Sergeant have returned?'

'They're staying in Delphi, Yannis says. Why they can't stay here I don't know. It would make things so much easier. Look, the Austrians…'

The group of men entered and took seats at a long table over by the window.

'Still minus Dr Schlange,' Cassie said. 'I'd like to talk with them. It's too much of a coincidence that Schlange has gone missing after Barbara Doukas was killed.'

The two women collected trays and joined the queue for the counter. Within moments several of the Austrians followed.

'Herr Freyer,' Cassie greeted the rotund Salzburgian.

'Ms Fortune, congratulations on your presentation this morning. Thank you for stepping into the breach. It was most illuminating – and what a massive budget for your programme. You must think ours a very small thing by comparison.'

'Not at all, Herr Freyer, change is always difficult to introduce. If our tax reforms gain traction, revenue should increase so we can justify our investment.' The carefully learned phrases rolled off her tongue. 'Has Dr Schlange turned up?'

'No,' the Austrian frowned. 'It's worrying. I thought at first he might be hung over, but now…' he lifted his palms in exasperation. 'And there is the woman's death. A local, I know, but I worry for Stefan.'

'Could he have decided to leave and not told anyone?'

'Oh no! He had to make the presentation, we were all relying on him. It could have been the last time he did so. He's applied for a new post – a very prestigious one – something he'd been working towards his whole life. Anyway he couldn't have left, how would he go, there's no available transport.'

'Do you know Dr Schlange well?'

'Not really. He's from Linz.'

Dr Wild, he of the sharp features and sardonic air, was standing behind Herr Freyer in the queue. He began to smile, though he looked down at his feet when Cassie caught his eye.

You always seem to be around.

'Er... is that far from Salzburg? Forgive me, I thought you worked together.'

'Oh yes, yes, but not every day,' Herr Freyer explained. 'Our project involved all the Austrian regions. Dr Schlange was an esteemed colleague, a pillar of the community, but I don't know him well.'

'Does he speak Greek, do you know?'

'A few words only, I think.'

The server behind the counter claimed their attention.

Having chosen her food Cassie asked, 'May we join you, Herr Freyer?'

With laden trays, Cassie and Helena made their way to the Austrians's table. She was surprised to see that the two Americans and Elise Forché had sat there too. They were watching her approach with ill-disguised interest.

'Hello again,' she said as she set down her tray.

'Hello, what's the latest?' Jim Norton asked.

'What do you know about the murder?' Elise added.

'Will we be able to leave tomorrow?' Mike Robbins chipped in.

'I don't know, the police want to interview people,' Cassie said.

'We saw her you know, the woman who was killed.' Elise bestowed the information like a secret. 'She was organising a visit to the Museum. She came round to see if we wanted to go on it, asking everyone. She was with that boyfriend of hers, the one who eventually took us to the temple site.'

'When?'

'Er... Monday morning,' Elise said. 'We said we'd go, but then it all changed, once the Minister arrived on Tuesday and the temple complex was opened up instead.'

'So she was here, in the guesthouse? Or at the Centre?'

'Here,' Jim said. 'As people arrived. She was greeting us.'

Cassie glanced at Herr Freyer and the other Austrians.

'Yeah, them too.'

'Why do *you* want to know?' Elise leant forward to see around Jim.

'Cassie's been asked to help,' Helena explained.

'Who by? The Security Chief?' Mike was sarcastic. 'You've made sure he's on your side, haven't you?'

Helena flushed and blinked rapidly.

Why do you make a habit of being a bastard?

'I wasn't aware that there were sides,' Cassie said sharply. 'And you have just alienated two people who may otherwise have been sympathetic towards you.'

'Cassie,' Helena nudged her, nodding towards the door.

Iraklidis stood there, scanning the dining room. He spotted them and walked over.

Mike concentrated on eating his dinner.

'Helena,' the Security Chief bent over and spoke to the interpreter in Greek. Then gave a curt nod to the other diners and left.

Mike raised his head.

'Why doesn't he speak English?' he complained. 'We all know he can.'

'Why should he, he's a Greek in Greece,' Helena said. 'You're the visitor here.'

'So's she,' Mike pointed at Cassie. 'Why does she get special treatment? She isn't police.'

'As Helena said, I've been asked to help by the Minister's advisor. I've had some experience of such matters,' Cassie said, looking Mike square in the face. She had plenty of experience dealing with pipsqueaks like him. 'We'll be interviewing everyone on our list of suspects tomorrow, including you, Mr Robbins.'

Mike blew the breath out through his lips.

'Well, I'll just take myself off and enjoy my food elsewhere,' he said, rising.

'Don't trouble yourself, we're leaving anyway,' Helena said. 'Aren't we, Cassie.'

◊ TWENTY

A bright flash of lightning lit the dining room as the women made their way towards reception.

One, two, three… Cassie automatically began to count the seconds before the thunder roll came. She reached eleven before the rumble sounded, so the storm was still far off.

'Yannis wants us to join him at the Minister's suite,' Helena said. 'The Professor wants to discuss things with you. I'll go and get an umbrella just in case.' She hurried up the stairs to her room.

Cassie wandered over to the windows. Outside, the horizon was backlit by a sheet of blue-white light, etching the outlines of the peaks opposite. The trees and boulders of the lower slopes were delineated sharply for a second or two then gone, swallowed up in the returning blackness. The terrace lights, little globes on pillars, did not penetrate far into the dark. There were no stars and no moon.

The slabs of the terrace were dry but were unlikely to stay so for long. Cassie hoped that the Athenian Treasury was covered over or any evidence it held would be destroyed by the rain when it came.

'Here.'

Helena handed her an umbrella.

The two women hurried down the steps and around the path to the Centre as more lightning punctured the darkness.

'Helena!' The Security Chief was waiting, looking out for them at the door to the private suite. He ushered them inside with an anxious look up at the sky.

In the living room Professor Matsouka was standing at the glass doors watching the lightning.

'It seems to be far off,' Cassie said as thunder rumbled again.

'Ah, you've been counting,' the Professor said. 'I too, but I'm told that doesn't necessarily work here in the mountains. Come, sit. Can I fix you a drink?'

'No, thank you,' Cassie said and Helena shook her head.

'Yannis has told us about Major Lykaios and her Sergeant,' he began. 'They're focusing on Delphi town, the victim's family and the environmental protesters.'

'Yes,' Cassie answered.

'You would focus elsewhere?'

'Most unlawful killings are carried out by people known to the deceased,' Cassie said. 'So no, the focus is correct.'

The Professor looked at her and raised an eyebrow.

'But I am frustrated by the lack of urgency,' she responded. 'We haven't begun interviewing people yet and the scene of the crime won't be properly inspected until tomorrow. That's three days after we think the young woman was killed. We won't have a pathologist's view on time of death or other details until then either. I understand that we are isolated here and that the geography is difficult, but...'

'I see,' the Professor glanced at Cassie, then at Iraklidis.

He's already said this.

'It's too late now, of course. We'll begin the interviews tomorrow,' Cassie continued. 'I fear, however, that the Major will not share any discoveries with us. Of course I may be wrong, but the victim's family may have vital information and we need to have it, especially if we are to keep to your timeframe.'

'I have tried to impress upon the Major that this *must* be a joint investigation,' Iraklidis said.

'But she is not within your chain of command. I understand. Hmm.'

They both waited as the Professor thought it through. Cassie wondered if the higher echelons of the Greek police force, like majors, were involved with Golden Dawn. She didn't see why not. That organisation couldn't have become so powerful if it only attracted the lower ranks. Having had an excellent relationship with the police in her previous investigations Cassie was unused to not working closely and openly with them. It struck her forcefully that she would not have been able to get any form of justice done if she hadn't been able to trust the police.

'I had hoped that we could set the course of this investigation and conclude things by the time we leave here, yet it seems the Major will not be guided.' Professor Matsouka rose, walked over to the sideboard and lifted the telephone handset. 'I would like an outside line please,' he said, then continued speaking to them. 'I will contact the Regional Chief Inspector. This will need careful handling. Ah yes...' He switched to Greek. There was a pause.

'Problem,' Helena said under her breath. 'He's asking when it will be repaired?'

The Professor replaced the handset.

'It appears that the phone lines are out,' he said. 'A problem elsewhere in the mountains. We don't know when they will be repaired.'

The lightning flashed again.

'So, we're on our own.'

And there's a killer on the loose.

◊ TWENTY ONE

To Cassie's surprise, Helena insisted on returning via the upper path. It was a quicker route back to the guesthouse, but less even and more badly lit than the lower path, and it would be easy to slip or trip in the darkness. At least the rain, which had been threatening to arrive all evening, was holding off, so the bushes and trees which lined the path were dry. One of the security men accompanied them – after last night's stalker, Iraklidis wasn't taking any chances.

'You're wondering why I wanted to come this way,' Helena said as they reached the metalled road. 'When I went upstairs earlier to fetch an umbrella I looked out of the window of my room. It faces away from the valley – I'm not a delegate, so I don't get a spectacular view,' she added. 'The lightning was quite something, though, and I was watching it. Then I saw lights, high up there on the mountain.'

'Are you sure?'

'Yes,' Helena said. 'I can't see Delphi town from my room, it's hidden on the other side of the ridge, so the lights weren't from the town, but I can see the slopes above it. That's where the lights were. And they were moving. There are, or were, people up there.'

'What were they doing at... what time was it?'

'Eight thirty, I checked my watch. Out on the mountain, with tempest about, it could be dangerous. I wanted to walk back this way so that we could see if they were still up there – you can't see the slopes above Delphi town from further down, on the other side of the Centre and guesthouse – but we should be able to see them from here.'

As if to order the sky blazed with an electric-white light.

Helena was right, the slopes above Delphi were visible, Cassie could even make out the path up to the Corycian Cave. There were no lights, not even when the dark returned, seeming blacker than before.

'Where were they?'

'About halfway up the visible slope,' Helena answered. 'They were moving sideways and upwards.'

'As if climbing the path?'

'Yes, though at the time I had forgotten that the path was there. Could it have been the police, following a lead?'

'Hmm, maybe, but the Major didn't seem to be in that much of a hurry to follow leads this afternoon.' Cassie was sceptical. 'We can't assume not. We'll ask her about it tomorrow.'

'I think the Major doesn't really want to co-operate with us. Even if she is up there, she won't share information. Yannis thinks so too.'

'Did he say so to you?'

'No, but I can tell.'

'Helena,' Cassie hesitated. 'This – relationship, between you and Yannis...?'

'I know, things seem to be moving very quickly,' the interpreter spoke rapidly. 'You probably think it's all too rushed, that we barely know each other, that we should take things gradually.'

Too right.

'I...'

What can I say?

Helena was making weighty decisions extremely quickly, but the Security Chief seemed to be genuinely smitten with her and she, it seemed, reciprocated. Maybe it wouldn't last, but if it did, the Embassy was unlikely to frown on the liaison. In fact, having someone with an inside track on the Minister of Finance's movements would be seen as advantageous. Helena might find she was offered a permanent contract, so her career, such as it was, would benefit. Freelance translating was a precarious profession, much depending on the goodwill of the Embassy, unless the individual hired themselves out to tourists and Helena clearly didn't want to do that.

But she doesn't really know him, doesn't know what she's getting into. She could be making an enormous mistake.

'We're neither of us young,' Helena was continuing. 'We've both been in love before; and neither of us was looking for this, quite the opposite. But it happened – and it's wonderful. Isn't that a good reason to make the most of it?'

Too late, she's already decided.

At a loss to know what to say without sounding scathing, Cassie said nothing. She squeezed Helena's hand.

'Thank you,' Helena said. 'It's not good to be by yourself all the time, Cassie.'

They'd reached the guesthouse and after arranging to meet at breakfast, both women retired for the night, Cassie to spend it alone.

◊ TWENTY TWO

Each time she closed her eyes Cassie saw Lawrence Delahaye, sitting in the chair opposite her bed as he had in the bedroom at Barton Street, right ankle over left knee, white skin stretched over hard muscle, watching her. Though her bed was warm she was shivering.

When she'd returned to her room that evening she had retrieved the pyjama top and put it back into its wrapper. It was evidence. She had to take it back to the UK.

She lay looking at the ceiling of her room, as lightning flooded the sky and landscape outside, shining stark through a gap between the floor length curtains.

This was what he intended, to get inside my head. Just as he did in Barton Street.

Cassie was under no illusion. She had escaped, had found the spirit and the energy from somewhere to get away. But before their flight from the police, he'd had the upper hand. After Andrew's death she'd gone to pieces and ceded control. And to control her was what he'd wanted all along, because he'd concluded, through complex logic which was wholly wrong, that she had the power to determine the next Prime Minister of the United Kingdom. That was her attraction for him, where her value to him lay, that underpinned whatever he said he felt for her. It was power he wanted.

Though, in a way, she had helped to determine the next PM, just not in the way he had thought.

It's why I'm here, in a guesthouse bedroom halfway up Mount Parnassus on my first mission.

Now she had to track down another murderer in order to ensure its success. The Professor had left her in no doubt about that. And the clock was ticking. It was Wednesday night and they were due to return to Athens on Friday. Only one and a half days left. With the phones down she couldn't even inform London of what she had been asked to do.

And Lawrence Delahaye? Where is he? Close by?

Could he have made an error and killed by accident? Maybe poor Barbara was in the wrong place at the wrong time. If so, he wasn't done yet.

Cassie suspected that he would want to enjoy his final triumph. So the guesthouse wouldn't give him the time or privacy he would like and it would be difficult to spirit her away, especially with storms and snow forecast. No, the pyjama top was probably just a reminder. It had worked, but alongside the pain and fear it had also awoken her anger, her desire for revenge. She *would* get even.

She needed to evict him from her mind. She needed clarity of thought and emotional disengagement.

She concentrated on her stalker. It was unlikely that this was Lawrence Delahaye. So who else could have followed her up the mountain road the previous evening? Was it Barbara Doukas's killer? And what had happened to Stefan Schlange? Would he be the killer's next victim?

Most of all she needed sleep. Cassie reached for the card of sleeping pills. Her hand hovered over the diazepam, but she passed over it and took up the blister tray.

THURSDAY

◊ TWENTY THREE

It was an unearthly sound, a prolonged and inhuman cry, ending abruptly.

Cassie sat bolt upright in bed.

Was that real? Did I dream it?

There was noise outside beneath her window, doors slamming, people talking in hushed tones. It was early, the sun wasn't up yet. Her watch told her it was just after seven o'clock.

Pulling her robe around her she stepped out on to the balcony.

In the half-light she saw people out on the terrace, kitchen staff and one or two guests. Others were on their balconies, clad in sleeping clothes and dressing gowns, shivering in the cold but too curious to remain inside. All looked perplexed, some a little scared.

The telephone in her room rang.

'Cassie?' It was Helena. 'Did you hear it?'

'It woke me. What was it?'

'It was a scream. We were awake, we heard it properly.'

Helena paused and Cassie could hear another voice speaking.

'Yannis is going to investigate. Shall I see you downstairs?' Helena said. Cassie was already pulling on her clothes with the phone still at her ear.

Ten minutes later she joined Helena in reception. By unspoken consent they both walked into the dining room.

The food counter was open and people were collecting breakfast, but there was a constant nervous chatter. Everyone was unsettled, no one seemed to be eating, not even the unflappable Austrians. Jim Norton and Elise Forché looked glum and worried.

'We thought it came from further up the mountain,' Helena said as they queued.

'I was asleep, so I couldn't say.'

'It was horrible.' The interpreter gave a theatrical shudder as they got to the counter. 'Do you think it had anything to do with the lights I saw? Someone was up there last night.'

'Perhaps.'

'Yannis may know,' Helena reached out her hand as the Security Chief approached and he took it in his own.

'It was a human cry, plenty of people heard it,' he said. 'Some people maintain that it came from the Phaedriades, the white cliffs beyond the temple site, but no one knows. There'll be a search, beginning in the area around the foot of the cliffs. Some of my men will help when it gets underway.'

'They are over fifteen-hundred metres high,' Cassie said. 'Anyone falling from the top would have had plenty of time to scream.'

'Thank you for that!' Helena said, a shocked half-grin on her face.

'Bring your drinks and come and look at the maps,' Iraklidis said. 'I want to know where the lights were which you saw last night.'

They returned to the small room next to the reception area.

Tightly squashed contour lines showed the sheer drop of the Phaedriades from the high plateau to the valley below on the map pinned to the wall. It also showed the Centre and Delphi town and the ancient track way up to the Corycian Cave.

'You told me that you thought the lights were moving up the path to the Cave,' he said to Helena.

'I think so,' she answered. 'Here, maybe...'

She drew her finger along the line of the path rising upward and to the right.

'What kind of lights were they? Self-contained or in shafts or beams?'

'I.... it's difficult to say.'

'Did they illuminate any of the ground around them? All around, or just ahead?'

'Ahead, just ahead.'

'Torches,' Iraklidis said.

'Or headlights, given how far away they were, but could a car travel up that path?' Cassie asked.

'Unlikely. Though a motorcycle might, or an off-road vehicle. Helena, did you mention this to anyone else?'

'Only to Cassie and you.'

'Good. I don't want people going up there to look for themselves. I'll send someone up there. We need to take a look at that track before any rain arrives.'

Beyond the window the sky was heavy with cloud. The previous night's promise of rain had not materialised, but it threatened still.

'I'd like to take a look myself,' Cassie said. 'Though I suspect the Major might take a dim view if we defer the interviews after making such a point about doing them quickly.'

'I've listed the people who were here on Monday,' Helena said, reaching for a folder in the desk drawer. 'And those who arrived later – check that one over first.'

'Then we can agree to their release,' said Iraklidis.

Without showing the names to the Major?

Cassie looked down the list of the later arrivals, she didn't recognise any of the names, other than those of the Minister and his party.

The list of those present on Monday was more interesting. It included Mr Marios and two conference organisers, all the Austrian delegation, Jim Norton and Elise Forché from the OECD, Mike Robbins, who was registered as an observer and twelve ECC/guesthouse staff, including Christos Katapodis, the night manager. About two dozen people all together. These were the suspects associated with the Cultural Centre.

'I think we should add Nico Vasilakis, the boyfriend. He was here with Barbara Doukas on Monday morning,' Cassie said. 'I'd like to speak with him and Ms Doukas's family too. The family of the victim is always important, even though that falls within the Major's area of the investigation. And I think we need to question everyone about Schlange's disappearance as well as the murder of Barbara Doukas.'

'Ok. So let's begin with Norton, Forché and Robbins,' Iraklidis said. 'Then we'll divide the others between us. You and Helena take the Austrians and I'll take the organisers and the Centre staff. Then you can join me for the night manager, when he comes in, given our unsolved little mystery.'

'There is another issue,' Cassie said. 'I have no authority here, nor does Helena, as Robbins made plain to us. It would be helpful if the Professor addressed people, he is the most senior politician here now that the Minister has gone. He could tell everyone what is going to happen – or perhaps hand over to you to do it, as the ranking officer – and explain about the Major and Sergeant.'

Iraklidis gave a half-smile. 'It's a long time since I did any traditional police work,' he said. 'But you're right. I outrank her.'

'You could then say that Helena and I are assisting.'

'You don't carry a rank?'

'Only a Civil Service one – Director.'

'Of what?'

'Well, there's a question. I work directly for the Prime Minister. It's difficult to explain, my role is an unusual one.'

'Cassie,' Helena ventured. 'Are you a spy? A – what do they call it – a spook?'

'Certainly not,' Cassie responded. 'I have been a sort of detective, working with the Metropolitan Police and with the British intelligence services. You could tell people that, if it helps.'

'Yes,' Iraklidis assented. 'With the Professor's authority and my own, that should be enough.'

◊ TWENTY FOUR

'Have a seat, Mr Norton,' Iraklidis said as Helena brought the American into the room.

Professor Matsouka had formally addressed the conference, explained what was going to happen and told the attendees that most of them would be allowed to leave immediately. Others would be interviewed before leaving. Given the weather forecast of storms and snow, everyone was keen to get away before it became too difficult to travel. No one wanted to get locked into a place of ill omen.

'Can we go home after this?' Jim Norton asked, with slight belligerence.

'Once the interviews are concluded we'll make decisions about who is free to go.'

'The weather is closing in and...,' Norton paused and took a deep breath, '...we don't want to be stuck here with a killer.'

'Let's get started then.' Iraklidis put his hands on the table. 'Why are you here, Mr Norton?'

'I work for the Organisation for Economic Co-operation and Development in Paris. The efficiency of public administration is one of my briefs, so this conference was an obvious call for me.'

'And Ms Forché?'

'Elise is OECD too. She's a translator. She normally works in French, Italian and Portuguese. But she's adding Greek to her portfolio.' A note of pride entered his voice when he spoke.

'And what of your compatriot, Mr Michael Robbins?'

'I don't know, can't say.' Norton stared straight at the Security Chief. 'We met here. I hadn't met him before the conference.'

He's not a good liar.

'If I may?' Cassie asked Iraklidis. 'Are you a permanent OECD employee?'

'No,' the American replied. 'I'm on loan from the US State Department.'

'And when does that loan end?'

'At the end of the financial year.'

'Next April. What will you do then, go back to the States?'

'Maybe.'

Does Elise know that I wonder? It would explain why she's so defensive.

'You and Ms Forché arrived... on Monday, is that correct?' The Security Chief took over again.

'On Sunday evening actually.'

'And Mr Robbins?'

'You'll have to ask him.' The eyes were front and centre again. 'He was at breakfast on Monday.'

'And you saw Ms Doukas shortly after breakfast in the lobby on Monday morning?'

'Yes, as we told Ms Fortune.' Norton's eyes slid sideways to rest on Cassie. 'We signed up for the Museum tour. Look, Mike Robbins is a jerk, but he's nothing to do with us. We've done nothing wrong. Elise will vouch for me and I for her on Monday night and we've taken part in lots of events since. There have been plenty of other people around to see us.'

Cassie remembered the argument between Elise and Jim on her first morning at the guesthouse.

'All Monday night?' Cassie asked. 'Didn't you go out for a walk?'

'Er, yes, but I was with Mike Robbins.'

'And Elise?'

'Was aiding and abetting a protester, you heard us arguing about that,' Norton snorted. 'You'll have to ask her about it. Typical of Elise to take matters into her own hands.'

'But she wasn't in your room when you returned?'

'No.'

'When did she return?'

'About five minutes after I did.'

'And Dr Schlange, did you speak with him, have any contact?'

'Not really. The members of the Austrian delegation all looked pretty dull, to be honest.'

'All right Mr Norton, thank you for your time.'

'Can we leave now?'

'Not quite yet, we need to conclude all our interviews, including Ms Forché,' Iraklidis replied.

The American got up with ill grace and left, Helena following.

'He's lying about something,' Cassie said.

'A connection with Robbins, maybe,' Iraklidis suggested. Then as the door opened, 'Ah, Ms Forché, please take a seat.'

The Frenchwoman slid into the seat indicated, her eyes flicking around the room. Her hands were clutched together in her lap.

'We have spoken with Mr Norton. Can you confirm what your relationship with him is?'

'I am his partner; we live together in Paris.'

'And with Mr Robbins?'

'I first met Monsieur Robbins this week when we arrived here.'

'Did your partner introduce him to you?'

'I don't know, I think we came across him in the dining room. A fellow American.'

'So Mr Norton didn't know Mr Robbins before?'

'*Non*, I don't think so.'

'Are you planning to return with Mr Norton to the United States next April?' Cassie asked.

'Jim's staying in Paris.' Elise Forché looked from Cassie to Iraklidis, defiant. 'With me.'

'Can you confirm that you saw Ms Doukas on Monday morning?'

'Yes, I told you this,' she said directly to Cassie.

'Did you see her at any other time?' Cassie asked.

'Yes, actually, I saw her on Monday evening.'

Cassie tensed. She sensed Iraklidis shift in his seat beside her.

'Where?' the Security Chief asked.

'Here, in the reception area.'

'At what time?'

'I'm not sure exactly, but it was when we came out of dinner, about nine o'clock or so.'

'What was she doing?'

'I don't know, nothing much. She was just here. The protest was starting.'

'Can you remember anything else about her?'

Elise shook her head.

'What did you do then?' Cassie asked.

'I went up to our room. Before you ask, Jim went out for a walk, with Mike Robbins.'

'The guesthouse was searched that evening, wasn't it,' she said. 'The protest leader Balasz Kouris managed to evade capture. Was that because you helped hide him?'

The Frenchwoman's cheeks turned pink. 'Yes, what of it? I hid him in our room and told the security guard who was knocking on all the doors that I'd seen no one.'

'At what time was this?' Iraklidis asked, frowning.

'About half past nine.'

'Then what did you do?'

'I checked that the coast was clear and took him to the laundry room where he was going to hide until the fuss died down.'

'What number is your room?' Cassie asked.

'Eleven.'

On the first floor.

'And when did Mr Norton return?' Iraklidis continued.

'He was in our room when I came back. He hadn't been outside for long, it was cold. Jim and I watched TV in bed later.'

'And you didn't see Kouris again?' Cassie pressed her.

'*Non.*' Her lips were pressed closed.

'Thank you, Ms Forché. You've been most helpful,' the Security Chief said.

'Can we leave now?'

'As I've explained to Mr Norton, we'll decide who can leave after we finish all the interviews.'

'When will that be?' The Frenchwoman asked as she rose.

'Later.' Iraklidis wouldn't commit himself. Helena ushered Elise Forché towards the door.

'Well, well,' Iraklidis said, sitting back in his seat. 'Barbara Doukas was here on Monday night.'

'And I wonder where Norton and Robbins went walking and why? The protest was beginning in reception, it was exciting and dramatic, yet they ignored it. Instead they took advantage of the distraction to scoot outside for an uninterrupted chat.'

'Could it have been Kouris in the room next to yours?' Iraklidis asked.

'The timing's right,' Cassie answered. 'But who was he with? Barbara Doukas maybe? Or Elise Forché, she might be being coy. Norton was acting very possessively when I came across them on Tuesday morning, they were halfway to a very public row. Maybe he found them *in flagrante* and they retired to another room. And Elise is learning Greek.'

'Something to pursue,' Iraklidis said. 'Let's get Robbins in before he has a chance to speak with Mme Forché.'

But Helena was already returning followed by a determined looking Mike Robbins, who sat firmly on the chair facing the desk.

'How long are you going to keep us all here?' he demanded.

'As long as is necessary,' was Iraklidis's swift reply. 'Mr Robbins, why are you at this conference?'

'I work for Greenforce Energy. We want to see what sort of renewable energy might find favour with European governments. This is one forum for discussion. As I'm sure you know, a lot of informal talk happens outside of the scheduled events – contacts are made, positions sounded out and so on.'

'What is Greenforce Energy, Mr Robbins?' Cassie asked.

'It's a new US company set up to exploit the business potential of a number of new technologies: solar, wind, that sort of thing. Up till now the Europeans have led the market. Greenforce Energy aims to challenge that.'

'When did you arrive here?' Iraklidis asked.

'Sunday night. You could have checked the hotel register.'

'We did. You met with your compatriot, Jim Norton, when was that?'

'Jim and Elise joined me at breakfast on Monday,' Robbins replied. 'I guess it's my accent, they could tell I was another American.'

'Did you know either of them before this conference?'

'Never met them before.' Robbins rattled out his answer.

'But did you *know* either of them?' Cassie persisted.

For the first time Robbins's gaze switched from Iraklidis to Cassie. 'I recognised Norton's name on the conference list.' His gaze switched back. 'He sometimes covers renewables at the OECD, but I hadn't met him, personally.'

'I understand that you and he went for a walk on Monday evening?' Iraklidis asked.

'Uh... yes, we walked around the terrace for a smoke. We didn't leave the compound.'

'Did you happen to see Barbara Doukas on your wanderings? Or Stefan Schlange?'

'I didn't know who the Schlange guy was until someone explained. The girl I'd noticed before, she was pestering people to go on some tour that morning.'

'Did you see her that evening?' Cassie repeated Iraklidis question.

'Dunno. Don't think so.'

'What did you do after your walk?' Iraklidis asked.

'Went to my room, watched some TV, drank some whisky.'

'Alone?'

'Yeah. The desk clerk would have seen me if I'd gone out. I'm on the ground floor.'

'Thank you, Mr Robbins,' Iraklidis said. 'We'll let you know when you can leave the Centre.'

Robbins left, grumbling under his breath.

'No one to vouch for him,' Cassie said. 'But then that applies to a number of people.'

'Why don't I trust him?' The Security Chief shook his head.

'Robbins is a bully,' Cassie said in a matter-of-fact voice. 'He's insulted Helena and me already – no, it's not serious – but he clearly has a problem when dealing with women who know more than he does. Or at least that is what he would like us to believe.'

'You think it could be something more sinister?'

'Possibly. It's speculation until we have evidence,' Cassie said. 'I just don't want us to take him – or anyone – at face value.'

'Good advice,' Iraklidis said. 'Let's carry on. I'll start on the Centre staff.'

◊ TWENTY FIVE

'Please come in, Herr Freyer,' Cassie greeted the head of the Austrian delegation as Helena held wide the door to the small meeting room. The interpreter followed him in, slipped across to a chair in the corner and picked up her notepad.

Freyer held himself stiffly upright. 'I understand that you are investigating the death of that unfortunate woman,' he said. 'But what about our colleague, Dr Schlange? He's missing, perhaps something has happened to him. Why aren't the authorities trying to find him?'

'They will, Herr Freyer, I'm sure, if he doesn't turn up. But as you know, the body which has been discovered is that of Barbara Doukas, a Museum employee. We believe she was killed on Monday night. You arrived on Monday?'

'Sunday evening, late on Sunday evening, we only just got here in time for dinner.'

'Barbara Doukas was here at the guesthouse on Monday morning, organising a trip to the Museum. Did Dr Schlange speak with her?'

'I suppose so.'

'Did you see her at any other time?'

'No. Not that I remember.'

'What about Dr Schlange, did he?'

'I've no idea, how could I have? He may have done. She was waiting for people in reception, as they left breakfast. She spoke with me then and some of the others. I didn't take much notice.'

You wouldn't notice very much if it wasn't to do with your own preoccupations.

'You told me earlier that you didn't know Dr Schlange well,' she continued. 'What do you know of his personal circumstances?'

'Stefan still taught at the university on a part time basis, although he had applied for another position recently, as I told you,' Freyer replied. 'He has a wife – a charming woman – married for almost thirty years, one daughter, though his wife's child, not Stefan's. He looked after her as if he was her father, but I know Stefan was very disappointed not to have children of his own. Has anyone told Frau Schlange that her husband is missing?'

'I understand that the police may contact their Austrian counterparts if necessary,' Cassie replied. 'When was the last time you saw Dr Schlange?'

'At dinner on Tuesday night – I sat next to you, remember. There was quite a lot of drinking, so when he didn't come down for breakfast I assumed that he was sleeping it off, but went up to rouse him because our presentation was at eleven. He was in the room next to mine. When he didn't answer my knock I came back down and asked the receptionist for a key to his room. I was worried. She offered to accompany me and when we opened the door the room was empty, there was no sign of Stefan.'

'Had Dr Schlange slept in his room?'

'It didn't look like it.'

'Did you all travel here together?'

'Yes, Stefan was part of the group. None of us had been here before. We were to leave today. Is there any chance of that, do you think?'

'It's possible, but not up to me to decide,' Cassie said.

There was a rap on the door and Major Lykaios entered, her Sergeant following.

'Herr Freyer?'

'Yes.'

'Would you come with me please?'

Freyer looked at Cassie then at the Major.

'We have found a body,' the Major said. 'We believe it to be that of the missing man. We must have formal identification.'

'Oh.'

Freyer slumped back into the chair. Helena poured a glass of water from the carafe on the table and handed it to him. He took it without seeing, then seemed to notice it and took several gulps. Helena took the glass from him as he stood.

'Very well,' he said. 'Take me to him.'

The Major and Freyer left and Iraklidis joined them, a sombre look on his face.

'A body?' Cassie asked him.

'What's left of one. It's badly battered I'm told, the skull smashed. He – you could tell that much – had fallen, or been pushed, from the cliffs. They found him at their foot.'

The punishment for sacrilege. Another ritual killing?

'We need Freyer's confirmation,' he continued. 'But the Constable says it's Schlange. The news will not be released until the dead man's family has been informed. The corpse isn't a pretty sight. Freyer won't be returning to the interview, so I suggest that you carry on through the list.'

'Do we have any idea what happened to the dead man?' Cassie asked. 'Did the fall kill him? Or was he dead before he went off the cliff edge?'

'Unknown.' Iraklidis shook his head. 'We've a good idea where he was before he went over the edge, just above the Castalian Spring, but we need to look at the top of the cliffs for physical evidence.'

'What could he have been doing up there?' Helena asked. Her face was bloodless.

'If we knew that, my dear, we'd be halfway to explaining how and why he died,' Iraklidis replied. He put his arm around Helena's shoulders.

'So, we have two violent deaths within fifty-six hours, in a place which hasn't seen a murder for over twenty years. Too much of a coincidence,' Cassie said.

'But what links Schlange with Barbara Doukas?' the Security Chief asked.

Cassie saw the question in the Security Chief's eyes, even if he was reluctant to voice the suspicion. Was there a serial killer at work in Delphi?

'What did Freyer tell you?'

'He hasn't seen Schlange since Tuesday night and Schlange's room hasn't been slept in, so Tuesday night was probably when he went missing. Freyer confirms that Schlange was in the group which spoke with Barbara Doukas on Monday morning. He speaks only a little Greek apparently, so he couldn't have been the man I heard arguing in the room next door to mine.'

'See if any of the other Austrians knows more,' the Security Chief said, as he rose to leave. 'I'll get back to interviewing the staff.'

◊ TWENTY SIX

Dr Josef Wild, sharp-faced, wiry and small, was the physical opposite of Herr Freyer. His eyes darted around the little room, resting briefly on the photograph, then he fixed his gaze on Cassie.

'Are you a spy?' he asked.

'No!'

'*Gut*, neither am I,' Dr Wild said with a smile. His accent was impossibly clichéd. 'I am responsible for the reorganisation in Tirol province, based in Innsbruck. Why was Dieter Freyer with the policewoman? Has Dieter been arrested?' There was a gleeful glint in his eyes.

A man who enjoyed upsetting the apple cart, Cassie thought. Not necessarily a bad thing in an academic but unhelpful in a murder investigation.

'No. Herr Freyer has been asked to identify a man's body.' She made her words harsh and cold.

'Stefan?'

'That's what Herr Freyer will determine.'

'*Mein Gott.*'

'Did you know Dr Schlange well? Herr Freyer does not, apparently.'

'Recently, no,' he said. 'But in his younger days, yes. I taught at the University of Linz with him.'

'Did he speak Greek, do you know?'

'Herr Freyer asked me the same thing only yesterday. I don't know, but I think he may have done. He was in Athens as an undergraduate back in the nineteen seventies, so it's likely, though he may have forgotten a lot of it.'

'Dr Schlange was here in Greece when he was a student?'

'Yes, though I think he didn't have that good a time. He wasn't happy talking about it.'

'Why do you say that?'

'Oh, just an impression I got,' Dr Wild said. 'I asked him about it when we arrived in Athens, but he dismissed it as just a short stay and changed the subject. Yet I know he was here for over a year.'

'And how do you know that Dr Wild?'

'I looked up his university profile.' The academic smiled at her mischievously. 'Before we came to this internet-less wilderness. He studied at Athens University.'

'What else did it say?'

'Not much. His life was a conventional one. There were rumours about his political allegiances, but personally, I think they were nonsense. Stefan was much too careful of how anything like that might impact upon his career. The same with his private life, he was a model of domesticity. Any wild oats were sown long ago.'

'Wild oats? That's an unusual expression to use these days, why do you say that?'

'I don't know.' Dr Wild looked perplexed. 'Maybe it's because I'm speaking English – I learned it many years ago. My usage is dated. Stefan, well he… he liked looking at women, especially if they were attractive. I've always imagined him to be something of a Lothario in his youth. Dear me, I make him sound interesting, but he wasn't, he was really quite boring.'

'He came to the temple complex with us on Tuesday afternoon,' Helena said. 'Do you know if he had signed up to go on the Museum trip, the one being organised by Barbara Doukas?'

'Yes, we all did. She was most charming. Such a dreadful shame.'

'When did you last see Ms Doukas?'

'When she was collecting names for the Museum visit.'

'Not since?'

'No.'

'And when did you last see Dr Schlange?'

'At the dinner on Tuesday. He was drinking far too much in my opinion, but then, it was a very strange evening. We all had something of a bacchanal,' he said. 'You left early.'

'Yes.' Cassie wasn't about to explain herself. 'When did you leave the party?'

'After you,' he said. 'Though not by much. It was late and we had the presentation the following morning. We all came back together. We caught up with the beautiful Amazon on the road.'

Meg Taylor.

'Do you speak Greek, Dr Wild?'

'No. I have learned how to say *efcharistó*.' He gave them a mischievous smile. 'Thank you in Greek. You may not have understood my accent. But that's about all.'

'What about your colleagues? Are any of them Greek speakers?'

'Not as far as I know, but then, why would they tell me?' He shrugged his shoulders.

'Thank you, Dr Wild. That's all for now.' Cassie rose.

The rest of the members of the Austrian delegation were subdued after the discovery of their colleague's body, all were anxious to be going home. They had all been at breakfast that morning, so couldn't have been directly responsible for Schlange's death.

After the last of the interviews Iraklidis joined them, bringing coffees.

'What about the Centre's staff?' Cassie asked.

'All of them claim to have alibis for the early hours of Tuesday,' Iraklidis replied. 'It's no surprise, this is a normal working week for them. They'd have been at home with their families. The Sergeant can verify what we've been told, to check out the alibis.'

'Have you learned anything useful from them?'

'Nothing we didn't know already,' he said. 'It looks like Schlange never made it back here from the restaurant on Tuesday night.' He paused. 'His ID and wallet were found in his jacket at the restaurant. It seems he left without them.'

'So where was he between Tuesday night and this morning, more than twenty-four hours later and without a coat?' Cassie said. 'I want to know what the Major has discovered up on the mountain.'

'She's due back here soon. We'll finish the interviews, catch up with her then go into Delphi to speak with Alecto Doukas, Barbara Doukas's mother,' Iraklidis said. 'We should also have the local doctor's opinion by then. Did you get much from the other Austrians?'

'Only one of them,' Cassie said. 'Dr Wild used to work with Stefan Schlange. He told us that Schlange studied at Athens University in the nineteen seventies and probably spoke Greek.'

'So he could have been the man you heard arguing in the next room,' Helena added.

'He also said that Schlange played down his time in Athens, suggesting that it was a short trip, but Wild looked up Schlange's educational profile and he says it was more like a year.' Cassie said.

'A year isn't such a short trip if Schlange wanted to learn about Greece,' Iraklidis said. 'If this was his area of expertise, then that would take a lifetime to master, so I don't see any contradiction there.'

'Hmm, but Schlange wasn't an expert on Greece,' Cassie replied. 'Though he could have wanted to be, back in the seventies, I suppose. Are the landlines repaired yet?'

'No.'

'Have you searched Schlange's room?' Cassie asked.

'Not yet.'

'I'd like to take a look,' Cassie said.

'We'll both look once the interviews are complete,' Iraklidis said.

'Aside from that, the Austrians were all together at dinner on Monday night and all retired to their rooms at about the same time,' Helena said, looking at her notes.

'Did they all stay there, I wonder,' Iraklidis said. 'We'll ask the night manager. But what about Schlange's death? Were any of the Austrians involved? No one else here knew him. His colleagues are the most likely suspects. Could this be the result of an academic rivalry? Schlange was supposed to be applying for a top job, wasn't he? Maybe one of them wanted to remove the competition.'

'Or maybe he saw something, or heard something to do with the death of Barbara Doukas,' Cassie suggested. 'And Barbara's killer realised.'

'The Austrians were all at breakfast shortly after we heard Schlange scream,' Helena said, shaking her head. 'They couldn't have been at the top of the Phaedriades ten minutes earlier.'

Iraklidis opened his mouth to speak, then closed it again.

'Right now I want to speak with the night manager,' Cassie said. 'Let's see if he tells us that Barbara Doukas was here on Monday night.'

'He's next,' Iraklidis said.

◊ TWENTY SEVEN

The night manager was composed and tidy as he was ushered by Helena into the room. He sat in the seat provided and crossed his legs, his fingers laced together on his lap. He was a neat man, Cassie decided, from his precise haircut and smooth skin down to his shiny polished shoes.

'You live in Delphi and have worked here at the Centre guesthouse for... eight years,' Iraklidis began. 'Is that right?'

'Yes.'

'Did you know Barbara Doukas?'

'Yes, she and I grew up here, we went to the same school. Most of the staff here knew each other from outside work. We're mostly Delphians.'

So he doesn't mention that they'd been lovers.

'Did you know Dr Stefan Schlange?'

'No. Not until he became a guest here.'

'Did you see Dr Schlange with Ms Doukas?'

'Yes, Barbara was here on Monday morning taking names for a trip to the Museum. All the Austrians wanted to go on it, including Dr Schlange, I think.'

'And that was the only time that you saw them together?'

'Yes.'

Iraklidis sat back, a cue for Cassie to take up the questioning.

'You were night manager on reception on Monday night.'

'Yes, I checked you into your room and sorted out another for your driver.'

'And you answered the telephone when I called down at eleven thirty about the noise in the room next door.'

'Correct.'

'I was told on the following morning that room eighteen was empty. Yet I heard two people arguing loudly in it.'

'With respect, madam,' the night manager leaned forward. 'I was not there, so I do not know.' He shrugged, looked at Iraklidis and raised the palms of his hands as if to say, 'Women, what can a man do?' Cassie's lips tightened.

'Was there anyone else moving around the guesthouse during Monday night?' Iraklidis asked. 'Any of the Austrians, for example?'

'No, not that I saw. They were all on the first floor.'

'So they would have had to come down the stairs into reception?'

'Yes, though there is a fire escape, but they wouldn't know about that.'

'You said you'd seen Barbara Doukas on Monday morning here at the guesthouse,' Cassie changed the subject.

The night manager bobbed his head.

'Did you see her at any other time that day?'

He hesitated for a second before replying.

'Yes.'

'When?'

'In the evening.'

'And?'

'Later that night.'

'At about ten o'clock.'

'Yes, how…?'

'Be careful what you say,' Iraklidis interjected. He managed to look even more threatening than usual. 'What was she doing on each occasion?' The night manager seemed to shrink back into himself.

'In the evening she said she'd come back to the guesthouse to look for someone.'

'Who?'

'I don't know, but she was asking questions about the ministerial party, where they would be staying and so on.'

'Then what happened?' Cassie asked.

'She went away. I thought she'd gone back to town, but she hadn't, she was still here. May I have some water, please.'

Helena handed the night manager a glass of water, which he sipped. They waited in silence, Cassie forcing herself not to lean forward. The seconds became minutes until she wanted to reach over and shake the story out of him. Then he seemed to make a decision and taking a deep breath, set the glass down in front of him. He lifted his head and spoke.

'She pleaded with me to give her a key to a room.'

'Which room?'

'It didn't matter, she said. It just had to be empty. A room which she could use.'

'So you gave her the key to number eighteen. The room next door to mine.'

Katapodis hung his head. 'Yes.'

'So you knew who was in the room,' Iraklidis snapped. 'Even if you weren't there. You've just lied to the police investigating a murder.'

Cassie could barely hear the night manager's whispered assent.

'And? Then what happened?' Iraklidis prompted.

'Ms Fortune rang to complain about the noise,' the night manager continued. 'I texted Barbara to tell her that she had to get out of the room quickly, that someone had overheard her.'

'What happened after that?'

'I don't know. When I returned to reception it was empty and the room key was on the desk.'

'You were probably the last person, aside from her killer, to see

Barbara Doukas alive,' Iraklidis said. 'Think hard before answering this question. Did she give any indication of why she wanted the room or what she was going to do?'

The night manager frowned in concentration but shook his head.

'No,' he said. 'I don't know, honestly.'

Cassie exchanged glances with Iraklidis.

'Can you think of anything which might help us find her murderer?'

'I've been trying. Barbara was a good person, she grew up here, her family is here. She's hard working and committed to the Museum. She didn't have any dark secrets, I can't think what befell her or why, unless it came from outside.'

'You may go,' Iraklidis closed the interview. 'But don't leave Delphi.' He sat back in his chair as the door closed behind the night manager, who had scuttled from the room. 'You were right about what you heard,' he said to Cassie. 'And now we can place Barbara Doukas in room eighteen at about ten o'clock, but who was the man with her?'

'Whoever he was, he was probably the last person to see Barbara Doukas alive,' Cassie said. 'And he may have been her killer.'

'Let's see what we can find in Schlange's room. We should do that before we meet the Major.'

◊ TWENTY EIGHT

The Austrian's room looked barely occupied. There were shaving articles and toothpaste in the bathroom and clothes hung up in the wardrobe, but little else. A newspaper lay on the bedside table beside a bunch of keys and the academic's closed laptop sat upon the room's long narrow wall table, a folder of papers lying atop it.

Cassie picked up each item, but they seemed unexceptional. She flicked through the papers. They were all notes for the presentation which Dr Schlange should have given. She pulled out all the drawers from the bedside tables and the desk.

Nothing.

She took the wheeled suitcase from the wardrobe. It wasn't

padlocked. Inside she found a couple of pornographic magazines. He must have brought those with him, she thought. What was it Wild had said? That Schlange liked looking at women, especially if they were beautiful or attractive. Cassie tossed them aside – enjoying pornography wasn't a crime.

'Anything?' Iraklidis put his head around the door to the room.

Cassie shook her head. 'Nothing out of the ordinary.' She weighed the bunch of keys in her palm. 'Forensics will examine the laptop, I assume. Until then we had best not touch it.'

'When they get here.' Iraklidis's tone had a sour tang.

'Are you going to allow the Austrians to leave?' Cassie asked him. 'There's something I want to check.'

'Herr Freyer has already spoken with the Professor.'

'Won't the Professor ask your opinion?'

'Yes, but we can't keep them here, we have no evidence against them. Even if they don't all have personal alibis for the early hours of Tuesday morning, the night manager confirms there was no one around. And they couldn't have killed Schlange. There'll be a diplomatic incident if we don't let them go.' Iraklidis held open the door. 'A minibus has been summoned from the valley for them, they'll probably be waiting for it in reception, I think.'

Cassie hurried passed the Security Chief, leaving him to lock the room. As she neared reception she heard the hum of voices. The Austrian delegation was waiting, impatient to leave.

Wild was over by the door, wearing a heavy overcoat and scarf. He raised an eyebrow as Cassie waved at him, beckoning him over.

'How can I help you, Fraulein Fortune?'

'Just one more thing, Dr Wild.'

The Austrian gave her a curious glance.

'I found a couple of pornographic magazines in Dr Schlange's room,' she said. 'It made me think about your remarks earlier about Dr Schlange liking to watch women and "sowing wild oats". Do you know if there was ever an issue at Linz University or elsewhere in regard to Dr Schlange? Harassment or inappropriate behaviour, recently or in the past? Were there any problems with complaints?'

'The university has all the correct procedures in place to deal with anything like that.'

'I'm sure it does, but...'

'I really can't help you.'

Dr Wild's face wore a closed expression.

'Then I'll have to mention this to Mr Iraklidis and Major Lykaios, Dr Wild. They might be reluctant to allow anyone who had information about the dead man to leave.'

The Austrian glared at her, his mouth twisting.

'I am unaware of any formal complaints,' he said haughtily. 'Though such things wouldn't be publicised. I know there was gossip, students used to call him "the goat", if that's in any way relevant.'

Cassie and Dr Wild looked at each other in silence. Finally Cassie spoke in hushed tones, 'It's the twenty-first century, Dr Wild. You know as well as I that what was permitted for a young, good-looking lecturer in the nineteen seventies and eighties is not permitted today to anyone, much less an older man. If he behaves like a goat, as he's called, then it can very much be relevant.'

It was slow and reluctant and his eyes shifted but he nodded in agreement. He was not going to lie to protect the reputation of his dead colleague.

'He had a reputation. It stifled his career. At his peak, when he should have been getting positions of influence, he didn't, though he was good enough. Everyone was cautious. No one wanted to be responsible for promoting a sexual predator. But as he aged, as we all age, he seemed to settle down and advancement once again became possible.'

'What kind of advancement?'

'It's not official. But I happen to know that he was on the shortlist to head a major European research agency.'

'Did he know this?'

Dr Wild blinked in surprise at this question. 'Of course he did. He applied for the job. He was interviewed. He had to submit statements. He was then interviewed again along with only two others, neither of whom had as strong a curriculum vitae as his.'

'So he could reasonably assume that he'd get it?'

He shrugged. 'There is little that is reasonable in these matters. But if he had, then it would be a triumphant end to a career that had long been stagnating.'

The delegation members stirred as a large coach drew up outside the reception. Wild pointed to his colleagues. 'Am I free to leave now?'

'Yes. Thank you, Dr Wild,' Cassie said.

◊ TWENTY NINE

Major Lykaios stamped into the small room, a scowl on her face.

'Major,' Iraklidis said as he rose and offered her his seat.

The Major hesitated, but took it. 'The local doctor agrees that the woman died during Monday night or the early hours of Tuesday morning. The pathologist is delayed. Do you have the list of conference attendees?'

'Delayed how? This is a murder, probably a double murder investigation!' Cassie couldn't believe it wasn't possible for the pathologist to make this a priority.

'There's been a large demonstration in Itea,' the Major replied. 'The riot police were called in and there's been at least one fatality. The whole thing is in the public eye. He's been diverted, there's nothing to be done about it.'

Cassie frowned and Iraklidis looked as if he was going to object, but the Major ploughed on. 'Now, the conference attendees?'

'Here.' Helena handed out copies of her lists. 'The people marked with an asterisk arrived on Tuesday or later, after the murder of Barbara Doukas. They have mostly left the Centre by now.'

'On whose authority?' the policewoman snapped. 'I said specifically that no one should leave until I agreed that they should.'

'On Professor Matsouka's authority,' Iraklidis answered, equally curt. 'If you don't agree, I suggest that you take it up with him.'

'You advise him!' The Major stood, glaring at the Security Chief. 'You advised this! Don't hide behind your boss. They may not have arrived before the death of the woman, but they were definitely here when Stefan Schlange died.'

True.

'Most of them, yes,' Helena admitted after a pause.

'So you may have let *his* murderer go free. The most obvious group of suspects for Schlange's murder are his colleagues, the people who knew him, the people within his own delegation! If that's so, the killer just got away with it.' The Major's dark eyes blazed with a dangerous light.

'The Austrians were all at breakfast ten minutes after Dr Schlange died,' Iraklidis said. 'They couldn't have killed him. And the two deaths are probably linked, or, were committed by the same killer.'

'This is political interference. I shall be reporting this to my superiors.' The Major almost hissed the words.

'What is the doctor's view of Schlange's death?' Cassie asked.

'He's reluctant to offer any view,' the Major replied sharply. 'The body fell almost fifteen hundred metres. It's very broken.'

'Was he alive when he went over the edge and is there any way of knowing if he fell or was pushed?' Iraklidis asked. 'Are there indications of a struggle?'

The Major hesitated.

'Unfortunately we haven't been to the top of the cliffs,' she said.

'What! Why not?' The Security Chief's arching eyebrows almost reached his hairline.

'My Sergeant spent much of his morning trying to organise some better protection from the weather for the first crime scene,' the Major said. 'I've been interviewing townspeople and the protestors and their leader, as we agreed. You could have sent one of your men to do it!'

The Security Chief said nothing, but he slowly clenched his fists.

'There are a lot of things to do,' Iraklidis said flatly. He addressed the Major again. 'Did you discover *anything* helpful? What about the protesters, for example?'

'They're the usual types,' she replied. 'One or two feature in previous reports, Constable Ganas is following them up. Kouris claims that he didn't know Doukas or Schlange and the protest took place here because of the presence of the Minister.'

'And the towns people?'

'No obvious suspects. Monday night was cold and unpleasant, most people were at home, shutters closed. Even those who live alone seem unlikely potential murderers.'

And why would they come to the Centre to speak with Barbara Doukas in the first place? Cassie thought. They could do that in town or in the privacy of their own home.

'At least we have made a discovery,' Iraklidis said, looking down his nose at the Major. 'Barbara Doukas was the woman in room eighteen. The woman Cassie overheard having a heated argument.'

'How do you know?' she responded.

'The night manager admitted giving her a key to the room,' Cassie replied.

The Major's eyes narrowed, then she said. 'Constable Ganas should be told.'

'And Barbara Doukas's mother,' Iraklidis said. 'Have you interviewed her, or Barbara's boyfriend?'

'Mrs Doukas is too distressed to talk with us,' the Major said. 'She has taken to her bed, her brother says.'

What?

Cassie cast a worried glance at Iraklidis, whose face flushed red. Helena bit her lip.

This simply isn't good enough. Surely the Major must see that?

The Security Chief spoke rapidly in Greek to Helena, who murmured 'Cassie, could we give them some privacy?'

'Of course,' Cassie stood and followed Helena out of the room, closing the door behind her. She had not gone even a few steps before she heard raised voices.

The two women sat on one of the reception's sofas.

'Helena, this isn't the way the police work in the UK,' Cassie said. 'So I can't really judge, but it doesn't seem very effective to me.'

'It isn't normal,' Helena answered, looking glum. 'I don't know what's going on.'

'I could understand why the Major wouldn't like our working with her, she would see it as interference,' Cassie said. 'But I don't know why she isn't pursuing the case more vigorously. She's without a permanent post and needs to find one. This is an opportunity for her. To show the Professor what she can do.'

And the clock is ticking.

'I don't understand it,' Helena frowned. 'I hope it doesn't rebound on to Yannis.'

'Is she incompetent, or is she being deliberately obstructive?'

Helena shrugged.

The door to the office opened. A grim-faced Iraklidis led the Major into the reception. 'We're going into Delphi,' he said.

◊ THIRTY

A heavy blanket of cloud lay on the mountain, deadening the sound of their footsteps as they walked to the police station. There was no dramatic view of the valley that afternoon.

Constable Ganas looked up when they entered. He sat to one side of a small gas fire at the back of the office, warming his hands. His face was tired and anxious, his grey-streaked hair unkempt and there were heavy bags beneath his eyes.

'Constable,' Iraklidis nodded to Ganas. 'We would like to interview your sister, Alecto Doukas.' He repeated his statement in Greek.

The local policeman answered and Helena translated quietly.

'He says that his sister is unwell and has taken sleeping pills. We cannot talk with her.'

Iraklidis drew back his lips with an intake of breath, responding with a flood of angry words. The Constable stared up at him, as if not seeing. The Major strode forwards to stand beside Ganas, placing her hand upon his shoulder and arguing with Iraklidis.

So now she's the Constable's ally.

The Major seemed set on opposing Iraklidis. Yet, Cassie thought, she must realise that he had the ear of the Professor. It was a dangerous course of action for her to follow, but the Major didn't back down. If anything it was Iraklidis who seemed the more hesitant.

'I think...' Helena muttered to Cassie as she watched the conversation. 'We could go and speak with Nico, the boyfriend, now. We can always come back later to talk with Mrs Doukas.'

'Good idea. Suggest it. Or better still, just say we'll come back later when she's awoken. Then we can go and find Nico without a minder accompanying us. Do you know where he lives?'

'Yes, I got all the addresses for the people on our list.'

Helena waited for a break in the discussion, which was becoming heated, then made her suggestion. Iraklidis shot her an exasperated glance, his brows drawn together.

'So your colleagues aren't as keen as you are, *Kyrios* Iraklidis, to speak with Mrs Doukas,' the Major said.

The Security Chief turned away, forming a fist with his right hand, which he punched into the palm of his left.

How far will she push him?

'We need to speak with Kouris before we go.' Cassie interjected, looking at Ganas and the Major.

She couldn't understand the short exchange which followed but it was clear that the Major didn't want them talking to the protest leader either. This time Iraklidis prevailed.

Constable Ganas led them all through a heavy metal door into the chilly jail. Balasz Kouris sat on the low truckle bed in the first cell. A bare light bulb dangled from the ceiling, augmenting the grey light coming through the barred window high up in the brick wall. A sickly odour of decay and decomposition hung about the room. Beyond the makeshift curtain of blankets there now lay two bodies.

The protestor's face carried livid bruises and he had a black eye. When he saw Iraklidis he stiffened. His eyes narrowed and he spoke.

'What's he saying?'

'He recognises Yannis from the motorcade and doesn't trust him,' Helena answered. 'I think he thinks this is political. He's afraid, of an "accident" happening to him, he says. He's being over-dramatic.'

Kouris's gaze travelled over the group and he frowned, as it came to rest on Cassie.

'My name is Cassandra Fortune,' she said, betting that he understood at least some English. 'I work for the Prime Minister of Great Britain. I was asked to help find the person who murdered Barbara Doukas,' Cassie pointed to the curtain of blankets. 'Her body was found two days ago. You probably overheard me conducting an examination yesterday.'

He looked at her with considerable intelligence.

'Nothing to do with me,' the prisoner said in English. 'I never met the woman, I didn't know her *and* I was locked up at the time.'

Not until after she died.

The Major responded sharply in Greek, but Kouris shot back a reply, adding, in English 'I told them already. I was at the protest at the Centre. We thought the Minister had arrived early so we decided on a sit-in. A "meet and greet", I believe you call it.' He grinned at them.

'Why did you think he'd arrived early?' Cassie asked.

'One of us saw a limousine arrive. Turns out it was the Olympian.'

'I arrived at the guesthouse when your sit-in was being broken up,' Cassie said. 'You disappeared. Where were you?'

The activist gave a mischievous grin. 'Hiding in a lady's room.'

'Number eleven,' Cassie said.

The Major stared at Cassie, Kouris wasn't the only one to look surprised.

'That was at about ten o'clock,' she continued. 'What did you do after that?'

'I hid in a laundry closet until the fuss had died down. Then I came back to the hostel where we are all staying.'

'At what time? Did anyone see you?' Iraklidis asked.

'About midnight and no, I don't think anyone saw me,' Kouris replied. 'People were asleep by then.'

Cassie exchanged looks with Iraklidis. 'I have one more question,' she said. 'It's about companies offering environmentally friendly technology. Have you ever heard of a company called Greenforce Energy?'

'Oh yes,' the prisoner smiled scornfully. 'The latest attempt of the big fossil fuel companies to greenwash their products.'

Cassie raised her eyebrows.

'It's a deception. So that the public thinks they are becoming more environmentally friendly. For example, "clean burning natural gas" is one of Greenforce Energy's promoted products to help reduce carbon in the atmosphere. It's partly true. It is 50% less 'dirty' than coal when it is burned, but what this doesn't acknowledge is the damage caused by the fracking required to access the gas. The fracking companies are here in Greece, just as they are in the UK.'

'I see.'

'If as little as three per cent of the gas escapes during the process, the impact on the atmosphere is just the same as coal. Why do you ask?'

'It may have nothing to do with the murder, but one of the people I spoke with yesterday is from Greenforce Energy and I thought he wasn't telling me the whole truth.'

'People eventually see their lies,' the protest leader said. 'Sadly, that doesn't stop them gaining contracts and putting pressure on governments. This is why we protest.'

'But why here? Specifically?'

'Theo Sidaris has already sold off prized state assets to the private sector. He's been too close to big global corporations. If there are

Greenforce delegates at the conference we were right to protest. What has Sidaris been agreeing with Big Oil now?'

'He may not have been agreeing anything,' Cassie said.

'You're in Greece, Ms Fortune. Here our politics happen in secret. We only get transparency if we maintain the pressure.'

'I could say the same about the UK, or indeed anywhere else,' Cassie countered.

'But it's worse here, there are backdoor deals done all the time, as there always have been. In the time of Demosthenes, King Phillip of Macedon had his paid informers and collaborators in Athens. In the time of the Generals there were plenty of collaborators who got away before the trials, warned beforehand. And probably now, in the guise of a European conference on administration there are the deals selling off our patrimony. Crimes are committed and no one knows about them. The only way the public gets to find out is if we make a deafening noise.'

'I'd hardly call those demonstrations deafening.'

'Wait until you see it on social media.' Kouris grinned and pointed to his bruised face. 'This helps.'

'At least you have that advantage, they didn't have social media in the 4th century BCE or even in the 1970s.'

'Greeks didn't need social media to understand how things worked. Everyone knew. There were too many collaborators who got away.'

'That's no one's definition of justice being done,' Cassie said.

'Justice isn't done. The powerful always get away with their crimes. When people suffer they call them tragedies, or tragic accidents. They despoil the planet for profit.'

'That's enough,' Major Lykaios said, standing in front of Cassie. 'You've asked your question.'

Iraklidis retorted in Greek, but this didn't faze the Major.

'He asks if you've finished?' Helena said.

'For now,' she replied. She needed to think about what Kouris had said.

Iraklidis accompanied them towards the door.

'We need to question Robbins again,' he said. 'And Alecto Doukas, Barbara's mother, but now I want to speak with Constable Ganas about the protestors, eliminate as many as we can. Shall I see you back here, or at the guesthouse?'

'We don't know how long we'll be,' Cassie said. 'We'll see you at dinner later. Best of luck.'

You'll need it.

With a sharp nod, Iraklidis stepped back into the room.

◊ THIRTY ONE

Cassie pressed the button marked Vasilakis on the door entrance panel and a scratchy voice answered the intercom. A little explaining from Helena resulted in the door clicking open and the two women entered and climbed the stairs. Nico lived on the second floor in a low-rise modern block near the lower edge of Delphi town. He was waiting for them on the landing and showed them into his apartment.

The living room was rectangular with double doors leading out on to a deep balcony which ran the width of the flat and overlooked the valley, as well as windows which looked back to the mountainside.

'What an amazing view,' Cassie exclaimed.

'It's pretty good,' Nico said, smiling shyly. 'Can I make you a drink?'

There was a small, fitted kitchenette at one end of the living room, where the young man proceeded to make coffee. He was pale and unshaven and had dark rings beneath his eyes. His black hair was already receding at the forehead and he seemed prematurely aged, though that may have been caused by recent events. It was only two days since his long-time girlfriend had been found dead in the temple compound, Cassie reminded herself.

He was also a potential suspect. In some ways perhaps he was by far the most likely suspect. A crime of passion, followed by deep remorse and a lifetime of regret, Cassie speculated. Yet why then would he kill Dr Schlange, unless that death was unrelated?

'Here.' Nico put steaming mugs down on a low table in front of the sofa where Cassie and Helena sat. His hands, Cassie noticed, were square, the fingers stubby. He took the only other easy chair. 'How can I help you?'

'Cassie's an investigator back in the UK,' Helena said. 'She's been asked to help the police.'

Nico turned to Cassie. 'So?'

'When did you last see Barbara Doukas?'

'On Monday lunchtime, at the Museum.'

'Not later that day?'

'No. She'd signed people up for a tour, to take place on Tuesday and she went back to the Conference Centre to catch the late arrivals. I stayed at the Museum, preparing. I was there until very late. It was important. We thought the Minister or his party might attend and we could impress him, maybe get access to more funding. Money's always tight, so this was an opportunity we couldn't let pass.'

'You were the person who reported her missing, I believe.' The young man nodded assent. 'That was on Wednesday morning. Why not on Tuesday night?'

'I did. At first I didn't realise that she was missing, I thought she was at home with her mother. When I realised she wasn't there I went to speak with Alex, Constable Ganas, Barbara's uncle. That was on Tuesday evening, but he wanted to wait to see if she returned to her mother's house before starting a full search.'

'Why wait? If Barbara had, say, gone for a walk and fallen, she would've been out on the mountain all Tuesday night.'

'That's what I said,' Nico looked down at his hands. 'I didn't see her all day. She wasn't at the Museum at all and wasn't at home later either. But he took no notice of me.'

'Why, Nico? Why wouldn't he listen to you?'

Nico stared into the liquid in his mug.

'Barbara and I, we've had a few disagreements recently. Sometimes I don't see her for days. It's nothing serious, just couple stuff, but I think Alex, Constable Ganas, thought she might have gone off in a sulk and been blanking me.'

Or you might have killed her.

'What were your disagreements about?'

'Mainly because I wanted to get engaged,' his cheeks flushed, 'but Barbara didn't.'

'Did she say why?'

'Sometimes I think she found Delphi too small. There aren't many career opportunities for the likes of her and me here. She would talk of moving to somewhere bigger, maybe Amfissa or, more recently, Athens, where the family originally came from. She went there to research the family history and I think she enjoyed it, the bright lights and big city, I think she would have liked to move there permanently, but didn't have the money. I don't understand that. I prefer a quiet life, a small community. I won't move from here, I like that it's a small town. She seemed more insistent this time, that she'd get away, but it usually came to nothing.'

The young man shrugged his shoulders. His mouth turned down at the corners and he blinked rapidly, as if he was trying not to weep. Then he inhaled deeply.

'Alex went to ask for help in searching from the Minister's security people, but not till Wednesday morning, after Barbara didn't come home on Tuesday night. I told the policewoman all of this – the Major. She spoke with me and with Barbara's mother when she arrived in Delphi.'

What!

'I had understood that Mrs Doukas wasn't seeing anyone at all right now. That she's very distressed, which is understandable and quite ill.'

'Oh.' The young man looked puzzled. 'But she didn't seem ill this morning, she was out with her brother and that Olympic runner.'

Meg? What had Meg to do with all of this?

'Are you sure?'

'Yes, I saw them in the Jeep. I couldn't sleep, so I came and sat in here for a while.'

'When was this?'

'Earlier today, at about seven o'clock, seven thirty this morning. I was surprised to see them out so early.'

'And where were they exactly?'

'Coming down into town along the track that leads to the Corycian Cave and the stadium.'

The young man gestured towards the window which looked back on to the mountain. Cassie could just make out the pathway climbing the slope.

'You're sure it was Mrs Doukas and Meg Taylor with Constable Ganas?'

Cassie caught Helena's eye.

'Yes, quite sure.'

'We haven't found Barbara's mobile phone,' Cassie said. 'Did she always carry it with her?'

'Usually, yes.'

'And her key to the temple complex is missing too, yet she must have used it to let herself in. You have a similar key don't you?'

'Yes.' Nico pulled open a drawer in the cabinet behind him and drew out a large bunch of keys. 'Here.' He selected a key of the standard metal type. 'Barbara's is the same as this. It was on her key ring.'

Cassie examined it. It was unexceptional.

'So where were you on Monday night?'

'At the Museum until late, eleven, midnight,' Nico replied. 'Like I said.'

'Was anyone else there? Anyone who can vouch for you?'

He shook his head in the negative. 'There's only Barbara and me during the Winter months, when the temple complex is closed.'

No alibi and, by his own admission, close to the scene of the crime at about the right time.

'Do you have any idea who might have killed Barbara?'

'No. She didn't have any enemies.' Nico sucked in a shuddering breath.

'What about in Athens, did you say that she had family there?'

'Not anymore. Barbara was born here in Delphi, but her mother and Alex came here as children. Alecto's house is full of photographs from years ago.'

'And their parents, Barbara's grandparents?'

'I don't know exactly, I'm not sure anyone does. Alecto doesn't talk about them, though I know Barbara asked her about them more than once. She was curious about her background. Athens always seemed more glamorous to her, she liked the connection.'

'What about politics?' Cassie asked. 'Did Barbara belong to any political party? Were there any causes which she favoured, women's rights, wildlife, environmentalism?'

'Not really,' he shook his head. 'She voted, but she wasn't interested in politics. She liked Greta Thunberg, thought whale hunting was wrong and wanted the Amazon loggers to stop, but she wasn't an activist of any kind. She wasn't any trouble to anyone. She spent more time looking into the past, like me, working at the Museum.'

Cassie looked at Helena. 'Is there anything else?' she asked. 'Anything I've missed?'

'I don't think so.'

'Thank you, Mr Vasilakis,' she stood. 'You've been a help.' Cassie was sure that Nico Vasilakis didn't realise just how much help he'd been.

'Let me show you out.'

◊ THIRTY TWO

Cassie strode away from Nico's apartment block. She waited until she was sure that they couldn't be overheard, then stopped and turned to Helena.

'What the hell were Alecto Doukas and Meg Taylor – Meg Taylor! – doing with Ganas on the mountain early this morning? And at around the time Schlange died.'

'I don't–'

'And why is the Major hiding things from us?'

'Ganas seems to be involved somehow too,' the interpreter added.

'I don't trust him. Is he Golden Dawn do you think? And then there's his sister, Barbara's mother, to whom we aren't allowed to speak.' Cassie raised her hands in frustration.

'Also, what's Meg Taylor's part in all of this?'

'The night manager told us that Barbara was asking questions about the Minister's party. We don't know why. She could have been trying to ensure their participation in a tour, or did she have another reason to contact them, or one of them, before she was killed?'

'Only Meg was at the Centre on Monday. Could Meg have known Barbara from before?'

'Or was Meg someone glamorous and powerful in Barbara's eyes, someone worth knowing. When we return to the Centre we need to focus on Meg and try and find a link between her and Barbara.'

'Yannis won't agree. He doesn't think Meg is involved.'

Yannis this, Yannis that. She's worse than a schoolgirl.

'His loyalty is to the Minister and the Professor and she is their close friend. So of course he thinks she isn't involved. But she is. He just has to face up to it.'

'He's only doing his job.'

'Is he? Or is it rather more than that? Iraklidis owes them his career, the Professor controls him, you've seen it. Take care, Helena, don't let a few nights of passion cloud your judgment.'

'At least we have some leads now,' Helena said, in a small, tight voice. 'I think we should share them with Yannis.'

'I agree. Primarily, he needs to know that the Major is withholding information and then to damn well do something about it. He must take this to the Professor. Find him. He may still be at the police station or may have gone back to the Conference Centre.'

'What about you?'

'I'm going to take a look at that path before it rains,' Cassie stated. 'Up the mountain, to where you saw the lights last night.'

'By yourself? What about the man on your trail?'

'If it rains we'll lose the tracks and any physical evidence.' Cassie raised her eyes towards the heavy cloud. 'I have to look.'

'Cassie, I don't think you should go. It's too dangerous...'

'It isn't for you to tell me what I should and shouldn't do,' Cassie reminded the interpreter, her tone shut down any discussion. Helena cast down her eyes, chastened. 'Look, I know the way I've been up there already, when I went to the stadium with Meg Taylor... I'll be fine. I'll see you back at the Centre.'

With a perfunctory wave she set off through Delphi town, striding out. Her mind was buzzing. She fizzed with frustration. There was too much at stake for her personally as well as for the safety of everyone around her and no one was telling her anything. Everyone was compromised by politics in one form or another, even her own interpreter, with her pathetic romance and her reporting back to the Ambassador.

Find something concrete – some physical evidence. She wanted to look at the path, to see if there were any traces from the previous night or other clues. More than anything else, she wanted to be alone to think through the case.

She set a steady pace as the road turned into a track and the track into a trail. The scrubby trees gave way to bushes, blowing in a wind which seemed to grow stronger as she climbed. The cloud cover was low and heavy.

Barbara Doukas was at the Centre on Monday morning, where she met with those conferencegoers who had already arrived, including the Austrians as well as the OECD pair and the greenwasher Mike Robbins. By evening she was back and looking for someone, asking questions about the ministerial party. By ten that night she was demanding that the night manager give her a room, room eighteen, where she met and subsequently argued with an unknown man, a Greek speaker. She, and whomever she'd been fighting with, left room eighteen at shortly after eleven thirty.

Did she go to the temple complex next? Was she accompanied and if so, by whom, the man who she had argued with? And why go there? It was dark and cold and a storm was threatening? Was there nowhere else she or they could go?

Concentrate on building the picture from what you know.

She had reached the place where the trail diverged and one path led to the stadium above the temple complex. She took the other, steeper path.

Why go to the temple site at all? If she came from the Centre, she'd walked through Delphi town. So Barbara's home wasn't a possibility. Whatever she was doing, she didn't want her mother to know about it. Barbara had a key to the gate, so could have let herself and any companion into the complex. What about the Museum, she had a key to that as well and it was closer to the Centre? Though, if Nico was working there she wouldn't need one.

Maybe she went there and he killed her? But then why go out into the night to put her body in the Treasury? Wouldn't there be places in the Museum where a body could be hidden? Perhaps she had planned to go there, but didn't want Nico to see her, or whomever she was with? So they went on to the temple site. The Athenian Treasury was one of the few almost complete structures in the complex and even without much of a roof it would have provided some shelter.

Cassie stopped and bent over, her breath laboured. The slope was very steep and the trail had grown rocky. The clouds seemed much nearer. She turned to look back down the path and was surprised at how high up she was. The buildings in Delphi seemed very small and she could just see a figure walking up its main street. Helena. Beyond the ridge lay the Conference Centre.

Helena needs to get her priorities sorted. This love affair is becoming annoying.

She pressed on. The trail began to switch back up the mountain, only the goat's path continued on straight.

Chances are that the romance won't last once they're back in Athens anyway.

Cassie scanned the trail, looking for tracks. This was approximately where there had been lights on the mountain on Wednesday night.

There!

The wide tyre tracks of an off-road vehicle were visible in the dirt of the track. Cassie pulled her telephone from her pocket and took a number of photographs. Not before time as she felt rain in the wind; a downpour would wash away any traces.

The trail branched into two again, the right-hand branch going across the mountain side to the Shining Ones, while the left-hand track turned back upon itself and continued up the mountain above Delphi town. This led to the Corycian Cave. From the corner of her eye she saw a movement above her and to the right.

It was a figure, clad in mountain walking gear, with hood raised and wearing goggles, she couldn't even tell if they were male or female. They were striding away from her along the path to the top of the cliffs.

Who the hell goes mountain walking in November on a day like this?

Could it be whoever had followed her the other night? Or someone else – her thoughts flew to the pyjama top added to her suitcase.

Focus on the task in hand, she told herself. Whoever it was has gone. The rain would come soon. Do what you're here to do. She took the trail to the Cave, scanning for more tracks.

She walked upwards into the cloud, a milky wet whiteness which clung to her hair and eye lashes. The hairpins of the track, with its sharp stones and flattened earth, became her whole world. The only sounds were of the whistling wind and the deadened scrunch of her footsteps. Then she gasped as she was met by a sharp wind rushing over relatively level ground. She had reached the top of the climb. Grey shapes loomed further off, rocky outcrops or further slopes, she couldn't tell.

She turned, but could see little of the way she had come, cloud covered all. The mysterious figure had disappeared completely.

There were way markers, cairns of rocks, for hikers to follow, but

Cassie could barely see from one to the next. She followed a stony path across uneven scrubland. Soon she joined with a track and entered a wooded area, dotted with firs and pines, the slope rising again. Outcrops of grey rock rose above the trees.

More tyre tracks – she photographed them. They looked the same as those she had seen earlier. So this trail had been used often in recent days. Was that linked to Barbara's murder?

There was a bright flash and she was momentarily blinded.

The lightning was immediately overhead. A deafening roll of thunder crashed, reverberating around the peaks. Rain began to pummel the earth. The tempest was all around her, it was as if she was inside the storm.

Was it a good idea to explore alone? Now where have I heard that before?

Cassie pulled up her hood, thrust her hands into her pockets and hurried along the path. The rain's intensity increased as the lightning flashed again. The Cave couldn't be far off. She would wait there for the rain to stop.

◊ THIRTY THREE

Through the murk Cassie spotted the cave entrance, a grey slab of rock hanging suspended at an angle above a black void. She picked her way through a jumble of boulders, rain bouncing at angles from the hard surfaces. Ducking beneath the overhang, she skittered down the slope inside the cave.

The blue-white beam of her phone light revealed a dirt floor. The gloomy light from outside didn't penetrate far within the cave, which was about twenty feet across, but widened out further in, its increasingly high roof breaking into dangling rock stalactites. She could see no end to it, her light swallowed by the blackness. Outside the thunder rolled, sounding a dull echo in the cavern.

Cassie swept the light from right to left, going over the uneven ground as she walked deeper in. On the third sweep she found what she was looking for. Nico had told them that this place had been home to people for thousands of years and it seemed that it still was. By the wall of the cave was evidence of recent occupation.

She hastened over and knelt to examine what was there – a couple of rough grey blankets, a biscuit-packet wrapper, an empty plastic container and a water bottle. A newspaper, two used syringes – no indication of what they contained – some dirtied and slightly bloody bandages, the backing paper from plasters and an empty tray of paracetamol.

Drugs? An addict or was someone injured?

She prodded the blankets with her foot and took multiple photographs.

A vivid flash of lightning lit the cave and Cassie blinked. As her vision returned to normal she heard a new sound from outside, the growl of an engine.

'Cassie!' Helena's echoing voice preceded her by only a few seconds as the interpreter half slid down the slope into the cave. She had acquired a transparent plastic cape with a hood, though she still wore her ordinary shoes. 'Thank goodness! We were getting worried about you, up here in the storm.'

'I'm fine.'

'You look soaked through!'

Right on cue, Cassie sneezed.

'Found anything?' Iraklidis appeared at the cave mouth wearing a similar cape, closely followed by Constable Ganas, whose hair was slicked down to his head. The Security Chief strode over and crouched to look at the collection of items. 'What's this? Who was here?'

'I don't know,' Cassie replied. 'But whoever it was may have been injured and was supplied with food, water and reading material.'

She picked up the damp pages of the newspaper, holding them by the corner. It was The Times, dated Wednesday 9th November, the editorial and letters page. It carried an editorial about the Athens Appeal Court decision on Golden Dawn, setting it within in the context of Greece's past.

You can't escape the past.

She took more photographs.

'An English newspaper?'

'Yep,' she answered. 'We need to dry it out, in case any fingerprints have survived.'

Helena translated what was being said for Constable Ganas. 'We can do that at the station, he says. He's going to take the evidence.'

'Careful!' Cassie said, as the policeman scooped up the detritus in the blankets. He seemed to lack any understanding of how to deal with evidence. Iraklidis frowned, his mouth drawn into a grimace.

Ganas carried his bundle outside, where the rain had reduced to a light but persistent drizzle. As they crossed to the police Jeep parked near the cave entrance, Cassie took a good look at its tyres. Once on board she checked the photo on her phone. They looked the same.

So the police Jeep, or one very like it, has been up here recently.

'What about the top of the cliffs?' Cassie asked. 'Could we have a look around before the rain obliterates everything?'

Constable Ganas climbed behind the wheel, ignoring her.

'It'll be dark soon,' Helena said.

'But the Jeep's got lights,' Iraklidis said. 'It might be fruitless, but I'd like to see the top of those cliffs as well.'

There followed an exchange in Greek and, reluctantly, the policeman put the vehicle into gear and switched on its headlights. They headed back through the stand of trees, then turned eastwards across the undulating plateau, trundling over the uneven terrain to the top of the Phaedriades. For all their reputation as shining cliffs, Cassie had mostly seen them in darkness, cloud and rain.

The wind whistled around the Jeep as it pulled to a stop. It wasn't quite dark, but low cloud obscured any view. Cassie was buffeted backwards by the wind as she climbed from the vehicle. She sensed open space in all directions. There was nowhere to hide here, only a few bushes and shrubs, it was very exposed.

'He says there's the cliff edge,' Helena shouted, translating needlessly, as Ganas swept his arm towards where the white-grey rock stopped and milky cloud raced in the beams of light from the Jeep. 'But there's nothing to see.'

Cassie stepped forward and bent to look at the ground. It was from here, or very nearby, that Schlange had plunged to his death. She couldn't see any disturbance of the earth and there didn't seem to be any signs of a struggle, but, in the murk and rain it was almost impossible to tell.

There were more tyre tracks, which looked the same as the others, belonging to the police Jeep or one like it. The Major had said that she hadn't been up here, but a Jeep seemed to have been.

Could Ganas have been up here without her? There was so much that didn't make sense in this case.

'Cassie!'

She heard Iraklidis call.

'It's getting worse, come on!'

The Security Chief was going back to the Jeep, where Ganas already held open a door. Helena was already inside. With a brief look back at the racing clouds, Cassie followed suit.

◊ THIRTY FOUR

The atmosphere in Delphi Police Station was thick and fuggy. Wet rain capes and Cassie's sodden outer clothing steamed on hooks or over the backs of chairs. The Constable made hot drinks as Iraklidis unrolled the blankets taken from the Cave and laid out their contents on a trestle table at the side of the room to await the forensics team. The two women sat close to the little gas fire. Cassie sneezed again.

'Where's the Major?' she asked, taking the tissue handed to her by Helena.

'Gone to speak with the local doctor,' Helena translated Ganas's reply. 'The bodies need storing somewhere more suitable than here and the nearest mortuary and funerary parlour is down in the valley.'

'The Major's absence may be useful,' Cassie kept her voice low and without inflection. 'We need to ask our host some questions. About what he did after his niece was reported missing on Tuesday evening and what he was doing up the mountain with his sister and the runner early this morning.'

Iraklidis looked up sharply from his contemplation of the objects on the table.

'This morning?'

'I was going to tell you,' Helena said, warily. 'We were told that the police Jeep was seen coming into town from the mountain road at about seven thirty yesterday.'

'We heard Schlange's cry just after seven,' the Security Chief said. 'And what about–?'

'Your Olympian is involved in this somehow Yannis whether you like it or not. We have to tackle her,' Cassie said. 'Otherwise we're not doing our job.'

The Security Chief opened his mouth to reply, but said nothing and closed it again.

'And we have to speak with the Constable's sister.'

'That I agree with.'

As Ganas handed round mugs of steaming liquid, his dark eyes flicked from one to another as they spoke, his expression hard to read. He drew up a stool and sat down by the fire, sipping his coffee.

'Ask him why he didn't start a search when Nico told him that Barbara was missing,' Cassie said.

Helena did so. The Constable's face took on a haunted look, even more haggard than before.

'He says he thought she was simply avoiding Nico. Apparently relations between them weren't as settled as Nico would have liked. Barbara and he hadn't been getting on so well for a couple of weeks. He asked his sister about her and went down to the Museum. When he realised that she really was missing it was too dark and the conditions too dangerous to look further. He raised the alarm first thing the following morning.'

'So he didn't go out on to the mountain to look for her?'

'He says not.'

'When did he begin searching?'

'Wednesday morning, as part of the general search. He went up to the Corycian Cave, but it was empty.'

'What about the top of the cliffs?'

'This morning.'

'But the Major said that they hadn't searched up there,' Cassie said. 'Which was infuriating.'

'He says he went up there as part of the search for Schlange.'

'Didn't he tell the Major?' Iraklidis said, aghast. 'Is no one telling anyone anything?'

Because no one trusts anyone else.

Irritated, Iraklidis took up the questioning. Helena translated for Cassie.

'What were you doing up the mountain early this morning, at the time of Dr Schlange's death?' The Security Chief was curt, his face immobile.

'I wasn't...'

'You were seen.'

'Who by?' Ganas challenged.

'It was almost seven thirty, people were getting up to go to work.'

'I went to check on my sister. She wasn't at home and neighbours said they had seen her go out. She likes to walk on the mountain sometimes. But it wasn't really light, so I went looking for her. I – I was afraid what she might do.' The Constable paused, frowning, then continued. 'I found her on the path above the temple complex. She had some wild idea that she should appeal to the old gods, to find Barbara's murderer.' He shrugged, raising the palms of his hands. 'She wanted to invoke the Furies to track down the killer and seek revenge. I'm afraid that my niece's death has... turned my sister's wits.'

He looked into the flames of the gas fire. Helena leaned towards Cassie to explain.

'Furies are deities of pure vengeance, a kind of ancient retribution. Invoking them is like calling upon God Almighty to smite all your enemies whether they actually deserve it or not.'

More old religious beliefs.

Cassie murmured thanks, although this wasn't news to her.

Then she asked Ganas 'You were accompanied by someone else when you came back to town?'

'Yes, the Olympic runner. She runs every morning. I've seen her. We gave her a lift back to town.'

'Where did you come across her?'

'On the path up to the Cave, beyond the stadium turnoff,' Helena translated his answer.

'Were you out on the mountain on Wednesday night?' Iraklidis asked. 'After dark?'

'No.' Ganas shook his head.

But who else could it have been?

'How many people in Delphi own vehicles which could climb those paths?' Cassie asked. 'At night?'

'There are a few,' Helena relayed his rambling response. 'The local garage has a Jeep and several people own trail bikes. Trail biking is a popular pastime. The Centre has a three-wheeler trail buggy.'

'You thought you saw vehicle headlights.'

'I certainly saw lights and they were moving.'

'We'll have to speak with the garage owner,' Iraklidis said. 'Ah, Major, you've decided to join us.'

Major Lykaios gave the Security Chief a withering look as she removed her rain cape, water spouting from it, and hung it up to dry. She didn't look surprised to see them.

'The bodies are to be removed to the doctor's surgery,' she said in English. Her eye was caught by the items on the side table and she strode over to it. 'What's this?'

'Evidence,' Iraklidis replied. 'Found in the Corycian Cave. Someone was sleeping there, someone who was injured.'

'And someone who spoke, or could read, English,' Cassie added.

Cassie watched the Major closely as she bent to look at the items, not touching them. She hadn't seen them before, that was clear, though she hesitated before straightening up. Something specific had attracted her attention. Cassie peered to see what it was, but couldn't tell.

'Why are you withholding information from us?' Iraklidis was unable to hold back any longer. 'You spoke with Barbara Doukas's mother and boyfriend. This is supposed to be a joint investigation.'

'It is my usual practice in murder cases to speak first with the immediate relatives of the deceased. I don't have to answer to you.' Major Lykaios answered, unrepentant. 'I spoke with them as soon as I arrived in Delphi, before I visited the temple complex, before I even spoke with you and Ms Fortune.'

'And you didn't think to tell us?' The Security Chief was growing red in the face.

'You were supposed to share information,' Cassie added.

'There was nothing to share. They told me nothing.' Something in the Major's tone made Cassie pause.

Even if that's true, you think they're hiding something. What else aren't you telling us?

'I want to question Alecto Doukas.' Iraklidis's jaw was set, he wasn't going to be deflected again. 'There are more questions which need answering now, like what she was doing up the mountain this morning.'

The Major shot him a surprised look.

'How...?'

'A witness.'

'You can't question her tonight,' the policewoman said. 'No one can. The doctor told me that he's sedated her.'

The Security Chief smashed his hand down on the top of the desk. The Major was stony faced, unmoved.

Cassie sneezed. Then muttered an apology.

'I suggest that you take Ms Fortune back to the Centre,' the Major suggested. 'She looks like she needs a hot bath. And I'm sure Ms Gatakis could do with a change of clothes.'

Iraklidis glared at her, a black look on his face. Helena touched his arm and murmured something.

'We'll be back tomorrow morning,' the Security Chief said, giving the Major a cold, hard stare. 'To speak with Mrs Doukas.'

As they gathered up their belongings, making ready to leave, Cassie slipped through the open door into the small jail, startling Balasz Kouris, who was lying on his bed reading a magazine. The Major's reaction to seeing the evidence table had made her think. The bare light bulbs gave the gaol a stark appearance, casting black shadows. Everywhere she smelled the clinging stink of decay. Even through her running nose Cassie felt its burn, it scorched her throat. She hurried across to the makeshift curtain and took out her phone to take a photograph of it.

The blankets were the same as those found in the Corycian Cave.

◊ THIRTY FIVE

Cassie sneezed.

A cold. That's all I need.

The guesthouse reception had been deserted when they returned. Large numbers of guests had gone home earlier in the day and the place seemed eerily empty, its hard surfaces echoing any sound. Cassie wanted a hot shower but trundled after the others into the small room off reception. Her head ached.

For the first time she considered if there was a political aspect to the killings? Otherwise what had the ministerial party to do with it? Professor Matsouka had insisted that the Minister leave immediately, so as to keep Sidaris safe from any murderer. But was there more to it than that? It seemed that at least one of them was involved.

If Balasz Kouris was telling the truth about Greenforce Energy – and there was no reason why he would lie – then Mike Robbins wasn't really in renewables. His appearance at the conference, to try and influence Theo Sidaris, might be the opposite of what she had assumed.

There was also a new element – the sleeper in the Corycian Cave. Had Schlange, the missing Austrian, slept there or maybe the mysterious walker she'd seen through the mist? Someone had followed her up the mountain road from the tavern on Tuesday night, another unresolved mystery. Maybe it was nothing to do with Lawrence Delahaye, but was linked to the two recent deaths? And what was the significance of the blankets in the cave being the same type as those in the jail? Maybe they were just from the same shop or supplier?

Stop! Too many questions!

'Cassie... Cassie.' Helena repeated.

'Sorry, what?'

'You found the tracks you went looking for?' Iraklidis asked.

'Yes,' Cassie replied. 'But the only tyre marks I found on the mountain tracks fit with the tyres on the police vehicle, which tells us nothing other than it was up the mountain, which you would expect.'

'That's no help.'

'But while I was climbing the path to the Cave I saw someone else up there. I couldn't see them clearly through the mist, but whoever it was wore outdoors gear.'

'The sleeper in the Cave, perhaps?' Iraklidis suggested.

'The figure moved fluidly, didn't look injured in any way,' Cassie responded. 'But yes, maybe. Are there any tourists in town?'

'Someone who couldn't afford a hotel room?' Helena speculated. 'A protestor?'

'Or someone who wants to stay away from any investigation,' Iraklidis said.

'There's one other thing too. The blankets in the Cave... they're the same as those in Delphi jail. And the Major has already noticed – I was watching her when she looked at the evidence from the Cave. She chose not to mention it.'

'What the hell is going on with that woman?' Iraklidis threw his hands up in the air. 'Why isn't she doing her job?'

'I can't imagine,' Cassie continued. 'She didn't examine the cliff top or the track leading up to it. And she didn't tell us that she'd spoken with the victim's mother and boyfriend – that's inexcusable. Yannis, I think that you need to look into her background and her ties to other organisations. Is she a Golden Dawn member? She might intend to smear the Minister with innuendo about the killing.'

And that certainly won't help me get him to London.

'Will you raise this with the Professor?'

The Security Chief didn't respond immediately.

'Let's give her the benefit of the doubt for the moment,' he said, eventually. 'I suspect that Constable Ganas isn't exactly co-operating with her. Policemen in these outlying locations tend to resent outside interference. The Major... well, she's an outsider. She would look upon your involvement as an imposition too, potentially politically inspired.'

'I never wanted to be involved!'

'Fine, but she doesn't know that. Then, as you say, there's the possibility that she, or indeed, the Constable, is a member of Golden Dawn.' Iraklidis's face clouded. 'If either of them is, they wouldn't look favourably on me, or want to help the Minister. '

'Ganas isn't telling us everything, I'd bet on that,' Cassie said. 'Neither he nor the Major are conducting themselves as police should. Did you notice Balasz Kouris's face? Ganas seems to have given him quite a beating.'

'Yes. Unfortunately, it happens. Local police in remote areas can be a law unto themselves,' Iraklidis said.

Cassie widened her eyes.

'I'm not saying it's right, just that it happens,' he snapped. 'Anyway I don't believe Constable Ganas murdered his own niece.'

'The Major should have examined the top of the cliffs as soon as the body was found at their foot,' Cassie said. 'Who knows what evidence has been missed. I strongly suggest that you speak with the Professor and get her to toe the line.'

Or I will.

The Security Chief glared at Cassie, but he said nothing.

He complained about her before and she's worse now.

'We were supposed to focus on the outsiders, the visitors,' Helena interjected, anxious to defuse any confrontation between her lover and Cassie. 'Can we do that? There were ten staying at the Centre on Monday night – seven Austrians, including Schlange, two Americans and the Frenchwoman,' the interpreter said. 'But we've ruled out the Austrians, so that leaves three.'

'And Meg Taylor,' Cassie said. 'Four.'

'The suspect list for Schlange's death is wider,' the Security Chief continued, ignoring Cassie. 'It includes the members of Barbara's family and her friends and neighbours in Delphi.'

'But what if the same person killed them both?' Cassie said. 'We can rule out Kouris from that, he was in jail, and the Austrians were all at breakfast, very shortly after we heard Schlange's scream, as were Norton and Forché. Setting that pair aside, that leaves Mike Robbins and Meg Taylor.'

Iraklidis opened his mouth to respond, but before he could speak blinding white lightning illuminated the underside of the heavy layer of cloud which lay across the sky, distracting them all. There was no thunder.

'The storm's a long way off,' Helena said. 'Let's hope it gets no closer, or more evidence will be destroyed.'

'If it hasn't been already,' Iraklidis said. 'Tomorrow we'll talk to Ganas's sister, Barbara's mother. I will insist.'

'There is also one other avenue to be explored,' Cassie said. 'Who was Barbara Doukas looking for when she returned to the guesthouse on the night she died? Why was she asking about the ministerial party?'

'Before we arrived,' Iraklidis said.

'Before you and the Minister arrived,' Cassie said.

'You've mentioned Meg Taylor a number of times now,' the Security Chief said pointedly.

'We need to ask her some questions,' Cassie kept her voice neutral, but firm. 'She's involved, Yannis, whether you like it or not. We have to tackle her.'

'Oh!'

'What!'

They were plunged into darkness.

Cassie remained still and, gradually, her eyes became accustomed to the lack of light. Even with the low cloud outside there was a little ambient light from the solar-powered garden lights and she began to make out the shapes of furniture in the little office room, of Helena and Iraklidis. He was moving round the desk, feeling for something, a drawer perhaps.

The beam of a torch shone into her eyes then away. The Security Chief's walkie-talkie crackled into life and a conversation in Greek took place.

'The electricity is down across the complex,' Iraklidis said, once he'd signed off. 'Maybe even in town, we don't know. One of my men has gone to find out.'

'There aren't many people still here are there?' Cassie said.

'The night staff, those conference attendees who we haven't yet let go and the remainder of the ministerial party and security, plus us. So about twenty people,' Helena answered.

'I must go over to the ministerial suite,' Iraklidis said, rising. 'The two of you stay together. Take this,' and he handed the torch to Helena. 'Someone will come over with another torch for me. See if you can find any battery powered light sources, lamps or something. Try the stores behind the kitchens.'

The Security Chief opened the door to the reception and Cassie saw a slim wand of light approaching the reception doors. Iraklidis hailed the man who carried the torch.

'Take care,' he said and kissed Helena's forehead. 'And remember, keep together. After checking the stores go to one of your rooms, *together*. There could be a killer on the loose. I'll be back soon.'

'You take care too,' Helena called after him.

A power failure might suit a killer very well.

'Now. Where's this storeroom?'

◊ THIRTY SIX

Cassie followed Helena and the powerful beam of the torch which she carried into the reception area. The solar garden lights outside shone a weak diffuse light through the doors and windows, not strong enough to cast shadows.

'We'll head for the kitchens,' Helena's voice quivered 'There are a number of service rooms just out the back there.'

They passed through the dining room and into the kitchens, torchlight reflecting from the steel surfaces, but the rest of the long room was completely dark. At the far end Helena pushed at a fire door which opened on to a small internal courtyard.

What was that?

There was a shuffling noise. Cassie and Helena froze, ears straining. The silence grew. Cassie shone her phone's slim wand of light around the walled space. Scrubby weeds grew between its concrete slabs, but it was empty.

'There's the storeroom.' Helena directed the torch at a door opposite. It was slightly ajar. 'Maybe we have company,' she whispered.

'If there was someone here, this is where they've gone,' Cassie also kept her voice low, but her heart was pounding as she crossed to the door and grasped the handle. 'Only one way to find out.' Taking a deep breath, she opened the door.

Her light played over row after row of open metal shelves, their ends facing toward the doorway. It bounced from the shiny surfaces of kitchen pans and a toaster; the shelves held all kinds of equipment. There were piles of crockery and linen, mobile heaters and hair dryers and lots of cardboard boxes. Air conditioning units were stacked to one side.

'There's all sorts here, we might be lucky,' Cassie said. She pointed at her chest, then at the ground at her feet, making sure Helena saw the gesture which signified that she would remain at the door. She shut off her phone light. Helena waved and entered the aisle nearest to them.

'I'll check what there is,' the interpreter said. 'More torches might be useful, if we can find any.'

Helena stepped past and began to go along the nearest row of shelving, while Cassie loitered, completely hidden in shadow. If anyone was in here, they were hiding, afraid of being seen. She was prepared to gamble that they weren't armed and, if they tried to sneak out, she hoped to slow them down enough to identify who they were.

'There are lights here.' She heard Helena's disembodied voice. 'Table lights, with boxes of batteries, just what we need.'

She could see the beam of Helena's torch at the far end of the first rack, furthest away from the door. Cassie tensed. If there was someone in the room this was their best opportunity to slip out. She sensed an alteration in the darkness to her left.

There's someone there!

'And some battery-operated party lights. They'll do for reception. We can set them up at the desk.'

Cassie flattened herself against the wall. She held her breath. There was definitely someone drawing closer to the doorway. Was that shallow breathing she could hear?

'No torches yet, but I think there's enough here to help.'

A dark shape slipped past and Cassie lunged. Her right hand grabbed a handful of fabric as she slammed the door, shutting whoever it was in the room. Her prey twisted and struggled to get free, but she held on.

'Helena! Here!'

The torch's powerful beam swung round to shine directly into her eyes. It also showed her captive. A pale, tear-stained face, surrounded by dark hair, gazed, screwing up her eyes, into the light. Elise Forché.

'Elise. What are you doing here?' Cassie relinquished her hold on the Frenchwoman but took care to stand between her and the door. 'And why were you running away? You've been crying. What's going on?'

Elise snivelled and wiped her hand across her nose, the fight seemed to go out of her.

'Come on, let's go back to the dining room,' Cassie said.

'Here, take this.' Helena loaded Elise with boxes and strings of lights.

They crossed the courtyard and went through to the dining room where Helena set up a lamp on one of the tables. In the small pool of light the Frenchwoman's face looked puffy and wan.

'What were you doing in the storeroom?'

'Nothing,' Elise answered.

'You must have been in the kitchens ahead of us and in the courtyard.'

'Yes.'

'Elise, there could be a murderer roaming around somewhere on this mountain, possibly in this building and you're behaving suspiciously,' Cassie gave Elise a cold stare. 'Tell us what you were doing or answer to the police.'

'I was looking for some booze,' Elise answered, sullen. 'I wanted to get drunk. The bar's locked, so I went into the kitchens. Then you came in and I went outside, but you followed, so I went into the storeroom.'

'Why'd you want to get drunk, Elise?'

'It's like you said. Jim's going back to the States. He's lied to me, now he's leaving me.'

'I'm sorry.'

Maybe she's better off without him.

'The bastard, He's been lying all along,' Elise angry words were belied by the tears running down her cheeks. 'He must have been arranging this with Robbins weeks ago. I sensed something was wrong, but I didn't want to know. I thought maybe he'd found someone else...'

'What has he arranged with Robbins?'

'To go work with him in the States. Mike Robbins wants Jim's contacts, in Europe and the OECD. Robbins is bad news, I don't believe he's in renewable energy at all.'

'Big oil and gas, I think you'll find,' Cassie replied. 'Petrodollars.'

'I should have known,' Elise said. 'Jim would never get to meet a Minister otherwise.'

'Hang on –,' Cassie said. 'Jim met with Minister Sidaris?'

'Yes,' Elise replied.

'You didn't say.'

'You didn't ask.'

'When?'

'Wednesday morning. Robbins was there too. I wonder what Balasz Kouris would make of that?'

So Kouris was right, the Minister was cosy with big carbon. A meeting at an out of the way conference on public administration wouldn't draw the attention of the Greek press in the way that an 'official' meeting in Athens might. It could also explain why Robbins was so insistent at the tavern that she tell him what the Minister had discussed with her on the previous evening.

She would have to speak with the Professor, if only to eliminate this aspect from their murder enquiries. There was also the French woman to consider. She may not have thought of it already, but it was only a matter of time before Elise Forché realised what incendiary information she possessed and how it might afford a way of revenging herself on her former partner. This secret meeting wasn't likely to remain secret for long.

What would the Professor do if he knew that Elise was aware of the meeting? Clearly the Minister and his entourage wanted to keep any talks with Big Oil hidden from Kouris and his supporters and the Greek public.

Wait a second. Did this explain why the Major was focussed on the protest leader?

Maybe she didn't have ties to Golden Dawn. Maybe she'd been working at the Professor's command all along. How perfect it would be if Kouris was the guilty party, the killer of Barbara Doukas. Kouris's precise whereabouts on the night of Barbara's murder were unknown. He could have been in room eighteen, having the shouting match late on Monday night. He was a strong suspect. Would the Professor organise for him to carry the can, pinning the murder on to a troublesome protester? He had shown himself to be ruthless when necessary, but would he go so far?

Cassie hoped not. But this hypothesis explained why the Major wasn't sharing information, and why she was unafraid of Yannis's influence with the Professor.

'Can I go now?' Elise asked, sulkily.

'Unless there's anything else you have to tell us?'

The Frenchwoman shook her head.

'Okay, you can go,' Cassie said.

'You could help us with the lights...' Helena left her remark unfinished as Elise got up and left.

'So, Jim Norton's dumped her and the OECD, he's going back to the States to work with Mike Robbins in petrochemicals. And he and Robbins met with Minister Sidaris.'

'They won't want that news getting out before they're ready.'

'Maybe,' Cassie replied. 'But I'm going to have to talk with the Professor about it tomorrow.'

That would be a very delicate and difficult interview, Cassie thought. She still needed Professor Matsouka on side if she was to fulfil her mission.

'Do I need to be there?'

'No, his English is quite sufficient.' The interpreter looked relieved. 'But, Helena, don't mention it to Yannis, please, at least not before I meet with the Professor.'

The interpreter frowned, but she slowly nodded acquiescence.

'Now, what about these lights?' Cassie got to her feet.

What the–?

Her vision swam. She sat again, her legs barely functioning. She felt weak and cold. Was this the result of getting soaked out on the mountain?

'You're shivering. You should get to bed,' Helena said.

'I'll be alright.'

'Come on. The reception's on our way. I'll put up the lights then we can go upstairs. Yannis will be back soon.'

A good night's sleep will sort me out.

With deliberate care Cassie got to her feet.

FRIDAY

◊ THIRTY SEVEN

'Cassandra, good morning!' An overcoat-wearing Professor Matsouka was effusive in his welcome. 'What can I do for you?'

He was alone in the living room of the ministerial suite. Beyond the large windows there was a clear blue sky but a battery driven heater was having to battle against the cold. The temperature had dropped dramatically overnight and the whole complex was still without electricity. Cassie wore a heavy pullover and gloves. She felt rested, but not quite as normal, maybe she was going down with something. In any event, the paracetamol she had taken would soon take effect.

'I wondered if you could clear some things up for me,' she answered. 'Delicate matters.'

'I see your Embassy colleague is not here.' He indicated that they should sit on the sofas.

'I would also like to speak with Meg, afterwards, if I may.'

'Unfortunately she isn't here. Out running. It's her normal practice in the mornings, even very cold mornings.'

Cassie gave a smile which she hoped signalled that they were in agreement.

'So, what are these delicate matters?' The Professor sat back, his arm stretched along the back of the sofa and legs crossed, looking at Cassie from beneath partly closed eyelids.

Here goes.

'I understand that Minister Sidaris met with representatives from US oil and gas corporations during his brief stay here,' Cassie began. 'This is, of course, no business of mine and I would not expect you to share any discussions with me. However, you should know that there is at least one individual who is sympathetic to the environmental cause and is aware of that meeting, who may choose to publicise the fact that it took place.'

'Exactly how you came by this knowledge interests me,' he said, eyes narrowing further. 'Great pains have been taken to ensure that this meeting was not in the public domain.'

'There are only a limited number of sources available to me, so Yannis Iraklidis will, doubtless, learn who told me. But I am not in a position to tell you. I came upon the information in the course of enquiries into the two recent deaths.'

Professor Matsouka frowned.

'My only concern is whether or not this meeting plays any part in the case,' Cassie continued. 'Major Lykaios has been focusing on the protest leader, Kouris, as a suspected murderer. He doesn't have an alibi for the night Barbara Doukas was killed, although we cannot find any connection between them. It may be, however, that casting suspicion on him might be convenient, given the meeting.'

'I don't believe that the Major knows anything about our meeting,' the Professor answered, after a pause. 'If she's suspicious of Kouris, it's for reasons of her own.' He sat, silently contemplating Cassie. Then he seemed to make a decision and began to speak.

'The Minister informed the Americans that ongoing attempts to persuade the Greek authorities to permit exploitation of natural resources by US hydraulic fracturing corporations will be unsuccessful. He has scheduled a meeting with the US Ambassador to repeat that message. Greece is one of the most seismologically active countries in the EU and as such cannot countenance any activity likely to precipitate earthquakes.'

That's a prepared line if ever I heard one.

'Thank you, Professor.'

'It is what the notes to our press release will say. I anticipate issuing it just as soon as we can, given no telephones, no internet and now, no electricity.'

'Is the town without electricity too, do we know?' Cassie asked.

'No, fortunately for its inhabitants,' the Professor replied. 'Yannis's men are trying to get hold of a generator there. I understand that the power is often cut, so many households have such things. Let us hope they find one and we have some heat and light and hot food today. Ah, here he is.'

The Security Chief gave Cassie a hostile look as he entered. His overcoat was unbuttoned and he straightened the scarf which was awry around his neck.

'Professor,' Iraklidis said. 'Another demonstration outside the Centre – my people had difficulty regaining access.' He passed his phone to the Professor, who held it out so that Cassie could see it too.

The recording showed a gang of protesters once again barricading the gates. They shouted slogans and waved placards saying 'GREENFORCE is GREENWASHING' in English alongside others using the spiky Greek letter forms.

The Professor's eyes widened. 'Is this our security breach?'

'If you mean Elise Forché,' Iraklidis said. 'I've just learned about her.'

He's not pleased. I don't blame him, but at least Helena knows which side she's on.

'She can't get any information out until the telephone lines are restored,' Iraklidis continued.

'Though she seems to have communicated with the protesters,' the Professor said, wryly. 'Fortunately, with the landlines down they can't get the story out more widely. We need to issue our communication to the news media as soon as the landlines are working again, then, whomever she, or they, speak to, the story will be old news. Now,' he turned to Cassie, 'what was it you wanted to speak with Meg about?'

Cassie hesitated. She didn't want Elise blamed for something she didn't do. Somehow Kouris had managed to speak with one of his group after she'd asked him about Greenforce. She also didn't want Meg forewarned about the questions she needed to answer and the Professor would undoubtedly tell her.

'Meg is in Delphi,' Iraklidis said. 'I'm told she is visiting Alecto Doukas, the mother of the young woman who was killed.'

Cassie's head whipped round as she looked from the Professor to Iraklidis. Someone else who had access to Alecto Doukas, while she didn't. And Meg Taylor wasn't above suspicion either.

'Ah yes, the grieving mother, I did ask Meg to extend our condolences,' the Professor said. 'It seemed appropriate.'

'We are going to speak with Alecto Doukas this morning and my men are calling on all households which own an off-road vehicle.'

'The lights on the mountain?' Professor Matsouka remarked.

'Exactly.' Iraklidis shifted his weight from foot to foot, impatient to proceed.

'Very well, Yannis,' the Professor rose. 'Report back to me later.'

There was a knock on the door and a member of the Centre's staff entered, carrying another heater. Cassie and the Security Chief left.

In the corridor outside Iraklidis rounded on Cassie. Slightly taller than she and much more physically powerful, he thrust his face close to hers, his eyes cold.

She remembered the ruthless determination with which he organised the removal of the demonstrators.

Don't underestimate this man, just because you've seen another side of him with Helena.

'The Major isn't the only one withholding information,' he said. 'I thought we had an agreement.'

'I'm sorry, Yannis,' she said. 'I was concerned that Elise Forché would be the unwitting victim of the Professor's anger.'

'Which you couldn't trust me to manage.'

'I didn't want to put you in that position.'

'So you made me look a fool instead.'

'I don't think you looked a fool. You made it clear that you knew who had talked.'

'No thanks to you. And I'm warning you, Cassandra. Don't try to turn Helena against me. You might have a powerful position in your own country, but you're in Greece now, my country, where I know the rules and I have the power. You're the outsider!'

The Security Chief stalked off in the direction of the guesthouse.

◊ THIRTY EIGHT

Iraklidis hardly spoke during the walk into town, even to a flustered Helena, who made several attempts to smooth things over.

Conflicting loyalties. I can't help that.

'Cassie, did you search all of the Corycian Cave?' Helena asked.

'No. I only had my phone light.'

'We didn't search it either, I mean, really search it,' Helena said. 'Maybe there's more evidence still up there.'

'Yes. Good thinking, it's worth a look,' Iraklidis spoke grudgingly. 'I'll get someone to go up there once we've finished here.'

They had reached the little police station.

Inside Constable Ganas was sitting by the gas stove with the Major and her Sergeant. Iraklidis got down to business.

'The proprietor of Delphi garage spoke with one of my men earlier this morning,' he said. 'He was able to tell us which of the townspeople had trail bikes and we have taken photographs of the tyres on all the vehicles.' He passed round a piece of paper which showed the photographs, together with Cassie's pictures of the tyre tracks. 'The tyres on the police Jeep are the only ones which match any of the tracks.'

'That means nothing,' the Major said, dismissing the Security Chief's point. 'The police Jeep went up the mountain. That's what it's for.'

But it means the Jeep was up there on Wednesday night or there's another vehicle like it which no one knows anything about.

'The other items you found in the Cave don't help either,' the Major continued. 'The local pharmacy sells bandages and medication; and bandages can also be purchased at supermarkets and convenience stores.'

'What about the blankets?' Cassie asked. 'Where did they come from? They're the same as the blankets in the jail, aren't they?'

Everyone looked at Constable Ganas.

'They're standard issue,' Helena translated his words. 'We get them from the regional police supply depot.' The policeman coughed discreetly. 'But – he says he's donated some to Delphi's fire and rescue colleagues and some of the more needy townspeople. Some may have found their way into a couple of the shops here.'

There was silence. Then the Major and Iraklidis both began speaking at once. The Major sounded angry at what looked like misappropriation of government supplies and, Cassie speculated, possibly minor corruption. Political bias she had been prepared for, but that Ganas might be corrupt hadn't occurred to her. Iraklidis, she suspected, just wanted an answer to the question.

'Is he saying that anyone could have bought the blankets?' she asked.

'Yes.'

'Where from?'

'Any shop which sells blankets, like the outdoor pursuits store,' Helena translated.

'How long has the Constable been, er, dispersing them?'

There followed a heated discussion in Greek.

'It seems this has been going on for quite some time,' Helena said. 'I'm not surprised. It's a way of spreading things around, I doubt it was for his personal profit.'

'Bottom line, anyone could have got hold of those blankets.'

'Exactly,' Iraklidis said. 'No help at all.'

'There's the newspaper,' Helena said. 'The Times of London published on Wednesday.'

'Aren't there newsagents in Delphi which get a regular delivery of foreign language newspapers?' the Major replied. 'There are usually plenty of tourists, for the Temple and for walking in the mountains, though it is getting late in the year for that now. Sergeant, something to check please.'

Sergeant Chloros nodded but didn't seem inclined to leave his place by the fire in a hurry.

'The Centre gets a delivery of international newspapers,' Cassie said. 'Though not until the afternoon of the day they're published and I guess that would be the case for the newsagents too. There will be one delivery a day.'

'So?' Helena asked.

'A copy was in the Cave just over twenty-four hours later,' Iraklidis said. 'Does that give us a timeframe for the arrival of the rough sleeper?'

'Maybe,' Cassie replied. 'But not necessarily. Has there been any progress on finding Barbara Doukas's missing mobile phone or her key to the temple complex?'

Blank looks met her question. No one had really been looking. It was not surprising, she supposed, the phone and key could have been disposed of easily by throwing them off the mountain and there simply weren't enough people to do a detailed search over many square kilometres.

'Nico said that Barbara usually carried her mobile with her,' Cassie continued. 'It's not at his flat. Has anyone checked that it's not at her mother's home? Did you ask Alecto Doukas when you spoke with her?' She addressed the Major.

'No.' The Major replied, her mouth pinched.

'It's time to ask now,' Cassie said. 'And there are other questions for your sister to answer, Constable Ganas. Like what Barbara Doukas said to her mother before going back to the Centre on Monday evening.'

'My niece didn't have to explain her comings and goings to her mother.' Helena translated the Constable's remark for Cassie.

'Nonetheless, she may have said something. I suggest we now go and speak with Alecto Doukas.'

This time not even the Major disagreed.

◊ THIRTY NINE

The tall, double-fronted Doukas house clung to a steep slope at the upper edge of Delphi town. Made of local stone, like many of the older dwellings, its window shutters were closed, except for those on the first floor.

'Alecto!' Constable Ganas called, as he opened one of the front doors. Cassie, Iraklidis, Helena and the Major followed him into the wide hallway.

As she filed up the heavy wooden staircase after him Cassie peered at the framed photographs hanging on the wall. Sepia coloured portraits of people in stiff poses, dressed in a mixture of early twentieth-century formal wear and Greek traditional dress. Family groups under vine-draped loggias, or seated in open topped, horse drawn carriages. School year line-ups in black and white, the too bright colours of 1970s photo stock showing pudding basin haircuts and wide ties. Alecto Doukas was the keeper of the family's memories, of its past.

Approaching the landing there were more recent pictures taken at family events, birthdays, a wedding. Cassie spotted what she thought was a childhood holiday photo of Barbara, russet-haired, vivid and alive, running away from the camera. There was a familial likeness running through many of the pictures, a wide forehead and narrow nose, which she recognised. Then she saw a family group. The colours of the photograph had faded but that didn't detract from the proud smile which lit up the face of a young man, whose joy leapt from the picture. He stood behind a beautiful young woman, her long hair dramatic against her pale skin, she fitted easily beneath his encircling arm. She too was smiling, as she held a baby wrapped in swaddling clothes.

Constable Ganas saw her looking at the photograph. He pointed at the baby then at his own chest.

'He says that's him as a baby,' Helena said. 'He says to look at the next photo, taken the same year, in 1973, his father outside Athens Polytechneion. The Constable is proud of his educated father.'

In the photograph the young man was standing by a sign to the side of a set of gates in a group of other young people. Cassie leaned forward to see the second group picture, but the others were pressing up behind her, so she carried on up the stairs.

They entered a living room on the first floor, a room containing too much dark wood furniture, with a fire burning in the grate of a stone chimney. It reminded Cassie of her great-grandmother's house, which she had visited as a child. Framed photographs covered every conceivable surface.

To the left of the fireplace Alecto Doukas sat in an upright armchair, her grey streaked auburn hair unkempt, her eyes hooded. She looked frail and weak, her face drawn and lined, skin pulled over her sharp cheekbones. Alecto Doukas was only in her forties, but today she looked much older.

Standing by her side was Meg Taylor, clad in running gear, who glanced over at them, eyebrows rising. She walked behind the armchair, to open one of the shutters more widely. The sunlight fell upon the right side of the grieving mother's face, showing the deep shadows beneath her eyes.

The Constable indicated that they should sit on a sofa facing the fireplace.

Iraklidis crouched down in front of Mrs Doukas and spoke quietly. Her gaze ranged around the room, showing a glimmer of recognition when she saw Major Lykaios, who moved to stand by the fire, elbow resting on the high mantelpiece on the opposite side of the fireplace to Meg Taylor.

Then the security man mentioned Cassie's name and the woman looked directly at her. Her eyes were cornflower blue.

Unusual. And that's where Barbara got her auburn hair from.

'I'm sorry for the loss of your daughter,' Cassie said. Translation wasn't necessary.

'Sit,' Helena whispered. She translated as Iraklidis took a seat and began.

'Mrs Doukas, where were you on Monday night?'

'Here, at home.'

'Did you expect your daughter to come home that evening?'

'She would or she wouldn't. Sometimes she stayed with Nico, her boyfriend.'

'What about the following evening?'

'No. Alexandros, my brother, told me that Nico was worried about her because he hadn't seen her all day. I became anxious.'

'Ask when she last saw her daughter,' Cassie said.

'On Monday afternoon.' The reply came. 'She came home at about four o'clock but went out again later. She had work to do at the Centre, she said.' Mrs Doukas was tight lipped.

'What did she tell you about that, Mrs Doukas? And how was she? We know, from people at the Centre, that she was upset earlier that day,' Cassie pressed.

'I don't know anything about that,' the woman answered, her feverish gaze fixed on Cassie's face. 'She was a good girl. She never hurt anyone.'

'Yes, but...'

'A fine, good-hearted girl.' Mrs Doukas rocked forward and back, beating at her breast with closed fists. She began to weep, tears flowing down her face.

'Mrs Doukas...'

'That's enough for now, Cassie,' Iraklidis said. 'It'll only make her worse.'

'We can't catch her daughter's killer if she won't help us,' Cassie muttered.

The Security Chief spoke quietly and firmly, persisting until the distraught woman's weeping subsided.

'Mrs Doukas, what were you doing out on the mountain early yesterday morning?' he asked.

The woman looked sidelong at her brother, an accusatory and vicious stare.

'I went for a walk.'

'Before sun-up, is that your normal practice?'

'No, but I wanted to go to the Temple. Dawn is a good time, it's better then.'

'Why the Temple?'

'It's a special place. The immortals are what they are, just because it's the twenty-first century, it doesn't change them. I wanted vengeance for Barbara's death. I'm her mother, I can call upon the old ones. She means the *Erinyes*, the Furies,' Helena added. 'I think she's deranged.'

Though her face was tear streaked, her eyes gleamed with a manic intensity.

Grief.

'There is vengeance,' she said, Helena translating. 'The *Erinyes* bring it and madness to those bearing blood guilt.' Mrs Doukas turned to stare at Cassie.

To me. She means to me.

Cassie's insides grew cold. She had caused a death, though she hadn't killed anyone. A shiver went down her spine.

She can't know. It's just a coincidence.

Ever since Lawrence Delahaye had Andrew Rowlands killed, Cassie had blamed herself for his death. It still lay heavily upon her. If she had not behaved so recklessly she would not have been captured and Andrew would not have been drawn in after her. He would be alive and they would be together.

Stop it!

Focus. Solve this mystery, before someone else dies.

Alecto Doukas was almost mad with grief at the loss of her daughter.

'And on Monday,' Iraklidis continued. 'What did your daughter speak with you about when she returned home?'

'Nothing,' the woman replied, sulkily. She began to rock once more, cursing under her breath.

'Do you have her mobile phone? Is it here?'

Alecto Doukas shrugged.

'Mrs Doukas,' Cassie asked, sitting forward. 'Barbara was at the Centre on Monday night, we know that she was with a man – we don't know who – and that they argued. Do you know of anyone who Barbara could have had a fight with, anyone whom she disliked or who disliked her?'

The grieving mother gave an almost imperceptible shake of her head, muttering and allowed her hair to fall down to shield her face from the daylight. Her fingers began drumming a rhythm on the arm of her chair.

'Did she have anything to do with the environmentalist demonstrations at the Centre? We know she was there when one took place?'

'No.'

'Did she know the organiser, Balasz Kouris?'

Alecto Doukas shrugged, her mouth turning down at the corners.

'What about politics? Did Barbara belong to a political party?'

The shake of the woman's head was more pronounced now, the drumming of her fingers on the chair arms quickened.

'Iraklidis.' Constable Ganas appealed to the Security Chief, clearly asking that his sister be left alone.

Reluctantly, Iraklidis rose. 'Leave it, Cassie.'

Cassie clamped her mouth closed. Then said, 'Barbara asked for the whereabouts of the ministerial party,' she directed her question at Meg Taylor. 'You were the only member of that party there on Monday. Did you see her?'

The runner's face flushed. She obviously hadn't been expecting the question.

'Yes,' she answered.

Everyone waited. Even Mrs Doukas turned to look up at the runner.

'She was looking around outside the suite,' Meg Taylor began to explain. 'She said she needed some help, but she didn't say what about. I thought she was just schmoozing and I gave her the brush-off.'

'Why did she come to you?' Cassie asked.

'I don't know. Perhaps just because I was there, but...'

'But?'

'I regretted not helping her. When I thought about it afterwards it seemed to me that she was really quite distressed. Maybe she hadn't just wanted to schmooze, maybe there was something else going on. So the following morning I ran over to Delphi, to this house,' and here she looked at Mrs Doukas. 'But Barbara wasn't here. We assumed she was with her boyfriend.'

By then Barbara was already dead, her body in the Athenian Treasury.

'The morning of the demonstration outside the Conference Centre,' Helena said. 'We saw you on your way back.'

Everyone was standing now, only Alecto Doukas remained in her seat.

The Constable spoke, insistent. 'Let me show you out.'

◊ FORTY

The Constable led them out on to the landing.

'Helena, will you ask him if there are any other photographs of him with his parents, and his sister, please,' Cassie said.

The interpreter started to speak with Ganas, but the policeman cut her off with a curt and vehement response. Cassie saw Iraklidis bristle.

'What?'

'He says not,' Helena turned to speak with Cassie as they descended the stairs. 'He wants us out of here.'

Surreptitiously Cassie drew her phone from her pocket and began videoing the photographs hanging on the wall as she passed them. She re-pocketed her phone before she got to the front doors.

Ganas saw them all out on to the street with only peremptory courtesy, before returning inside.

'Satisfied?' The Major rounded on Iraklidis and Cassie. 'She told us nothing we didn't already know. That was a waste of time.'

'I'm not so sure about that,' Cassie replied. Iraklidis shot her a quizzical look. 'It's interesting that Barbara was at the ministerial suite. Meg, did you see Mrs Doukas again after you came up here on Tuesday morning?'

'Yes, as it happens,' the runner answered. 'I came across her and the Constable yesterday morning, when I was out running. They were in the police Jeep on the mountain and gave me a lift to town.'

Hmm, was that answer a little too pat?

There was a flash of lightning followed by a roll of thunder.

'The storm's finally arrived.' The Security Chief looked up at a sky now black and lowering. 'So much for searching the rest of the Cave. There may be more evidence still up there.'

'Look, I could run up to the Cave now, have a look around, see what I can find, if you want.' Meg began stretching exercises.

'I wonder if–' Cassie began, but Iraklidis cut her short.

'I'll send a man up with torches to meet you there,' he said. 'And bring you back down.'

'OK. See you back at the Centre,' Meg said and waved as she set off, loping up the steep slope behind the Doukas house.

'Yannis,' Cassie said, drawing the Security Chief to one side, leaving Helena standing with the Major. 'I think you ought to get someone to the Cave right away, on a trail bike or in the Jeep, perhaps? I don't think we should allow Meg to search alone.'

'You're determined to finger Meg Taylor, aren't you? I've told you, your suspicions are ill-founded,' Iraklidis replied, his mouth a thin line. 'Meg wouldn't hurt anyone.'

'She might not harm anyone intentionally, but I can see her anger spilling over if she thinks something is wrong or unjust. Especially given that she refused Barbara's request for help.' Cassie held her ground. 'And I think she is perfectly capable of protecting someone, if she feels that's the right thing to do, including by appropriating evidence.'

'You suspect Ms Taylor?' Major Lykaios joined them.

'I suspect everyone, Major. No one is above suspicion,' Cassie replied. 'I'll go up to the Cave myself.'

'You've already got a cold,' Helena said. 'And you'll never catch up.'

'I know, but Yannis's man will catch up with me and take me to the top.'

'The Constable can take you,' the Major suggested.

'Let the Constable stay with his sister,' Cassie said emphatically. Iraklidis gave her a sidelong look.

'Ok. I'll send someone after you,' he said. 'And take care, this storm looks like a really bad one.'

◊ FORTY ONE

Cassie had only gone a hundred yards above Delphi town when the first thick drops of rain fell. She quickened her pace, but the weakness she'd felt the night before still lurked and she was reluctant to push herself too hard. On the other hand, she didn't want to get wet; she had a cold already. She broke into a trot. At least the Cave would be dry.

Thunder rolled, echoing from the sides of the valley, ricocheting from the sheer rock of the Shining Ones. In the open on the mountain Cassie was, once again, getting drenched. Beneath the hood her hair was slick and plastered to her head, her jacket was waterproof but her jeans were already sodden. It wouldn't be long before her trainers were too as she skidded on the path, setting small stones tumbling.

The temperature was dropping as she climbed and a mist was forming. Hard electric-white sheets of lightning flashed across the sky, casting night-black shadows and making stray wisps of cloud take semi-solid form. She could see only a little way ahead, but occasionally the cloud lifted and she saw forked lightning bolts crackling around the top of the mountain. She stood, gasping.

Getting to the Cave now seemed impossible. She turned around, but the path was very steep and already water was sluicing down it, taking dirt and rolling stones in small rivulets. Going back looked equally difficult. She took a careful step. And then another. Her weight-bearing foot slipped sideways as the footpath became a slurry of gravel and she staggered to retain her balance. The path was no longer safe.

Better head for the stadium, then follow the path down to the road, the route she had taken with Meg the other day. Cassie swung right along the path to the stadium – it was easier going across the mountainside and soon she reached a copse of firs and cypresses, the tree roots twisting across the path. At least here the trees gave a little shelter.

A sharp crack sounded behind her and Cassie smelled the acrid tang of burning. As she turned to look, a fir tree slowly toppled to the ground, its trunk broken and smouldering. Cassie leapt aside, avoiding the branches. No, the little wood wasn't a haven.

She began to half jog along the path, screwing her eyes against the blinding rain. Ahead she could just make out the trees around the stadium. Rain bounced from the ancient running track and its stone seats as she reached the long oval.

Cassie kept to the northern side, taking what shelter she could from the trees. On the southern side, where the mountain fell away, she could see only a space filled with cloud and mist, illuminated by the eerie white lightning. She shivered, feeling increasingly icy.

Press on.

Past the starting blocks at the far end the descent to the foot of the Shining Ones began. This was the path which, she now remembered, led across the scree field.

It had been difficult to cross that when the weather and the ground were dry, it would be dangerous now. She slowed. Was there any other way down? She didn't think so. The path grew stonier and sloped away, disappearing into the mist and the driving rain. It would soon reach the scree field, with its loose stones and pebbles. In what seemed like only a few strides she was there and she crouched down to look at the ground. The sheen of moving water reflected in the latest flash of lightning.

She had to cross it if she was to get off the mountainside.

Begin slowly, get as far as possible, then, if it starts to slide, run like hell.

She calculated that she should head always to the left, away from the drop to the temple complex below. How far it fell she couldn't remember, but she didn't want to find out.

Feeling for secure footholds between the pebbles and stones Cassie started out. She stretched her arms out for balance and bent her knees, as water sloshed into her trainers. If she recalled aright, the scree was only about twenty feet wide, then the path re-established itself. She just had to keep upright and step gradually across.

Keep going. You can do it.

There was a vivid series of flashes and she heard a cracking sound behind her. Another tree had been hit by lightning. Amidst the sound of the storm there came a splintering as it fell to the earth. Beneath her feet, the ground moved.

A mini avalanche of pebbles and stones began. Cassie felt her feet sliding from under her body. She took one step, trying to find solid purchase, but the whole slope was beginning to slide. If she didn't do something she would slide with it and, once she started she wouldn't be able to stop, not even when she reached the edge of the drop down to the temple site.

Run!

She shifted to balance on the balls of her feet and shoved herself off, high stepping across the scree, focusing on her feet, her arms still outstretched. For a while she made headway and sensed the looming presence of the cliffs ahead of her. But in a heartbeat her feet were swept from beneath her. She was sliding down the slope.

Stones pelted her head. Cassie tried rolling to her left. She grabbed at anything, her nails scraping at the ground, her toes digging in for a foothold. Part upright, she managed to scramble, crab-like across the tumbling water and pebbles, gaining a few feet closer to the cliffs. A tree trunk fell past her and she was swept back on to her previous trajectory by another pulse of mud and earth.

Frowning against the rain, she gasped for air and scrabbled for a hold of any kind, but anything she grasped immediately began to slide. Below, to her right, the scree ended, disappearing into the milky whiteness.

Do something! Shift your weight. Throw yourself towards the cliffs.

As she drew nearer to the edge Cassie stabbed her heels down hard and thrust her body leftwards. For a moment she teetered, trying desperately to balance and step or roll to the left, but her clothes and shoes, wetly heavy, were pulling her down. The moving scree took her feet from under her again and she toppled back to the ground.

There was nothing she could do. She was going to go over the edge.

◊ FORTY TWO

Falling.

Through earth and branches, stones and water, a mass of matter cascading down the mountain. Cassie rotated her arms and legs, flailing in a furious attempt to break the air and slow her fall.

Then her spine jarred as she hit something more solid and a shard of pain pierced her left leg. Still she fell, buffeted and pummelled. As her progress slowed, she realised that she had fallen on to a mass of debris which was forming a mound at the foot of the drop. It had broken her fall.

Still alive!

Though not for much longer if she didn't manage to claw her way off the mound, as more earth and pebbles showered her. Cassie pushed herself upright and tottered forward, her right foot sinking into the unstable surface, followed by her left. Pain shuddered through her leg and hip.

Helped by the constant flow of stones and smaller rocks, she limped downward until she reached solid ground. She leaned against a huge block of stone, part of the base of a larger structure now destroyed, and looked back. The mountainside had shifted, the landscape changed; the Phaedriades still loomed above, but the path and scree had gone, replaced by a long slope reaching down into the temple complex. The landslide had toppled the chain-link fence and deposited her inside, above the temple terrace, the open area in front of the Temple itself. Only three days ago she had stood there, listening to Nico.

She blinked as lightning flashed, etching masonry and columns in shadow, accentuating their solidity. Thunder rolled, echoing around the temple complex lay. Now there were flakes of snow in the rain. Cassie shivered, she was wet through and she also needed to check out her left leg and foot.

Must find shelter, or I'll freeze to death.

The most complete structure in the complex was the Athenian Treasury, where Barbara had been found. Cassie didn't relish the thought of sheltering there and anyway, it was open to the sky. Was there anywhere enclosed?

What had Nico said?

There were several small nooks in the lower levels of the Temple. Perhaps she could shelter in one of those.

Cassie heaved herself towards the temple terrace on her one good leg, wincing with pain and clutching at the broken walls and columns for support. Her jaw was set, but a cry escaped as she struggled across and a dagger of pain scored her leg. The cloud had closed in and, just as up on the mountainside earlier, she could barely see her way, as tendrils of mist floated ghost-like amid the ruins. The surfaces of the stones were slick and slippery with wet fir needles and Cassie tried to step on the pebbly ground where she could.

She found a broken branch and slotted it beneath her left arm. It wouldn't take all her weight, but it helped her reach the terrace, where the six giant columns on the temple base reared high above her, wreathed in cloud. Up the ramp, on to the flat base of the temple portico.

Cassie saw the solid stone base give way to a small labyrinth of low stone walls and roofless chambers at a lower level. She hobbled down into the lower paths, the temple floor now being at waist height. Some of the marble slabs were missing and the path dropped even more. Here the remaining flagstones protruded out, creating a small covered niche which disappeared beneath the temple floor.

That'll do.

On her hands and one knee Cassie crawled inside, her left leg dragging behind. Her palms pressed down on a plentiful carpet of dry pine needles. She reached as far as she could go and rolled round, drawing her right leg up. Her refuge had an earthy smell, but it was dry, the tight-fitting flagstones above kept the water out.

Looking back she could see that outside, the rain was turning to snow, settling on the stones of the temple to form a carpet. With any luck it would keep the temperature higher below ground. She could wait out the storm here, wet or not, then try and get back down to the road, if her leg allowed, once the storm had passed.

She felt her left hip, flexing its muscles and those in her thighs. All were working alright. Then she stretched and flexed her knee joint, pushing her leg down on the ground with her hands. The problem was at ankle level. It was Meg Taylor's fear, Cassie remembered, breaking an ankle running on the scree. Cassie hoped her ankle wasn't broken.

She could still wiggle her toes, which was a good sign, but it hurt to flex her foot muscles. Maybe it was only a strain. She felt around the ankle, stroking and probing it tentatively. She winced as pain cut through her and jerked backwards, banging her elbow on a stony protuberance.

Ow!

The stone moved and Cassie reached out to steady herself, but it wasn't there anymore. She was falling again, falling backwards. The wall at her back had given way and there was nothing behind it. She screamed as her leg was dragged across the edge of her refuge and she plummeted downwards.

◊ FORTY THREE

Shock and pain shuddered through her body as she hit the ground hard. She shrieked.

Her cry diminished to a whimper and she opened her eyes. At first she could see nothing in the blackness. Then her eyes adjusted and she could make out a dull, slate-grey light about ten feet above. That must be the gap she had fallen through. The dirty light revealed a section of the ceiling and upper wall of a rocky cavern.

Where am I?

She ran her hands over the ground around where she lay. It was flat, made of some sort of stone. Her fingers found straight lines where flagstone met flagstone. A man-made floor. So this was part of the Temple.

She shifted her position to reach inside her jacket pocket for her phone and felt the smooth surface of its hard case. Extracting it, she sighed with relief. It seemed unbroken. The phone's blue-white torch light flicked on, its beam creeping over rock and stone.

She was lying in an underground room, roughly rectangular in shape, but with walls of natural rock. Cassie placed the phone on the floor and heaved herself into a sitting position. Her left ankle was throbbing and she was badly winded, her back aching from the fall. She didn't even try to stand, but managed to haul herself across the floor to sit against one of the walls. Her phone told her that it was a quarter to one and the temperature was thirteen degrees.

Iraklidis would have dispatched his man up the mountain by now, especially given the severity of the storm, but he wouldn't find her in the Corycian Cave or anywhere else. The others had no way of knowing where she was. She wasn't entirely sure where she was either.

Again she shone the beam of light around her shelter. There was nothing here. Nothing at all, no pine or fir needles on the floor, no cobwebs. Why? Had this place been closed off for... who knew how long, decades, may be centuries. The air was dry, but had a tired quality. The light picked out what looked like shaped or sculpted elements in the rocky walls, niches and flat surfaces carved by humans, though she would need to examine these more closely to be sure. There were also faint markings or pictures drawn on to the rock of human figures, animals and symbols.

Could this be the *adyton*, the sacred room of the Pythia? Where the oracle would be visited by visions from the god? Or even older, a chapel to Gaia the Great Mother?

No one knew that this place existed.

How long could someone survive without food and water?

I could die here.

No, the others would launch a search for her. They would find the landslip and would search the temple site. They might be forced to wait out the storm, it would be dangerous out on the mountain, but it was only a question of time. She would be found. Briefly, she wondered what had happened to Meg Taylor. Had she reached the Corycian Cave?

There was nothing she could do but wait. The only obvious exit was high in the wall near the ceiling, it was out of her reach and she couldn't climb up to it, especially with her ankle so unreliable and painful.

Until the others found her – and they would, she told herself – she was sheltered from the storm and snow and, as far as she could judge, in a safe place. Not too uncomfortable, if it wasn't for the increasing pain in her leg. She might be here some time.

Save the phone battery.

She switched off the phone plunging herself into darkness. Again her eyes became accustomed to the darkness, the only illumination from the hole through which she had fallen.

Think of something else. The murders.

But she couldn't concentrate. Her ankle throbbed with the rhythm of her heart. Her teeth were chattering and she was losing feeling in her extremities. She shook from pain and cold.

What was that?

It was a noise, a scuttling. She held her breath, waiting to hear it again.

There might be ways into the room, cavities in the rock. Maybe some other creature had found its way in, out of the storm and the cold. She was prepared to share her bolt hole and there wasn't much she could do about it anyway. She resisted the urge to switch on her phone light.

Cassie hurt all over. She placed the back of her hand to her forehead and felt the perspiration. She was running a temperature too. She was thirsty.

She laid her head back against the stone and closed her eyes.

◊ FORTY FOUR

Gradually the light changed within the cavern, there was a pearly shimmering within the darkness. She was able to see the stone wall opposite her and the air was heavy with the sweet fragrance of thyme and jasmine. Her head no longer pounded and the pain in her ankle had gone, but she couldn't move it. She couldn't move any part of her body, but it didn't seem to matter.

Across the room the outline of a figure gradually became discernible. It was a man, naked, his white skin drawn tight over powerful arm and shoulder muscles, black wiry hair on his chest and legs. He was sitting, bony right ankle over left knee in a pose she was familiar with. He turned his head to look at her, dark eyes glittering, his face devoid of emotion.

Why's Lawrence Delahaye here?

He spoke, but she heard no sound. Now he looked angry, frustrated, his hands chopping the air, his movements sharp and violent. He was berating her.

'You need to decide what you want, Cassie.'

Andrew's voice!

'Andrew! Help me!' She shouted, though she made no sound.

The darkness did not answer. Then Delahaye was extinguished and the same sheen created another figure.

Andrew?

No. This figure wasn't as broad shouldered and clean cut as the policeman, nor as languidly graceful as Delahaye. The elegant man sat, legs neatly crossed, leaning forward with an elbow resting on his knee, his chin set on his hand. A questioning pose.

Rob? What are you doing here?

Her ex-husband, the closely cut beard and light brown hair flecked at the temples with grey, in his moleskin trousers and brogues looking every inch the successful professional that he was. The last person she would have thought of. He gazed at her with a polite and curious air, detached and slightly sorrowful, one eyebrow raised, then shook his head, eyes full of hurt and pity.

'Why are you here?' she shouted, to no effect on the figure, which shimmered and dissolved. The blackness was absolute again.

Hallucinations.

How ridiculous.

Probably the product of a combination of things: a stress reaction, fever from her cold and the culmination of reaction to the events of recent months. Inwardly, Cassie began to smile. She was in the shrine of the Temple of Apollo and she was seeing visions. Yet she had no idea what they meant.

It would be so good to see Andrew.

The familiar ache returned.

There was that sound again. Not so much a scuttling as a slithering or gliding. Why couldn't she move her arm to reach her phone and find out what was there?

Because this isn't real.

The sound was closer, then further away, to the other side of the room. It seemed to be in both places at once. A pale, dirty light illuminated a movement over the flagstones and Cassie's heart leapt into her mouth. It was a snake. A huge snake.

The *Pytho*, the giant snake fought by Apollo when he took the shrine from Gaia.

The blunt triangle of its head rose above heavy coils of scaled flesh and a split tongue flicked into the perfumed air. The serpent, sacred symbol of fertility and life, the umbilical cord to the earth, the snake of healing, a reminder of death.

The European python is extinct. It isn't real.

Cassie was transfixed by the swaying motion of the head, which reached forward, gliding over its own coils towards her. The snake slid over the flat flagstones. She couldn't move.

It isn't real, it isn't real!

A rushing, beating sound filled the air and a huge bird swooped down across the serpent's path which hissed and backed away. The enormous eagle, taller than Cassie as she lay propped against the wall, turned its gold-ringed eye upon her. At the same time a shadowy grey form padded forward from the blackness on the other side of the snake. A wolf.

All three creatures fixed their gaze, their eyes round, slitted and oval, on Cassie's own. Their stares were intelligent and unwavering. Light shimmered around the eagle and its form changed. It grew taller into the form and with the features of a woman. The viciously sharp beak became a high bridged nose and the jaw-line sharpened; her filthy hair was long and wild, its tendrils snake-like on the scabrous skin of her shoulders, which were barely covered by the rags she wore. No, the tendrils moved of their own accord, snakes rearing and hissing. It could have been Meg, but not Meg. Her eyes were a burning yellow, her hands claw-like and grasping at the air.

By her side the python reared and thickened in the light, forming the body of another woman, the slit eyes blue. Alecto Doukas, half mad with grief, wholly alien in her drive for revenge. Her eyes sparkled, cold and hard, ringed with bruised shadows above cadaverous cheeks. The wide headband that she wore around her brow squirmed and writhed. Another snake.

Beyond this figure the wolf had transformed into another whom Cassie recognised. It was the Major, but not the Major, whose anger paled in comparison with the intense fury of this creature, her every limb contorted and stiff with rage. Her black eyes fathomless, her black hair flowing, glistening down her back, entwining with torn robes and wrapped around her waist beneath pendulous breasts. Her fingers and hands were encrusted with blood up to the wrists and her pointed teeth were bared in a snarl.

The Furies. The *Erinyes*. Pure vengeance, pure hate. They dragged their prey, screaming, down to Hades and eternal torment, having hunted him or her to the brink of madness.

The light flickered, splintering the vision of the monsters. Then the wolf turned and padded into the darkness. Beating heavy wings the eagle took to the air and the snake, its great body winding, scales flexing, slithered away.

They were gone, but the shimmering light remained. Another figure formed. It was a woman, dressed in a long Greek chiton, perched on a high, three-legged stool. The Pythia. Seer. Prophetess. The Oracle of Apollo herself. Cassie recognised her from a photograph of an ancient bowl in the Guide attached to the conference papers. Her dark hair was bound by leather ribbons, drawn back from a luminous face of ethereal beauty. She stared fixedly at Cassie, whose skin prickled. The hairs on the back of her neck rose.

She can see me. The Pythia can see me.

'Ask me your question,' she said, her voice echoing.

'I cannot pay you,' Cassie answered. 'I have no treasure.'

'You have paid already and will pay again,' the Pythia said. 'He who learns must suffer. Ask your question.'

'How do I solve this mystery. Where do I look?'

'You have already seen. Look again. Look for the crimes which are no crimes.'

What the hell does that mean?

The shimmering light began to flicker.

'Wait, Pythia, I must ask...'

'Quickly.'

'Are they hunting me for Andrew's death? The Furies?'

'No, those furies are your own.'

'And will I ever see... Wait!'

The light faded and the vision ended. Darkness returned.

Cassie felt tears on her cheeks. Her rest of her body was numb and immobile. And she didn't care. She just wanted to sleep. To sleep and never to wake.

◊ FORTY FIVE

There were noises, coming from above. Voices. She could hear voices.

Cassie was slumped against the wall, she struggled to sit up. Her neck and shoulders had stiffened and she bit her lip in pain as she straightened. Her ankle throbbed. She wondered how long she had until they actually got close enough to her to hear her. Maybe she could sleep a little more.

The noise increased. With a groan of pain, Cassie shifted her head to look up. Clean shafts of white light cut through the darkness at ceiling level, then blackness returned. The air was stale, no longer perfumed. The long miserable night of wracking fever and cold had finally ended.

'Here–' she croaked, her mouth and throat dry. 'Here! I'm here!'

All went silent.

'Here!' It was a yelp more than a yell, but she'd shouted with as much force as she could muster. 'Here!' she tried again.

There was a babble of sound. Then–

'Cassie?' Iraklidis's voice.

Cassie felt tears welling, stinging her eyes, but no tears came. She didn't even have the energy to cry.

'Where are you?'

'Underground room,' she shouted, though it emerged as a gasp. 'A hole at the back of a niche beneath the temple floor. I can see torchlight coming through the gap.'

'Yes... I think we have it!' The Security Chief's voice drew nearer.

Then the beam of a powerful torch was shone through the gap in the wall, swinging round and down until it picked her out. She raised her hand to shield her eyes, grimaced at the pain, and squinted.

'Thank God we've found you.' Iraklidis sounded relieved. 'Are you alright? We've been searching for hours.'

'I'm ok,' she lied automatically. 'Just hurt my ankle.' It took so much energy to speak loudly. 'In the landslip. Badly jarred when I fell in here. I think I have some sort of flu, but otherwise ok.' Her voice died away to a mutter.

She heard him laugh.

'I'm coming down,' he said, as the light was blocked. 'How far down is the floor?'

She switched on her phone and focussed its light on the wall, illuminating the legs of the Security Chief as he squirmed backwards through the hole lying on his stomach. She tried to straighten up so he didn't find her a complete wreck. It's just an ankle thing, she practiced in her head.

'About... your feet are about six foot above the floor now. You'll need to lower yourself more. Be careful.'

'It's ok. There are others here, they're holding me.'

The blue-white beam of light showed her Iraklidis, a rope under his arms, being lowered to the floor. His feet touched the ground and he shrugged off the rope, which was swiftly pulled upwards.

'What is this place?' he asked, as he knelt at her side.

'Don't know,' she answered. 'Maybe I've discovered the Pythia's chamber. Ow!' She grimaced as Iraklidis slid an arm around her waist. She felt the hard muscle of his arms as he gently pulled her to his chest and she smelled his odour, a mixture of male sweat and lilac, Helena's perfume.

Andrew. I didn't see Andrew.

As he eased her into an upright sitting position she felt hot tears escaping from the corners of her eyes.

'Sorry, I'm sorry' he said. 'I'm trying not to hurt you.'

That wound wasn't made by you.

'Cassie, are you alright?'

No. Not alright. Haven't been for a long time.

'Yes, yes, I'm fine.'

'There's a medic coming down, from Delphi's mountain rescue team. I didn't think this was the sort of thing that the local doctor would relish, clambering around on the mountain.'

Sitting on his haunches Iraklidis shone his torch around the chamber. He gave a low whistle.

'You know, I think maybe it *is* the *adyton*. Seen any visions?'

Well...

'We'll have to get Nico down here.' She heard the humour in Iraklidis's voice and could almost see that flashing white smile.

He's jollying me along. They must have been so worried.

'I've been thinking, Yannis,' she said. "Bout the case.'

'Cassie! Cassie!'

That was Helena's voice. She had come to find her too.

'I couldn't keep her away,' the Security Chief said.

A scrabbling at the entrance hole preceded another set of legs and a man wearing a first aid backpack was lowered to the floor. He knelt by her side and began to examine her, while more equipment was sent down.

'My ankle,' she pointed to it.

'I'm going to support it.' The medic's voice had an antipodean twang. He wrapped an inflatable bandage around her lower leg and heel and began pumping it up. 'How's your neck and your spine?'

'Bruised. All over. I fell on my back. You Australian?'

'Kiwi,' he said. 'We need to get you on to a stretcher, just in case,'

Together Iraklidis and the medic strapped Cassie on to the stretcher, placing her neck into a brace. Now she could hardly move.

Again.

The small chamber grew crowded as two more of the mountain rescue team arrived. Bright helmet lights threw dramatic shadows on to the stone walls. Together with Iraklidis and the medic they prepared to lift the stretcher. Cassie felt herself rise, the rocky ceiling drawing suddenly nearer and she was edged, floating it seemed, towards the exit hole. She heard the sharp snap of a rope being attached to the bar above the crown of her head and the stretcher was pulled through the hole.

The cold air hit as she emerged and she gasped. The sky above was a clear and deepening blue. It was after sunset. Hands raised the stretcher and carried it along.

Still today, yet it seems like days since the storm.

'What time is it?' she asked.

'About six.' It was Helena, sounding shaken. The ground was being crunched underfoot.

'Meg alright?'

'Yes, she got to the Corycian Cave and waited until Yannis's man arrived, looking for you. He brought her down in the Jeep. It was snowing by then.'

'She find anything?' There were questions she wanted to ask Meg.

'No. Don't worry about that now.'

'I crawled in to shelter then fell. Stone moved. Landslide must have shaken things loose.'

'The Professor was very angry,' Helena sounded contrite. 'With Yannis and me, especially. I think he was afraid he'd have to answer to your Prime Minister.'

Cassie felt her face crack with a smile. 'You shouldn't have worried, I'm not that important. Where're we going?'

'Back to the Centre, rather than the doctor's surgery.'

Too many bodies there already.

'It's not much further and the doctor's waiting.'

'I've informed the Professor of your rescue.' That was Iraklidis's voice. 'He's very pleased.'

'Good. Look, thought about the case...'

'Don't think about that now,' Helena replied. 'Concentrate on getting better.'

My God, I really must look awful.

Cassie could visualise the exchange of glances between the interpreter and the Security Chief.

'The Professor will expect me to...'

'I'm sure he won't expect anything,' Helena was trying to sound reassuring.

'I want to discuss things with you both,' Cassie said. 'Is there power yet?'

'A generator provides heat, but we're trying not to overload it, so it's torches and battery powered lights,' Iraklidis replied. 'All the roads are closed, by the snow and the landslide. The authorities in the valley will be sending diggers and clearing equipment, but for the moment we're stuck here.'

'With everyone else,' Helena said. And though she sounded brave, Cassie could hear the shiver in Helena's voice.

◊ FORTY SIX

'Relax,' the Kiwi medic said.

The local doctor, a short, stocky, grey-haired man, packed away his stethoscope and snapped shut his medicine bag. A light-weight metal crutch stood propped against the bedside table. The doctor spoke and the medic translated.

'You're in one piece, but you've been badly bruised and shaken. Your back, shoulders and leg will hurt for a while and there are painkillers by the side of the bed. What you need now is rest. Here's a silent alarm.' The medic placed a button medallion on a long cord over her head. It sat on her sternum and she examined it. 'It'll only work over short distances because the signal's so bad up here. But it'll bring someone if there's an emergency. Not that you should need anyone. The doctor's given you a mild sedative, which should help you to sleep.'

Not sure I want to.

'No visitors. At least not until after you've had a good rest,' was the medic's parting shot as he closed the door behind them.

She half sighed, wincing at the pain this caused in her upper back. She was propped almost upright again, this time on a mound of pillows in bed in her own room in the guesthouse. A hump beneath the duvet was her puffer-cast leg. Her eyelids felt heavy, so she closed them.

Once again she saw the three terrifying Furies, seeking out those guilty of blood crimes, to destroy them horribly, without understanding or mitigation, in a self-perpetuating cycle of violence.

'The rule of law is fundamental, without it there is chaos.'

Andrew's voice.

They had been in the incident room at New Scotland Yard, when she had just joined the case, with Daljit and the team. Outside the Thames had sparkled in the September sunshine. Only two months ago. Andrew had always pursued justice, even for those whom the system forgot, never giving up. She would do the same. She had vowed to track down Lawrence Delahaye and bring him to trial.

If she was honest with herself, she had to admit that her vow had as much to do with revenge as with justice. Delahaye had Andrew killed, yes, but he also got inside her head. He had won. That was what she couldn't stomach, that was why she wanted vengeance, almost regardless of justice for Andrew. Yet she had sworn her oath, made her promise.

As long as her quest was about revenge, she would run into trouble and be consumed like the Furies, hateful creatures from a more brutal age. They were what you got if you rejected justice under the rule of law and sought mere revenge.

An Oath Leads to Mischief.

One of the Delphic maxims. Maybe she had ought to take note, she thought.

What of the Pythia? What did she say?

'You have already seen.'

What is it that I have seen which gives me the key to this case?

Cassie began to run through her head all the events since she had arrived in Delphi, all that she had seen.

It's hopeless. There's just too much, it could be anything.

The Pythia was famous for her cryptic and often misleading pronouncements. Was this one of them? And what were the "crimes which are no crimes"? Wrong doings, betrayals, what?

Why was she, Cassie asked herself, half smiling, trying to fathom the meaning of a mystic from her fevered dreams?

Exhausted, she drifted off to sleep.

SATURDAY

◊ FORTY SEVEN

'You asked to see us both,' the Professor said. He sat, his legs neatly crossed at the ankles, on one of the sofas in the ministerial suite. Meg Taylor was sitting, looking cool and elegant, in one of the armchairs. 'Are you sure you're feeling up to it?'

'Yes, thank you, Professor.'

Cassie sat on the sofa opposite, Helena by her side. The diazepam she had taken as soon as she had risen meant that she felt clear headed and the paracetamol kept the pain from her ankle under control.

Iraklidis stood to prowl around the room, to get a coffee, to look from the windows, to sit back in an upright chair. He'd been against interviewing Meg in the presence of the Professor, indeed, he'd been reluctant to agree to interview her in connection with the case at all. In the end Cassie had wagered that his security personnel couldn't tell him exactly the time that Meg had left the tavern on Tuesday night. When Iraklidis had returned from speaking with his men, it was without the exact time of Meg's departure, but with an appointment to see Meg and the Professor.

'I hear that you've made quite a discovery,' Professor Matsouka continued. 'If not the *adyton* itself then a new chapel, certainly.'

'Did the god speak to you?' the former athlete asked, smiling. 'Though no, of course, Apollo's not here at this time of year.'

'I can understand why,' the Professor's tone was dry. 'Now, what is it that you want to ask?'

'I'd like to ask you both about Tuesday night, the night at the tavern.'

'What about it?'

'I left the tavern at approximately eleven forty,' she said. 'I think you had already left by then?' She looked at the Professor.

'Yes. But Yannis,' he raised his hands and looked at the Security Chief, 'you know this, your men accompanied me back here.'

The Security Chief gave a sharp nod.

'Were you also accompanied back?' Cassie turned to Meg Taylor.

'Er... no, actually.'

Cassie glanced at Iraklidis. He didn't return her look, his expression was closed.

'What time did you leave?'

'I'm not sure. Not long after you, I think.'

Cassie looked at the Security Chief again.

Come on.

'My man outside the ministerial suite noted your return at twelve fifteen,' Iraklidis said from between clenched teeth. 'They didn't see what time you left the tavern.'

'Ok, so, maybe I left later,' the runner said. 'I walked up the road with some of the Austrian delegation.'

'They came across you on the road,' Cassie said. 'They didn't leave with you.'

A frown creased the former athlete's brow, just a suggestion of irritation.

'Why do you want to know? Surely you don't suspect me of being the murderer?'

'The murderer of whom? Did you leave the tavern alone?'

'Yes.'

'Shortly after I did, you told me, but you didn't catch me up, nor did you catch up with Yannis and Helena, who left immediately after I did. In fact, one of the Austrian's, a Dr Wild, remembered catching up to you.'

'So?'

'How did that happen? You're much fitter than they are and you weren't drunk. You walk faster. So what were you doing on the road that allowed them to catch up with you?'

'It was a lovely night–'

The Professor said something rapidly in Greek, his eyes on Meg Taylor. She snapped back. The tension between the two grew, as neither said anything more. Helena cast a questioning glance in her direction and Cassie shook her head slightly. She wasn't going to end this impasse.

Meg unleashed a torrent of words. Her chin was raised and she pushed herself up from her perch and began to stalk towards the door. The Professor spoke one word.

'Theo.'

Theo Sidaris, Minister and heir to the leadership. Meg's relative.

Meg pulled up short, then spun round, but she hesitated to speak.

She knows she has no choice but to tell him the truth.

'I did leave shortly after you,' she said after a pause. 'But Schlange was on the road. He seemed to be waiting.'

The Professor sat forward, an astonished look upon his face.

'I think he originally followed me,' Cassie said, prepared now to help the former athlete tell her story. 'It wasn't a criminal from my past, just a man trying to take advantage of a woman walking alone down a darkened road.'

'Yes,' the runner said. The tension left her and she sat down on the sofa. 'He made various remarks, suggestions, then he lunged at me. I was able to skip away. But I miscalculated and he grabbed me.' Her lip curled. 'We struggled. He was stronger than I expected.'

'Megaera,' the Professor reached out a hand, but the former athlete ignored him.

'Dr Schlange fell from the road, down the mountain.'

Iraklidis, the Professor and Helena all began to speak at once, until the runner raised her hand for quiet.

'I – I tried to see where he'd gone, if he was hurt. But it was impossible in the dark. The slope is steep there, but it's not sheer and there are bushes and rocky outcrops; he couldn't have fallen far. Then the Austrians arrived.'

'You didn't tell them about their colleague. Why?'

'I don't know. I guess I thought he deserved what he'd got. He'd attacked me, after all. He was an arrogant man. And I thought he'd be ok, he might even have been waiting for us all to go, so that he could climb up and slink back to the guesthouse without his colleagues knowing. Even if he wasn't, at that point I didn't care.'

'But by the time you saw me the following morning you had already changed your mind.'

'Yes.'

'You were late meeting me for our seven thirty jog. Had you already been to look for him?'

'Yes.'

Silence. Then she spoke again.

'He was badly bruised and his right side was injured, his shoulder and hip, where he'd fallen. He'd spent the night on the mountain, it had been clear and very cold, so he had lost the feeling in his leg.'

'Why didn't you report this?' The Professor was on his feet, walking back and forth. 'Or tell me, or Yannis, or even Theo?'

'I did,' Meg said. 'The man assaulted me. He should face justice. I reported it to the local police, to Constable Ganas.'

◊ FORTY EIGHT

Iraklidis began to berate Meg Taylor who retorted angrily. Helena turned to Cassie, a look of amazement on her face and the Professor threw his hands up in the air with an oath. A security man rushed into the room, gun in hand, only to retreat again, embarrassed.

'Wait! Calm down!' The Professor instructed loudly. 'You reported this to the police? So why haven't we been told about it?'

'The Constable asked me not to say anything,' Meg replied. 'Barbara's body hadn't been discovered then. Delphi is only a small town; its crimes are typically small. Yet suddenly a woman is killed and another is assaulted. Ganas thought the two were connected and I thought he was right. He had a witness to the second crime – me, its victim. To him it made sense that Schlange should be questioned about Barbara's disappearance. I must say, it seemed logical, though I wanted Schlange charged with assault, so I was all in favour of his being arrested and charged.'

'Why didn't the Constable do so?' Iraklidis asked.

'I think Ganas was afraid that Schlange would be taken to hospital out of his reach and he probably wouldn't get the chance to question him again. That wouldn't help find Barbara. The Constable didn't want to lose him. Wasn't Schlange something important in his own country?'

'I think he was about to become more important,' Cassie said. 'But he could still have been charged and extradited, justice is international these days.'

'I know, but I don't think the Constable has a lot of faith in international justice, or any kind of justice which wasn't within his own hands. Especially if the suspect was powerful and protected.'

'What happened then?' Cassie asked.

'Ganas collected Schlange in the police Jeep and took him to the police station.'

Early Wednesday morning. Yes, that fitted.

'But then Barbara Doukas's body was discovered,' Iraklidis said. 'That must have changed things. Her corpse was taken to the jail. We saw it there in the early afternoon.' He looked at Meg Taylor. 'There was no sign of Schlange then.'

Meg shook her head. 'I don't know anything about that.'

'But you were involved later that evening,' Cassie said.

'Yes.' She shot a worried glance at the Professor.

'Ganas asked you to accompany him,' Cassie prompted.

'Yes and as I discovered, he had taken Schlange up to the Corycian Cave.'

The Professor raised his hands, then dropped them again.

'Ah! Those were the lights which I saw on the mountain,' Helena said. 'Belonging to the police Jeep.'

'Probably, I don't imagine there was any other vehicle out then. It was a vile night, tempest all around.'

'So the Constable had what – kidnapped Schlange?' Iraklidis said, angrily. 'The man's a policeman. He's sworn to uphold the law! What was he doing?'

'He may, by then, have arrested Schlange,' Cassie said. 'I suspect he will say that he had. On suspicion of the murder of Barbara Doukas. I think he'd found something, something in Schlange's room perhaps. Ganas was here at the Centre on Wednesday evening, remember. But why did Ganas want you there?'

'Possibly because I speak both English and Greek,' Meg said. 'And as a witness, perhaps, that he wasn't harming Schlange or as some form of insurance with the powers that be.' She looked, shamefaced, at Professor Matsouka. 'He also wanted help in tending Schlange's wounds. As an athlete I have a pretty good understanding of human biology.'

'The small collection of medicines and bandages which we found...'

'Exactly. But I think, above all, he wanted me to see that he wasn't hurting Schlange.'

'He was keeping the man prisoner!' The Professor was aghast. He wrinkled his lips. 'Why didn't you tell me, Megaera? This was a murder.'

Meg avoided meeting his eyes. 'It's the shame of it. I – I was afraid that I'd be blamed. It's ridiculous, I know, when he attacked me, but the victim of that sort of assault is often blamed. And I was afraid that I'd be prosecuted just when I'd got my life back on track. You know how things work. I'd be crucified in the press. Theo's enemies would have a field day taking pot shots at me. And then, the longer it went on the more difficult it became to tell you, the more culpable I became.'

'You should have told me,' the Professor was insistent. 'For Theo's sake, if not your own'

'I know.'

'Don't you understand? Now it'll happen anyway, only it will be worse!' The Professor took a deep breath and closed his eyes for a moment, struggling for calm. 'The involvement of a policeman will make this case even more difficult, especially given the criminalisation of Golden Dawn. When he's apprehended the press will latch on to it and he will be portrayed as either a backward-looking bogeyman or a victim persecuted for his traditional, time-honoured beliefs. Is Ganas a member? Do we know? Can we find out? Where is he now?'

'I assume he's at the Delphi Police Station,' Iraklidis replied. 'He should be detained.'

'Agreed,' Professor Matsouka responded.

'He does have the Jeep, one of the few vehicles capable of getting out of here,' Cassie said. 'But he doesn't know we're on to him. As long as it stays that way he's unlikely to flee, leaving his sister here, in her grief. We need to take him by surprise.'

'I'll go and organise my men.' Iraklidis strode from the room.

◊ FORTY NINE

'This shouldn't take too long,' Iraklidis said to Helena.

'But it could be dangerous.' Helena's shoulders sagged.

They were in the guesthouse reception. Cassie watched from one of the sofas, her leg raised. She had slit the seam on her jeans so she could wear trousers.

'I'll be back before you know it, with Ganas in custody. Stay here with Cassie.' The Security Chief kissed Helena's forehead and accompanied by his men, left for the town.

Meg Taylor wandered into reception from the dining room, carrying an open packet of biscuits.

'Have they gone? Has Yannis told the Major about the Constable's imminent arrest?' she asked. 'She might be able to help.'

The former runner looked astonishingly relaxed, munching to replace energy. Cassie was perplexed. Such a complex character. Driven, yet content enough to snack after telling them about being a key witness in a murder investigation. Intensely private, but always on show. Tough enough to fight and walk away after shoving a man down a mountain, but decent enough to search for him the following morning even if he had attacked her.

'I don't think so,' Helena said. 'How could he? There aren't any phones. Ganas is armed. And remember what he did to that poor demonstrator, Kouris.'

'I don't think Constable Ganas is a threat,' Meg responded.

'Why?' Cassie asked. 'He probably killed Schlange.'

'Oh no. As it happens, when Schlange screamed, Ganas couldn't have pushed Schlange off the cliff edge. He was with me,' the former athlete said.

'You can give him an alibi! Why didn't you tell us?' Cassie asked in amazement.

'I didn't think about it and no one asked.' Meg eyes were cold as she looked down at Cassie. 'You don't know everything, do you?'

Bloody hell.

So Ganas wasn't a cold-blooded killer. Iraklidis was going to arrest the wrong man! This could be very embarrassing for the Minister, Iraklidis being his Head of Security and wholly in his camp. Sidaris and Matsouka wouldn't have to look far for someone to blame and there would go any chance Cassie had of getting them to London.

We must warn Iraklidis.

There must be some security men around on the walkie-talkie system. Or…

'Meg, wait!' She called after the runner, who retraced her steps. 'Do you still have a key to the perimeter fence?'

'Yes, do you want it?' Meg reached into the bag on her shoulder and produced the key on its ribbon. 'Though I can't see you getting far.'

'Thanks.' Cassie took the key. The former athlete walked off in the direction of the ministerial suite. Helena turned to Cassie.

'Shouldn't Yannis know what we've just learned before he tackles Ganas?' she said.

'Yes,' Cassie replied.

'So how do we follow them?'

Cassie smiled. Helena was game. 'Pass me my crutch. The Centre has a three-wheeler trail buggy, Ganas told us.' She smiled and handed

Helena the keys. 'I got the night manager to bring it round earlier to transport me places. It's parked round the side. Can you get it?'

In ten minutes they were at the gate in the chain link fence.

'So this is the other way out of the grounds,' the interpreter said, as she closed it behind them and climbed back in to the driving seat of the buggy.

'This path will take us over the ridge and to the top of Delphi town,' Cassie said. 'It's quicker than going round by road, though the terrain's rough.'

'Are you sure you can do this?'

No. Not sure I'll even get as far as the town.

Cassie's back and shoulders were hurting, the painkillers were wearing off. The buggy's wide tyres deadened the impact of the terrain, but it was only going to get worse and her ankle, propped against the skeleton of the vehicle, was already throbbing.

'Of course. Come on.'

As they crested the ridge Delphi lay below them. It was quiet, with a few faint weekend morning sounds, the drone of a motorbike, the clattering of a metal blind. The local refuse wagon was crawling its way around the streets. Overhead the sky was blue, yesterday's storm seemed far away.

'If Ganas didn't kill Schlange,' Helena said as she put the buggy into a low gear and started down the steep slope, 'who did?'

Ow!

A sharp pain stabbed her ankle as the buggy lurched and Cassie gasped.

'Cassie, you can't go any further.' Helena braked and the vehicle came to a halt, perched ungainly on the path. 'I can drive more carefully, but then we won't get there in time.'

'You're right, you go on ahead. It's important to tell Yannis about Ganas. I'll follow on foot, I'll catch you up, I've got my crutch.' Cassie clambered from the vehicle. 'I'll be fine. Look, there's Yannis and his men.'

Through the branches she caught sight of red roof tiles, indicating where the town began. In the town below a group of men could be seen walking up the main street.

'Go, go. Quickly! He needs to know.'

Helena pulled away, a look of concentration on her face, down the slope to the town. Cassie could follow her progress until she disappeared into a stand of pine trees fifty yards below.

She stepped forwards, cautiously testing her ankle and slowly made her way with her crutch down the path. At the trees a slippery carpet of wet pine needles further slowed her progress. It was ten minutes before she emerged on to a hard-surfaced lane. This intersected a larger road close by, which led to the police station. Cassie limped along more quickly, ignoring the pain. Iraklidis and his men would be there by now.

Turning the corner she could see the front of the police station up ahead. Outside the two-storey building, a large wheelie bin stood on the pavement awaiting the rubbish cart. A bulky security man was backing out of the door, his gun held in both hands and pointing back into the building. He dropped his arms as another man, a colleague, also backed through the door.

Cassie tried to increase her pace even more, hobbling ungainly along the pavement until she was level with the police station. The first security man had seen her, she ignored his wave to keep her away and crossed the street towards him.

'What's going on?'

The man answered in Greek.

Damn it, I can't understand!

'Hostage,' was the only English word she could make out.

Oh no, not Helena, please.

Cassie scrutinised the police station. If she wanted to know what was happening, she'd have to get inside. She recalled that the front door opened into a reception area, with the small office visible through a plate glass screen, behind the desk. In the left-hand wall, not far beyond the screen, was the door to the jail cells.

The protestor, Balasz Kouris, was still there. Had he been able to hear what was going on? She was sure that, at times the Constable left the jail door ajar. So it was possible. There was a window in Kouris's jail cell, she might be able to speak with him from outside.

'I'm just going round the side,' she said to the security man, pointing to the side wall and limping as quickly as she could towards it.

The narrow space between the buildings was litter strewn and Cassie smelled the acrid tang of urine. About halfway along was a barred metal gate preventing access to the rear of the building. Under normal circumstances she could have climbed it with ease, now that was impossible. But the window she was looking for was on her side of the gate, a small oblong high up in the wall. She found an up-turned wooden crate lying in the alley – that would do to stand on.

'Mr Kouris.' Cassie knocked on the glass, teetering slightly. She could only just see through the window. 'Sir, can I speak with you please?'

There was no answer.

She knocked again. The top of a man's head rose into view, a startled expression on his face.

'Mr Kouris, it's me, Cassie Fortune. We spoke about justice the other day, do you remember?'

She received a grunt by way of acknowledgement. The glass was thin, she could hear through it.

'What's going in inside, sir? Can you tell?'

'I heard a group of men arrive, there was noise. Then a woman's voice, but not the policewoman, I didn't hear her at all.'

So not the Major.

'Then doors banging, people going out the front. Still people in there.'

'Do you know who?'

'No.'

Cassie looked at the gate barring her way then back down to the street. The two security men were standing on the pavement opposite, watching her.

'This is going to sound like a very stupid question, but do you know if there's a back way into the building?'

'Yes,' Kouris chuckled. 'Some of my more intrepid followers checked it out, planning a jailbreak – I told them it wasn't a good idea. I'm more use where I am. There is a rear door into the back yard. It might be open, I heard the Constable putting out the rubbish earlier. He came out along the side here.'

'Thank you, sir,' Cassie said as she stepped down, jarring her ankle. She let out a yell of pain.

One of the security men was crossing the road with a determined look upon his face. He was coming to get her. If she was going to try the back entrance she had to do it now. She reached for the gate and to her surprise, it opened. Without thinking, she slipped through and the catch clicked into place as she drew it closed behind her.

◊ FIFTY

Cassie picked her way across the rubbish-filled yard, taking care where she placed her crutch. She dared not risk making a noise, alerting those inside. The door Kouris had mentioned was in the centre of the back wall with a barred window to the left of it. She reached for the door handle. Had Ganas bothered to lock it after putting out the rubbish? Was it her lucky day?

Yes!

She hopped inside. Sunlight from the window showed a corridor running forwards away from the door and a staircase. To the left was a small space leading to another door. She limped along the corridor, being as quiet as she was able, until she could hear voices.

That was Iraklidis, trying to persuade, but with underlying tension in his voice, then Ganas, gruff but not conceding. Iraklidis spoke more loudly, prompting Ganas to respond.

'I'll go, I'll go!' Helena's voice, speaking in English because Ganas couldn't understand it. That was quick thinking, and brave too.

'No. Helena!'

'Don't shoot him. Please. I couldn't live with myself if someone died or was even hurt because of me.'

A line of yellow light fell across the floor and wall ahead. The door to the office was opening. They were going to come this way.

Ganas gave instructions, presumably to Iraklidis, who was still in the office. He had, she assumed, his pistol pointed at Helena, but where did he mean to go and how? There was nothing back here but the yard and alleyway.

The other door must lead somewhere.

Cassie retreated to the space by the window to the second door. She could hear Ganas and Helena in the corridor behind her. Reaching for the door handle she sent up a silent prayer. It opened.

Beyond was darkness. She stepped inside and closed the door.

Her phone light showed wooden shelves to each side, shelves stacked with junk and piles of grey blankets, Ganas's supply. There were steps going down into a basement.

Cassie steadied herself, leaning on the walls as she descended. At the foot of the stairs a dull, grey light came through a narrow grill high up in the wall. Further on, her phone's beam of light reflected in the red brake lights of the police Jeep. She was in a basement garage, where the Jeep was kept. That was why Ganas was coming here.

The only escape route.

Cassie hobbled towards the Jeep. She could see the glint of the key in the ignition. Should she take it?

Too late, she heard Ganas and Helena at the door above. He had a gun. She couldn't risk confronting him.

I must hide. Where?

The interpreter was pleading with the policeman as, back in the office, Iraklidis was shouting, presumably to his men outside.

Ganas was going to take the Jeep. If she wanted to help Helena, the Jeep was where she had to hide. Cassie reached for the cargo boot handle and pulled it up. She heard the basement door open. Switching off her phone light, she climbed into the boot space and pulled the overhead roof closed.

◊ FIFTY ONE

Fluorescent lighting flickered on, but the cargo boot was in shadow. Cassie listened hard, trying to hear what was going on above the hammering of her own heart against her ribs. Already her ankle had begun to hurt and she wanted to shift position but she dared not. If Ganas looked directly into the back of the Jeep he would undoubtedly see her. Any movement would attract his attention.

Running her hands around the space she felt a number of large water bottles, a backpack, a box, probably a medical kit and a pile of blankets. There were footsteps alongside the vehicle and voices, first Helena, with Ganas close behind her. The front driver's door opened and the vehicle sagged a little. That must be Helena, sliding across to the passenger side. Then another, deeper dip as Ganas got in and slammed the door. Central locking clicked on.

I can't get out now, even if I want to.

There was a beep, followed by the low drone of an electric motor and a clanking. Probably the garage door opening. Ganas was doing something, she could feel his weight shifting.

'Ouch!'

That was Helena. Followed by Ganas speaking. What was going on?

Then the Jeep engine rumbled into life and the vehicle reversed as the handbrake eased. Ganas was going to accelerate out through the garage door as quickly as he could. Cassie felt him slam his foot down and the Jeep jumped forward, engine roaring, out of the garage, bumping up a ramp and onto the street. Without warning, she was flung against the back of the cargo boot, the tyres spun and the SUV screeched around a corner. Wedged between the back of the rear seats and the rear of the boot, Cassie's bruised shoulder blades took the main impact. She cringed in pain, desperate not to cry out. Her one good foot was braced against the frame of the vehicle.

They were climbing a steep gradient now, going up the mountain. She had to stop herself sliding. There had been maps of the area in her briefing she'd only glanced at, but she knew that this was all national parkland. There was a large ski centre, but that was closed until December.

There would, however, be plenty of places where someone like Ganas could hide for the winter. Lodges and hiking chalets, hunting cabins and wildlife hides, isolated but within a relatively short drive to some sort of village or hamlet for essential supplies. If it came to it, she suspected, Ganas could hunt for his food.

The Jeep braked to a halt and the engine was switched off. Cassie could see tree branches above them. Was this it? Surely he would want to get further away than this?

When Helena began to speak, Ganas shushed her. He was listening.

Then she heard it, the drone of motorcycle engines. Iraklidis must have commandeered the trail bikes in Delphi and he and his men were following the tracks of the Jeep in pursuit.

The engine started up again and the Jeep began climbing again, travelling at breakneck speed. Cassie was bounced around, until she re-jammed herself in place, holding on to the internal tow bar to keep hidden.

She was almost shaken loose by a huge jolt. Pain shot up her leg and she bit back a cry. Now the Jeep was no longer climbing they were on flattish ground, so they must have reached the plateau. Yet, if anything, the going was tougher than before. Had they turned off the trail to go across country? It wouldn't stop the bikes pursuing them, though their trail might be harder to follow over rough ground. What was Ganas planning, where was he going?

Tree branches were slapping against the windows of the Jeep. Cassie didn't dare raise her head to look, but the sky was no longer to be seen through the rear window. They had entered another copse or wood.

The engine died. Ganas got out of the Jeep. Where was he going?

Cassie blinked against the bright light as the cargo boot roof opened.

When her vision adjusted she found herself looking down the barrel of a pistol.

◊ FIFTY TWO

The Constable gestured with the pistol that she should get out of the cargo boot.

'Ok, ok,' she said. She pushed herself up and clambered out, ungainly, over the lip of the boot. Ganas watched, his expression suspicious and wary.

She raised her hands above her head.

'I'm unarmed. I don't have a weapon. No gun.'

'Cassie, is that you?' Helena's voice.

'Yes. I was hiding in the boot.'

'He's telling you to get in.' Helena hardly needed to translate Ganas's instructions. Cassie exaggerated her limp as she walked round the Jeep. 'Back seat. Cassie, he'll probably–'

As she climbed into the back seat the Constable produced a plastic cable tie and bound her wrists together in front of her, then closed the door.

'He says to put your leg up on the seat,' Helena said.

Cassie wriggled around in order to do so, grasping the head bars of the passenger seat in front. When she had settled she was surprised to see dark flakes of something adhering to her fingers. She brought them to her face and sniffed.

Blood.

The unmistakable metallic odour. But whose was it? Barbara's? Or Stefan Schlange's?

Her ankle was aching badly, but it was a great deal more comfortable in the back seat than in the cargo boot. Helena was belted into the front seat and her hands were also bound, but the interpreter turned to address her directly as the Jeep moved off again.

'Are you ok?'

'Yes. Where he's taking us?'

Ganas could drive over the mountain trails heading north. But if he was trying to outrun his pursuers and leave the area, what would he do with Helena and herself?

'I don't know, but he seems to know his way.'

'I suspect he knows the mountain,' Cassie replied. 'Just as well for us he does. Driving over rough mountain ground at the sort of speeds we've been doing could be suicidal.'

The Constable grunted in the affirmative.

'*Katalavaineis!*' Helena exclaimed.

'He understands!'

How much had he overheard when we thought he couldn't understand us!

He spoke in Greek and Helena translated.

'He says you don't need to worry,' she said. 'Oh, look.'

They had emerged from the trees and before them lay a snowfield, pristine and glistening. Cassie screwed up her eyes against the glare of sunlight reflecting white and crystalline from the snow, which stretched away to one rocky ridge then another. The Jeep swung left and Ganas drove along the edge of the wood, not entering on to the whiteness. They drove in silence.

'Where are we going?' Cassie asked, wanting to break the spell.

'He says we'll see soon enough,' Helena translated. She hesitated then continued. 'Cassie, I think he's glad you're here.'

'Can you tell him that I only want to know what happened? I know a lot already, tell him that I just need him to fill in the gaps. I'm not here to condemn him. Be clear, I want to be sure that he understands.'

The Constable ended the rapid exchange which followed, he seemed to want to concentrate on driving. In the distance Cassie could make out the black line of a metalled road, elevated three feet above ground level and relatively clear of snow. They were converging with it and Ganas positioned the Jeep alongside, then accelerated up the steep slope with ease.

The vehicle sped along. He was putting as much distance between them and their pursuers as he could. Cassie squirmed round to look back at the rapidly diminishing tree line. There was no sign of any pursuit. Iraklidis had been outmanoeuvred, at least for the present. Yet he wouldn't give up and the Professor would give him whatever resources he needed to find them. The chances of Ganas getting away and staying away were very small, which he must already know.

The Jeep was slowing and Cassie spotted a turning coming up on the left, running down from the raised road into the snow field. They descended between walls of compacted snow and it was no longer possible to see the countryside around. Before long they arrived at a row of modern chalet-style houses, ski-lodges. They were boarded up and Ganas drove straight past.

The road dwindled into a track and there were no more buildings, but the Jeep continued. The terrain grew wilder and, even lying on the back seat of the SUV, Cassie was jounced around. Eventually they entered a pine forest, but this didn't slow them down, the Constable obviously knew every trail and byway. Pine branches flailed against the Jeep as it passed, the sky a patch of blue high up above them.

Then, finally, the Jeep came to a halt.

They had arrived.

◊ FIFTY THREE

The Jeep had stopped in an overgrown clearing deep in the woods. As the engine died, silence took its place.

Ahead was a wooden building, its walls silver with age beneath a moss-covered roof. Shuttered windows gave it a blind and secret appearance and tall weeds grew up around its walls. The cabin seemed to be a part of the forest vegetation which surrounded it.

'Out,' the Constable ordered, as he opened the car door and cold air filled the Jeep. He gave instructions in Greek.

'We're to follow him,' Helena said, climbing out. 'Let me help you.'

Together Cassie and Helena followed Ganas into the cabin, Cassie hobbling badly. It was dark and cold inside, the windows closed and the air stale. They clung together as Ganas lit a pair of battered antique oil lamps. In their glow Cassie could see more of the surroundings.

The room was furnished with wooden furniture from the 1950s. Thick tartan rugs covered a sofa and chairs arranged around an oval coffee table. There was a brick fireplace and chimney, with kindling already in the grate. Ganas knelt to set a fire going.

He spoke to them over his shoulder.

'He says he'll power up the water supply pump. Once the water's running we can make hot drinks,' Helena translated. 'The kitchen's through here.'

Off the main room at the back of the cabin, the kitchen had a shuttered window, a stone butler's sink and an ancient gas cooker. Helena got the gas cylinder working, while Cassie looked in the cupboards. Empty, except for a jar of solidified ground coffee and some herbal tea bags. The water pipes clanked and shuddered as Helena turned on the tap. A dribble of brown liquid spattered into the sink, then clear, icy water spurted out.

'Well done!' Cassie said.

The interpreter called through to Ganas, who appeared at the door. He took a Swiss army penknife from his pocket and advanced on Helena. The interpreter paled, then her chin came up and she stared at the policeman, daring him to do his worst. He shook his head gently and cut the band around her wrists. He said something as he freed her, prompting Helena to smile.

'He says that everyone says you're a spy,' she said. 'I've told him it isn't true. Says he hopes you don't have a license to kill – he's watched too many James Bond films. It's a joke. Don't worry I've told him you're not.'

'*Efcharisto*,' Cassie said as the Constable cut her restraint. 'Licensed to limp is more like it.'

The Constable smiled, tentative. He looked to Helena to translate for him.

'He says we'll get a fire going and air the place. Then we can sit and talk. He wants you to tell him what you think happened.'

'I can do that,' Cassie replied, enunciating clearly. 'He does know, doesn't he, that they won't stop searching for us until we're found?'

'He knows,' Helena said. 'But he says it won't be easy for them to find us here. The cabin is well concealed and no one knows its whereabouts. Someone could stand within fifty yards and not see it. By the time they gather enough people to conduct a full scale, detailed search he probably thinks he'll have time to be far away.'

That might be a miscalculation.

She felt the slight weight of the alarm medallion against her sternum. Would the police walkie-talkie frequency pick up its silent signal?

'I don't think he's planning to run. That would mean leaving his sister,' Cassie said, rubbing her wrists. 'Because she was involved too, wasn't she?'

The Constable waved his index finger, shrugged his shoulders and returned to the living room.

'He says be patient, he'll tell you everything as soon as we're settled down.'

◊ FIFTY FOUR

A log burst with a crack as loud as a gunshot and Constable Ganas prodded the fire with a poker. Warmth spread through the room, where Cassie lay on the sofa, with Helena and Ganas in armchairs on either side of her. Indifferent to the noise and to the smoke flowing up the chimney, Ganas seemed confident that they would not be found. Either that or he didn't care if they were.

Thus far he'd treated them well, but Cassie was all too aware that his attitude might change, especially if he was threatened. She glanced at her watch. It was half past two.

'Will you tell me?' Helena translated Ganas's request.

'Yes.' Cassie put her mug down on the coffee table and eased her position.

'Tell him to correct me if I'm wrong. When Nico came to you on Tuesday evening, I think you weren't sure if he was right. Relations between he and your niece hadn't been good for a while, but you went to check with your sister anyway. And you found that your niece was, indeed, missing, but by then it was too late to begin a public search, so you had to wait. That must have been hard to do, especially for your sister.'

Ganas sat forward on the edge of his chair, his elbows on his knees.

'He says it was one of the most difficult nights of his life.'

'I can imagine,' Cassie said. 'Then Meg Taylor came to you on Wednesday morning with the tale of the assault on the mountain road the night before and you had to defer beginning the search for Barbara and instead go with Meg to find Schlange.'

The Constable nodded and spoke.

'He says he had never gone to bed,' Helena translated. 'He was already up when Meg arrived to make her complaint. It was very early.'

'It must have been,' Cassie replied. 'I'd arranged to go running that morning with Meg at 7.30. But she was busy beforehand. She reported the altercation with Schlange of the night before and she took you to where he lay, incapacitated, on the mountain slope.'

He nodded again.

'Together, you brought him back to the police station and left him there, while you went to start the search for Barbara. You can't have put him in a cell or Balasz Kouris would have seen him. What did you do with him?'

'Left him in the back of the Jeep.'

'So that was his blood I found just now?'

'Did you?' The Constable looked surprised. 'I thought I'd cleaned it all up.'

'Then your niece's body was found and you began to suspect that her murder and the assault on Meg Taylor were connected.'

The Constable twisted his lips into a sardonic half smile.

'Even stupid, uneducated small-town cops might work that one out,' Helena translated.

'I don't think you're stupid, Constable Ganas, though you're content to let people think you are, people like the Major, for example,' Cassie said. 'Who you don't trust. You wanted to question Schlange about the murder of your niece, but he was injured and would certainly be taken away to hospital – where's the nearest? Amfissa? You thought that you wouldn't get another chance.'

And you were probably right.

'It was my *only* chance,' Helena translated. 'The Major I didn't know at all, she could have been Golden Dawn, for all I knew, I couldn't trust her.'

'So you drove him up to the Corycian Cave.' She paused. 'Why there? Why didn't you take him to your sister's home, for example?'

'He says he couldn't trust his sister to look after Schlange, if she thought he had anything to do with Barbara's murder. He feared what she might do. He had to put him somewhere safe, but somewhere he couldn't escape or get help. He was going to bring him back to the jail as soon as he'd questioned him.'

'I see. You left Schlange there on Wednesday night. You lied when you said the Cave was empty. When you were at the Centre that evening for our case conference you searched his room didn't you?'

'Yes.'

'And found something incriminating.'

'Yes. My niece's missing key. It was an ordinary looking key and Schlange had put it on to his key ring, kept it – as a memento, a trophy perhaps. He didn't see that it had a splash of red paint on it, dulled to a rusty colour now, maybe, but quite distinctive to anyone who was used to seeing the key. I wasn't the only one who would recognise it, my sister would too and Nico.'

'I see. So now you had evidence. Did you confront Schlange with the key?'

'Yes.'

'And...'

'He denied knowing it was Barbara's, said it was just a key he had found. He claimed to have put it on his key ring to keep it safe before handing it in at the guesthouse desk, but he forgot all about it.'

'Did you believe him?'

'No.'

'Why not bring Schlange back down to the jail and charge him?'

'He says at that point Schlange seemed delirious.' Helena translated. 'He didn't think he should move the Austrian.'

'When did you tell your sister about him?'

'On Wednesday night when I returned to town. She insisted on seeing him, but it was already late. I persuaded her to wait until the morning.'

'So you left before sun up on Thursday morning? In the Jeep. Did Meg go with you?'

'Not initially. We met her on the mountain, running, on our way to the Cave. I asked her to come with us.'

'And when you got to the Cave it was empty. Schlange had gone.'

Ganas stared at Cassie, suspicion in his eyes.

'How can you know that?' Helena translated his words.

'An educated guess,' Cassie replied. 'You were all looking for Schlange when you heard his cry.'

'Yes.'

'Where exactly was your sister?'

'Alecto was helping with the search. It was difficult to see, the sun hadn't burned off the cloud and mist. So we spread out and were walking towards the top of the Phaedriades. I swear we were nowhere near the edge. Meg Taylor will swear it too.'

'Perhaps you didn't need to be near the edge.'

Helena frowned at Cassie, not understanding.

'Did you find Schlange?'

'No. We didn't see him.'

'But you heard him?'

'Everyone heard him.'

'Then you all came back down to Delphi.'

'Yes.'

'Why didn't you collect the things from the Cave?'

'I'd taken the Jeep towards the cliffs, we just got in it and came back directly. The Cave was out of our way and, to be honest, I didn't think about it. None of us did. We were too shocked. We hadn't wanted the man to die, we wanted him to answer our questions.'

'Thank you, Constable Ganas,' Cassie said. 'I'll try to ensure you get a fair hearing when they catch up with us. Because they will catch up with us, you know.'

Ganas smiled though his eyes were still sad.

He knows.

Cassie shifted position, she'd grown tense and had become uncomfortable. She winced at the twisting pain. The ache in her ankle had lessened, thanks to painkillers from the medical kit, but her back and shoulders were still tender.

'You need a proper lie down,' Helena said. She spoke with the Constable in Greek, then said, 'I'm going to make up a bed. I'll air some sheets.'

So saying, she rose and went into another room.

◊ FIFTY FIVE

Ganas watched her leave, then leaned forward.

'Yannis Iraklidis,' he said, his voice lowered. Furtive, he looked back at the door through which Helena had passed. 'Delphi, before.'

'Iraklidis was in Delphi before this visit?'

Ganas nodded in the affirmative. 'Security.'

'To discuss the security arrangements at the Centre, the Museum and the temple site?' Again Ganas nodded. She wasn't surprised, it would be standard practice to bring a couple of men and do a reconnaissance. 'You met him?'

'Yes, and Barbara.'

'Barbara was at the meeting?' In the absence of the Museum Director, perhaps.

'Yes.' The policeman struggled to find words. 'Barbara.' Then he wiggled his body, with a hand on his hip and smiled.

'She... what? She flirted with him?'

The look of disapproval on his face and a crude, if universal, gesture told Cassie it was rather more than that. So, Yannis Iraklidis had slept with Barbara Doukas.

A girl in every port. Had Barbara fallen for Yannis, just as Helena had?

'Here,' Helena returned to the room and placed some folded sheets over the back of an armchair. 'We'll need blankets.'

Ganas rose. He went outside, to get some blankets from the police Jeep, she assumed.

This explained why Barbara and Nico weren't getting on so well, if Barbara thought she had found someone else, someone who lived in Athens. Cassie's mind was racing. Iraklidis hadn't been in Delphi when Barbara was killed, he couldn't be the murderer. And he'd been with

Helena when Schlange had died. Yet he undoubtedly had information pertinent to their enquiry, which he deliberately hadn't volunteered. Why? What was he afraid of?

If the Major knew about this it might also explain why the Security Chief was reluctant to report her to the Professor.

Helena perched on the edge of the sofa.

'Come by the fire,' Cassie encourage her. 'Tell me what happened in the police station this morning.'

'When I arrived Yannis and two of his men were inside, trying to arrest the Constable. I surprised them, I think, and Ganas reacted first, by grabbing me and drawing his pistol. He made the others back off, then he persuaded them to leave the building, but Yannis wouldn't go. It was stalemate. I don't think any of it was pre-meditated.' As she shook her head the black curls fell around her face. 'Then Ganas took me through into the garage and we drove off.

'Was the Major there?'

'No.'

'Hmm, I wonder where she was.'

The fire crackled as a log disintegrated and collapsed.

'Helena, can you tell me about what Greece was like in the 1970s?'

'Of course, everyone knows,' the interpreter replied. 'Why?'

'The photographs in Alecto Doukas's house, of the Ganas family, set me thinking.'

'It was a turbulent period,' Helena began. 'Like so many. After the military coup in '67 opposition to the military dictatorship was driven underground, but by 1973 people had had enough. First the navy mutinied, a mutiny which was viciously put down. Then the students occupied the campus of Athens university, the Polytechneion, and called for a restoration of democracy. The Generals sent in the tanks. Democracy was restored in 1974. But it was too late for many of those rounded up and "disappeared", in the navy and both before and immediately after the student uprising.'

'What happened then?'

'Eventually there were trials, the biggest since the Nazi trials at Nuremberg, of the senior military, their political stooges and those who had supported them. There were plenty, Golden Dawn isn't the first right-wing extremist party to gather support in this country.'

'That's what I thought. It was the basis of the editorial in Wednesday's Times.'

'So what happens now?' Helena asked. 'The Constable doesn't seem inclined to continue onwards.'

'I think he knows he'll be found,' Cassie responded. 'He just wants to be sure he's not fingered for the crime, but now he knows that we know he isn't the murderer.'

'Ganas is afraid of being made a scapegoat and he kidnapped Schlange because he couldn't see that he would get justice any other way. Kouris was afraid of unexplained "accidents". Even the police don't trust each other. This isn't how I thought the system worked. I used to believe that justice would be done, maybe not all the time, but in the main.' Helena's head drooped. 'Now I'm not so sure.'

What can I say? This isn't my country.

'If it's anything like the UK,' Cassie chose her words with care, 'it probably is. Though whether or not you agree with that might depend on who you are and your experience of it, which does undermine the whole idea. The law has to apply equally to all, or it's reduced for everyone.'

'What will happen to the Constable?'

'He's broken the law and is involved in someone's kidnapping and, possibly, death.'

'Meg Taylor said...'

'But Meg Taylor is involved too. We can't trust her either. Look, I don't know what'll happen. There will have to be an inquest or inquiry into the deaths at least.'

The Constable reappeared carrying blankets. Helena rose to take them into the bedrooms.

Cassie returned her gaze to the fire, which was now burning strongly. Not for the first time, she pressed the button on the alarm around her neck. If the police were nearby it might help them find the cabin.

'*Kyria.*' Ganas took a seat on the other side of the fireplace.

'Constable,' she said, shooting a quick glance towards the bedroom door. 'You told me about Iraklidis's earlier visit to Delphi, two weeks ago.'

The policeman nodded.

'Do you know if Nico knew about Barbara and Iraklidis? Or suspected?'

The policeman shook his head from side to side.

'One night,' he said. 'Iraklidis.'

'He was only here for one night?'

A one-night stand. Still, a lot could happen in one night.

'What about–'

'This is the police! This is the police! Constable Alexandros Ganas come out with your hands above your head. I repeat, come out with your hands up!'

◊ FIFTY SIX

Cassie struggled to her feet as the voice continued in Greek. Helena appeared in the bedroom doorway, mouth agape and eyes wide. The Constable went to stand at the side of the front window and peer between the shutters beyond the glass.

She joined Ganas at the other side of the window. She couldn't see very much, the cracks in the shutters were narrow, but it was clear that there were a number of vehicles outside, not just the Delphi police Jeep and the trail bikes. Either the roads must be open again, which was unlikely, or they had come over the mountain from the north. She could see armed men and she thought she make out the Major, holding a megaphone.

'Looks like it's the Major,' Cassie said. 'That's why she wasn't in the jail yesterday.'

Ganas looked across at her his eyes large and sad. He began to unstrap his pistol holster.

'Helena, make sure he understands what I'm saying,' Cassie said to the interpreter. 'Translate exactly, please.'

'Ok.'

'Ninety-five percent of hostage situations are resolved without injury or fatality. So we have a very good chance of getting out of here alive.'

Helena translated, glancing at Cassie as she did so.

'You must not go out first,' she said to Ganas, slicing her hand horizontally in the air to indicate a negative. 'Regardless of what the police say. We'll tell them that Helena is coming out first. Then you. Then me, finally, with your pistol, empty of bullets.'

'Shouldn't you go first. You're the most important?' Helena translated.

'No. If there's a trained negotiator there, they will always try to get the hostage taker to give himself up first. If that doesn't work, they'll then try and get the weakest hostage released, anyone injured or sick, or any children. Given my leg, that's me. Then the rest of the hostages, then, finally, the hostage taker. That's the FBI protocol, it's internationally recognised.'

'But we're not going to do that?'

'No. We minimise risk if Ganas goes out before me. Specifically, we minimise the risk to him.'

'Why?'

'They don't know who else is in here. He might have an accomplice, so if Ganas goes out before me any attack on him puts me at risk. That's why they won't do it. It increases his chances of staying alive.'

Does it decrease mine?

For the first time Cassie considered her own safety.

'I'm warning you – don't try and turn Helena against me... You're in Greece now, my country, where I know the rules.'

It might be in Iraklidis's interest that an accident occurs. He wouldn't be held accountable. Then, best get Helena out there, just in case. Her presence might deter him and she could act as a witness if an "accident" did happen.

'Come out!' The Major spoke through the megaphone, in Greek and in English. 'Or we have no choice but to come in and get you.'

'That's not in any manual,' Cassie said. 'It might be the Major getting bullish. I get the feeling that the Constable's not her favourite person at the moment.'

I'm probably not top of her list either.

'No, nor Yannis's neither. He'll be worried,' Helena said. 'About us both.'

The megaphone voice had begun again.

'We have to do this soon.' Cassie looked at the policeman and waited. He had to choose and his decision could determine all their futures.

'Let's hope they follow the protocol,' she said, as much to herself as to anyone.

Then she exchanged a look with the Constable. His gaze was fearful but resigned. Indescribably sad. He handed his pistol to Cassie.

She emptied the bullets out on to the coffee table and tucked the gun into the waistband of her jeans.

'Right. Repeat what I say in Greek,' she said to Helena. 'Loudly. Now, I'll open the door. Are we ready?'

◊ FIFTY SEVEN

'Don't shoot! We're coming out!' Cassie shouted as she pulled the cabin's front door open, back against the interior wall.

The sun's rays shone across the small clearing in front of the cabin directly through the rectangle of the open door. She flattened herself against the door and inched forwards to look out. She could see two police jeeps, in addition to the one belonging to Delphi, in the shadow of the pine trees. There were armed police, at least a dozen of them, crouched behind the vehicles open doors.

'Helena Gatakis will come out first,' Cassie yelled. 'Ok, Helena.'

She smiled at the interpreter, who had come to stand by her side. 'It'll be ok. Go out with your hands above your head. Walk straight forwards, slowly. Someone will get you, probably Yannis.'

Helena returned the smile. She took a deep breath, raised her hands high and stepped into the oblong of light. There was a shouted order from outside. Then Helena stepped into the clearing. Cassie lost sight of her after about three paces.

She'll be fine.

Unless someone's stupid, panicky or trigger happy.

The silence stretched.

'I'm ok! I'm ok!' She heard Helena's voice.

She released her breath with a relieved sigh. Now for the more difficult part.

'Constable Ganas is coming out next! He is unarmed. Repeat – he is unarmed! Tell them Helena!'

Ganas came and stood next to her. He rubbed his unshaven chin with his large hand, grimacing, then held out his hand to her. She squeezed it, wanting to reassure, but he knew the score. A policeman, apparently gone to the bad, he would get little sympathy. There would be people, including within the police service, who wouldn't care what happened to him as long as it was bad. The insiders within the justice system would probably throw the book at him, especially if he'd been foolish enough to be political. She dreaded to think what life in prison would be like for him. If he survived.

He gave her a small nod, pressing his lips together, then stepped into the rectangle of light with hands raised. As he walked through the door he lifted his arms high above his head.

Instructions were rattled out via the megaphone. Cassie couldn't understand the words but could imagine what they were – 'Keep your hands in sight at all times.' 'Walk towards us.' 'Present your wrists when asked.' The Major had read the handbook.

'Ok! Cassie, he's in custody, but he's ok!' shouted Helena.

Cassie withdrew the pistol, opened the barrel and held it by its trigger guard in the thumb and forefinger of her hand.

'I'm coming out now. I'm the only one left in here. I'll be holding the pistol in my left hand.'

Here's hoping. Fingers crossed.

She raised her arms and stepped into the bright rectangle of light, screwing up her eyes against the blinding sunshine. The sun seemed to be much sinking, how much time had passed, what time was it? Too late, she couldn't look now.

The ground was muddy and slippery with snowmelt. She concentrated on keeping her balance, dragging her left leg behind her and keeping her hands in the air. She could see little beyond the ground immediately in front of her, though she knew the vehicles and the police were there. She could hear Helena calling, then heard Iraklidis's voice as she limped forwards.

Before she'd gone more than halfway towards tree line she was surrounded. A policeman took away the gun, holding it carefully and placing it into an evidence bag. Helena hugged her and, for a moment, Iraklidis looked like he was going to do so too. He embraced Helena instead, wrapping her in his arms.

Groundless fears.

This was the second time she had been rescued in two days and Iraklidis had been involved on both occasions. Perhaps she had misjudged him.

And he doesn't know I know.

She was led over to the small ring of vehicles, where she found the Major and her Sergeant, as well as police she hadn't seen before.

'Where did all these people come from?' she asked. 'Are the roads open?'

'No. Not on the Delphi side of the mountain,' the Major answered, her habitual sour look displaced by a contented expression. 'But they're not blocked to the north. The telephone lines are working again, that's how we got back-up to come over the mountain. How are you feeling?'

'I've felt better.' Suddenly her back and shoulders felt sore again and her ankle throbbed. 'I'm very tired.'

'You need to get back to the Centre. Sergeant!' The Major issued a series of orders to the Sergeant and the other police. 'I'm going back north with the others to collect the pathologist. I'll bring him up over the mountain today as long as we have enough light left. The mountain tracks will be too dangerous after dark.' She watched as Ganas, handcuffed, was being taken to one of the jeeps. 'He'll be arrested and jailed.'

'Deal gently with him, Major,' Cassie said. 'He hasn't killed anyone, Meg Taylor will attest to that. Also, he should be taken to Delphi, we still have questions for him.' When the Major looked as if she was about to argue, Cassie added. 'The Professor will want to speak with him too.'

The Major pursed her lips as Ganas shot Cassie a grateful look.

'He kidnapped you and Helena,' Iraklidis said, brow furrowed, as he gripped the interpreter tighter. 'Not that either of you should have been at the police station at all!'

'Actually he didn't kidnap me, I stowed away for the ride,' Cassie answered. 'And I don't think he meant any harm to Helena either. He was only scared. As for being at the police station, we came to warn you that you were going to arrest the wrong man.'

You've got some explaining to do yourself.

The Security Chief looked at her over Helena's head, a question in his eyes.

'It's true, Yannis,' Helena said, looking up at him. 'He would never have harmed us.'

'You don't know that my dear. You'd be surprised what so-called harmless people are capable of.'

'When pushed,' Cassie said. 'Or when it suits them.'

The Security Chief shot Cassie a sharp glance as he opened the Jeep door for Helena, but she didn't respond. She was just too tired. She climbed into the rear seat and put on her seat belt as Iraklidis took the driver's seat and turned the ignition.

As she sank back into the leather of the back seat for the second time that day, Cassie looked down at her hands. They were clean of dried blood, she had washed them in the cabin kitchen, but they were shaking. This case was taking its toll. She focussed on controlling the tremor, breathing deeply and regularly, commanding her muscles to relax. The shaking stopped.

Now all she wanted to do was to get back to the Centre and have a hot shower, then to rest and unwind. But there was much to do before she could really do that.

◊ FIFTY EIGHT

'I'm very pleased and more than a little relieved to see you both alive and well,' the Professor said, smiling. 'You seem, Cassandra, to lead a life full of adventure. First a landslide, then a hostage taking. Not what I expected of a Prime Ministerial envoy.'

'I hesitate to remind you, Professor, that my adventures here in Delphi have been in pursuit of the murderer at your request,' Cassie stressed the last three words. Her response was jokey and polite, but made a point. She wasn't about to accept any criticism of her conduct when all she was doing was at the Professor's behest.

'Touché,' Professor Matsouka raised an eyebrow and crinkled his lips to stifle a smile. 'I cannot deny it.' His expression changed. 'And we are grateful to you, myself and the Minister.'

'Happy to help.'

Not entirely true, but hey...

They were sitting in the ministerial suite, Cassie and the Professor on one sofa, Iraklidis and Helena on another, with Meg on a third. Constable Ganas had been locked in the spare cell in his own jail, something which the occupant of the other cell found darkly comic. A pathologist would be arriving within an hour or so to conduct a full post-mortem on the body of Barbara Doukas and the remains of Stefan Schlange. A forensic team was expected too, though Cassie doubted that there was anything much left for them to find.

The room where they sat was filled with light from the setting sun, creating long shadows on the carpet. Iraklidis held Helena's hand in his.

She had showered and felt better for it, but the mirror told her that the tension and danger of the preceding days was beginning to show, quite apart from her physical injuries. Her eyes were red-rimmed with tiredness and tension and her skin was pallid beneath its outdoor tan. The doctor had checked her over and advised rest.

She had taken more painkillers so her back and shoulders no longer pained, but the inflatable cast on her ankle still irritated her.

Don't forget the real objective here.

'And I hope to see you and the Minister in London soon.'

'You will, Cassandra,' the Professor replied. 'You will. Now, has everything been resolved?'

'Not yet. It's almost certain that Schlange was somehow involved in or responsible for Barbara Doukas death,' she answered. 'Constable Ganas found his niece's key to the temple complex amongst those belonging to Schlange. The Austrian claimed he had found the key, but Ganas didn't believe him. The pathologist will be here soon and whatever is under the dead woman's fingernails should yield DNA to confirm if Schlange was her killer or otherwise. If it doesn't and given that both are deceased, with little likelihood of finding any more physical evidence, we may never prove who did it.'

The Professor looked at Cassie, expectant. 'There's more?' he asked.

'There are still pieces of the puzzle missing and I would rather we had the full story before we return to Athens, as, I'm sure, would you. We still don't know exactly what role Schlange played in Barbara's death or how he died, who killed him and why. The case isn't complete.'

'So where do we look next?' The Professor wasn't giving up. The full glare of publicity would be focussed on any inquiry and he didn't want to leave anything to chance.

'We know some of what happened to Barbara,' Cassie summarised. 'She met with a man in room eighteen, the room next to mine, on Monday night. She argued with him so loudly that I complained. Then they had to go elsewhere, probably to the temple complex.'

'Outside on the mountain?'

'I suspect she may have wanted to go to the Museum, but that plan had to be abandoned when they found the Museum occupied by Nico working late. So they had to go on to the temple site. Just how she induced her companion to meet her in room eighteen in the first place who knows, an implicit promise of sex perhaps, Barbara wasn't above using her physical charms to get what she wanted. She had something of a track record for doing that.'

Cassie shifted her weight and overtly looked at Iraklidis. She waited. The Security Chief sat very still. His eyes were wary, his jaw tight. In confusion, the Professor, Helena and Meg swivelled their gaze to Iraklidis as well.

As the silence lengthened Iraklidis scowled. 'What do you mean?'

'You neglected to mention that you met Barbara Doukas when you visited Delphi to carry out a preliminary security check.'

'I met her, yes. What of it?'

'Constable Ganas told me that you did rather more than that.'

Iraklidis swore with harsh vehemence. Cassie didn't understand the oath, but understood that his wrath was directed against her as well as the Constable.

The Professor snapped out a comment.

'She practically threw herself at me. She was an attractive woman, I'm only human,' Iraklidis argued.

Helena snatched her hand from Iraklidis grasp, folding it into a fist in her lap. Her lips were white, so tightly were they pressed together.

Too bad.

'You didn't think to tell us this? Privately, perhaps?' Cassie glanced Helena's way. 'It is material to the case.'

'I knew she wanted to go to Athens, and I had a good idea that that was why she was so... why she was behaving the way she was. That's all. I thought she wanted a weekend in the capital, some fun, no strings attached.'

He turned to face Helena and began to entreat her, ignoring the others in the room. Helena refused to look at him, eyes shining with unshed tears.

'The woman wouldn't leave me alone. She called and texted, wouldn't take "No" for an answer. She was trouble, I wanted no more to do with her. You can check my phone, it's all there, in my email account. Look.'

He pulled out his phone and opened up his email. They began to huddle around it, but the Professor sighed in frustration and turned on the TV in the corner of the room, plucked the mobile out of Iraklidis's hands and bluetoothed it to the TV. They all watched as the Professor scrolled down the emails.

'There,' Iraklidis said. 'That's the thread.'

Cassie could only watch them read it; she certainly couldn't understand it. Helena's eyes were focussed in intense concentration. Memorising the messages, Cassie surmised.

The Security Chief's angry expression gave way to weariness. 'I've thought it over many times since. She wasn't interested in me and wasn't about to trust me. She wanted to use me, as I used her.'

'You realise that you have been withholding evidence in a murder investigation, Yannis,' Professor Matsouka admonished. 'For whatever reason.'

'It wasn't material to the case, I thought–'

'That's not your judgment to make.' The Professor's voice hardened. 'And it would all have come out anyway.'

'I know.' Iraklidis looked at his shoes. 'I hoped we'd all be back in Athens by then.'

And I'd have gone home. So an interpreter wouldn't be required.

But Iraklidis was fooling no-one but himself if he thought he'd get away with that. The press would have got hold of it or the political opposition. He'd have risked his job and his career for nothing. He'd risked it because he cared so much about what Helena would think if she knew about his fling with Barbara Doukas.

The Security Chief glowered at Cassie his mouth twisted.

'Oh!' Helena gave a cry of surprise. 'Look, Barbara attached some photos. And look…'

The TV screen showed an image. Of a young man standing beside a set of gates.

'That's the same photo as is on Alecto Doukas's stairs,' Cassie said.

'Alex Ganas's father when he was young, outside the Polytechneion with his friends... wait a minute. Can you enlarge that, Professor?'

The image expanded, getting slightly blurry.

'Look, second from the left,' Cassie said. A tall, slim figure with floppy blond hair and bright blue eyes.

'That's Schlange!' Meg said.

'Yes, I wonder if Barbara recognised him too. Nico said she was curious about her family history. Maybe that was what they were arguing about. Dr Wild told us Schlange didn't like talking about that period in his life.'

'That doesn't mean we can be sure he killed her,' Iraklidis said. 'Only the DNA will tell us that.'

'We'll see,' Cassie looked at Meg Taylor. 'He was a quick-witted man, cold-blooded enough to follow a woman along a dark mountain road with a view to accosting her, but he miscalculated when he tried to accost you, Meg. Ganas filled in the details for us about the Corycian Cave. He told us how he and his sister came across you, running on Thursday, and how you joined them.'

'Yes.'

'Can you tell us what happened when the three of you began looking for the missing man? You fanned out and were walking towards the top of the Phaedriades...'

'You seem to know it all already,' Meg said. 'We searched around the entrance to the Cave and found his tracks. He'd headed into the scrubby trees on the plateau towards the cliffs. So we started after him. It was misty and wet, we were walking through low cloud. I was the most westerly, Ganas in the centre and Alecto Doukas out to his left.'

'Could you see the others?' Cassie asked.

'Sometimes. At other times they became indistinct in the mist, Alecto especially, as she was furthest away.' Meg brought her brows together in irritation. She didn't like being interrupted.

'We beat the undergrowth, scaring the birds, trying to ensure he wasn't hiding, waiting for us to pass,' the former athlete licked her lips. 'We were hunting him, I felt uncomfortable about that.'

'Uncomfortable,' Cassie repeated the word. 'Yet you left him out on the mountain on Tuesday night?'

'I was in a rage then. He's everything I hate about–' with an apology in Greek to the Professor, 'about successful men. They betray their wives's trust, harass their students, jump women in the dark. And get away with it! Then they'll turn on a woman if she isn't their idea of female. Men like that destroyed my career. So yes, I left him on the mountain side. It was freezing that night and I'd hoped he'd get really, really cold, maybe even be hurt. I admit I thought all those things and then I walked away. Served him right. And now, it seems, he could be a murderer.' The outburst dwindled away. After a moment or so of silence, Meg spoke again, but quietly, almost hesitant. 'Anyway, at one point there was some sort of commotion beyond Alecto and we stopped. But she shouted that it was all alright, so we carried on. It was shortly afterwards that we heard the scream.'

'Think carefully before you answer my next question,' Cassie said. 'Could Alecto Doukas have pushed Schlange off the cliffs?'

Meg's eyes glazed, she looked inwards.

'No,' she answered eventually. 'We weren't near enough to the edge for her to be able to do that. Even though we couldn't see it, I knew where the cliff edge was because of the scream. It must have been twenty feet in front of us. And besides, Alecto's small and Schlange would have fought her. He was a tall, strong man, even if he was injured. On Tuesday night I was surprised by how strong he was and he was drunk then.'

'But if it wasn't Alecto Doukas who pushed Schlange off the cliff edge, who was it? Or was it an accident?' The Professor asked.

'I don't know,' Cassie answered. 'It's one of the loose ends that need tying up. But first we need the pathologist's opinion.'

'Very well,' the Professor said. 'The roads will be open shortly, I hope, and we will be leaving as soon as they are. This case needs to be resolved before then.'

◊ FIFTY NINE

Cassie stood at the full height windows in her room, looking out on the remains of the spectacular sunset. The last rays of sunlight were painting the white snow of the very top peak opposite with orange. The Centre and the guesthouse were in shadow. Dusk was falling and the temperature was dropping, so she didn't venture on to the balcony.

Julie Anderson

Since her arrival here, less than a week ago, two people had died and several lives had been blighted. The past had, it seemed, reached out to echo down the generations of the Ganas family. Stefan Schlange was prime suspect in the murder of Barbara Doukas. He had her key to the temple site and had almost certainly argued with her, if the sounds Cassie had heard in this very room indicated anything. Could he have been afraid of her, of something she knew? Or was there more to it?

She puzzled over what her next move here in Greece should be. There were answers to find in Athens about Schlange's history and his relationship with the Ganas family.

Cassie began to assemble her clothes and travelling items, preparing to repack the small suitcase she had only unpacked last Wednesday. Within, in its transparent covering, was the pyjama top.

At least she now knew what had happened on the mountain road. Her shadow had been Stefan Schlange, not Lawrence Delahaye, nor one of his creatures. She was mightily relieved, but she wasn't about to let her guard down. Delahaye would, she was certain, be coming after her, it was only a matter of time. She would track him down, but that was for another day.

Briefly her thoughts went back to the walker in the cloud and mist on the mountain. They had thought he might be the man in the Cave but knew now that the man in the Cave was Schlange. This was still a mystery.

The whirlwind romance between Helena and Iraklidis now appeared to be over. The interpreter had refused to speak with her lover after they left the ministerial suite, despite all his entreaties. She had shown considerable resolve; just as she had shown resourcefulness and courage earlier in the day. Helena had turned out to have a lot more backbone than Cassie had originally given her credit for. Cassie had some sympathy with the Security Chief, what he did he had done before he met Helena. Yet it revealed him as someone who used women casually for his own pleasure and was prepared to deceive, not just Helena, but Cassie and the Professor too. Would he even keep his job?

It's better that she knows. She's better off without him.

It was also now obvious how the Major had manipulated the Security Chief. She had threatened to tell them all, including Helena, about his earlier visit to Delphi and his involvement with Barbara Doukas. Yet there was definitely something else. Cassie couldn't put her finger on it.

Time was running out. The pathologist and the Major were expected at the police station later that evening. Everyone would be leaving the following morning, when the road would, it was anticipated, be cleared. It was likely that she would have to remain in Greece for an inquest or something similar, if the case was not resolved.

Nonetheless, the Minister and his party were coming to London. Her first mission for David Hurst had been successful. Not without effort and at some cost – she felt as if she had been put through a mangle, her joints stiff and aching, her ankle still in its cast. But she'd done it.

She acknowledged to herself that she really did need to take some leave and rest. It would be good to be back in Clapham, to see Spiggott again, to give her all the cuddles she could want, to be in her own place. A longing to be in her own home sliced into her with unexpected ferocity, an almost physical need.

But she couldn't go home yet. What was the Greek procedure for an unnatural death?

The telephone lines were working again, so she could contact Siobhan and request some research. It was early afternoon in London. Cassie picked up the handset from the telephone on her bedside table, pressed Reception and asked for an outside line. Not long after she had keyed in the number, she heard Siobhan's voice.

'Hello! What's going on? Why haven't you rung me?'

'Siobhan, it's so good to hear you,' Cassie said, with feeling. And it was. Very good. She realised how isolated she had felt.

'Are you alright?'

'Yes, well, I've got some bumps and bruises because of the landslide and hiding in a car boot before being taken hostage by a man with a gun hasn't exactly helped, but–'

Cassie began to laugh as Siobhan shrieked.

'I've been batting back requests from all over the place,' Siobhan said, when she eventually calmed down. 'Number Ten wants an update and the Foreign Office. Even someone from the Ambassador's staff has been in contact and they're in Athens!'

'There was a blizzard and we were cut off, with the telephone lines down,' Cassie explained. 'Completely isolated. Not before my suitcase turned up, by the way. Thanks for that.'

'I didn't do anything really,' Siobhan replied. 'So, anything to pass on?'

'Tell Number Ten mission accomplished and tell the Foreign Office, but Number Ten first. We have to give them the good news and not let the Foreign Office take the credit. Tell them I'll give more detail when I can. It'll be easier when I'm back in civilisation tomorrow evening. I'll be in touch then.'

'Ok. What about the Ambassador? Do I contact him too?'

'No. I'll suggest to Helena that she does that,' Cassie said, then clarified. 'The interpreter. It'll get her some brownie points and she deserves them.'

'What else can I do?'

'Find out about what happens over here when an unnatural death is reported. I don't think they have coroners and inquests but there must be something, I need to know the procedure and the jurisdiction, particularly if I'm going to have to attend whatever it is. Plus, everything you can glean on Dr Stefan Schlange of Linz University.' She spelled out his name. 'Especially his formative years,' she paused. 'He studied in Athens.'

'Inquests or similar? What's been going on? Has someone died?'

'Yes, there have been a couple of deaths, one was definitely a murder. I'll tell you about it when we have a secure line. Look, I must go now. Fax through anything which isn't confidential. Bye.'

'Ok. Cassie… take care. Bye.'

There was one more thing to do. When the outside dialling tone returned she punched another UK number into the phone, she needed to get a name and address.

◊ SIXTY

Cassie took each stair tread one at a time as she descended the stairs. The reception area was empty, save for one solitary figure, Elise Forché. She looked up at Cassie from where she was sitting, an anguished expression on her face, lips turned down.

She's still here?

She had forgotten Elise, Jim Norton and Mike Robbins in the recent dramas. Of course, they couldn't leave the Centre either. As Cassie reached the foot of the stairs, Jim arrived to sit opposite Elise. He fidgeted, shifting his position and looked even more uncomfortable when he noticed Cassie's approach.

'How are you?' he asked as he stood. 'You were caught in the landslide, we heard.'

'I'm okay, thanks,' Cassie answered. 'Bumps and bruises mostly.'

'Your leg–'

'Isn't broken, fortunately. I'm told the road should be cleared tomorrow morning, then we can all go home. You're going back to Paris?'

'Er, yes.' Jim cast a hopeful glance in Elise's direction. The Frenchwoman shifted her gaze and stared out of the window into the dark. 'Via Athens. You?'

Cassie nodded. 'I suspect I'll have to hang around for the legal proceedings.'

Jim's eyes focussed right, over her left shoulder and Cassie turned to see Mike Robbins entering reception from the corridor to his room. He grunted in their direction but continued on into the cafeteria.

'You're going to work for him?'

'Yeah, in Washington,' Jim answered.

'Even after if you weren't successful with Minister Sidaris?'

'So you know about that too,' the American grimaced. 'Seems there's not a lot you don't know.'

'I don't know who killed Stefan Schlange.'

'Can't help you with that, I'm afraid,' he said, then lowered his voice. 'I – I've asked her to come with me.' He glanced once again at Elise. 'There are plenty of translating jobs in the Beltway. Mike's said she can even work for Greenforce if she wants.'

'Do you think that's likely?' Somehow Cassie couldn't see Elise Forché working for Big Oil, although Jim was right, there would always be translation work available in a place like Washington.

'I don't think she'll come. I didn't want to deceive her,' he continued. 'But Mike was hell bent on secrecy.'

Not a bad man, just a weak one.

A pinched smile on his face, Jim turned to sit down beside Elise.

Cassie crossed to the dining room. Helena was seated by the tall windows, alone. Another woman disappointed by a man. Cassie half raised her hand in greeting but received no response. The interpreter was staring out on to the terrace and beyond into the night, twirling her fork in some pasta.

She felt a twinge of guilt as she helped herself to some food.

Maybe it's you she doesn't want to speak to?

It had been part of Cassie's strategy to maximise the public shame and shock, so as to surprise the Security Chief into confessing. It was necessary. She hadn't considered the impact that would have on Helena.

Looking round the dining room she saw Mike Robbins taking a seat and she joined him instead.

'What do y'all want?' he drawled.

'To talk to you,' she answered. 'And you can drop the misogynist act, Mike. I have a suggestion which you may find useful.'

He grunted, but he was listening.

'Before I tell you what it is, I want you to answer one or two questions.'

'Shoot.' The Texan continued eating.

'On Monday evening you and Jim went for a walk after dinner,' Cassie began. 'Where did you walk to?'

'Nowhere in particular, just round the grounds. I wanted to see where the Minister was lodged.'

'Did you see Barbara Doukas on your perambulations?'

'Huh, yes, as it happens. She was outside their suite, trying to schmooze her way in.'

'Jim didn't mention that.'

'Jim didn't notice anything, he was too frightened that his Frenchie girlfriend would spot us.'

'What was she saying? Barbara? And don't tell me you don't speak Greek, Mike, the Minister is widely known not to speak English. Your company wouldn't have sent you if you couldn't understand what was being said.'

Robbins shrugged. 'The Doukas woman was asking after the Security Chief, Iraklidis. Seems she wanted his help. He certainly has a way with the ladies. Just as well your friend should find that out now.' He waved his hand airily in Helena's direction.

So Iraklidis was Barbara's target. Only when he wasn't there, she tried Meg.

'I'm told your overtures to the Minister weren't successful,' she said.

The American grunted. 'Who by?'

'Never you mind.'

Robbins bared his teeth in an unpleasant smile.

'But then, that's what'll be in the Press Release.'

Robbins's face took on an entirely neutral look, devoid of expression.

'What if you didn't really expect to get agreement at this meeting,' she proposed. 'What if it was just a precursor, to opening less-public channels for discussion. Not with the Minister himself, of course, that would be much too dangerous for him, given public opinion at the moment. With a trusted advisor maybe, like the Professor.'

Robbins put down his fork, slowly and deliberately.

'And in a neutral venue,' she went on. 'Like London, for example.'

His stare grew intense.

Yes, that's it.

'I will, of course, be advising government colleagues on the visit of Minister Sidaris and his party. My colleagues in the trade department have their own contacts in your industry, mainly, though not exclusively, with British companies. I imagine that they will find this intelligence very useful.'

'And your suggestion is?'

'That you contact your British counterparts yourself. A joint British-American approach would be much more acceptable, with Greek or other European partnership.'

Greece needs cheap energy and there are clearly ongoing negotiations, she'd reasoned earlier. At least if the EU was involved better environmental standards would be applied and Britain might get a little something from it too.

'I don't think so.'

'I do. Otherwise you might find that you can't manage a meeting with the Professor in London, whereas your British competitors can.'

Robbins's mouth turned down at its edges.

He could force things, but that wouldn't sit well with Professor Matsouka. He has little choice. And…

'Your European liaison man could be Jim Norton,' she said, rising. 'He doesn't need to move to Washington at all. Goodbye Mr Robbins. Perhaps we will meet again in London.'

◊ SIXTY ONE

Cassie clambered out of the ministerial limousine and hobbled in an ungainly fashion after Helena. Wet pavements and the puffer-cast on her leg made it difficult to move quickly and she caught up with her just outside the police station building. The interpreter hadn't slowed until she could no longer avoid it without seeming rude and insubordinate.

'Helena, wait.'

The interpreter stood, saying nothing, in the pool of light from the lamp above the door.

'My PA back in London tells me that the Embassy has been asking her for up-dates. Now we have telephone lines again it might be politic for you to contact them. Let them know what's happening.'

'I have, just before coming here.'

'Good.'

Oh well, so much for an olive branch.

They walked into the police station together, neither speaking. It was, Cassie mused, always the fate of those who brought bad news to be blamed.

The Professor had remained at the Centre, but Iraklidis and Meg Taylor had accompanied Cassie and Helena. Inside, the Major and her Sergeant together with a short, bespectacled man, were sitting on upright chairs near the small fire. At every available opportunity Iraklidis's eyes sought Helena's, but, Cassie noticed, the interpreter kept her gaze lowered, avoiding looking at both the Security Chief and herself.

The Major stood to make the introductions.

'Dr Niarchos, the pathologist,' she gestured towards the newcomer, who gave a small bow.

It was clear that she already questioned him. This meeting was for their benefit.

'Pleased to meet you, Dr Niarchos,' Iraklidis said. 'Have you conducted your examinations?'

'I have conducted a full autopsy on both cadavers.' The pathologist spoke English.

'Sit, please.' The Major resumed her seat and the others followed suit, except for Iraklidis, who hovered behind Helena.

'Barbara Doukas died from asphyxia due to strangulation after a short struggle,' Dr Niarchos said. 'A week ago, sometime during the night of Monday and Tuesday – I'm sorry, after all this time I can't be more precise than that. She fought her attacker and I'm hopeful that the matter under her fingernails will provide DNA. This has been sent to the laboratory at Amfissa.'

'It will still yield DNA?' Cassie asked.

'It should,' the pathologist answered. His precision with words reminded Cassie of Bill Pottinger, the forensic pathologist she had worked with in London.

'Was she raped or abused?' she continued.

'I don't believe so.'

'Are there any indications on the body of who the murderer might be?'

'Ms Doukas wasn't a large, or especially strong, young woman and finger marks on her upper arms suggest that her assailant was someone considerably larger. A man or a large boned woman. That's all I can say.'

It'll all come down to the DNA.

'If that is all regarding Ms Doukas?' the pathologist asked, and no one had any further questions. 'I'll move on to the remains of Dr Schlange. Multiple fractures to legs, arms, ribs and spine. Skull fractured – all consistent with a fall from a great height. Interestingly there were signs of his being injured before the fall, with healing already having begun.'

No one gave any indication of having known about the earlier injuries.

'Were there traces of any medication in his body?' Cassie asked.

'Yes, he had been taking opiates, they were still in his bloodstream.'

'I don't suppose his killer left any traces?'

'Not that I could find,' the pathologist replied. 'The injuries from the fall would have eradicated just about everything.'

Cassie sat back.

'Does anyone else have questions for Dr Niarchos?' The Major looked around the assembled group.

'When will we get the results from the lab?' the Security Chief asked.

'Within a couple of days, I hope.'

'Have your forensic colleagues found anything?' Cassie asked.

'I believe fingerprints were taken from the head rest in the police

Jeep, the first victim's key and the items found in the Cave, as well as your suspects and the bodies,' the pathologist replied. 'And blood samples where appropriate.'

'Thank you, Dr Niarchos.' The Major rose, as did the pathologist. 'Are you staying here overnight?'

'Yes. I'll be going down the mountain tomorrow when the road opens. I'll be making my report to the public prosecutor. There will be an inquiry.'

'Sergeant, could you take Dr Niarchos to the guesthouse, where a room can be arranged for him.'

The Sergeant accompanied the pathologist out of the jail.

'Where does that leave us?' Meg said, eyebrows raised.

'It confirms what we already believed,' Cassie replied. 'Last Monday night Barbara Doukas was murdered, the DNA test will tell us definitively if Stefan Schlange was her killer. I have insufficient knowledge of your legal system to understand what happens next. In the UK, the coroner would formally record the murder, but I doubt that the killer would be prosecuted if he was already dead.'

'Do you think that's going to satisfy Alecto Doukas?' Meg Taylor asked.

'I suppose not,' Cassie said, thinking about the Furies. 'But I'm not sure what would. Justice isn't merely vengeance, though there's an element of retribution and of reparation. Schlange had a family too, what of them?'

'We still don't know the facts of his death,' Iraklidis said. 'Presumably, it'll all come out during the inquiry which Dr Niarchos mentioned.'

'Where and when will that be held?' Cassie asked.

'An investigating prosecutor will be appointed. Usually in a case like this that would be in Amfissa,' the Major answered. 'But, given the nationality of one of the deceased, your own involvement and that of one of the ministerial party...' she indicated Meg Taylor, '...it's more likely to be the capital.'

For the final act of the drama.

It seemed fitting that the denouement should be played out where Schlange's involvement had begun so many years ago.

'There are a couple of things I'd like to do first,' Cassie said. Everyone looked at her, expectant. 'I'd like to speak with Constable Ganas again. Can we bring him in?'

◊ SIXTY TWO

Alex Ganas sat beside the little gas fire, self-consciously holding his handcuffed hands before him. Cassie was pleased to see that he hadn't been subjected to the same indignities Balasz Kouris had.

'Constable Ganas,' she began. 'I think you can help us clear up one or two things.' She extracted her phone from her pocket.

The policeman grunted assent and took the phone when it was handed to him. He looked at the screen.

'I saw it on your sister's wall,' Cassie said, referring to the photograph she had called up. 'Your niece had seen it too. She sent it to Mr Iraklidis. Nico told us that she had been delving into family history.'

Ganas looked at Cassie from the side of his eyes, his head slightly bowed.

He knows. And now he knows that I know too.

'Do you think she recognised him?'

'I don't know,' he said, Helena translating. 'I didn't recognise him myself at first. It was only when he was in the Cave and began raving about the past that I began to wonder where I'd seen him before.'

'When was your sister Alecto born?' Cassie asked. 'She wasn't in any of the family photographs I saw yesterday. They showed only your parents and you.'

The Constable gave a sad smile. 'October 1974.'

'And the date of the student uprising was?'

'November 1973.'

'When did you realise that you and your sister didn't have the same father?'

Helena gasped.

The Constable hesitated for a moment, then answered. 'I've been suspicious about my sister's paternity for a while,' he said. 'We look very different. People made comments, even when we were children.'

'Your sister has blue eyes,' Cassie said. 'That's quite rare here. As far as I could see, no one in all those family photographs had blue eyes, even the black and white photos showed dark-eyed people. Neither did either of the parents in your family photograph. It's a recessive gene so it could have been a genetic throwback, but it more likely indicates that you and your sister didn't share a father.'

'My father, whose photograph you have seen, went missing shortly after the student uprising,' the Constable said. 'Schlange had blue eyes like that.'

Iraklidis shook his head in amazement and the Major leaned forward, her mouth slightly open, transfixed by the conversation.

'Many went missing, I understand,' Cassie said. 'Taken by the regime.'

'Is that what you think happened to your father?' Iraklidis asked the Constable.

'Yes. But if my father was taken, he couldn't be Alecto's father too. That had to be someone my mother knew and trusted, someone already close to her, who was there when my father went missing.'

'And offered comfort?' Iraklidis said. 'Did you consider that she may have been coerced?'

'Yes, it was a lawless time, or rather, those who were supposed to enforce the law broke it when it suited them. It wouldn't surprise me if rape happened. But Philo, our mother, wasn't part of the uprising, she was at home looking after me. It was in the following months that Alecto was conceived.'

'So, a friend or neighbour,' Cassie said. 'Or a fellow student, as you've already considered.'

'I tried asking family members, our parents's contemporaries, but many had died or moved on and those who remain don't speak of that time. Many of the official records were destroyed, undoubtedly to protect the identity of collaborators and fellow travellers. Certainly the university's records have huge gaps.'

'You checked?'

'Yes, I used official channels, as well as doing my own research. My sister doesn't know about any of this, by the way,' Ganas continued. 'She doesn't know anything about what happened to my father, the man she thought was her father. I didn't realise that my niece was trying to find out too.'

'Is that what she wanted my help with?' Meg said, aghast. 'On Monday night when she came to the ministerial suite? And I turned her away.'

'She was probably looking for me to ask me the same,' Iraklidis said, shamefaced. 'I wouldn't help her either.'

Helena sniffed.

'Did you question Schlange about the past?'

'I tried,' Ganas replied.

'He was raving by then,' Meg said. 'Hallucinating and delirious. He didn't make any sense at all. I urged the Constable to get him to a doctor, even though the man had assaulted me.'

'Is that what you thought?' Cassie raised an eyebrow at Ganas.

'I wasn't sure,' the Constable licked his lips. 'I wondered if it was all an act. It was possible that he had an infection in his wound, but – I think he was a clever and a calculating man. He would do whatever he had to in order to ensure his release. He wasn't going to answer my questions.'

'Thank you, Constable Ganas.'

The Constable was returned to the cells.

'Cassie, when did you realise?' Helena asked, her hauteur forgotten.

'That Stefan Schlange could be Alecto Doukas's father?' Cassie replied. 'The photographs started me off. There were no family groups containing both Ganas and his sister and their parents. Alecto didn't feature at all. Then I began thinking about why Barbara Doukas was killed. Was it random, a coincidence, or was there a specific motive? She had a mighty argument with someone in room eighteen, so she knew something, or was going to do something, which that man wanted to prevent or alter, maybe? The question then was, who was the man in room eighteen? For a while I thought it might be Kouris, but there were no links between him and Barbara. Then we found that Barbara's family came from Athens, where Schlange had attended university and we discovered that Barbara planned to go there.'

Cassie glanced at Iraklidis, who flushed.

'You would have been doubly useful to her,' she said to him. 'As someone who could show her around, but also someone who had access to records and data.'

'But, if Stefan Schlange was the father of Alecto Doukas, Cassie,' Helena began. 'It means that...'

'Schlange may well have killed his own granddaughter.'

There was a small silence as that realisation sunk in.

'So he jumped then? Suicide?' Iraklidis said.

The action of a man overcome with shame. You might think that Yannis Iraklidis, but would Stefan Schlange?

'Maybe,' Cassie answered. 'Or maybe not. Schlange may not have known that she was his granddaughter. She certainly didn't know and couldn't have told him.'

'The idea of a ritual killing was completely wrong then?' Helena said.

'Yes, I confess I was way off there.'

'So why was she placed like that?'

'I don't know.' Cassie shrugged. 'Some trace of religiosity perhaps, because of the location. We'll never know. And we still don't know what happened to Stefan Schlange. I don't like that. Neither will the Professor.'

'Time has run out Cassie,' Iraklidis said. 'Our investigations conclude when we leave and we leave tomorrow.'

◊ SIXTY THREE

The others had gone ahead and only the Sergeant remained in the police station office when Cassie slipped through the side door into the little jail. Both prisoners looked up as she entered. Cassie pointed to Kouris and the Constable lay down on his truckle bed.

'Mr Kouris, I wanted to thank you for your help the other day,' she said to the activist who had risen and now was standing close on the other side of the cell bars.

He shrugged. 'I have no fight with you.'

'Nor I with you, though I confess that you were my main suspect for the murder for a while,' she smiled at him. 'But, in fact, you are exactly as you seem, an environmentalist trying to force a democratically elected government into greater transparency. How did you manage to get the word out about Greenforce, by the way?'

'The same way I told you what I could hear inside,' he said, glancing up at the small rectangle of black window. 'Did they cause a stir?'

'They did enough to get some more publicity,' Cassie responded.

'Good.' He smiled.

'So what's next for you? Have you been charged? Will you be?'

'I doubt it, a high-profile court case would generate even more publicity. No, they'll probably let me out soon. We'll carry on, trying to find out what's really going on, exposing the wrongdoing in the hope that public pressure forces change. It's what we believe, we can't afford to allow fracking in Greece.'

'Hmmm, if I were you, I'd keep an eye on what various OECD personnel might be doing,' she suggested, circumspect. 'And where they might be going next. I met a fellow at the conference, a Jim Norton, now he's an interesting chap. A US State Department employee, on secondment and moving on from the OECD next year I'm told.'

Balasz Kouris raised an eyebrow. 'Well, thank you, Ms Cassandra Fortune, envoy of the Prime Minister of the United Kingdom,' he said, and chuckled.

Job done.

'Goodbye, Balasz Kouris.'

Cassie turned to leave, meeting the Sergeant in the doorway.

'They're waiting for you,' he said. 'What's so funny?'

'Nothing. Nothing at all.'

Athens

TUESDAY

(one week later)

◊ SIXTY FOUR

The District Court was in the back of a local government building near Omonia Square. The square lay at the end of the road running straight to the Acropolis and the Areopagus, the ancient hill where trials had been held since the 5th century BCE. At the foot of the hill the classical temple to the *Erinyes* or Furies stood beside a basilica dedicated to Dionysus.

Cassie could see the distant escarpment but lost sight of it as the taxi drew up to the kerb outside the court. She spotted Helena sitting on a stone bench to the side of the double doors into the building, waiting. She wasn't the only one. There was a huddle of people, some carrying cameras, others talking into mobile phones. Press, probably waiting for the Minister.

But Sidaris wasn't scheduled to attend that day. Maybe it was Meg, the glamorous Olympian, they were after? She climbed from the car and the press pack surged across the pavement towards her.

What? Me?

Cameras clicked and microphones were thrust at her, but Cassie ignored them all and barged through the scrum towards the doors, neither listening to nor looking at any of them. At the edge of her vision she saw Helena heading in the same direction too.

As the doors swung closed behind her, Helena was at her side. Two security guards took up position at the doors.

'The press won't be allowed in until just before it starts,' the interpreter said. 'But I don't understand why there are so many here and why, forgive me, you are of such interest?'

'Not sure. They're probably after Minister Sidaris or the Professor, or even Meg Taylor,' Cassie said, but she had a sinking feeling in her stomach.

'I think the others are already here,' Helena said, leading her along a wide corridor. 'They will have come in through the side entrance, I checked it out yesterday.'

'Thank you,' Cassie said vehemently. 'I'm very grateful for your help.' And she was.

The chill between them had thawed a little since their return to Athens. Helena seemed to have decided to forget Cassie's cruel exposure of Iraklidis's liaison with Barbara Doukas; she certainly didn't refer to it.

The two women were no longer thrown together for sixteen hours a day and each of them had some space, which may have helped. Maybe the Embassy had told Helena to be helpful. For whatever reason relations had improved, but the ease and friendliness which Cassie had once felt in Helena's company had not returned.

It's my fault, I could have done things differently, but I was too mean spirited and envious.

How could I have been like that? How?

Professionally, they still worked well together.

'Once we've finished here, I'm going to visit this man,' Cassie handed a business card to the interpreter. 'He's a private investigator and I'm told he's good. I want to try and find out what happened to the Ganas family and Stefan Schlange back in 1973. To tie up the loose ends.'

'I think that would help Alexandros and Alecto Doukas, especially Alecto,' Helena scrutinised the card. 'To know. We should all understand how we got to where we are.'

Oh yes, I realise that now.

'Anyway, if the Embassy asks about his invoice, this is what the expenditure was for.'

'Ok,' Helena said. 'But the inquiry first, what do you think is the best result for us?'

That Professor Matsouka and the Minister aren't involved any more.

'That the whole cycle of killing and revenge ends, with as little fuss and publicity as possible,' Cassie replied. 'Barbara Doukas was unlawfully killed by Stefan Schlange, who is classed as a deceased offender and therefore cannot be charged. I fear it's unavoidable that Alexandros Ganas will be prosecuted, the question is, what with?'

'He's not a bad man,' Helena said.

'I know and he was under an immense amount of emotional pressure, but he did wrong, even if he didn't kill anyone. Good people do bad things.'

Her phone rang. It was Siobhan. She was using the secure number.

'Excuse me, Helena, I have to take this.' Cassie veered to the other side of the corridor as she took the call.

'Siobhan. What's up?'

'Hi Cassie. I've got David Hurst for you.'

Cassie put her shoulders back and stood up straighter as she heard the low baritone of the Prime Minister.

'Cassie? David. How are you? I'm told you've been in the wars.'

'A landslide,' she replied. 'On Mount Parnassus.'

'Maybe the gods are trying to tell you something,' he chuckled.

Maybe they are!

'But you're okay now?'

'Yes, though...'

'The media?'

'How did you know?'

'We received prior warning that the UK press was going after you again and I've managed to keep a lid on that here. In Europe, Germany and Spain are supportive, but some of the rest of the EU is less anxious to help, so...'

'Prime Minister, if I've become the story then I must resign.'

'Oh no, I'm not having that. This is being orchestrated to achieve that very thing.'

'But...'

'I'm not losing my most effective envoy. The visit of Minister Sidaris and party has already been arranged for next month. Not an official visit, but within the rules, a return to old haunts and some Christmas shopping, with a little business to do too. Well done Cassie, this was better than I hoped for. It gives me plenty of time before the Greeks take over the Presidency of the Council.'

'Thank you, Prime Minister. I'm glad to have been of some assistance.'

'I want you to host the visit, oversee everything, the nuts and bolts. You know them now, know what would interest them, what they'd enjoy. After Christmas, well, it may be time for you to take a back seat for a while, get some rest. Take on something else in the spring.'

Am I being eased out, side-lined? Already?

'When are you returning?' Hurst asked.

'As soon as the inquiry into the deaths is over.'

I want to see justice done.

'Ok, keep my office informed and come and see me when you do.'

'Will do–' But he had rung off.

'Cassie, come on.' Helena was frowning. 'We need to go in now.'

'Ok, ok, I'm coming. It was my boss, that's all.'

Helena's mouth made a round "o".

◊ SIXTY FIVE

Courtroom C of the Omonia District Court was an airy room, warmed by a series of clanking radiators. Usually used for family, administrative and minor criminal proceedings today it held a public hearing to determine by what means, when, and where the two recent deaths had occurred. The examining judge would then decide whether or not to initiate criminal charges.

A desk on a raised dais was at the front of the room for the judge and a small dock for witnesses, with formal desks for legal representatives. The judge had already taken his seat on the bench when Cassie and Helena slipped in and sat on the nearest row of chairs. A lean man in a smart suit, his skull almost visible through his very short grey hair, sat at one of the advocates' desks.

On the front row of chairs were the potential witnesses, Professor Matsouka, Meg Taylor and Yannis Iraklidis sitting together, then Major Lykaios, with a hand-cuffed Alexandros Ganas and his sister, Alecto. Mr Marios the conference organiser sat behind them, with Dr Niarchos the pathologist. On the other side of the central aisle a tall woman with greying blonde hair was accompanied by a female companion, a younger version of herself.

Frau Schlange and her daughter.

The killings, the peculiar nature of such a public hearing and its press coverage meant that the court room was full. Under normal circumstances such an enquiry wouldn't have been in public and wouldn't even have taken place for months. Cassie identified the Professor's hand in expediting it. Above and to the rear of the room was a crowded press gallery.

The judge looked to be in his late thirties or early forties, a round headed man with a neat dark beard. Helena whispered a translation as he spoke.

'This is the formal introduction of the inquiry into the death of Barbara Doukas. The identity of the deceased is verified by her mother and uncle. All potential witnesses have been sworn. He's going through the circumstances now... how she went missing and her body was found. The investigation which followed...' Cassie heard her own name mentioned, which prompted a frisson in the press gallery, some sitting up and whispering. Yes, they were being paid, or otherwise directed, to focus on her involvement in the case.

'No mention of Yannis's preparatory visit,' Helena said, tight-lipped.

'That's good, Helena,' Cassie said, smiling in an effort to look sympathetic. 'For lots of reasons. It doesn't muddy the waters of the case.'

Helena sniffed. 'The judge has cut to the chase. Forensic evidence found on the body. He's calling the pathologist.'

Dr Niarchos stood and went to sit in the dock to one side of the bench. The judge asked questions and Niarchos answered. Again, Cassie heard her name – Niarchos must be explaining about the early examination of the body. The judge glared up at the press gallery as there was a slight stir. Silence returned.

'The DNA analysis shows that the matter under Barbara's fingernails belonged to Schlange,' Helena whispered. 'He was, Dr Niarchos says, undoubtedly her attacker and killer.'

The suited man sitting at one of the desks raised his hand, asking, Cassie assumed, for permission to question the pathologist. He looked professional and grave, as befitted the proceedings.

'Attorney Agathon,' Helena explained. 'Representing the Schlange family. He's asking how accurate the test for DNA is after seven days.'

Dr Niarchos answered at length.

'As accurate as it would be after two days or three, he says. DNA doesn't decompose. But...' Helena's eyes widened.

'What?'

'Schlange's DNA and that taken from Barbara Doukas confirm that they were close relatives.'

There was a shuffling and murmuring in the well of the court as people whispered to each other. The newspapers had reported the previously unknown familial relationship between the dead man and his alleged victim. A stifled sob came from Frau Schlange, who placed her head in her hands and was comforted by her daughter.

As there were no more questions Dr Niarchos returned to his seat and Major Lykaios took his place.

'The Major's describing the investigation, going over the dead woman's movements on the night she died. Schlange's having the deceased's key to the temple complex in his possession is evidence of his involvement.'

Again Attorney Agathon intervened and this time the judge replied.

'He's asking if the key has been identified as that belonging to Barbara Doukas by independent witnesses,' Helena said. 'The judge confirms that it has, including by the Director of the Museum.'

'I suspect he'll be asking a lot more questions when it comes to Schlange's death,' Cassie said.

He looks sharp. I hope our witnesses are up to answering his questions, especially Ganas.

'Is that it?' Cassie asked, as the judge appeared to already be summing up.

'I think so, yes, Barbara Doukas, unlawfully killed by Stefan Schlange.'

The judge was rising from his seat.

'Ten-minute recess,' Helena said. 'Toilet break.'

'That was quick,' Cassie said, checking her watch. The whole proceeding had lasted barely two hours. There had been no mention of Schlange's youth in Athens, or his involvement with the politics of that time. 'I guess the DNA evidence was too compelling.'

Cassie and Helena slipped out into the corridor, along with half the people sitting in the public seats. It was quite a scrum.

'Excuse me,' a blonde woman in sunglasses squeezed by, followed by a tall, bearded man in a blazer, also in sunglasses, wearing a straw trilby.

'Tourists.' Helena wrinkled up her nose. 'Can't they find better ways to spend their holiday? Cassie, the press isn't only here for the Professor, or even Meg Taylor. They're here for you, aren't they?'

'It's possible,' Cassie replied with a sigh. 'On my last case before this one, back in London, the media were used against me and the police by the same man who wants me dead.'

'And you think he's doing it again?'

'Yes.'

'But isn't he on the run now?'

'Yes, but he's still extremely wealthy and has plenty of leverage and contacts.'

'So he can still do you harm.'

'I fear so.'

'It's going well so far.' It was Yannis Iraklidis's voice.

He arrived at Helena's side, looking for a response from her. The interpreter said nothing and looked straight ahead.

'Yes. Let's hope it's as clear cut with Schlange, but I doubt it will be,' Cassie said, just as the usher came to stand by the doors to the courtroom. 'We had better go back in.'

◊ SIXTY SIX

The low buzz of chatter in the courtroom dissolved into quiet as the judge retook his seat. Attorney Agathon was studying his papers. The other desk remained empty, there was no legal counsel for Meg or for the Constable and his sister.

Wasn't that risky? Presumably the Professor, or whoever was advising him on the law, knew their business, but Cassie was surprised that counsel hadn't been appointed. Exactly what had happened to Schlange was still unknown, it was a loose end.

Cassie noticed Iraklidis sit down beside Helena rather than return to the others, occupying one of the seats vacated by the tourists, but she didn't have time to think about him, she was too busy trying to work out the Professor's strategy. He was bound to have one. She hoped that Ganas wasn't going to be thrown to the wolves.

Helena leaned closer and began to translate.

'The judge is running through Schlange's arrival at the conference, when he was seen late on Tuesday at the Tavern. His body found on the morning of last Thursday at the foot of the Phaedriades cliffs. He died of injuries consistent with a fall from those cliffs. The Major's going to give more details about the investigation now.'

Major Lykaios took up position in the dock.

'She's saying that Schlange accosted Meg Taylor on the road from the tavern and fell down the mountain slope. Meg went to look for him the following morning to check that he was alright and, when she found him, injured, reported the whole incident to the police.'

That might get Meg off the hook, but it puts the focus on Ganas.

'The local policeman rescued Schlange and took him to the police station for questioning and to receive medical care. Shortly afterwards, however, the body of Barbara Doukas, niece of Constable Ganas, was found and brought to the police station to occupy the only available cell.'

Attorney Agathon raised his hand.

Here we go.

'He's asking who witnessed the 'attack' on the mountain road. The Major says no one, but that witnesses saw Schlange afterwards and he was injured, which the pathologist confirmed.'

It was clear from his repeated glances towards Meg Taylor that Attorney Agathon was going to insist that he question her. The judge appeared reluctant to allow him to do so.

'Oh!' Helena said. 'The attorney says that if the injuries Schlange sustained when he fell down the mountain contributed to his death, Meg Taylor should be charged as an accessory.'

So, he's going for her because of her connections.

'She'll have to take the stand,' Cassie said, just as Meg rose from her seat. She looked as elegant as always, neat and stylish, but her face was paler than usual. Helena translated the evidence she gave to the judge, though they'd heard much of it before. Meg described leaving the Tavern, the unlit mountain road, a drunken Stefan Schlange waiting for her and his lecherous intent.

'At first I didn't feel threatened, I thought I could get past him and I could certainly outrun him.' There was a sprinkling of laughter in the courtroom. 'But I miscalculated and when he caught me I found it difficult to get free. I shoved him and he staggered backwards, falling at the edge of the road, down the slope.'

'What did you do then?' Attorney Agathon rose to his feet.

'I tried to look for him, but there wasn't enough light for me to see by. Then a group of the Austrians came round the bend and I went back to the Centre with them.'

'Callously leaving Dr Schlange on the mountain, injured, perhaps unconscious, perhaps dead?'

'It wasn't that steep and I thought he was probably waiting until we'd all gone, to avoid the humiliation. I realised later that he could be hurt and early the following morning I went to look for him. I found him, a little way down the slope. He seemed to have damaged his leg and needed medical attention, so I ran into Delphi and reported it all to the police.'

'Did any of the Austrians see Dr Schlange attack you? Or hear the attack perhaps?'

'I don't think so. They gave no sign of having done so.'

'They could have helped you find Dr Schlange. Why didn't you ask them to?'

'It was late, they had all had a lot to drink. I don't think that they would have actually been any help. In fact, they might well have hurt themselves.'

'Why were you on that road in the first place, Ms Taylor? Why were you in Delphi?'

'As an adviser to the Minister on sporting and cultural events,' she replied. 'Unpaid. I was a sports administrator as well as a runner.'

'In your adopted country, not the country of your birth,' the lawyer added. 'And it was a position from which you were forced to resign.'

Meg Taylor winced but said nothing.

'You are related to Minister Sidaris, I understand, and a regular member of his entourage.' The lawyer was about to go on, but the Judge intervened. There was a staccato exchange and the Attorney sat again.

'He says that this is an inquiry into Dr Schlange's death. If there is to be a prosecution it will happen subsequently,' Helena said. 'He's telling the attorney to limit his questions to matters concerning the death. I don't like the Attorney.'

Attorney Agathon is turning this into a political trial.

Now a clean-shaven Constable Ganas took the stand. He wore a navy suit so new Cassie almost expected to see its price tag. Ganas was the man easiest to attack. Would the lawyer do so?

'Dr Schlange was in your jail, Constable,' the lawyer said. 'Yet I understand that you took him to a mountain cave. Is that correct?' Ganas agreed. 'Why?'

'I believed he was connected with the murder of my niece, Barbara Doukas, as the court has found he was,' he said. 'I arrested him. When I searched his room I found, in his possession, my niece's key to the temple complex. It had been put on his key ring. A souvenir or trophy. I wanted to question him about it and about what happened to her and there was no room in the jail. I planned to return him to the jail once I'd questioned him, but it didn't work out that way.'

'Nonetheless you took an injured man to a cave, high on a mountain in winter?'

'It was the first place I thought of and... I didn't want to compromise anyone else. I'm trained in first aid, I knew his injuries weren't life threatening, I took bandages, medication, blankets, food and water. The Cave isn't like what you think; it was lived in for many years.'

'The man should have been in hospital. You took him to a cave.' The lawyer spoke calmly and his words were all the more powerful for it. He addressed the judge. 'The family will pursue this through the civil courts, sir, seeking reparation for breach of duty by the police under Human Rights legislation.'

The law applies to all, equally. Even murderers.

'He killed my niece!' Ganas looked close to tears and he was becoming enraged.

'You still have to observe due process, Constable' the judge said. His voice was soft, but it hardened as he continued. 'As a policeman the standards applied to you are even higher than to the general populace. Standards which you have, it is clear, fallen far below. Go on with your story.'

'I wanted my sister to see him, to help me question him about Barbara,' Ganas continued, after getting himself under control. 'But when we arrived at the Cave early the following morning he had gone.'

'And what did you do then, Constable? Did you alert your colleagues? Or tell the local doctor that an injured man was missing?' the lawyer asked.

'I didn't have the chance,' Ganas was again indignant. 'We tried to find him, looking all across the plateau and towards the cliff top.'

'Who was 'we', Constable?'

'My sister, myself and *Kyria* Taylor.'

'Ms Taylor, the Minister's friend and relative, again. How did she come to be there?'

'She was running on the mountain. When I saw her I asked her to help us.'

'To see your prisoner in the Cave?'

'He was the main suspect for the murder of my niece,' Ganas said. 'I thought it would be better to have an independent witness.'

'And one who is the confidante of a Minister of State.'

'To tell you the truth, at six o'clock in the morning halfway up a mountain, it didn't occur to me!'

The judge banged his gavel as there was a tittering in the courtroom.

Cassie's mind was racing. Agathon was focusing on the more outlandish aspects of the case and on Meg. When would he transfer his attack to the Minister, or would he await any subsequent trial for that, when he could get even more publicity?

Helena was translating again and Cassie tuned in.

'–visibility was restricted by the mist and low cloud. Minutes later we all heard his scream.'

At the judge's instruction Ganas stood down, to be replaced by Alecto Doukas.

She wore a suit of faded black in a style at least ten years out of date. Her eyes were sunken and ringed by shadows and her sharp cheekbones created hollows in her cheeks. Cassie half expected her to wring her hands and tear at her clothes and hair, so closely did she resemble a portrait of old-fashioned mourning.

'Mrs Doukas,' the judge began. 'Tell us what happened before Dr Schlange screamed.'

'We were pacing forward, the mist all around us. I couldn't see Ms Taylor at all and even Alex was only visible sometimes.

'Then what happened?'

'I found him,' Alecto Doukas said.

Helena gasped as she translated.

So did Meg Taylor and half the people in the room. Dr Niarchos leant forward in his seat. Iraklidis was staring at Alecto Doukas. Her brother, the Constable was white faced with shock.

'He appeared out of the mist. He was limping, but otherwise he seemed ok. I told him "I am the mother of Barbara Doukas, the woman you murdered." "Barbara Doukas?" he said, as if he didn't even remember her name. "My only child," I said to him. "Now I will not have grandchildren. Our family will die out." "Your brother is the policeman, Ganas?" Schlange said. "Come closer, let me see you." I wasn't afraid. I walked up to him.'

'What did he do then?'

'He stared at me. He seemed astonished, then he said, "My God, you look like her, though you're taller and your eyes are blue."' Alecto smiled.

'I have many old photographs at home. One shows the man I'd

thought of as my father standing next to his friends from his student days, before he went missing. One of the friends is tall and blonde with blue eyes. I've looked at that photograph so many times without really seeing it. But when I saw the man before me at the cliff top, even after forty years or more, I recognised him. That was when, for the first time, I realised he could be my father.'

Alecto's voice shook with emotion. She stopped speaking and breathed deeply. The courtroom was so quiet her ragged breaths could be heard, even near the back where Cassie and Helena sat. Then she continued.

'I realised after he did, I think. He'd worked it out, put two and two together. But I hadn't, not at first. I was still searching for some sort of revenge for what he had done. Not a civilised trial, when he would be treated with kid gloves, supported by expensive lawyers. I couldn't work out how to hurt him in the way that he had hurt me, when suddenly he turned on his heel. He ran away. He ran off the cliff.' She sobbed. 'But I didn't even want that. I wanted him alive to suffer.'

'I am his daughter, conceived years ago, after the student rebellion. You can see it when you know – my eyes are his.' She looked straight at the lawyer, then into the well of the court, so that everyone could see her startling blue eyes. 'He knew what it meant – he had killed his own grandchild.'

Noise erupted from the public and press gallery as people turned to their neighbours to exclaim or comment. The banging of the judge's gavel went on for some time, with a court official shouting for order. Finally, order was restored.

'When you came across Stefan Schlange did you tell your brother and Ms Taylor that you'd found him? They were searching for him too.' Attorney Agathon was on his feet again.

'No,' Alecto cast down her eyes, then raised them. 'I told them that the noise they had heard was nothing, that I'd disturbed a goat.'

'But you hadn't. You'd found the man you were all searching for, he was there in front of you. Why did you lie?' the lawyer persisted. 'Unless you have something to hide.'

Major Lykaios stood.

'Because I told her to,' she said.

◊ SIXTY SEVEN

The court usher stood and yelled for silence, but to no avail. Noise overwhelmed him, swamping the courtroom. The judge banged his gavel, again and again. Constable Ganas began to remonstrate with the Major, Meg Taylor was exclaiming, loudly, to no one in particular. Dr Niarchos shook his head from side to side, bemused.

Ignoring the noise round her, Cassie looked straight at Major Lykaios. *She'd followed them.*

Finally, the noise subsided and the judge recalled the Major to the stand.

'I didn't trust Constable Ganas, so I didn't want Mrs Doukas to alert him to my presence on the mountain. I wanted to apprehend Dr Schlange myself,' she explained. 'I'd followed them up the trail. The heavy mist deadened all sound, including of my Jeep. By the time I got to the plateau, I could see that they'd already found the Cave empty. I waited to see what they'd do next and, when it became apparent that they were going to search towards the top of the cliffs, I cut across the slope and got there not long after they did.'

The Major's hands drew a picture in the air as she recounted events.

'They spread out in a line. In the mist it wasn't hard to skirt behind them. Ganas was in the centre, with his pistol, his sister to his left and Ms Taylor to his right. The weakest of the three, physically, was Mrs Doukas. If Schlange was somewhere on that promontory and could see them, she would be the one he would confront, the one he would try to get past. So I stayed close to her.'

The Major paused, weighing her words.

'The promontory has only scattered vegetation. No trees; it's too exposed to the wind. I walked behind Mrs Doukas, where the ground slopes away to the left, before you get to the sheer cliffs. We were all hunting in the whiteness, though I was unknown to the other hunters.'

'I heard something happening ahead so I drew my pistol. The mist was particularly thick at that point and Schlange came out of nowhere, moving at a shambling run. I thought he was going to attack Mrs Doukas, but instead she spoke to him. He stopped and stared, transfixed, facing her, so close he could almost touch her. They talked and I crept closer.'

'He fled. I didn't have to threaten him, or fire my weapon, he simply turned around and limped away into the mist. Mrs Doukas cried out and her brother called to her. She turned around, searching for him in the mist. That's when she saw me and I put my finger to my lips. A few minutes later we all heard Schlange's cry. He must have run off the edge. It's easy to lose your sense of distance and direction when there are no landmarks, and you can only see a few feet in any direction.'

'And when you realise that you've killed your own granddaughter,' Cassie muttered, under her breath. 'Those whom the gods would destroy, they first make mad.'

And yet... Something still bothered her. Schlange didn't strike her as the type to commit suicide. He had murdered a young woman then returned to the Centre and the conference as if nothing had happened. On the following afternoon he'd walked past the building where her dead body lay, asking questions of the tour guide and engaging in the historical discussion alongside others who were unaware that she was there. That took a cool head. He'd then gone partying that night and looked for another woman. Was he the type to kill himself from shame?

There was a silence, interrupted only by the sound of Alecto Doukas, weeping.

'Regardless of what he may have done, Stefan Schlange should have stood trial, not be driven like an animal to his death.' The lawyer was pressing on, giving what sounded like a formal summing up. He paced up and down and declaimed, in a fruitless attempt to catch the attention of the courtroom. 'His fate was sealed as soon as he was taken from Delphi Police Station up to the Cave. Ganas couldn't then let him go for fear of the consequences. That the policeman, his sister and the Minister's friend didn't push him from the cliffs is almost immaterial, he was there because of Ganas and he and his accomplices hounded Dr Schlange to his death.'

Cassie watched the Professor, who was following the attorney's every movement.

'I request that this case is referred on to another court, to pursue a criminal trial for manslaughter. It is clear that, despite their close connections with the ruling party, certain individuals have a case to answer. Not even the most powerful are above the law and even the political elite cannot evade justice in a democracy.'

A fine speech, but is it justice he's serving?

The court was completely silent. Everyone waited for the judge to reply.

'These are proceedings to determine how Dr Schlange met his death,' the judge's voice was stern. As Helena's translation paused Cassie sat forward. 'As prosecutor in this case I find that Stefan Schlange's death was accidental. Whether or not due care was taken by those representing the authorities in their treatment of him is subject to question, in particular under the European Convention of Human Rights, Article 2 and, in consequence, there may well be further proceedings in another court.'

There was a hubbub in the courtroom. The court official demanded silence as the judge stood.

◊ SIXTY EIGHT

'What happens next?' Helena asked.

The courtroom was now almost empty. A group, consisting of Professor Matsouka, the Major, Meg Taylor and Alecto Doukas were waiting for the crowd to disperse. Constable Ganas had been taken away to the cells.

'I don't know enough about the Greek legal system to say,' Cassie replied. 'I suspect that Attorney Agathon will be advising his clients that they should seek a prosecution for criminal manslaughter.'

'So it isn't over,' Helena said.

'No, that family's tragedy has another act to play out yet,' Cassie replied. 'I just hope the Constable doesn't become collateral damage in a political dogfight.'

'Frau Schlange and her daughter deserve justice too,' Iraklidis said. 'And justice needs to be seen to be done. But the murderer is already dead and not killed directly by anyone's hand. Ganas will be charged, but this verdict is probably the least damaging to him.'

'When is he likely to be tried?' Cassie asked.

'The Attorney will press for an early trial so as to maintain momentum,' Iraklidis answered. 'We'll see whether or not he gets one.'

Somehow I don't think that'll happen.

'He'll also be pressing for the most serious charge.'

'Agathon's trying to make political capital?' Cassie asked. 'Why?'

'He may have sponsors in the opposition, or in the Minister's own party. There are always rivals. And it's a way to advance one's career, of course. The judge will be aware of that.'

If the Professor's applied some gentle pressure, he's not going to tell us about it.

Major Lykaios walked over to them, followed by Meg Taylor and Alecto Doukas. The three women stood together. Iraklidis twisted his lips.

'You were working the case by yourself all along,' he said with rancour.

'That's why you wouldn't stay at the Centre, why you stayed in Delphi town,' Cassie said. 'And which was where, incidentally, you garaged the SUV you and the Sergeant came in.'

Iraklidis stared at Cassie.

'How did you think they got to Delphi in the first place?' she said to him, then addressed the Major. 'You saw Constable Ganas and Ms Taylor when they went up the mountain on Wednesday night.'

'How did you know?' the policewoman asked.

'When I was questioning Constable Ganas in the police station just before we left Delphi Meg Taylor described Schlange as 'raving' while he was in the Cave. She had seen him of course, but that was the first you would have heard of her doing so. But you didn't react; it was no surprise to you. Which meant that you knew that she had gone up to the Cave with Ganas,' Cassie replied.

The Major half smiled as she nodded assent.

'Besides,' Cassie continued. 'In any murder the family of the victim is always the first port of call for any policeman or woman. An experienced investigator would always begin with them. So that's where you started and you realised, very quickly, that the answer lay there.'

'I believed that they were hiding something.'

'Did you follow them on Wednesday night?'

'No, I didn't know the way and it was dark. But I saw Ganas drive the police Jeep from the station with his passenger and take the mountain track. I thought the answer might lie up on the mountain, a view that was confirmed when Ganas returned and had an emotional and angry conversation with his sister.

Alecto began to protest, but the Major forestalled her. 'You really ought to keep your shutters closed.'

Cassie recalled the living room of the Doukas house, with its window shutters thrown back. Although the house lay at the top of Delphi town, anyone on the first floor of the buildings on the other side of the street would be able to see straight into that living room.

'So the following morning you lay in wait,' Cassie said.

The Major gave a thin smile. 'It was cold and unpleasant, believe me, at five in the morning. I didn't know which track they would take, the one to the Cave, or the one to the stadium, so I watched at the fork in the paths. The Jeep took the former.' The policewoman raised an eyebrow at Meg Taylor. 'I confess, I hadn't expected your involvement.'

'As you know Barbara asked me for help on Monday night,' Meg reminded the Major. 'I refused her.'

'So you felt guilty and bound to aid her uncle.'

'And it played out as you said.' Cassie smiled. 'I thought you were focusing on Balasz Kouris as a suspect because it was politically convenient to do so. In fact you were trying to distract us, throw us off the scent.'

'Not really, but I was trying to keep the politicians well away from the case at all costs,' the Major replied. 'Political interference ruins justice, which must remain impartial. You saw how political ambition skewed a case here today. Unfortunately, it's impossible to exclude politics altogether, especially when the police are, themselves, involved.'

'And you had leverage over our Security Chief here, too,' Cassie said.

'Yes, Ganas told me about the earlier visit to check the security arrangements and it wasn't difficult to wrest out of him the story of what happened between his niece and Iraklidis. He liked Nico Vasilakis – the boyfriend – and was very disapproving,' the Major explained, as if the Security Chief was not standing there. 'Given Iraklidis's infatuation with Ms Gatakis, he was anxious to avoid that coming to light.'

'Yannis!' Helena exclaimed, looking at Iraklidis. 'So that's why you wouldn't press the Professor to bring her into line.'

The Security Chief flushed and said nothing.

The Professor summoned Iraklidis and Meg with a beckoning wave.

'I must go,' Iraklidis said to Helena, lingering.

Helena gave the briefest of nods in acknowledgement, her face closed. Yet it was enough to please the Security Chief, who favoured them with a flashing smile before he walked off.

Cassie raised an eyebrow.

Will she take him back? Maybe she should.

Helena sniffed. 'I'd better report back to the Embassy,' she said and began to leave.

Cassie watched her take a few steps. Then, to her own surprise, she called out to the interpreter, who stopped and looked back. Cassie didn't know what she was going to say but she walked up to Helena.

'It's none of my business, Helena, what you do and who you do it with. It's entirely up to you. But I want to tell you this: I would give anything to bring back the man I lost. If I could go back in time, if I could change only one thing about my whole life, I would do whatever I could to keep him alive.' She paused, unsure of the right words to convey what she was trying to say. 'He wouldn't have to be with me, he'd just have to be alive and well. If that was the deal that the universe offered me, I would make it.'

Cassie blinked back tears, acknowledging the pain lying just below her skin, a churning morass of loss and guilt and rage. 'But the universe doesn't work like that. He died. Don't make the same mistake.'

Helena looked confused.

I can't blame her.

'What I'm trying to say is this. Yannis did a stupid thing, but he did it for the right reason. Yes, he should have told us earlier about Barbara and we should have known about the emails sooner because they would have helped with the case. That, however, was the only mistake he made. He fell in love too and did something stupid as a result. You must consider forgiving him for that. If you don't, you might never forgive yourself.'

Helena's expression softened. 'Thank you, Cassie,' she said.

◊ SIXTY NINE

Euripides Street was a narrow road off one of Athens's larger boulevards, made even narrower by the cars parked along both its sides. Tree roots erupted from broken paving slabs as the branches strained upward to find light. Cassie stepped round them, taking care. She no longer wore the puffer-cast, but her ankle was tightly strapped, bandages hidden under her trousers.

The street was of twentieth century blocks and the further along she walked the more squalid it became. Cassie consulted the piece of paper on which the address was written.

Filipos Krateros, 3rd floor, Stafsi Building, Euripides Street.

The Stafsi Building was at the furthest end of the street, a nondescript concrete edifice, its blank façade scattered with air conditioning machines like acne. Cassie took its tiny lift to the third floor. Krateros's office was dark and dingy, housing a cheap modern desk, with an old telephone directory supporting one of its legs. Files and papers were piled high upon it. An inner door was ajar, a rasping male voice emanating from it, speaking rapidly in Greek. The voice's owner appeared in the doorway seconds later, mobile at his ear.

Krateros was broad in the beam and of middle height. Black curls framed a face both flat and bulbous, with a nose askew and sharp, darting black eyes. The private investigator had left her a message on her phone asking her to come to his office. Back at the European Conference Centre she had phoned an ex-colleague in London and asked him who was the best man in Athens for a quiet investigation. She'd been given Krateros's name. She hoped this shrewd, tough brick of a man had managed to unearth the facts about what happened back in the 1970s.

'Hello,' she said. 'I'm Cassandra Fortune. We spoke on the phone.' Krateros ended his call and offered his hand, which she shook. They settled in chairs and he passed her an envelope, carefully sealed. She took it, almost holding her breath.

'Stefan Schlange,' Krateros said. 'I spoke with some of my contacts again to try and trace him. Some remembered him as being a particular friend of Alexandros Ganas at the Polytechneion. One man, who was involved in student politics himself, recalled that Schlange and Ganas had been active in an underground student society. It was societies like that which spear-headed the uprising of 1973.'

So Schlange <u>was</u> involved.

Krateros was waiting to speak again. She stopped fingering the envelope and gave him her full attention.

'May I ask what all this is about? I'm curious.'

'You'll have seen news reports of the murder of Barbara Doukas,' she explained. 'Stefan Schlange killed her. The question I need answering is, why? Only then will I understand what happened to Schlange.'

Krateros smiled and settled back in his chair to listen.

'At first I wondered if he had assaulted Barbara and feared that she would accuse him,' Cassie continued. 'But this idea didn't hold water. What I heard in the room next door to mine, where they met, didn't sound like an assault. Even if it was, he could simply have denied it and it was her word against his. Barbara was a twenty-six-year-old professional and independent woman who slept with whom she chose to, living in a rural, socially-conservative town. She might not have been believed.'

Cassie glanced at Krateros, who nodded slowly.

'Then I remembered a conversation I'd had about justice – particularly justice in 1974, when many of the collaborators with the regime of the Generals escaped before their trials. This is where your investigations come in.' A sweep of her hand invited Krateros to continue.

'Members of societies like the one that Ganas and Schlange belonged to were rounded up after the tanks were sent in, many of them never seen again,' he explained. 'Alexandros Ganas was one of those taken, Schlange was too, but he was released when others were not.'

'Because he was Austrian?'

'I spoke with someone at the Austrian Embassy and it seems that there were representations made on Schlange's behalf in '73 – my contact found the old file.' He indicated the envelope he had given to her.

Cassie opened it and took out the paper file, riffling through its contents. A photograph caught her eye, of Alexandros Senior with a group of friends. Next to him stood the tall, lanky figure of a young Stefan Schlange, blond then, but with the same cornflower blue eyes. It was similar to the photograph in Barbara's email to Iraklidis, the one on Alecto Doukas's wall.

'The intervention of the embassy may have saved his life, but the interesting thing is that he didn't then go back to Austria. The embassy tried to repatriate him, but he wouldn't go. Schlange stayed for another two months at least, until January '74. The address the Embassy had for him is in the file. It's the same address as for Alexandros and Philomeni Ganas.'

'The same address as before the rebellion, or different?'

'He moved in there after he was released from detention.'

'There might be lots of reasons for that,' Cassie speculated. 'He'd lost his earlier place or he hadn't paid his rent. It would have been natural for Philomeni to offer a home to her missing husband's friend. Alecto Doukas, the daughter of Philomeni, is almost certainly the result of an affair between her mother and Schlange.'

She paused to think things through.

'Constable Ganas told me he believed that Schlange was his sister's father and I wondered how Schlange would react if he thought that this would become widely known. Would such a youthful transgression, the comforting of his friend's widow, be held against him? How would it damage him? He may not even have known that he had a child. Indeed, he and his wife had been unable to have children, something one of his colleagues, Herr Freyer, told me was a cause of sadness to them both. A newly discovered daughter could have been welcome news. Would this coming to light be a secret worth killing for? I doubt it, it could be a reason for rejoicing. So, it couldn't have been this which frightened him so much that he killed Barbara to keep it quiet.'

'I think I see where you're going,' the detective said with a wry smile. 'By January '74 the dictatorship was already crumbling. Word was getting out about those who had "disappeared" and how the authorities had got their names in the first place. When the government fell months later there were arrests and, eventually, very public trials, including of those people involved in suppression of the uprising of the Polytechneion students. But a lot of individuals got away before the trials began, including small fry.'

'That's what I was told,' Cassie said. 'There were plenty of people who collaborated with the dictatorship and their police. If Schlange was one of them and he had betrayed his fellow members of the society to the authorities, he wouldn't stick around to be named. The families of all those who disappeared or died would be out for his blood, seeking old fashioned vengeance. Nor would his relationship with beautiful Philomeni continue if he was identified as the man who had betrayed her husband in order to seduce her.' She paused to think. 'Stefan Schlange sold out his fellow students for entirely selfish and personal reasons. I think it was this which was so frightening to him, that he would be identified and universally despised as a collaborator and destroyer of young lives.'

She recalled Balasz Kouris saying that so often the crimes of the powerful were not deemed to be "crimes" at all, but in this case the perpetrators, if they'd been caught, had answered for what they had done. Stefan Schlange hadn't. The Pythia had told her, to "seek out the crimes which are no crimes" – betrayal wasn't a crime, it was a choice. An evil one.

'Schlange never had to answer for what he'd done, never stood trial,' she continued. 'If it had all come out, it might not have led to criminal charges, but it would almost certainly destroy the rest of his career and possibly the rest of his life.' Krateros looked puzzled so Cassie filled him in. 'Schlange was on the cusp of achieving one of his goals in life, to become the head of a prestigious organisation after a lifetime of... underperformance.'

'So he killed Barbara, who he thought knew about it all.'

'I think so,' Cassie said. 'Though I don't think Barbara knew very much when she confronted him, she was just searching for facts about her family. Even so, once it was out in the open more and more facts would come to light and she was a determined young woman, she would have kept digging. He knew that. And he knew he would have been finished.'

'So he killed his own granddaughter.'

'I don't think he knew she was his granddaughter at the time. He didn't know until he met her mother, Alecto, on the cliff top. I think it was then that he realised what he'd done.'

'And he wanted to die, to take his own life?' Krateros said.

'Maybe, though I don't see Stefan Schlange as a self-sacrificing type.' Cassie thought of Barbara, placed like a sacrificial victim in the Athenian Treasury. 'Maybe he just ran off, then slipped.'

'His death was poetic justice then.'

'Not for Alecto,' Cassie countered.

'Nor for her own mother, Philomeni,' Krateros added. 'Philomeni Ganas committed suicide not long after her daughter was born. I wonder if she suspected.'

Suicide!

And with both parents dead or missing the young Ganas children were sent to relatives in Delphi. Where the older of them, the boy, grew up to be the local policeman and his sister married a local man and had a daughter. It was a tangled web, a tragedy indeed.

'Thank you, Mr Krateros, for your research. Send your invoice to the British Embassy, please. I'll see that it's paid.'

'Ok.' The detective moved round the desk to show her out. 'Are you returning to England soon?'

'Yes, tomorrow.'

He hesitated. 'You know that someone followed you here?'

What!

'When you told me you were coming, I was out of the office on another job,' he said. 'I didn't get back until just now – I only got here before you because you walk so slowly. You have been injured I think.'

'Yes.'

Krateros produced his phone and showed Cassie a photograph. 'Do you know this man?'

It was the man from the court in the blazer and sunglasses, who had sat with the blonde woman, next to Helena.

She shook her head. 'He was at the inquiry earlier.'

'Come.' The detective lead Cassie to an office situated at the front of the building. After a word in Greek to the secretary there, he crossed to the window and looked up and down the street.

'There,' he said, standing back. 'In the doorway of the pink apartment block opposite and to the right. Do you see?'

'Yes.'

The man stood in the shadow thrown by the canopy of the building, but it was definitely him, the man from the court. He was wearing dark glasses again and a hat, though this time he looked less like a tourist, more like a slightly down-at-heel businessman.

'Do you know him?'

'No.'

'Is there any reason why someone should be following you?'

Oh yes.

'No. I'm just a civil servant.'

'My advice to you,' he said. 'Go back to your hotel and speak with your Embassy. Tell them about this. I'll send you the photograph and–' he took another. 'This one too. Make sure you're on your plane tomorrow.'

'Thank you *Kyrios* Krateros.'

'Filipos.'

'Thank you, Filipos.'

'Let me call you a cab.'

◊ SEVENTY

Cassie slid back the metal lattice of the lift and pushed the door open. She had managed to dissuade the private detective from calling her a cab and also from accompanying her back to the boulevard where she could hail one. Before she stepped out on to the pavement she stood at the side of the doors and checked the street. Her shadow was still there, leaning in the doorway of the pink apartment block, reading a newspaper.

She had absolutely no intention of running away.

The street was becoming busier, as people made their way home from work and cars passed up and down. If she was going to confront him, this was the time to do it.

She pushed open the door and went jauntily down the steps to the pavement. From the corner of her eye she saw her watcher fold his newspaper, making ready to tail her along Euripides Street. In the roadway a car halted, its driver trying to reverse into a space which looked too small for it. Another driver honked his horn, wanting to pass. People watched as the driver of the second car lowered his window and started to harangue the driver of the first.

Perfect timing.

Cassie dashed across the road and hurried, as best she could, towards the pink apartment block. Her watcher jerked upright and leapt down the two steps to the pavement.

There's something about the way he moves. I've seen him before.

The man was walking very quickly along Euripides Street, long legs stretching. He was drawing ahead, Cassie could barely maintain the five-metre distance between them. She broke into a lop-sided run, her ankle precluding anything more, as she skipped around broken paving stones and tree roots. He was definitely getting away.

'Sorry. Sorry.'

She redoubled her efforts, trying to dance through oncoming pedestrians, but, invariably, barging into some of them, producing a flurry of protests. Up ahead, her watcher seemed to have no trouble forging through. He'd be at the boulevard in another fifty paces.

What? Where's he gone?

The watcher had disappeared. He was no longer on the pavement and he hadn't reached the boulevard, so he must have turned off Euripides Street, gone down a side turning. Cassie slowed her steps. Confronting him in a busy street full of people and cars was one thing, chasing him down a quiet side street or empty alleyway quite another.

Cassie reached the entrance to an alley. The narrow passage was the depth of the block and about ten feet wide. Completely in shadow it was difficult to see very far along it from where she stood on the sunlit street. A few large dumpster-style dustbins lined one side, amidst weeds, litter, cardboard, the usual detritus of a back alley. No movement save a few scavenging birds. No sign at all of the watcher, but this must be where he'd gone.

There was no way that he could have made it to the far end in the few seconds before she'd arrived. She stepped out of the sunlight, all senses alert for any sound, any sight, any movement. On the right of the alley was the blank concrete wall of the apartment building, the other was built of brick, behind the dustbins. There might be a door further along, but Cassie couldn't see one.

He must be among the bins.

She began walking, cautiously, by the concrete wall, stepping around the rubbish, trying not to breathe too deeply the smell of decomposition as she scanned the left-hand side of the alley. She jumped as a startled cat shot out from beneath a pile of cardboard, yowling.

Passed the first large rubbish bin. No one there. The second was jutting far out into the alley. Cassie pressed her back against the concrete wall in order to get around it.

Crash!

She threw herself forward as the bin smashed against the concrete wall. She'd almost been crushed. Off balance, she hobbled a few feet further, then steadied herself against the wall. On the other side of the alley, only feet away, stood the watcher.

'Dear me, only just fast enough,' he said, in the irony-filled drawl of the English public school. He grinned and removed his hat. The sunglasses he put in his breast pocket.

Peter Bradley!

'But then I must be getting slapdash, I never expected you to turn the tables.'

The fair hair, slightly thinning, the high, wide brow, the ramrod straight stance and precision of movement; intelligence services, ex-military and one of David Hurst's little group of operatives. Cassie had met Bradley during her last case.

'What the hell are you doing here?'

'I think that's obvious, don't you?' Bradley's grin grew wider. Then it froze. He whipped a semi-automatic pistol from his jacket pocket and pointed it back down the alleyway. 'Come out! Hands in the air!'

'Ms Fortune? Are you alright?'

'Filipos!' She gestured angrily at Bradley to put the gun away. 'I'm fine.'

The barrel of a pistol came into view beyond the rubbish bin, followed by the private detective, who kept the weapon pointing at Bradley's chest.

'It's okay, Filipos, I know this man. He works for the British government.'

Krateros lowered the pistol and clicked on the safety catch.

'Peter Bradley, this is Filipos Krateros, a private investigator who has been most helpful to me.'

'Mr Krateros,' Bradley nodded as he adjusted and pocketed his pistol.

'I thought you might try to unmask your follower,' Krateros said. 'And that you might need some help.'

'Mr Krateros was only trying to protect you,' Bradley said. 'Say 'Thank you' nicely, Cassie.'

Fuck off.

'I *am* grateful for your concern,' Cassie said, ignoring Bradley. 'But it really wasn't necessary.'

'Hmm.' The Greek looked unconvinced. 'I'll be on my way, then.'

'It really would be better, thank you, Filipos.'

Krateros retreated up the alleyway.

'Another knight in shining armour,' Bradley said. 'You do seem to attract them. Though I'm sorry that D.I. Andrew Rowlands was killed, he was good policeman.'

Cassie said nothing.

'Hurst sent me.'

'To check up on me?' she bristled.

'To find out what was going on. No word for days, the murders made all the European papers. He was concerned.'

Bradley manoeuvred the large bin back to its usual position. They walked back towards Euripides Street. Cassie's ankle was hurting after her jolt.

Damned if I let him see it.

'I spoke to Hurst yesterday,' she said.

'I'd tell that secretary of yours not to blab quite so much, if I was you. She doesn't help matters.'

Siobhan had always been discreet in the past. What could she have said?

'I saw you in court,' Cassie said.

'Shame. I thought I was unmemorable.'

'Try not to wear sunglasses in November. The beard's good though.' She glanced across at Bradley, the closely shaved red-gold-grey beard suited him. 'Who's the blonde?'

'Embassy Cultural Attaché.'

Odd that Helena didn't recognise her, she knew all the Embassy staff. Then something else occurred to Cassie.

'Was it you on the mountain? On Parnassus? Walking in a thunderstorm. What madness was that?'

'Yes,' Bradley smiled. 'You were doing the same.'

'I was looking to record evidence before it disappeared,' Cassie said.

'I was looking out for you.' His chin rose slightly. 'Though you shouldn't have seen me – that damn mist.'

'Well, you can go back to London now and report that I'm fine and everything is in hand.'

Cassie wanted rid of Bradley, she didn't want him hanging around

Athens after she had left. They'd reached the boulevard, now choked with rush hour traffic, headlights already shining in the dusk.

'I fly tomorrow,' he said. 'Same flight as you.'

Damn.

'I'd ask you to dinner, but I'm afraid I'm already engaged. The blonde.'

Good.

'Don't apologise, I'm busy anyway.'

Cassie was to have a gala dinner with Minister Sidaris, the Professor, Meg Taylor and Helena. Given that the ministerial visit to London was already organised for within a month, this would be less of a farewell than she had envisaged, more of an adieu.

She hailed a cab. 'See you tomorrow afternoon at the airport,' she said, leaving Bradley standing by the roadside.

◊ SEVENTY ONE

'To Cassie!' The Minister raised his glass.

'To Cassie!'

Light glinted from glasses filled with fizzing with champagne raised in Cassie's direction by those sitting around the large round dining table. She flushed, smiled and tried not to look uncomfortable. They sat in a private room of a restaurant in central Athens, frequented by the political class. The food and wine had been excellent and the Minister had called for toasts. It was quite the celebration.

Cassie sat on Theo Sidaris's right and she'd enjoyed speaking with him throughout the meal, filling in the gaps in what he had been told about the case by the Professor and smoothing the way to discussions in London. He was an intelligent and amusing dinner companion, someone who had a life outside politics.

The Professor sat across the table from her and he joined in the toast with enthusiasm. His wife, a small, thin and obviously intelligent woman sat by his side, with Meg Taylor on the other. Between Meg and Sidaris was the Minister's wife. Both wives would accompany their husbands to London and, as they had already told her, they were looking forward to doing some Christmas shopping. Helena, who sat on Cassie's right, was coming along to interpret for them, although, as far as Cassie could see they both spoke English well. Yannis Iraklidis rounded out the party, seated on Helena's right.

'So all the mysteries are solved,' Sidaris said. 'And, it seems, the Temple at Delphi has a newly discovered layer.'

'I don't know about that, Minister,' she replied. 'Nico, our guide at the temple site, said ultrasound imaging had already identified chambers beneath the Temple. I just happened to fall into one of them when the mountainside moved.'

Sidaris chuckled.

'Surprising how you just happened to fall, like Alice down the rabbit hole,' he said. 'And you just happened to be in Delphi when we had a murder and a mystery to solve. You have the knack of being in the right place at the right time, Cassandra. Are you sure you're not a prophetess?'

Or the wrong place at the wrong time. Depends on how you look at it.

'No, Minister,' she smiled at him. 'Besides, my namesake came to a sticky end and no one believed her when she was alive!'

'You'll never have that problem,' the Minister replied. 'David Hurst chose his envoy well, I will congratulate him.'

'Thank you, Minister.'

'When we all meet again in London,' the Professor called across the table. 'You will be our host?'

'I believe so, yes,' Cassie replied. 'Together with the diplomats – you'll have a full schedule. Aside from business, you must tell me what you would like to do while you are there.'

This prompted a barrage of suggestions. Cassie noted opera, Selfridges, Ronnie Scott's and Covent Garden (more opera, that was the Minister). The Professor had a yen for a return visit to the London School of Economics, where he and the Minister had studied. She would arrange something.

Iraklidis would be coming too; he was the Ministerial Security Chief, after all. Things between him and Helena seemed to have improved. Cassie hoped interpreter had given consideration to her impromptu outpouring outside the courtroom.

Who am I to give advice on relationships?

She observed the couple. Iraklidis was humble, not pushy, but he was quietly persistent and working hard to ensure Helena's comfort, passing her a dish, filling her glass, keeping the conversation going. Helena was fully aware of it and he knew that she was. Each seemed hyper-sensitive to the other. Whatever had passed between them since the inquiry yesterday had made a change. Would she keep him at arm's length? Did she really want to? Or would she take him back?

Cassie hoped so. Why turn happiness away?

She would find out soon enough. The ministerial party would arrive in London within a month and be staying at the Savoy. Iraklidis was overseeing security from the Greek side and someone would make arrangements on the British side, Cassie hoped it was someone she knew and could trust. The visit was not an official one, although some official business would take place.

Don't think about that now. Enjoy tonight.

She looked around the table, at faces flushed with wine and bonhomie.

'May I make a toast?' she asked the Minister.

'Of course,' Sidaris replied.

'To Dionysus Chthonios.' Cassie raised her glass to laughter. They were Greek, they recognised Dionysus's other name: it meant the god "underground". 'And his cousin, fleet footed Apollo!'

'Dionysus Chthonios and fleet footed Apollo!'

WEDNESDAY

◊ SEVENTY TWO

Cassie trundled her small suitcase on to the travelator, this time she wasn't going to let it out of her sight. She'd spent the morning shopping to buy small gifts, for Siobhan, for her mother and sister and her neighbour, who'd been looking after Spiggott. She also had a collection of newspapers reporting on the court proceedings and translations provided by Helena. She wanted to know what they were saying about her, what the world knew.

The tiled patterns and images flowed past as she stood. Athens airport seemed quieter than on the previous occasion, with fewer people in the general areas. Now she was headed to Departures, glad that, so far, she hadn't come across Peter Bradley.

He had been helpful on her previous case, but she was under no illusion, circumstances were different now. Bradley had his own career to consider. Like her, he answered directly to David Hurst and he would view her as a rival.

Was he telling her the truth? That Hurst had been worried when the murder made the news? Even if the PM had sent him to Greece for that reason, that wouldn't stop Bradley playing his own game, checking up on her, trying to finesse things his way. She replayed her conversation with Hurst over in her mind. He hadn't mentioned Bradley and he could have done, but then they had been diverted by the subject of the media. Anyway, it was up to David Hurst what he did, though it might make her job more difficult if he set several hares running the same course at the same time.

Think of something more pleasant.

The dinner the night before had been an enjoyable success and she was pleased at the apparent thaw between Helena and Yannis. She wished the couple well but cringed with embarrassment when she considered how she had behaved towards them. It was envy, pure and simple, however she rationalised it to herself. She had envied them the happiness they had found. And she had seriously underestimated Helena.

Be more positive.

She had accomplished her mission, the first for her new boss, who was very pleased with the outcome, whatever Bradley's involvement. What's more, she had solved a murder investigation along the way – a achievement by anyone's standards. Then there was her intervention in the petrochemical aspect, another trick taken; she would have to look up "zemiology". Plus, she had, inadvertently, found an unknown part of the Temple of Apollo.

Not a bad reckoning.

She began to pay attention to the images of Greek gods drawn in the tiles alongside the moving walkway. The Olympians were shown first – Zeus, Athena, Apollo and others of that clan, then the Titans, like Prometheus with his gift of fire and Atlas, holding up the world on his shoulders. The heroes were portrayed too, Heracles and his club, Achilles with his bow and Jason with the Golden Fleece. Then the older, pre-Hellenic deities like Gaia, the Great Mother, Oceanus with his water spirits and the demi-deities, like the Furies. They were there, drawn on the tilework with their names.

The image burned itself into Cassie's eyes and brain.

She walked back along the walkway to regain her place in front of the mural then slowed her pace to a crawl to remain directly in front of it, walking slowly backwards so that she never progressed. The three Furies, drawn in the Greek redware style, their hair and arms entwined with snakes, their hands grasping and bloody.

'Signora, questa è la direzione sbagliata.'

She had walked into a family of Italian tourists.

'Mi dispiace, mi scusi,' Cassie said.

She hitched her suitcase over the side of the walkway on to the floor beyond it and quickly followed it, perching on the guide rail and swivelling around before dropping to her feet. The Italian family laughed, the little boy cheering. Her ankle jarred and she winced at the pain. Grabbing the suitcase, she walked back to look again at the image.

They were outlined, red and white against black. The Three Furies: Alecto was "unceasing anger", Megaera, "jealous rage" and Tisiphone, "furious vengeance". Alecto Doukas, Megaera Taylor and Tisiphone – that, she remembered, was Major Lykaios first name. Alecto, eyes glittering, held the tablets of memory, her role to never forget the wrongs of the guilty. Megaera, with her long snake hair escaping its bonds, would track down the betrayers and the oath-breakers, and Tisiphone, black-haired and snarling, was the huntress of murderers.

She must have seen this, Cassie realised, on her arrival in Athens and it resurfaced as her vision, or fever dream when she lay beneath the Temple of Apollo. The real Megaera, Tisiphone and Alecto were not fury-like at all. She acknowledged to herself that, just as she had underestimated Helena, she had also completely misread these three women.

Meg Taylor had struggled with her grudges and had chosen to move on and live her life, not remain bitter and hidden. Cassie would try to help Meg's rehabilitation in the UK and speak to a couple of contacts in PR and Sport England.

The Major rejected vengeance. She chose to be an agent of justice, impartial and objective, an agent of law, regardless of the pressures to be otherwise. Her reward was a rather more permanent position, courtesy of the Professor, where her competency and discretion would be appreciated.

And Alecto Doukas, what of her? She had sought vengeance, a desire arising from her grief so raw and near the surface. What Filipos Krateros had discovered would help her, Cassie hoped, providing some certainty for the keeper of family memories. Meg said that the bereaved mother, and she was a bereaved daughter too, derived some comfort from the presence of Nico Vasilakis, Barbara's boyfriend, a Delphi man through and through and also grieving. He was trying to involve Alecto in the work at the Museum and temple site.

And what of herself? What of her own inner furies?

Envy or jealousy had made her unfeeling towards Helena and Yannis, disregarding of Jim and Elise, she had realised, because she hadn't accepted her own loss and was in pain, like grief-filled Alecto. She hadn't come to terms with Andrew's death.

Anger still fuelled her, not reason, because she hadn't objectively examined her previous downfall, as Meg had. She didn't really know what had gone on years ago, back at GCHQ, that had brought her career down. Had she failed because she wasn't good enough, as she had believed? Or was her downfall as a result of unseen malign forces, as Meg's had been.

Nor had she considered how she had treated others, including those close to her at that time, like her ex-husband, Rob. Looking back, it was obvious to her that though she had valued their marriage, she had not valued it as much as she had valued her career. Even so, Rob had tried to make it work. He was a decent man and loved her; entirely reasonably he refused to come second all the time. Their break-up had not been pleasant. Why had she seen him beneath the Temple?

I wonder what he's doing now. I hope he's happy.

Was she to make her peace with him? She suspected that he wouldn't welcome any contact from her. Besides, their break-up was linked irretrievably with memories of her downfall and disgrace.

Perhaps that was what she needed to address – her own past. Like Meg Taylor or Stefan Schlange. Meg Taylor had and could now get on with the rest of her life. Schlange hadn't and it had killed him. If she didn't confront and made peace with her past, one day it might come creeping up to ambush her when she least expected it.

Now, working directly for David Hurst, she might never have a better opportunity to look into what had really happened three years ago, as a way of coming to terms with it. Many of the people who had been involved then were still in place now. Though it could be seen as getting her own back. Forget that, it *would* be seen as getting her own back, even if that wasn't what she was doing.

So, she would have to be very careful. Like the Major she would be an agent of justice, not vengeance. She shouldn't confuse the two. The same applied to her response to Lawrence Delahaye.

She could also find out how Rob was doing. Her sister was still in contact with her former husband, her mother as well, perhaps, she wasn't sure. She would go and visit the family home, maybe at Christmas, the dreaded annual family gathering. She could stomach it for one year.

She had a lot to sort out when she returned to London.

'Know Thyself.'

Cassie headed off towards Departures and the First Class Lounge, not using the moving walkway, but walking and with a lighter step. There was much to do.

A F T E R W O R D

Oracle is a work of fiction. The characters and events within it are the products of my imagination. Some elements do, however, bear a similarity to my own visit to a conference on public administration held at the European Cultural Centre at Delphi in the 1990s, though not, of course, the deaths. The Centre has a wonderful and very scenic position outside Delphi town. Its interior may have changed since my visit, but *Oracle* shows it as I remember it. The conference took place in November, as does that in the novel, when the weather could have been kinder. It was as a storm raged on the mountain and the lights were flickering that someone suggested that it would be a great place to set a murder mystery. Over twenty years later, when my publisher asked me to write one, Mount Parnassus and the amazing Temple of Apollo immediately sprang to mind.

The incident with the motorcade and the herd of goats actually took place – at least I remember it doing so. The 'tavern' where the Dionysian bacchanal occurs in the novel is based on a real restaurant about fifteen minutes walk from the Centre. The cold, star-lit walk up the mountain road, back to the Centre, was stunning.

As with *Plague*, its predecessor, *Oracle* chimes with current times. The greater politicization of police forces, from the U.S. to Europe, is an ongoing danger to the delivery of justice and, therefore, to democracy. During the writing of it, however, the judgment of the Athens Appeal Court in the case of Golden Dawn, the former far-right Greek political party, was given. Golden Dawn was found not merely to be an illegal organisation, but a criminal one and its leaders jailed. An independent UN investigation had earlier concluded that many Greek police were members of it.

The events of the 1970s in Greece are well documented and made headlines around the world. The trials were the largest since the Nuremberg trials of the Nazis after the Second World War. Those charged included the instigators of the 1967 military coup and those responsible for the quelling of the Polytechneion uprising of 1973. Many were sentenced to death, commuted to life in prison. It was, and remains, widely believed, that many guilty individuals got away beforehand.

Thousands of tourists visit Delphi every year, as they have for millennia. It has an excellent modern museum, in addition to the Cultural Centre. Much of the history of both town and temple can be found on-line, however, I found *Delphi; A History of the Centre of the Ancient World* (Princeton University Press) by Michael Scott an invaluable resource. I have, I am afraid, taken liberties with the architecture of the Temple by having Cassie make an unlooked for discovery beneath its flagstones. I trust that Apollo and his cousin Dionysus will forgive me.

The *Erinyes*, or Furies, appear widely in early Greek legend and drama, becoming the *Eumenides*, or 'Kindly Ones' in Aeschylus play of that name, the third of the extant *Oresteia* plays. Opening in the portico of the Temple of Apollo at Delphi, it concludes in Athens, with what might be the first representation of a jury trial scene in Western literature. It celebrates justice, as opposed to vengeance or retribution, a distinction I too wanted to make. I used the Oxford World Classics version of the *Oresteia* (OUP) translated by Christopher Collard to inform *Oracle*.

Cassandra, daughter of King Priam of Troy is a character in *Eumenides*. Beloved of Apollo, she was given the gift of prophesy but was cursed with never being believed. As my Cassie says, female characters in Greek tragedy tend to come to sticky ends so she's anxious not to be compared to one.

There are many representations of Megaera, Alecto and Tisiphone in art, from ancient times on, including depiction of their role in *Eumenides*. They were commonly shown as monsters with snakes for hair and glittering eyes and that is how the English poet, John Dryden, described them in his ode *Alexander's Feast* or *The Power of Music* (1697). They were forces of nature from a more brutal time. A modern reading of *Eumenides* can, however, discern the prejudices of countless ages in how they and other females are depicted.

ACKNOWLEDGEMENTS

I would like to thank a number of people with expert knowledge, who have been generous with their time and expertise in advising me on aspects of *Oracle*.

Very many thanks to Maro Nicolopolou, Head of Conferences & Artistic Programmes, the European Cultural Centre of Delphi for her invaluable feedback and help with the setting. This was especially important in the year of COVID when I couldn't get to Delphi to look for myself and was forced to rely on memory.

Thanks to Sharon Hartles of the Open University's Harm & Evidence Research Collaborative (HERC) and member of the British Society of Criminology. She is currently conducting research on Primodos at the University of Strathclyde in the relatively new discipline of zemiology.

I must also thank Katie Isbester and Madeleine Simcock-Brown at Claret Press, who made this book what it now is and were as passionate about it as I was. Thanks too, to Charley Bennett, Giulia Battini and Lauren Johnstone, also of Claret Press.

As always I must thank Annette Souter and Myfanwy Garth for their unceasing support and help. The latter holds in her West Country safe the last lines of *Opera*, the third book in this series, which I sent to her during the writing of *Plague* and which I now have to work towards.

Many thanks for similar reasons to the friends who read early drafts of *Oracle*: to Roger Eastman, Helen Hughes and Sue Pither, the latter the convener of the Ivydene Bookworms. The members of that book club and some others were kind enough to read and comment upon early drafts of the manuscript. The members of Clapham Writers Circle have also been unwaveringly supportive, while acting as critical friends. To Dave, John and the others, very many thanks.

And, as always, thanks to my husband, Mark.

ABOUT THE AUTHOR

Julie Anderson is a professional writer who organises literary events in her spare time. Formerly a member of the UK's Senior Civil Service, she worked in Westminster and Whitehall for a variety of government departments and agencies, including the Office of the Deputy Prime Minister. This is her second of a series of political crime thrillers featuring Cassandra Fortune, civil servant and GCHQ investigator. The first in the series was 'Plague'. Her previous novels include the historical adventure stories 'Reconquista', long listed for the 2016 Mslexia Children's Book of the Year Award and its sequel 'The Silver Rings'. Julie is Chair of Trustees of Clapham Writers the organisation responsible for the annual Clapham Book Festival, a celebration of books and reading in south London and she also curates other literary events across the capital. She lives in Clapham.

Website
www.julieandersonwriter.com

Twitter
@jjulieanderson/twitter

Pinterest
www.pinterest.co.uk/andersonjulie4

Claret Press shares engaging stories about the real issues of our changing world. Since it was founded in 2015, Claret Press has seen its titles translated into German, shortlisted for a Royal Society of Literature award and climbed up the bestseller list. Each book probes the entanglement of the political and the everyday—but always with the goal of creating a page turner.

If you enjoyed Julie Anderson's mysteries, then we're sure you'll find more great reads in the Claret Press library.

Subscribe to our mailing list at **www.claretpress.com** to get news of our latest releases, bespoke zoom events and the occasional adorable photo of the Claret Press pets.

Claret ▶ Press

Lightning Source UK Ltd.
Milton Keynes UK
UKHW010721210321
380690UK00002B/108